THE INSTITUTE
(ASCENDANCY: BOOK 2)

By

D. Ward Cornell

Dedicated to my family and friends who have been very supportive through this adventure, especially those that have been willing to read the manuscripts and give me feedback.

Thank you all for your support and encouragement.

Special thanks to Theresa Holmes whose help has been a game changer.

Table of Contents

FOREWORD

This is the second book in the Ascendancy series. The first book, *Revelation*, was a joy to write and the reader feedback has been very gratifying. If you have not read *Revelation*, I would recommend that you do. It will provide context for many of the things that happen in this book. But whether or not you have read *Revelation*, I hope the following short synopsis helps whet your appetite before plowing in. Please enjoy!

...

In *Revelation*, the Intergalactic Confederation of Planets reveals itself to humanity. Their Ambassador, Michael, takes over every television and radio in the world to make his announcement, offering gifts and warning of pending threats that humanity is unlikely to survive without Confederation assistance.

Although Michael and his Revelation team are not human, they have taken human avatars, fully functional human bodies that they occupy. At first no one believes that Michael is a representative of an Intergalactic Confederation. He looks like a normal 35-year-old, is known to be a US citizen and owns an important company in San Diego. But that changes quickly.

The evening of the Revelation, the US President orders a raid of Michael's ranch in Hawaii. The raid goes very badly. Several FBI agents are injured or killed trying to approach the ranch on a trail that had been closed and was known to be hazardous. Michael and his team rescue the FBI agents, healing the wounded and bringing the dead back to life.

The morning after the Revelation, Michael and his team appear on Good Morning America. They heal Sergeant George Butler, a quadriplegic injured in Afghanistan, introduce food replicators and a new clean energy technology, then demonstrate how they will reverse climate change.

Israel becomes the first nation to form an alliance with the Confederation, after Michael puts a protective shield over Israel that thwarts an Iranian nuclear attack.

One by one, nations ally with the Confederation. But Michael cannot intervene in human affairs until he has alliances with at least half the Earth's population.

That changes when North Korea deploys and demands the surrender of South Korea. Dozens of nations ally with the Confederation in time for the Confederation to stop the invasion.

In the aftermath, Canada agrees to be the host country for the Confederation's Embassy on Earth. The Confederation leases a 100 square mile tract of land in the Mackenzie Mountains in the Northwest Territories, where it builds its Embassy. The Embassy becomes the home of the Earth Alliance, which is the primary interface between the Confederation and the nations of Earth. It also becomes home to the Ascendance Institute, which is the educational arm of the Confederation and manages Confederation technology transfer with humanity.

Following is the story of The Institute...

PROLOG

He could sense the presence of the Enemy. They were very close, yet hidden as if behind a veil. This was the mystery that he still had not penetrated.

The Enemy had first been discovered around 300,000 years ago. It was an old species, but nowhere near as old as his own. His was ancient. Sadly, his species had died out millions of years ago, and to the best of his knowledge, he was the last of his kind. Nonetheless, he still had purpose. Two million years ago, he had discovered an adolescent species, which he had adopted as his own. They referred to him as the Ancient Sentient.

Under his guidance, they had grown up to become the founding and dominant species of the Intergalactic Confederation of Planets, which now represented over 10,000 intelligent species, spanning over 1,000,000 planets across three galaxies. It was during their expansion into the Milky Way that they discovered the Enemy.

The Enemy was a parasite, one that could descend on a planet and completely consume it, stripping all its resources in a matter of years. Until recently, the Enemy had not been sapient. They were not intelligent, self-aware, or technologically able. But that had changed a millennium ago when they consumed a world that held an intelligent species and, by some means that he did not understand, had acquired their memories.

Five years ago, the problem got drastically worse when they consumed a planet that held a very intelligent species with nascent faster-than-light technology. They also acquired knowledge of a planet that he knew to be the most important planet in the three galaxies, a planet known as Earth. He could not allow them to consume Earth. If they did, then they would become the masters of the universe.

Recently, it had been discovered that the Enemy was extra-dimensional, meaning they could move between dimensions. That was why the Enemy appeared as smoke, or as dust. They wove between this dimension and four adjacent dimensions, like a snake writhing across the sand.

3

As he cast his thoughts back to his search, the Ancient Sentient had an epiphany... *The Enemy must come from a higher dimension. A different space-time continuum. That's why they seem to get closer and closer, then fade away without being seen.*

He returned to the place where they seemed closest, then cloaked himself and began moving through adjacent dimensions one at a time.

And, there it was, the Enemy home world. Adjusting his senses, he discovered that here they were solid and shaped something like an Earthly squid or octopus. If the Confederation brought the fight here, this blight on the universe could be stopped once and for all.

APPEARANCE

[Tuesday, 08.20.2030, 3:00 PM] KEELE PEAK, MACKENZIE MOUNTAINS, CANADA

It had been a beautiful morning. The air was cold and clear; the Sun blindingly bright; not a cloud in the sky. The perfect day for a summit attempt.

Alexi Santos had led the team that made the summit today. They were halfway decent mountaineers and had done a respectable job making the final ascent up the southeast ridge of the mountain.

They were now about halfway back down, and the weather was turning against them. Clouds had formed in the sky and the wind had started blowing. Following standard protocol, Alexi doublechecked the climbing ropes that bound the party together. Then she took the lead following the last of the ridgeline back toward base camp. As the storm intensified, the team's mettle was tested. Several men fell or were blown off the ridge, but their lines held them together. And each time, the one who had fallen was helped, or pulled, back up.

...

Alexi was a Confederation android, an Artificial Intelligence (AI) driving a human avatar. Her official job was head of the outfitting concession at the Intergalactic Confederation of Planets Embassy in Northwest Territories, Canada. As part of the Confederation's treaty with Canada, they'd been granted a 100 square mile tract of land in the Mackenzie Mountains. It was a very remote and inhospitable tract of land located 'close' to the geographic center of the human population on Earth. Its remoteness made the land available. Its location reduced travel time to all but a few of the world's capitals.

In granting this tract, the Canadian government had asked the Confederation to allow tourism to this part of their country and to offer outfitting services for the adventurers that wanted to travel there.

Amazingly, no humans had come forward to set up this operation. So Alexi, a Confederation citizen, had volunteered. Alexi rose to fame during the liberation of North Korea. She'd been part of the team that went in to clean up after the arrest of the former dictator. She'd helped set up the prisoner of war camps that housed the invasion

5

troops, which had been staged near the South Korea border. She then led the teams that liberated North Korea's notorious slave labor camps.

The outfitting concession had a half dozen certified expedition leaders, but Alexi had been the first approved by the Canadian commission that had oversight responsibilities for tourism in Canada.

...

As the expedition approached the last difficult descent before their shelter, massive gusts hit the team. It was not clear how anyone could make it down this cliff face without being blown away.

Alexi, who had figured out how to shelter thousands of troops in cold winter environments, never left home in the Mackenzies without bringing a shelter with her. She pulled a box from her pack that looked a lot like the power pack that came with the average portable computer. With her team gathered around her, she anchored it in the foundation dimension and activated it. A dome, maybe 20 ft. in diameter, glistened to life around them. The wind stopped, the snow deflected off the dome, and warmth from the small heater settled in.

Alexi used her implants to connect into Embassy security. She reported her situation and they advised her of the updated forecast. The blizzard would last another two days. Twenty feet of snow were predicted for the mountain. The center of the storm had stalled to the southeast of them, so the wind would be coming from the northeast.

This is trouble, Alexi thought. *The wind will come up over the steep part of the ridge and deposit all its snow right on top of us.*

By her calculations, a thirty- to fifty-foot snow drift was about to form right here. The shield could hold that weight. It, plus their personal thermal shields, would even keep them warm. Nonetheless, they would suffocate with no way to exchange air through the snow.

"We can't stay here," Alexi shouted.

The men looked at her incredulously.

Then reversing herself, she said. "Stay here. I can get help in time." Then, rope and carabiners in hand, she walked through the shield into the storm.

...

As Alexi first emerged, the wind nearly blew her away. But placing her back to the dome wall, she shimmied around to the leeward side of the dome until she found the first anchor point that was somewhat sheltered from the wind. She clipped a rope to the shield's anchor point, then walked to the edge of the cliff—the one they couldn't climb down—and leaped.

The mountaineers in the shelter saw her being swept up by the wind and immediately despaired. What they didn't know was that Alexi wore a Confederation climbing harness, an anti-gravity device similar to the Fabulous Flying Overalls that had made Sergeant George Butler famous. The climbing harness had an anti-grav drive that allowed Alexi to fly, regardless of the direction of the wind.

Navigating the storm was still tricky, but she made her way down to the dome at base camp and anchored the climbing rope she had brought. She clipped onto the rope, now anchored at both ends, and used the anti-grav drive to propel herself back up to the mini dome on the leeward side of the ridge. Snow had already piled up several feet.

Still clipped onto the rope, she walked through the shield to find pandemonium and despair inside. The temperature had been dropping and the snow piling up. The men were convinced they were going to die.

"Guys. Man up," she said. "I've connected a rope between the domes. The dome at base camp is safe. I can shuttle you down one by one. It'll be a wee bit bumpy, but a great ride nonetheless."

She beamed. "Who's first?"

A moment passed without any volunteers. Alexi was dismayed. Staying here was certain death. By comparison, riding down was safer than sitting in a rocking chair and watching the world go by, just more fun.

Seeing that none of these wusses was going to volunteer, she grabbed the closest member of the team, clipped him on, and then dragged him out of the dome and over the precipice.

Poor Henry, she thought, as he screamed the whole way down. *But, what a wuss.*

She purposely came in high, penetrating the shield, then made a smooth landing. Henry still fell when she let go of him. Shaking her head, she said, "Henry! Make yourself useful. Make some coffee for the others and turn on some lights. It'll be getting dark before too long. Next one will be down in about five minutes." Then she ran out of the dome and flew back to the others.

One by one, the men came down. On each return she found the snow against the mini dome stacked higher and higher. As she came in to get the last member of the team, disaster struck. The rope she'd been using to guide her flight suddenly went slack. Panicked that she might lose the rope altogether, she grabbed it where it passed through the carabiner she'd used to clamp on. She quickly tied on to the rope in a way that would prevent it from coming off completely, but in the process lost her bearings.

Suddenly the rope snapped tight, knocking the breath out of her. As she came back to her senses, Alexi couldn't help but laugh at herself. *Here I am. Attached to a rope. Using an anti-grav drive to hover someplace downwind of the rope's anchor point. I don't even know which end I'm anchored to. Hopefully, it's the mini dome. Otherwise, I'll never find it again.*

As the blizzard intensified, visibility dropped to zero. With no other option, Alexi started reeling herself in hand over hand, using the anti-grav drive to relieve the pressure of the wind while still keeping the rope taut.

...

Jack was worried. It had been a long time since Alexi left with Steve. Something must have gone wrong and he was running out of time, the mini dome was nearly covered in snow. And he was freezing.

...

Alexi suddenly hit snow. She'd been pulling herself in, but here the rope was just coming out of a wall of snow. After a moment of puzzlement, it occurred to her. *This must be the mini dome, covered in snow.*

I can use the taut rope like a knife. She thought, directing the anti-grav drive to move up and down, left and right. Slowly, she sliced off layers of snow until the rope finally hit the dome and she could see the light within.

"Yes!" she shouted. It was indeed the mini dome. Jack was still alive. As she pulled herself in the last 20 feet, the wind suddenly shifted and she went flying into the wall of stone to the northwest of the dome. She'd placed the mini dome here intentionally, hoping proximity to this part of the cliff would give them some shelter from the wind.

There was a loud crack and searing pain in her right leg. Ironically, hitting the wall killed her momentum and blocked most of the wind. She fell twenty feet straight down, landing on the injured leg, which bent unnaturally. She struggled to get up on her remaining good leg, took two hops, then fell into the dome and passed out.

...

Jack saw Alexi fall next to the dome and went to help, but the dome was not keyed to allow him to pass through it. As she fell over into the dome, he grabbed her and pulled her the rest of the way in. Looking at her leg, he saw that it was mangled and bleeding copious quantities of blood. He got the Confederation first aid kit, then wrapped her leg as they'd been instructed during safety training. When it was secure, he pushed the button on the wrap that would tighten it, isolating the broken bone and infusing nanobots. When he finished, he saw that he was sitting in a puddle of her blood, which had begun to freeze. Then, shivering uncontrollably, he passed out.

...

Alexi woke from a very pleasant dream. She'd been flying on a rope, using it to slice up snow. *Where do dreams like that come from?* she wondered.

She opened her eyes and took in the scene. Jack was out cold and covered in partially clotted, frozen blood. "What the hell happened to you, Jack?" she asked. Rousing herself, Alexi attempted to help him. That's when she realized she was the one that was injured. Jack was the one that had applied the first aid. "Thank you, Jack," she said out loud, then "What a wuss."

"We're not out of the woods yet, are we Jack?" she said to his inert body. "Let's take inventory. The anti-grav drive must have been broken when I hit that wall. Going to need to fix that."

Scanning the perimeter of the dome, she noticed that they still had Jack's rope and another one. *Must be Henry's. I did yank him out of here kind of suddenly,* she thought.

"Looks like we have enough rope, if I can fix the grav-drive, Jack," she said. Jack was still out cold, but talking to him helped keep her calm.

Slowly and awkwardly, Alexi took off her parka, then her outer mountaineering shirt, revealing the anti-grav harness. It looked more or less like a standard climbing harness.

Slowly, and somewhat painfully, she removed the grav-drive. The problem was immediately obvious. The power unit was damaged. The casing had cracked, breaking the connector that powered the lift generators. She disconnected the power unit from the rest of the harness and was relieved to see that the lift generators and their connectors were intact. The part that had broken was the socket on the power unit.

"Good news Jack. I only need to swap out the power unit, and I never go anywhere without at least one spare."

She grabbed her parka, fished through it until she found the spare power unit, and then attached it to the harness. The unit beeped. It was alive and functional. "Looks like we're back in business, Jack," she said, somewhat surprised that he hadn't come back around yet.

Alexi put the harness back on, secured it, and then levitated up off the ground. Her leg made several loud popping noises. "Not liking the sound of that, Jack," she said.

She went over to Jack and spotted his problem almost immediately. He was suffering severe hypothermia. At some point the power pack on his thermal shield must have either come loose or been broken. She patted him down looking for where he had put his power pack. He had the type that strapped on, so could be located anywhere as long as it was in direct contact with his skin.

Slowly, she worked his parka off and started patting him down again.

"Found it!" she shouted. Jack had placed the unit in the small of his back. It was held in place by a strap that wrapped around his torso just below the rib cage. The strap had come loose. Alexi quickly tested the unit to make sure it still had power. It did. She readjusted the strap and confirmed that his thermal shield was now active. A quick scan showed that Jack's core temperature had dropped to 85 degrees.

"Oh, Jack. You're in trouble, my friend. Let's see if we can save you."

Moving as quickly as she could, Alexi redressed Jack, then herself. Not wanting a repeat of her interview with the rock wall, Alexi reached through the dome from the inside and tied a new piece of rope to the anchor point on the exterior of the dome. Then from her rescue supplies, she put a buoyancy assist belt on Jack, reducing his 'weight' to about 30 lbs. The beauty of the buoyancy assist was that it offset gravitational pull on his body without applying a force vector the way the anti-grav harness did. She strapped Jack onto her back using four carabiners to lock him in place. Then, ropes attached, she 'dialed' the anti-grav to max and went flying out of the dome into the storm.

...

"Hey guys. I think we're in trouble. Check out the rope. It's slack and flopping around."

Several of the other guys looked at the anchor. The rope had clearly broken.

"Don't worry," Phil said. "She found her way down the first time. She can do it again."

"I don't know," Henry said. "Visibility is terrible. The wind is a lot worse. And it's starting to get dark. We need to do something."

"Dude, none of us is Alexi. If she's having trouble, then we have no chance."

Henry started pacing. It always helped him think.

"Lights!" he said with conviction. "In a storm, your own lights are almost worthless because they light up the snow around you. But someone else's lights can help because the snow brightens where they are. How many lights do we have? Can we aim them toward the mountain?"

Someone else piped up. "What about the radio? Can we call for help? Surely the Confederation has some type of technology to help?"

Once he'd snapped on the last of the lights, Henry started searching around and found the spare communicator. He had no idea how to operate it. It seemed that Alexi just talked into it and it worked.

"Hello," Henry said. Nothing. He started tapping on it, whistling into it, pressing every surface, saying random distress words... "Mayday! Mayday!" Then, "SOS! SOS!"

One of the other guys said, "Try 9-1-1."

"There are no buttons, idiot!" Henry said, starting to get a bit testy.

"I meant, say '9-1-1.'"

"Oh. Good idea," Henry said contritely. "Sorry about that."

Then he shouted... "9-1-1, 9-1-1" ...into the device.

"Embassy Operator. Please state the nature of your emergency."

Everyone was dumbfounded that this had worked. Then Henry quickly explained to the operator what was going on.

AMBASSADOR'S OFFICE

"Michael, we may have a problem." Pam came into his office. Michael served as Ambassador from the Intergalactic Confederation of Planets to the Peoples of Earth. He was Lorexian but occupied a human avatar. Pam was his assistant. She was an android. They had worked together for about 20 years.

"I just got a call from the Embassy emergency operator. They got a call from a member of the Keele Peak summit team. They said that Alexi had saved them, but she is now missing, along with the last person on their team whom she was attempting to rescue."

"What are we doing about it?"

"They need your approval to take one of the shuttles to launch a search and rescue mission."

"Approved." Michael said. "But they are not to take any exceptional risks."

NEAR KEELE PEAK, CANADA

Alexi was getting close to the point of calling for help. Jack had been strapped to her back for 30 minutes now and he was at serious risk of death or permanent disability from hypothermia. Then she saw something. Light within the shadow of the peak.

It must be base camp. They've lit it up for me! She thought, suddenly a little more impressed by this team.

She headed for the light, pushing the anti-grav drive as hard as she could. It really wasn't designed for this, but it had just enough power to overcome the wind.

The light got brighter and brighter and the form of the dome could now be discerned. It was about 100 ft. below her and maybe 500 ft ahead. *Time to trade altitude for speed*, she thought, turning the anti-grav drive to push parallel to the ground. She shot forward and fell precipitously, now that the grav drive wasn't holding her up anymore. A moment of that and she adjusted the grav drive to arrest the fall.

The grav-drive could produce about 2G of force and arrested the fall maybe 10 ft. above the ground. But the wind at this level was a lot lower and she was coming in toward the dome way too fast.

Perfect! she thought. About one second from impact with the dome, she flipped the anti-grav drive to slow her down. They still shot in through the wall of the dome a little fast. Alexi tried for the perfect parachute landing, coming in gently at a running speed, having completely forgotten about her broken leg.

...

It had been about two hours now. The mountaineering team was afraid that Alexi and Jack had been lost. The Confederation emergency operator had told them that a shuttle was inbound and would attempt to land. But sensors indicated that the wind speed was too high. A rescue team would transport down to the dome to prep the survivors for extraction while the shuttle conducted low altitude scans in an attempt to locate Alexi. It was clear they didn't expect to find her.

With all the lights on at their maximum settings, the team could see nothing outside, other than snow landing on the dome and drifting down the side or just blowing away.

Suddenly there was an incredible noise. It was Alexi whooping as she came in for a landing with Jack on her back.

"This is the way it's done boys!" she yelled as she came in for what looked like a running landing.

Her left leg planted. "Yes!" Alexi yelled.

But as the right leg hit, it completely folded up, bending 90 degrees about one third of the way between knee and ankle. Alexi and Jack came down hard, Jack on top. They slid and hit a classic government-style gray metal desk. There was a loud crack and a trail of blood where they had slid.

Henry still had the communications device in his hand and shouted, "Shuttle! Shuttle! We have Alexi and Jack, but they are badly injured. Emergency extraction required! Emergency extraction required!"

Moments later, two men in rescue garb appeared in the dome and headed straight to the spot the rest of the team was pointing at. A third appeared near the team.

They detached Jack and one of the techs immediately started triage. "Rescue shuttle. I have Patient 1. Male, the one they call Jack. Severe hypothermia. Core temperature below 85 degrees."

The other had started his assessment of Alexi, whom he had met before. "Rescue shuttle. Patient 2 is confirmed to be Alexi Santos. Multiple compound fracture of the right leg. Broken radius in left arm. Possible broken ulna in same arm. Concussion. Significant blood loss. She needs immediate evacuation."

While the med techs had been doing their assessment, a third member of the rescue team had tagged the other six team members. The seven of them transported up moments before Alexi's assessment was complete.

The pilot, in consultation with the Embassy, did an emergency site-to-site transport, sending Alexi, Jack and their rescuers directly to the Embassy's emergency medical facility from the base camp dome.

AMBASSADOR'S OFFICE

"Michael?" Pam said. "They found Alexi and the man she was rescuing. Both were in rough condition and were transported directly to the hospital. Doctors say the climber is stable. Alexi is in critical condition but expected to recover."

13

"Thank you, Pam."

...

Sarah would be coming by his office in about a half hour. She now headed Media Relations for the Embassy. Michael and Sarah had met a day after the Revelation. He had appeared on Good Morning America the morning after the announcement. Sarah had been the lead host that day. Within a week of that first meeting, they had fallen for each other. Now they were the world's most talked about power couple.

They had a dinner reservation at Chef Marco's restaurant in the building next door. *Only one more thing I have to accomplish before I can enjoy the rest of my evening*, Michael thought.

Suddenly, his office was bathed in brilliant light and a thunderous voice echoed in his mind. "Michael. I must speak with you."

It was the Ancient Sentient. Michael turned to look but was overwhelmed by the brilliant light and sparkles of color at the center. He found himself transfixed.

"I'm sorry to have come in my energy form. But the matter is urgent and the time short," the voice rumbled.

"Excellency. Your presence is always a gift."

"Unfortunately, I come with news of the Enemy. And it is not good.

"Those in your space-time continuum have acquired faster-than-light transportation and have found your coordinates. The main mass of them are still over 100 years away, but the leading contingent will arrive much sooner.

'Worse, they have figured out what Earth is." He paused for effect. "They know that Earth's core has high concentrations of transluminide. I would not be surprised if the first arrived in just a few years."

A shudder ran through Michael.

At the edge of his perception, he heard a thump. But in his transfixed state, it did not register in his consciousness.

"But that is not the bad news."

"What could possibly be worse?" Michael stuttered.

"I've been roaming the high dimensions and finally found the Enemy's home world. Through normal space-time it is close. If the Enemy had the ability to cross the high dimensions the way that I do, they could be here in hours. But they cannot. Nonetheless, the transluminide in the Earth's core draws them like bees to clover.

14

"If we are to have any hope, we must strike first. Humanity is an aggressive species, well-suited to war. Their planet has the greatest preponderance of transluminide in the known universe. So, our assault on the Enemy home world must launch from Earth. And it must be decisive.

"Begin building your army. I will be back to deliver the technology you will need as soon as I can. The fate of the Confederation will be decided here."

...

Michael returned to his senses, standing where he was when the Ancient Sentient had appeared. His eyes finally focused on the clock on the far wall. 7:14.

"Oh, no," he whispered to himself. "I'm late for dinner." He turned toward the door and saw Sarah lying unconscious on the floor.

His scans showed nothing wrong with Sarah, but those results were misleading. No one in the Confederation understood the undeniable impact that the Ancient Sentient's presence had on people, but the impact was real, even if it was not understood. When the ancient one presented himself in energy form, Michael lost all sense of time. But he'd never lost consciousness. For the vast majority of others, they blacked out as soon as he appeared. Most came back to themselves within minutes of his departure, but some remained unconscious for hours, days, even weeks.

Wake up, Sarah. Michael pushed, before even thinking about what he was doing.

She stirred but did not wake.

Wake up, Sarah. Michael pushed again, this time more gently and compassionately.

Sarah stirred again, her eyes fluttering open.

"Where? Where am I?" she asked, fogginess evident in her voice.

Michael took her hand and said softly, "You're in my office."

"What?" Then she looked around. "Why am I on the floor?"

"What's the last thing you remember?" Michael asked gently. "Do you remember coming here?"

Slowly, Sarah's memories started to return. "We had a dinner date tonight. You were tied up with an emergency, so I was going to meet you here..."

"Do you remember coming into the office?" Michael asked.

"Uh... I opened the door to the outer office and saw that no one was in the reception area. So, I came down the hallway and saw bright

15

light under your door." A long pause. "I thought that was weird. The light was too bright. So, I ran down the hall and knocked on the door." A pause… "This feels like a dream. I opened the door and you were facing a cloud, brilliantly lit with beautiful sparkles of color inside." Some hesitation… "I called your name, and the cloud cast its attention on me. I felt so small…"

Suddenly, wide awake, she stood and looked at Michael intently. "Michael, what was that thing and what did it do to me?"

Michael took her in his arms. She was shaking. "It's OK." He whispered. "It's OK."

He kissed her on the cheek and stepped back a little so he could look her in the eyes. "That is the person we call the Ancient Sentient. He is immensely old, the most respected elder in the Confederation. Millions of years ago, he figured out how to leave his physical form and exist as pure energy. I met him for the first time during my study of the Roman Empire."

Suddenly, understanding kicked in. Sarah might be a less-than-devout Catholic, but she had finished her catechism. Michael, realizing that Sarah had put the pieces together, made a face. "I probably shouldn't have said that."

"Michael, that looked like what was described in the Bible as the Transfiguration. Were you there? You told me you were in Palestine at that time. Were you at the Transfiguration? Did you know Jesus?" She asked, more as an accusation than as a question.

"It's not like that," he said.

"What do you mean, 'It's not like that!'" she asked, hysteria building.

"OK. OK." A long pause. "You understand why it is forbidden to talk about this, right?"

Sarah started to protest. Michael held up his hands in surrender.

"OK. OK. What I meant is that what you saw is not what you think it is. Yes, I was in Judea at the time the Transfiguration occurred. I was in Jerusalem that night. But I was not a participant. I was on another hilltop within viewing distance. And what I could see from that distance matched the accounts you were taught. But the important part is that the Ancient Sentient was standing next to me in his physical form. And even he was shocked by the power and purity of what we were both seeing across the valley. What you saw tonight was a speck of dust by comparison."

A long silence, then… "How does the Ancient Sentient do that? How can he exist as pure energy?" Sarah asked.

Michael laughed at that question, then sobered. "I have no idea," he replied, awe and dismay clear in his voice.

"Have you asked him?"

"No, but he knows I want to know. So he told me that it's something that cannot be taught. It's something that needs to be learned. Only a handful have learned to do it. He is the last of his kind that we know to be living. If you should ever be in his presence again, ask him. He will respect that."

Michael took Sarah by the hand. "Still interested in dinner? We've completely blown our reservation, but I bet they'll still give us a table."

CHEF MARCO'S RESTAURANT, CONFEDERATION EMBASSY COMPLEX

Dinner at Chef Marco's was fabulous as always. The chef was in town this week, and greeted them as soon as they came in. He'd prepared a special menu 'just for them' and reserved a table on the upper level that had a beautiful view over the valley. The sun had just set, and the Northern Lights were putting on their fabulously ethereal display.

One of the things that Michael had learned early in their courtship was that Sarah loved fine red wine. Chef Marco had learned that also. He'd put the word out to the premium wineries around the world that the Ambassador frequented his restaurant and loved fine red wine. Pictures of him enjoying their wine might get back to those that submitted samples or made rare bottles available for purchase.

Prior to his courtship with Sarah, Michael had refused almost all forms of alcohol. But when it became clear that it was not acceptable to refuse wine when having state dinners in foreign capitals, Charles had developed a nanobot therapy that held blood alcohol to 0.015%, no matter how much was ingested. The nanobots would also reduce blood alcohol levels to zero within 5 minutes of receiving the command.

Tonight, Chef Marco presented an old bottle matched to the main course, a 2005 'Soul of the Lion' from Daou Vineyards in Paso Robles. Sarah nearly swooned over this offering. Michael, who had finally started developing a taste for fine wine, simply marveled at 'the human ingenuity and artistry that could create such a thing,' words that ultimately showed up in a review written by Chef Marco.

…

17

As they walked back to the Ambassador's residence, Sarah snuggled up and said. "Thank you for such a pleasant evening."

AMBASSADOR'S RESIDENCE, CONFEDERATION EMBASSY COMPLEX

As soon as they were back in the Residence, Sarah took his hand and led him to the bedroom. Michael had come to love Sarah in a way he'd never known before. Part of that was the physicality of human contact. But the larger part was the mental connection they had formed. As they came together, Michael would push his affection and desire for her. Knowing that Michael would read her, Sarah sent the same emotions back.

Although it was something that had become a defining part of their relationship, Michael did not understand the science of it. Lorexians had nascent telepathy, something enhanced in Ascendants by their training and implants. Michael had an acute ability to 'read' others, particularly humans. But he was one of the very few that could push thoughts and emotions to others.

In contrast, humans had no telepathy. Yet, over the last five years, Michael had become so connected to Sarah that it was as if she had become telepathic also. When they made love, they truly became one, minds and bodies connected. It was a connection neither wanted to lose.

...

Despite the late night, they both woke early.

"I know," Sarah said meekly.

"Know what?" Michael asked.

"They're coming, aren't they?" Michael started to deflect, but Sarah cut him off. "Michael. I know. I hear your thoughts. I see your dreams."

Michael stood there, speechless.

"I want to enroll," she said.

This statement puzzled Michael. He had asked her several times if she would consider enrolling in the Institute and taking Ascendance training, but she'd resisted. And he'd finally accepted that as her choice. "May I ask why?"

"I don't want to lose you."

"What!?" Michael said, not understanding.

Sarah smiled at that. "Michael, if you just opened your senses to me, you would know."

"Better for both of us if you tell me," he said tenderly.

"With life extension therapy, I have what... 100 more years? You have hundreds of thousands. But you will be lost the day I go. I sense the fear in you while you sleep. So, I need to be here. I need to be part of the fight when they come. If I'm not, you won't be either. Then, everything will be lost."

Michael was overcome by his love for this woman and as that affection leaked out, she folded herself into his arms.

BRIEFINGS

PRESENCE PROJECTOR, AMBASSADOR'S OFFICE

"Mi-Ku. To what do I owe this pleasure?" asked the Admiral, holding out his paw to bump.

"Jo-Na, my friend. So good to see you." Michael bumped his own paw against the admiral's.

Michael and the Admiral were lifelong friends. They'd grown up together on the new Lorexian home world. 'Mi-Ku' was Michael's familiar name from his youth. 'Jo-Na' was the Admiral's.

The Confederation's projector rooms allowed each of them to be in their respective offices, yet see, speak and interact with each other via real time holographic projection. On the Admiral's end, he interacted with Michael in his native Lorexian form, not his avatar.

"I have news of the Enemy, and a request I'd like to make of you."

"Sounds like trouble. What can I do for you?"

"The enemy has acquired superluminal transportation."

"What? How? How did you determine this?"

"The Ancient Sentient discovered this during his travels. They consumed a small, technologically advanced planet about 1,000 light-years from Earth."

"In the area where we have been on patrol?" asked the Admiral.

"Maybe 50 light-years away from there."

"Yet, they escaped our scans," the Admiral complained.

"Apparently," Michael commented. "And the Enemy got more than just spacecraft. Apparently, the species they destroyed had previously visited and catalogued Earth. They had also determined that Earth had large deposits of transluminide."

"So, they are on their way to you. How long before they arrive?"

"Unknown, but their top speed is apparently only 10-times light, so we have some time to prepare."

"I assume you will start colonization efforts shortly?"

"Possibly, but that will not be a viable solution."

"Why not?"

"If I can hold that question for a minute, there is another piece of news to share."

"And that is?"

"The Ancient Sentient also found the Enemy home world."

"Where!"

"He did not tell me exactly. Only that it is close to Earth, but difficult to get to. There is some cosmological anomaly that isolates them and has kept them hidden."

"I'm not connecting the dots here, Michael."

"Remember during the Revelation, I told you that 'this planet holds a few secrets that are restricted above your grade?' I wish there were a way to get your help without having to give you that last piece of information. It is only known to two people."

"The Central Council does not know?" the Admiral asked incredulously.

"No. It is too important. Too secret. It's the reason the Ancient Sentient asked me to come to Earth." Michael paused before continuing, "I'm sorry, my friend, there is no going back once it is revealed and it will complicate your life beyond your ability to imagine."

No response.

"The Earth's molten core..." A long and regretful pause, "has high concentrations of transluminide."

"WHAT! How high?"

"There are at least 10^{23} kilograms of transluminide in the Earth's core. Could be much more."

Silence.

"That's why we can't evacuate. If the Enemy gets ahold of that much transluminide, there will be no place to hide. Not in the Milky Way. Not in Andromeda or Triangulum for that matter. Not anywhere. We must make our stand here."

"You know I have to report this up the chain of command."

"Yes. But do you think it's prudent to report something like this before you've had a chance to verify any of it for yourself?" Michael asked.

Another long pause.

"You have a plan I assume?" the Admiral said.

"It's not fully formed, but the basic idea is to arm humanity. They are much more aggressive than we are and have the cunning to pull this off. We'll start mining the transluminide and stockpiling a large reserve. Then we'll use it to put up a protective shield around the Earth, and ultimately to cross the cosmic barrier and destroy the Enemy's home world.

"That's where I need your help. Your Armada has the manufacturing capacity and the core battleship and weapons designs we need to battle the Enemy. The Ancient Sentient will be providing the new technology that will allow us to cross the barrier," Michael said.

"Why hasn't he disclosed this to the Central Council?" the Admiral asked.

"He is afraid that the Confederation will attempt to steal the Earth from the humans, destroying themselves and the humans in the process."

A long thoughtful silence.

"OK, Mi-Ku. I will help you. But I need to think this through. My captains and their crews will sort out what's going on well before you've finished what you need to do. Word will leak back to the Confederation. So, we need a plan that will get us far enough along that they want to join us, not fight us, when they find out."

"Thank you, Jo-Na. I knew I could count on you."

EARTH ALLIANCE HEADQUARTERS

"This meeting will come to order," called the Earth Alliance President, Binh Lee, as he pounded his gavel.

President Lee was Vietnamese. He served as the ceremonial head of the Earth Alliance. Every nation allied with the Confederation had been given two seats in the Earth Alliance's House of Ambassadors. From the House, fifteen members were chosen to serve on the Earth Advisory Council, no two from the same country. One additional member of the House, from a country not seated in the Council, had been chosen to be President. The Council was currently composed of ambassadors from Canada, the only permanent member, Brazil, China, Egypt, France, Germany, India, Israel, Japan, Poland, Russia, South Africa, Thailand, United Kingdom and United States.

Today the Advisory Council would receive a strategic update from Michael.

"Today's meeting is classified Top Secret. The material we discuss cannot be shared with anyone outside this room. As a reminder, if any information from today's meeting should become public, the Ambassador who leaked the information will be expelled from the

Alliance. The country that Ambassador represents will not be allowed to replace the Ambassador until the next session of the House of Ambassadors is seated. They will also be ineligible to have a representative on the Council for a period of 10 years. Anyone who does not wish to comply with these terms can wait in the isolation room," a door to that room opened, "until this meeting is over."

After a few moments, the door to the isolation room closed.

"Michael, if you will..." President Lee offered Michael the podium.

As Michael took the podium, he said, "My friends. I received some news yesterday that requires immediate action. It is imperative that it remain secret until we have decided how to respond."

"It's the Enemy, isn't it?" Ambassador Kosinski asked. Piotr Kosinski was a well-known diplomat from Poland. He had been a contender in the 2025 Presidential election there but had withdrawn from the race shortly after the Revelation and had sought the Confederation Ambassador job instead.

"Yes. It is. The Enemy recently captured FTL technology from a world they just consumed about 1,000 light years from here. Unfortunately, the species they destroyed had knowledge of Earth. So, instead of drifting in this direction at one-quarter light speed, they are coming here directly at 10 times the speed of light. Our previous estimate of onslaught was 4,000 years. It is now 100."

"Surely, 100 years is more than enough time to prepare a defense," said Margaret Whitaker, the Ambassador from the United Kingdom.

"Uncertain," Michael replied. This caused a great deal of commotion in the room.

With his hands up, Michael said, "Please. Please, let me continue." As the room settled, Michael added, "This is only the first of three things I have to share with you. None of them are good news."

The room became morbidly quiet. "We have also discovered, after centuries of searching, the Enemy's home world. It is close to Earth, but thankfully no easy or direct path exists between the two. Cosmic phenomena that human science does not know about yet block the direct path. If it did not, Earth would have been overrun millennia ago.

"Lastly, the Earth holds vast quantities of a very rare substance that the Enemy needs for survival. No other planet is known to hold even a fraction of the amount on Earth. Therefore, the Enemy will not stop its pursuit of Earth until the very last one of them has been destroyed.

"This third fact is by far the worst. If the first two were the only problems, then relocation would be an option. But this last piece of bad news means that we cannot abandon Earth, because if we do, the Enemy will become so powerful that there will be no place left to hide."

"Does that mean we have no hope?" asked Chinese Ambassador Hang Jiao-long.

"By no means." Michael said. "We have a great deal of hope. It will be difficult. There will be loss. But we have a great deal of hope. And ironically, because this is a threat to the entire Confederation, we will have a great deal of help."

"So, what must we do?" asked Sato Daichi, Ambassador from Japan.

"At this point, I do not have a complete plan. However, I know several elements of the plan that I would like to discuss with you." Michael paused, looking to the Ambassadors for permission to continue.

"Please continue," said Erika Schmitt, Ambassador from Germany.

"As a reminder, the entirety of today's discussion is classified, including the next disclosure, which could cause great harm if it were to become generally known."

"Continue," the German Ambassador repeated.

"First. The very rare substance that the Enemy needs is a material known as transluminide. It exists in great quantities on Earth. It is also the active ingredient in Confederation power systems. We must begin mining and refining operations to produce large quantities of refined transluminide. If we do this, then we will have the energy resources to fight, and we will have the financial resources to procure additional help from Confederation members."

"Second. We must develop a military space force to search out and destroy the Enemy ships in transit to the Earth.

"Third. A colleague has recently developed technology that will allow us to transit directly to the Enemy home world from Earth. We must industrialize this technology and corresponding weaponry, so we can launch a preemptive strike to destroy the Enemy home world."

Numerous voices started speaking, but one cut through them all. "How can we possibly afford this?" asked the American Ambassador, Paul Lewis.

"Transluminide," Michael replied. "It is the most precious material in the Confederation. There is more undeveloped transluminide on Earth than there is on any other planet in the three galaxies. Much more. That is why this information must remain secret. If it were to become generally known, even the Fleet might not be able to protect us from the hordes that would show up to steal it."

"What do you want from us?" asked the Russian Ambassador, Anton Petrov.

Michael went on to explain.

AMBASSADOR'S OFFICE

Michael arrived back at his office feeling good about the meeting with the Alliance Council. He had received approval to create a space force, start mining operations, start recruiting, and to host a press conference to make the announcement.

A couple of members had asked for space force bases in their countries and the right to populate those bases with their own troops. A committee would be working that issue.

As he walked in, Pam called out. "Michael, you received a call from Stephanie Davis while you were out. She said that she would be available until about 4:30 Hawaiian time if you wanted to give her a call back. She did not state a purpose, only said it was something you would be interested in."

"Let's see what she has for us," Michael said with a smile. "Can you get her and connect her to my line?"

...

Michael had barely sat down when the phone rang. "Stephanie. What a pleasant surprise."

Stephanie Davis served as Director of the WM Keck Observatory, which operated two of the giant telescopes located at the top of Mauna Kea, the tallest mountain in the Pacific. Stephanie and Michael had met over 10 years ago, before the Revelation. They had worked together on the supernova observation; the one that had consumed Michael's home world 2.4 million years ago, but whose light had only reached Earth the day before the Revelation.

"Michael, I cannot tell you how good it is to hear your voice. Thank you for returning my call. How is Canada treating you?"

"I love it up here, but the Big Island will always have a special place in my heart. How are things with you and the family?" Michael asked.

"June just started 11th grade. We will be hosting the back to school barbeque on Sunday. Seems like only yesterday that we were hosting it for her first-grade class. But everything is so different this year with John off to college and all. Have you seen him yet?"

John Davis was Stephanie's oldest child. He had graduated with honors from the Parker School in Waimea last year and had been accepted into the Engineering School at the Intergalactic Confederation's Ascendance Institute.

"In fact, I have," Michael replied. "I spoke at a social event for incoming students this morning and saw him in the crowd. Thankfully, he was still there after the formalities and I had a chance to catch up with him. I was very excited to hear that he was accepted into the Engineering School and of his interest in medical device design. Professor Reed is working miracles there. I would love to see John become part of that."

"Thank you for looking after him, Michael."

"How could I not?" Michael asked. "So, to what do I owe the pleasure of this call?"

"We finally closed the study of the Lorexian supernova. As you probably know the light has dimmed enough that our telescopes just aren't the right ones to continue the study. The study has been moved to the James Webb Space Telescope and the imaging should be incredible."

"Indeed, it should," Michael said. "I'm kind of surprised that you kept the study going this long."

"Webb had a little trouble coming up and we were getting remarkably clear images until recently. But with Webb up and our image quality falling away, it made no sense for us to continue." She paused. "Anyway, I'm calling to tell you that our computers were being upgraded and as the old ones were being uninstalled, the two thumb drives you gave us were removed. I had promised to return them to you or have them destroyed. So, what would you like me to do with them?"

Michael had forgotten about the thumb drives. "Is it OK if I have someone from the ranch, probably Kale, come pick them up?"

"Sure. I'll be here until 4:30 this afternoon. Have him come to reception and ask for me. I'll tell them to expect him." Again, she hesitated. "So, can I ask what these things are?"

Michael laughed. "You promise to give them back, once I tell you?"

"I think you can trust me, Michael."

"Remember when I told you that these would not work for any other observation?"

"Yes, you said something like they were keyed to this position."

26

"Indeed. They were. And are. The devices are linked to another computer of mine that is connected to a pair of highly directional, high-resolution gravimetric wave detectors. My computer could match the timing to the light, and the enhancement software could use the gravity data to enhance the visual image. I couldn't tell you then, or until we had sufficient alliances, because I didn't want the US Government tearing the island apart searching for gravimetric wave detectors. Similarly, the communications link between the two has some extraordinarily rare and expensive components that I didn't want in the hands of the US Government."

"So that's why the resolution is fading!" Stephanie exclaimed. "The supernova remnant has moved relative to the sun and your gravitational wave detectors are no longer aligned."

"Always knew you were the smart one." Michael complimented her. "Changing gears, have you considered taking sabbatical to come up to the Embassy and do the introductory professional course in stellar cartography? You would be great and would have a lot more to offer Keck when you got back."

"You're a good friend Michael. Can I take you up on that once June has graduated?"

"Any time. You'll have a priority slot when you're ready to take it."

...

"Michael!" Kale exclaimed. "So good to hear from you." Kale Iona served as the ranch's handyman. He was huge, muscular and Hawaiian. No one ever gave him trouble. He was just too big and friendly. When he left the ranch, women always gawked at him. What none of the humans knew was that Kale was an android.

"Kale, my friend, how are things at the ranch?" Prior to the Revelation, Michael had split his time between his home in San Diego and his ranch on the Big Island of Hawaii. In the weeks immediately before and after the Revelation, the ranch had been his main base of operation.

"Everything is good. Some scientists from the University of Hawaii finally found the cause of the centipede infestation along the trail north of the ranch. A couple months back, they did some remediation, which they think will hold. Now that the issue is finally settled, we have been given approval to refill the reservoir. That has been a big help. The state has even re-opened that portion of the trail.

"Other than that, things are very quiet here."

"Good news about the reservoir." Michael said. "Hey, I have something I need you to do for me."

"Name it, boss." Kale replied good naturedly.

"Can you run up to the Keck Observatory this afternoon? The Director has two thumb drives to return to us. They were used during the supernova observation. She will be there until about 4:30 this afternoon. Just ask for her at the front desk."

"Will do. I look forward to seeing her again. Been a while."

"Thanks, Kale."

MEDIA RELATIONS, CONFEDERATION ADMINISTRATION BUILDING

The phone rang and Sarah saw that the call was from Michael.

She picked up the phone with a smile. "Hi, this is Sarah Wright."

She hated the formality of that greeting when she knew it was Michael. But one morning shortly after she'd started, she greeted him with a somewhat saucy, "What can I do for you sweetheart."

She had been shocked to find out that the call was on speaker and the Emir of Dubai was in Michael's office with him. Michael invited very few people into his office. It was Michael's policy to take meetings in his conference room. Everyone had laughed and thought it was funny, but the next day the Confederation's worst kept secret showed up on the front page of every tabloid.

"Hi," Michael said, very affectionately. "Can you set up a press conference for Friday? I have two big announcements to make, then will take questions. I'll get you info on the announcements tomorrow, so you can do a simultaneous Press Release."

"Will do. Just enough time left this afternoon to get word out to the right people. You can tell me more tonight."

"Thank you, Sarah."

INVENTION

[Thursday, 8.22.2030] CONFEDERATION SCHOOL OF MEDICINE

Dr. Jackson Reed was a professor at McGill University in Montreal, Quebec. He served as Head of the Diagnostic Radiology Department but was currently on assignment at the Ascendance Institute in the Confederation Embassy Complex. He had been in New York the week his friend and fellow professor, Winston Chu, was scheduled to be on Good Morning America. Chu had been promoting his book 'Technology for a Green New Deal.' Dr. Chu had graciously arranged for tickets, so Jackson had attended the show. He'd been seated about five rows back from the disabled veterans and saw the healing of Sergeant George Butler up close. From that day on, his number one goal had been to study Confederation Medical technology and get involved in its conversion for human use.

As a department head at McGill, and with the recommendation of his friend Winston Chu, Professor Reed had won a position in the Imaging and Diagnostics Department as a researcher. Although technically part of the Medical School, most of his time was spent in the Engineering School, where he was adapting Confederation medical technology for human use.

When he first arrived, he, like all the other humans, had been overwhelmed by everything he saw. But he quickly got involved in a project with Professor Gupta, a Confederation medical doctor. Within a year they had a prototype of a new imaging system that could be used by human doctors. Now, four years later, it had gone into production. All radiologists in the current class were being trained to use it. Every radiologist that completed the class would be given a unit to take back home to their practice.

His current project was to develop a human-controlled system for medical nanobots.

CONFEDERATION SCHOOL OF MEDICINE

Professor Sadira Gupta served as head of the Imaging and Diagnostics Department at the Confederation's Medical School. She was an Ascendant on her 19th post-Revelation mission. Earlier in her career, she had aspired to be an Ambassador. But long ago she

29

realized that bringing 'advanced medical technology' to young species brought her a lot more joy than helping them settle their petty, self-interested squabbles.

She'd been part of one of the early missions to Earth and had led the first team to sequence the human genome. Her work had paved the way for the first human avatars. Michael had driven one of those avatars on his first mission to Earth during the Roman Empire. When she heard that Michael was going to lead a Revelation team to Earth, she petitioned the Confederation for a role at the Medical School they would open there. Michael had called her five years ago and asked if she still wanted the job. The rest was history.

Having been on 18 previous post-Revelation missions, Professor Gupta knew how to take imaging from Confederation scanners and work with engineers from post-Revelation species to convert it to a format compatible with their technology and medical practices.

She arrived on Earth six months after the Revelation and began teaching almost from the first day. A few months later she met Jackson Reed. From their very first meeting, she knew that he was the one that would bring the human-operated scanner to life. That scanner was now in production and being shipped out as quickly as they could train doctors to use them.

The first prototype of their next collaboration, a human-operated controller for nanobot therapy, was going into live testing today and Michael would be there to participate in the first procedure.

PROCEDURE ROOM, CONFEDERATION SCHOOL OF MEDICINE

Michael was excited about the procedure that was going to be done today. It was a simple one and would be performed on someone he knew very well, Alexi Santos. They had worked closely together on the liberation of North Korea.

Earlier this week, Alexi had rescued a climber who had become stranded during a snowstorm. She'd been grievously injured in the process. Her wounds were healed at the hospital within hours of her return, but some scar tissue had formed on her Achilles tendon. The scar tissue was causing quite a bit of residual pain. When she heard that a human doctor had developed a nanobot-based surgical procedure, she volunteered to be his first patient. Alexi liked to be the first to do everything.

As Alexi was wheeled into the treatment room Michael could hear her complaining. "This is really stupid. Even with the injury I can run faster than any of you and could probably take all of you at once in a wrestling match. I do not need to be wheeled around in a wheelchair."

Then, seeing Michael, she said, "Hi Michael. Are you the one behind this wheelchair nonsense?"

Michael could not help but to laugh at her spunk. "Good to see you too, Alexi. But I don't actually work at the hospital, so in this case, I may be innocent.

"On a more serious note, thank you for volunteering today. Professor Reed will be doing the surgery. Professor Gupta will be assisting. And I have override authority on the nanobots, so I can shut this down at any point if there is any indication that something is going wrong."

"Thank you for expediting the approval process on this device," Alexi said. "Even after five years, there are still too many North Koreans suffering from old wounds. I promised President Park that I would do everything I could to continue helping his people while I was on assignment here. So, I hope this works."

Alexi had worked closely with former General Park of North Korea, to establish prisoner of war camps for his troops when the Confederation stopped their planned invasion of the South. Once the troops were safely sheltered, Alexi and the General worked together to liberate North Korea's notorious slave labor camps. Ironically, they met when Michael and Alexi went in to arrest the former chairman. Alexi had taken the general into custody and had held him captive those first several hours. Then she'd become his partner through the transition, forming a very close relationship.

As Professor Reed wheeled his contraption into place, Alexi commented, "That does the same thing as Michael's scanner? It's like a hundred times bigger!"

"You know why, right?" The professor smiled at Alexi.

"Ah..."

"I'll give you a clue. How does Michael know what he's doing when he uses his scanner?"

"I have no idea how Michael ever knows what he's doing. That's why he is Michael and I am me," Alexi replied, which made the professor laugh.

"OK, point made. Michael sees the images the scanner creates through his implants. Similar with the controls. I doubt his perception is quite like viewing an image or clicking buttons on a screen, but without implants, humans need to see the images on a screen and issue commands through a computer interface. That's why my device is a lot larger. See how big the screen is?" He turned the device so she could see it.

"Cool. Is that my ankle?"

"Yes, ma'am."

"Dude. That's like five times the size of my ankle."

"And that's not even the close up. Watch while I zoom in on the scar tissue."

"Oh, man. That's really screwed up!" Alexi said.

"And exactly the reason it hurts."

"Maybe I do need the wheelchair," she said. The rest of the staff laughed.

"OK. Enough fun and games. Dr. Gupta, would you please administer the nanobot cream on Alexi's wrist? I'll take the ankle."

"Why apply cream to my wrist?" Alexi asked.

"The wrist gives the nanobots quick access to your blood. There are other spots on the body, like the inner thigh that would also work, but most people find that to be more invasive. And, before you ask, we apply the cream in two places so we can attack the problem tissue from two sides."

"OK. I am going to start directing the nanobots to their targets." Michael and Dr. Gupta got a faraway look in their eyes as they used their inner vision to watch the nanobots go to work.

"You might want to slow the nanobots down a little," Michael said. "Too many in the same spot can cause the patient a lot of pain. If you slow it down, the patient will still feel it. But it will be more like itching than being stuck with a knife. Although Alexi might prefer being stuck with a knife."

"Alexi says that's not nice," Alexi said. "Ah... It is definitely starting to itch."

"Want to see what the nanobots are doing?" The professor turned the screen toward her.

"Not a good idea," murmured Michael.

Alexi looked at the screen and saw a cloud descend on the tendon, which had previously looked like it was covered in scales. Slowly the scales disappeared with an occasional larger piece seen floating away. Then she noticed white smoke appearing above her ankle.

"Am I on fire or something?" she asked.

"No. Just the nanobots exiting back out through your skin and self-destructing."

Alexi looked back at the screen and saw that the cloud had disappeared, and that the tendon was clear of scales.

"Wow. That was cool. Are we done?" She started to move.

"No. Please stay still. We need to get the rest of the nanobots out first." Dr. Reed put a hand on her shoulder.

"But I feel great!" She squirmed a little more.

"Alexi please. We need to get all the nanobots out. Any of this type that get left behind are ultimately going to run amok and really start messing with your insides."

Five minutes later, they were done, and Alexi was on her way, walking under her own power.

...

"A quick debrief?" Michael asked.

They all gathered around the screen. "First of all, congratulations. That was the first nanobot-based surgery performed by a human on a live human body, and I think it went well."

"Agreed," said Dr. Gupta.

"Regarding Alexi's comment earlier about size... This is clearly a prototype; one that seems to work amazingly well. If we wanted to make ten more to start training additional doctors, how would you go about it?"

"I'm not sure I'd do too much different," Professor Reed said. "This type of set-up with the screen and computer mounted on a cart is fairly common in hospitals and clinics. The backward part of this prototype is the scanner mounted on the articulated arm. We needed to do that for our prototype scanner assembly because it's cobbled together. But now that we know the components needed, we could package the scanner in a smaller package, which could be held with a smaller arm. I see nothing that would prevent the device from eventually being handheld. But that is probably a little more engineering work than we would want to put in the critical path for training."

"I might be able to help with that." Michael said. Pressing a button on his collar he said. "Jacob, are you available?"

Jacob was an AI located in Tel Aviv, Israel. His primary responsibility was shield defense. But since peace had broken out, Jacob had started providing design and replication services.

"Here, boss. What can I help you with?"

"I am here at the Institute's Medical School with Dr. Gupta and Professor Reed. They have developed a variant on my medical

33

scanner-controller. The core device is essentially the same, but they have added an interface to human computer systems. Their prototype is too large to be handheld, but I'm thinking that it could probably be miniaturized to something about the same as mine if it were made in a replicator. Do you have time to help them with that?"

"Yes, I do. Things are really slow here, so I'd welcome the work."

"OK. I am sending you Professor Reed's contact information now. Please send him yours. I'm guessing he can get back to you in a couple hours."

"Done," Jacob said.

CONFEDERATION ENGINEERING LAB

Professor Jameson MacLellan served as head of the Spacecraft Propulsion Systems department in the Institute's Engineering school. The professor was neither a Jameson nor a MacLellan, and the circumstances that led him to this position could only be described as a fiasco.

The Professor (a Lorexian whose familiar name was Ka-Tu) was a high-ranking Confederation physicist, whose life had been turned upside down when his wife died unexpectedly at the relatively young age of 179 years old. He still loved physics, but with his wife gone, his passion for life had slipped through his fingers like grains of sand.

One day, he saw an advertisement targeted at Lorexian senior citizens approaching retirement age. It was from the Ascendancy and offered fast-track training that would enable seniors to become diplomats. It also guaranteed graduates placement as a diplomat serving a young species. Although he had never considered such a thing before, the idea had instant appeal. So, at the relatively advanced age of 195, he entered the Ascendance Institute on New Lorexi. The Confederation's new streamlined program for seniors allowed them to complete the program quickly, so they would still be alive to share their experience with a young civilization.

Ka-Tu had completed the program at age 209 and applied for the position as Consul General to Scotland on Earth. He had heard through the rumor mill that the Ancient Sentient was behind this mission and that Michael, one of the most respected members of the Confederation Council, had been appointed to the Ambassadorship.

Ka-Tu went through the process of qualifying in a Scottish avatar but, on route to Earth, word reached him that an error had been discovered during treaty negotiations, namely that Scotland, as part of the UK, could not have a Consul General. Therefore, his choice was to accept a position as Associate Consul to the UK for Scotland (a position well below his rank). Or he could take the only position open at his rank: Head of the Spacecraft Propulsion Systems department in the Engineering School, a job he was more than qualified for because of his previous career.

Unable to bear the thought of going back to New Lorexi or staying on Earth in a lower-level position, Ka-Tu had accepted the job as Head of the Spacecraft Propulsion Systems department.

When he arrived on Earth, six months or so after the Revelation, he was astounded at the natural beauty of both the planet and the embassy. He also found that he really liked his new human body and most of the humans he'd met. But most of the students coming through the Propulsion Systems program were not doing that well; none seemed to be mastering even the basics regarding faster than light propulsion systems. Then he met Eugene Xu.

[THREE MONTHS EARLIER] BALTIMORE, MARYLAND

Eugene Xu was a professor of Aerospace Engineering at Johns Hopkins University. He was a first-generation natural born American citizen, his mother and father having emigrated to the United States from China in the 1980s. His specialty was spaceship propulsion systems, a field made completely obsolete by the Revelation.

Eugene, who was eligible for a sabbatical starting in the spring of 2030, applied for a sabbatical fellowship at the Confederation's School of Engineering. His hope was to learn enough to salvage something of his career.

CONFEDERATION SCHOOL OF ENGINEERING

Ka-Tu was a bit disappointed with the Confederation staff that he'd been assigned. They were all brilliant. But none of them were having much success as teachers. The problem seemed to be the disconnect in the levels of education. His colleagues seemed unable to abstract their knowledge down to a level where the human students could understand them, and their highly intelligent, but under-educated, students were not happy about it. So he decided to teach the introductory course himself.

The course sequence was relatively simple: Combustion Drives, Ion Drives, Gravity Drives, Trans-Dimensional Drives, then Discontinuous Transition Drives. All so simple.

Most of his students already knew more than he wanted them to about Combustion Drives. Even the thought of those sent shivers down his spine. Who in their right mind would put a payload on top of a rocket propelled by a controlled explosion going on right underneath it?

Similarly, most of his class, drawn from the top human institutions, knew more about Ion Drives, and their seemingly infinite permutations, than he wanted them to know.

But the lessons that followed would be his students' first exposure to the theory behind and the properties of the main propulsion systems in use throughout the Confederation.

Ka-Tu first met Eugene Xu after his lecture on Gravity Drives. Eugene had come up to introduce himself after the session, then quickly cut to the chase.

"Professor, thank you for taking us through the overview on sub-light-speed propulsion systems. But I'm really hoping we will be taught about drive technologies that will take us to the stars. Are we going to cover that in this course?"

"Of course, we will. In fact, we'll be starting that in the next session." Ka-Tu replied.

"Yes!" Eugene exclaimed.

The excitement in Eugene's response was palpable, and contagious, at least for Ka-Tu. And for the first time since his wife's death, Ka-Tu found purpose.

This is a fabulously intelligent species that has not yet lost its curiosity, Ka-Tu thought to himself. *Maker be praised that I have landed here. Why did I ever consider the diplomatic corps?*

...

Eugene had been looking forward to this day since the moment he'd seen the lecture title on the syllabus. Trans-Dimensional Drives. He wasn't sure what a trans-dimensional drive was. But from the context of the rest of the course material and the professor's earlier remarks, he thought this was the main workhorse for FTL travel in the Confederation.

A fellow student had given nicknames to all the Confederation technologies. He referred to this one as the Warp Drive.

For the most part, students tended to arrive at class early and today was no exception. But conversation among the students buzzed with more excitement today than in any previous session. When

36

Professor MacLellan walked in, the class broke out in spontaneous applause.

"Good morning!" said the Professor. "And what a nice welcome. Earlier this week I overheard one of you saying that you hoped we would be discussing Warp Drive this week. I had not heard that expression before, so looked it up and discovered that it came from a TV show called *Star Trek*. I'm curious, how many of you are *Star Trek* fans?" He asked.

All the hands in the room went up.

"Well. I have good news for you. Today we will be discussing the Confederation's version of the Warp Drive." More applause started to break out, but the Professor put his hands up saying, "Wait! Wait! Before you get too excited, I have some much better news." A hush fell over the room. "I spoke with the Ambassador yesterday. And he approved a field trip for our class." A pause. "On Saturday, we will be heading out on a short excursion to Alpha Centauri, including multiple orbits of Centauri A, Centauri B, and one of Centauri B's planets."

The room exploded with applause and cheering that the Professor let run for about 20 seconds. Then he raised his hands to quiet the class. "The purpose of our trip will be to demonstrate and experience Gravity Drive within the inner system, followed by Trans-Dimensional Drive through the outer system, which will include a sling shot around Saturn and past the Oort Cloud, then Discontinuous Transition Drive to our destination."

After more cheering and some questions about the trip, the Professor started his lecture on Trans-Dimensional Drives, more than once slipping and calling them Warp Drives.

PRESS CONFERENCE

[Friday, 8.23.2030] EMBASSY, PRESS ROOM
When Michael had announced the presence of the Confederation on Earth, he'd promised a press conference in the first week. It actually happened on day ten, something the press never quite forgave him for. So, when the Embassy was built, he included a press room to make press conferences a little easier for him logistically.

At first, he held weekly press conferences, announcing the accomplishments of the week. But after a couple months, the press conferences devolved into meaningless Q&A sessions focused on rumors and gossip. Over time the sessions became less frequent. Now there was a monthly press conference conducted by a spokesman, who would put out a statement and take questions on the statement.

Today was different. A press release put out two days ago announced that Michael would be making two announcements of consequence this week and would answer a limited number of questions. As Michael approached the door to the press room, he could hear the commotion in the room and wondered if this had been a good idea.

He opened the door and the cameras started flashing. He walked to the podium. He smiled, waited for five seconds, then started speaking. "My friends. Let me start by thanking those present for being here today and thanking everyone who is watching or listening for your time and attention. I have two announcements to make this morning. Then I'll take limited questions.

"My first announcement relates to Medical Technology. As many of you have undoubtedly heard, Confederation medical scanners have now been configured for use by human doctors. Every doctor in the current class will be trained how to use this device. And each one will be given a scanner to take home. Ten thousand units will go out at the end of the month. Another ten thousand, possibly more, will go out every month thereafter until every human has access to this technology." The room got noisy as people shouted questions, but Michael put up his hands to calm the room.

"As good as that sounds, there is more. Yesterday, the first human doctor performed the first procedure using the surgical version of the scanning device. This is the same type of device that I used to cure Sergeant George Butler five years ago. Over the next week or two, ten more prototypes will be put into service. These will be used to train the current class of human doctors at our Medical School on Confederation surgical techniques. By the end of the year, we hope to have 50,000 human doctors trained and equipped to use this technology." Once again, the room erupted with shouted questions and other noise. After about 10 seconds, Michael continued to the second announcement.

"I have a second announcement to make. Today the Earth Alliance announces the formation of a human Space Force. Five years ago, when I announced the Confederation's desire to ally with the nations of Earth, I told you that there was a distant threat approaching the Earth, one that could possibly destroy it, if you were not prepared. I also said that even though that threat was a long way off, we would need to start preparing in the next couple of years. Well the time to start preparing is upon us.

"Initially the Space Force will explore and patrol the Solar System. The scientific knowledge accumulated in the first couple of years of its work will more than compensate for the human time and talent that will be taken by the Space Force. But I expect the first mission outside our solar system to begin within a year. And it is my fervent desire that the Space Force can be made capable of taking the fight to the Enemy within the next 10 years, so that the Enemy can be defeated before they even get close to Earth.

"The Space Force will be a volunteer organization; no one will be compelled to join. However, it will be a military organization, not a civilian one. Anyone who would like to volunteer will be welcomed. We hope to draw heavily from current and former members of allied armed services. Recruitment centers will open starting this evening in Alaska and Hawaii and tomorrow in the rest of the world. They will be located at, or near, major airports around the world. We will be putting out daily press releases announcing the locations and hours of the recruitment centers.

"Thank you for your time. I will now take questions."

Every hand shot up, as the room exploded with questions. Michael saw Keoni Gates raise his hand and said, "First question to Keoni Gates."

When Michael first met Keoni, he had been a local reporter with the Fox affiliate KHON in Honolulu. He did two interviews with Sergeant George Butler at Michael's ranch in Hawaii, which catapulted both George and Keoni onto the world stage.

"Michael, thank you for taking my question. Does the fact that we are starting up the Space Force now imply that the threat from the Enemy is more imminent?"

"Yes and no." More noise erupted. "Please, let me explain," Michael said, and the room started to settle.

"The original plan was to start the Space Force after two years, as I told the world in interviews shortly after the Revelation. That we have waited five, almost five and a half, years might lead you to believe that the threat is less imminent. Sadly, that is not true. I got word a few days ago that the Enemy destroyed a technologically advanced world about 1,000 light years from here in the general region of space where we knew the Enemy was active.

"The civilization that was destroyed was very advanced. They had faster-than-light travel and had managed to stay hidden from us, so we didn't know of their plight until it was too late to help. The bad news is that this civilization knew of Earth and had previously sent a probe to Earth. During their collapse, the Enemy captured their technology and their knowledge of Earth."

He paused.

"An advance Enemy force is now headed directly for Earth. With the faster-than-light technology the Enemy now has, we expect them to arrive in 80 to 90 years." Once again, the room exploded with questions.

Having already gone with a reporter he knew, Michael pointed to a reporter that he didn't know.

"Jill Larson, Toronto Star. How could there be a civilization that the Confederation did not know about?"

"I'm sorry. I don't know the answer to that question. The Confederation first became aware of this situation a few days ago. The Fleet is on route to the planet to investigate. We will let you know more when we know more. Next question." Michael said, pointing to a reporter that he'd met before and knew to be fair.

"Jack Williamson, Chicago Tribune. How will the Confederation be helping us in this fight?"

"Thank you for that question, Jack. The Confederation will be providing extensive assistance. No resource will be spared. The Fleet is

40

establishing search grids to find the Enemy. They are also establishing picket lines along the expected routes. Our leading scientists are working on enhancing our detection technologies and developing better weapon systems. The Confederation's manufacturing facilities in this sector stand ready to build humanity a fleet of its own to handle close-in defense. We are also looking at plans to make offensive attacks against known enemy strongholds in the hope of diverting their attention away from Earth.

"But please understand… We only learned of this a few days ago, so the only thing I can say with certainty today is that the Confederation will stand with the Earth until the Confederation's dying breath."

"Next question." Michael pointed to another reporter.

"Kung Mei-Hua, China Global Television Network. How will the Human Space Force be funded?"

"Thank you for that question, Ms. Kung. The Human Space Force will be funded according to the terms of our treaties. Loosely speaking, that means the Confederation will cover the costs of creating and operating the fleet. The costs that will be left to the nations of Earth are two fold. First, the cost of the land used for the ground-based military bases located in your country and the salary for citizens of your country serving in the Space Force under your flag. Said more colloquially… If you want a Space Force Base in your country, then you have to lease us the land at a lease rate of 1 cent per year, or the smallest denomination of your currency. The Confederation will cover the cost of developing and operating it. Similarly, if you want personnel serving in the Space Force to be designated as service members from your country, then you need to pay them according to your tradition. All their costs of living will be covered by the Confederation while serving in the Space Force."

"Next question," Michael pointed to another reporter.

"Miles Jeffery, BBC World News. Michael, can you tell us more about the new surgical device? What it does? How it is different from the one you use? How it was tested? That sort of thing."

"Thank you for that question, Mr. Jeffery. Let me start by saying that I'm very excited about this development. The medical part of this device is identical to the one I use. It has a dimensional resonance imaging system and a surgical nanobot control system. The only real difference between the new device and mine is the user interface. I connect to mine telepathically. The images simply appear in my mind and I control its function through my thoughts. The new device connects to a flat panel display to show an image that the human doctor can see with his eyes. Both the device and the display are controlled by a computer that has the normal selection of user interface devices: mouse, touch pad, keyboard, touchscreen, etc.

"Regarding testing, the active medical portion of the device is unchanged and has been used for millennia. The human interface part has gone through months of simulation but was used on a live person for the first time this week. For those of you that follow local news, there was a daring rescue of a stranded mountain climber earlier this week during a blizzard near Keele Peak. The rescuer, Alexi Santos, was grievously injured. Confederation doctors did the first round of surgeries immediately following the rescue. The final surgery was done at the Institute's Medical School. It was done in a treatment room by Dr. Jackson Reed of McGill University's School of Medicine. Dr. Sadira Gupta and I were in attendance.

"I am excited about this because the Confederation only has about 1,000 doctors available to treat humanity, so waiting times are very long for patients suffering from conditions that are not imminently life threatening. By the end of the year, we expect to have 50,000 doctors trained and equipped to do this work in their home countries. Very exciting! Next question." Michael pointed to another reporter.

"Jonathan Omeruo, Kameme TV, Kenya. May I say thank you for coming to Kenya last year to meet with our leaders and help negotiate the peace that has now taken hold." Applause broke out across the room.

Michael used the interruption to say. "Jonathan. Thank you for that reminder. Meetings and outcomes like that are what makes an ambassador's life worth living. What question can I answer for you?"

"Kenya is going through a period of unprecedented peace and prosperity, as are most of our neighbors. My question is... How long can this last? Many in Africa fear this is temporary, and that the Confederation will eventually abandon us."

"Please leave Mr. Omeruo's microphone on," Michael said. "Jonathan, do you know how old I am? And what my life expectancy is?"

Omeruo thought for a moment then said. "Shortly after the Revelation, I saw a news clip in which I think you said that you were 20,000 years old but didn't expect to live to be one million. Did I remember that correctly?"

"More or less. I am closer to 25,000 years old and, as you say, my life expectancy is less than one million years. Within that context, let me answer your question. I will fight for the Earth and for the people of Kenya until my dying breath. Africa will not revert to its former state. I stake my life on that statement."

The room broke into thundering applause.

"Thank you for your time today. I will give you updates as things change." Michael said, as the lights dropped and the door he was to exit through cracked open.

HONOLULU, HAWAII

Keanu Tajima felt... restless. That was the best word he could come up with. It started five years ago, the night he participated in the raid on Michael Baker's property on the Big Island. He'd never heard of Michael before that night. Now of course, everyone knew who Michael was, the Ambassador to Earth from the Intergalactic Confederation.

The night of the raid was the night he died. A stupid death, taken down by centipedes on a trail marked as a hazard to human life. According to his teammates, he had been dead for about 20 minutes. Cold to the touch. No pulse. Then, Michael... resurrected him... for lack of a better word. For the last five years, he had drifted. His fitness reports from the FBI dropping a little more every year.

He'd lost his girlfriend. Couldn't blame her for wanting to get away from him. He wanted to get away from himself. He'd lost most of his connection to his family.

As he waited at the bus stop for the ride into town, the thought of getting on his paddleboard and making a final trip out into the ocean, just would not go away.

The bus came. He climbed on and took a seat and, moments later, the bus started rolling. Out of the corner of his eye, he saw the newspaper one of the other passengers was holding up. The article had a picture of a spaceship and was titled, 'Earth Alliance Space Force. Experienced Volunteers Wanted.'

...

A half hour later the bus stopped, and Keanu got off. As he walked toward the building entrance, his friend and colleague, Jim Ryan, came up next to him.

"Hey, Ryan." Keanu said.

Jim had also been part of the FBI Team that had attempted to raid Michael's ranch the night of the Revelation. Jim had been part of the team on the south trail. He did not get injured and had participated in the rescue of the team on the north trail.

"Did you hear?" Jim asked. "The Confederation is starting up a Space Force. Just announced this morning. They are looking for volunteers. I think I want to sign up. There are interviews this afternoon at the airport. Qualified candidates can ship out tonight for additional interviews at the Embassy. Interested?"

Jim had been suffering as much as Keanu from the events of that night. Maybe this was a good idea.

APPLIED REACTIONS DEPARTMENT, SCHOOL OF ENGINEERING

Valerie Jensen was an Ascendant. Her familiar name was Va-Re. Like many of the other professors at the Institute, she had signed on with the Ascendancy in the hopes of becoming a diplomat, only to find out that it fundamentally wasn't who she was. In some sense she was the ultimate anti-diplomat. Her education in chemistry, coupled with two very bad diplomatic assignments, had led her to fantasize about devious ways to just blow stuff up. Those fantasies had led to a checkered career of continuous reassignment and an eventual transfer from the diplomatic corps to the Ascendance Institutes established on new worlds.

About five years ago, she'd been contacted by Michael and asked if she would consider a position as Professor of Applied Reactions at the Institute on Earth. 'Applied reactions' served as the Lorexian name for weaponry. She would have ample time for research during the first couple years and would have access to significant funding during that time. There would be no teaching requirement at first, but her contract would specify five classes per week.

Va-Re had accepted almost immediately. The administrator of her current Institute had made it very clear that he wanted her gone. And Michael, as a sitting member of the Central Council, had the resources to do as he promised.

Once the contract came through, Va-Re researched every destructive technology known to 10,000 species. Years earlier, she had determined the vulnerabilities of the Enemy. Over the last five years, she'd gone crazy devising truly devious ways to destroy trans-dimensional creatures.

On arrival at the Embassy on Earth, she received her appointment with the Institute and was given a well-equipped lab in which to do her research. After four years of research, she had finally been given a class to teach. The initial course schedule had just one section. It was offered on Tuesdays and booked into a room with seating capacity of 30. When she was told of the arrangement, she thought, *if I actually get 30 students, it will be the largest class I've ever taught.*

HONOLULU INTERNATIONAL AIRPORT

Jim and Keanu got out of the car near the International Departures entrance. They'd decided to splurge and spend $50 for a Lyft to the airport. After all, if they were accepted, they wouldn't be coming back. And if they weren't accepted, then maybe tonight would be the night to head off to Australia on their paddleboards.

A sign marked 'Earth Alliance Space Force' pointed to a long line that started at the end of the terminal and stretched down around the corner to parts unknown. They got in line and waited nervously as the line slowly progressed.

Jim smacked Keanu on the arm pointing. "Look, it's a shuttle taking off. I wonder if Elsie is piloting it." Elsie had been the pilot of the shuttle that rescued Jim and Keanu's teams that night. Jim still remembered his brief conversation with Elsie. He had thought about her many times since then.

They finally went around the corner where they could see the people doing the check-in and initial screen. Manning the desk was none other than Mark Patterson, the team leader on the North Trail that night. Keanu had been part of Mark's team. Both of them had died that night. Unable to control his excitement, Keanu broke ranks and went running forward, waving his arms and shouting, "Patterson!"

Mark got up from the desk and went to meet Keanu.

"Brother! Can't tell you how good it is to see you again!" Keanu said. "Didn't think you'd made it."

"I'm told it was a miracle that I did. Are you here with anyone else?" Mark asked.

"Yes. Ryan is holding my place in line." He pointed back to where Jim stood.

"Come on. Let's go get him." Mark turned to his partner at the desk and said, "Cover for me. We'll be back in a minute."

45

They grabbed Ryan, then headed back to the desk. A couple big guys started to protest but quickly shut up when they saw that Patterson was wearing an Earth Alliance uniform with colonel's bars.

"I can't tell you how glad I am to see you guys. I spoke with Michael earlier today and he told me to get you on the next shuttle if you came in."

Seeing the question in Jim Ryan's eyes, he added. "Yes. They are still the same people we, well you anyway, met that night. They took me in and healed me against all odds. Put me through physical therapy. Then enlisted me to join them at the Embassy in Canada.

"Michael is going to be very happy to see you. He has said from the first day I met him that you two were destined to be part of the Confederation. I'm glad we're going to get to work together again. This time on the right team."

RIVERSIDE PARK, CONFEDERATION EMBASSY COMPLEX

Sergeant George Butler led a team of veterans in the final stages of their recovery. They were running a marathon around the entire length of Riverside Park in the embassy complex. George was a veteran of the conflict in Afghanistan, discharged from the US Army after having his C4 vertebrae fractured in a suicide bombing incident. On the morning after Michael's Revelation announcement, George had been seated with the disabled vets in the studio audience of Good Morning America. He'd been quadriplegic with no motion below his neck. Michael had wanted to heal someone that morning and he'd wanted the most dramatic healing imaginable, so he'd chosen George.

George was the first of many cured by Michael during the Revelation, and soon became a spokesman for the Confederation. His notoriety as a recovered quad and spokesperson for the Confederation, eventually led to an appointment as a coach in the Recovery Program at the Institute's medical school. As a Congressional Medal of Honor recipient and the first recovered quadriplegic ever to complete the Ironman competition in Hawaii, he was an inspiration to the vets he worked with at the Institute.

As George ran, his thoughts fell back to those days, the healing, meeting his sweet Noelani, competing in the Ironman.

...

"George, you can do it," Noelani said. "You've done the miles on the treadmill. You've done the miles on the bike. Try swimming."

Some weeks later, they'd started swimming together at the Hapuna Beach Park. The sight of Noelani in a bikini was enough to get George to do anything.

Over the next year, they'd completed the qualifying races. Then they ran the race, Noelani at his side the entire time. In truth, it was a bit of a blur until the final stretch along Ali'i Drive. The professional athletes had finished hours ago. He was in the middle of the amateur pack. But people lined Ali'i Drive, cheering him on. When they crossed the finish line, the announcer said. "Sergeant George Butler, you are not just a Medal of Honor recipient... You are an Ironman!"

"Noelani Manoah of the Big Island of Hawaii. You are an Ironman."

As the volunteers came to offer them towels and assistance to the recovery area, George fell to his knees and pulled a ring from the light chain around his neck and asked, "Noelani, will you marry me?"

The TV cameras had caught the image of George on his knees and the image had gone viral.

The memories brought a tear to George's eyes.

Today, his wife Noelani was once again running with him and his team. Noelani was a Confederation medical tech who also worked with recovering patients. She was also an android. Under Confederation law, androids were full citizens with full rights. Most first contact species struggled with the personhood of androids. But from Day 1, George would have none of that. Noelani was his soul mate. And nothing would ever dissuade him.

FIELD TRIP

[Saturday, 8.24.2030] SPACE FORCE COMPLEX

The Embassy complex was huge, 100 square miles in total. The vast majority had been fully built out. But even after 5 years, the complex was only 60% occupied. To a degree, that was intentional.

From day 1, Michael had known they would need to build a space force. He also knew that it would initially be housed at the embassy.

Now that Space Force had been authorized, Michael had started powering up sections in the northwest portion of the Embassy Complex; sections that had not been assigned yet. The timing could not have been better. More and more volunteers were arriving every day. They already had over 25,000 and several member nations were pledging troops. The US alone had pledged 25,000. China, not to be outdone by the US, also pledged 25,000. The UK and France had each pledged 10,000. Russia pledged 2,000. And President Park of North Korea had pledged 1,000.

Multiple challenges came with such a rapid expansion; facilities, supplies, command structure... And that was just the basic logistics. At the top of the list, Space Force needed spaceships and weaponry.

SHUTTLE PAD, EMBASSY TRANSPORT CENTER

A group of about 30 students had assembled near one of the gates at the Embassy's Transport Center. Sitting on the other side of the gate was the Ambassador's personal shuttle. It was actually a Fleet Military Escort that had been converted for civilian use. It was the largest spacecraft currently on Earth, as well as the only one suitable for interstellar flight.

Eugene had only been to the Transport Center once before, on the day he arrived from Baltimore. What surprised him about it today was how busy it was. Shuttles were coming in, discharging up to 50 people, then taking off again as soon as the landing area cleared.

Two hundred or so people had arrived on shuttles since he'd queued up here at the gate. Most of them were lined up in a similar queue at a gate about a quarter mile away. Only they were trying to get into the Embassy complex, not leave it.

48

A commotion rippled through the assembled students as the door to the shuttle opened and a flight attendant walked over to Eugene's gate. The gates here were unlike gates at any airport he had been to. They looked like metal doorways just sitting in the middle of nowhere. The fence around the Transport Center was a force field, invisible to the eye, but much stronger than a cement wall. The force field was marked by a red line on either side of it. Where the gate was, the red lines would turn green when the gate could be traversed.

All non-human Confederation staff could just walk through the force fields. They were keyed in some way that Eugene didn't know about. The flight attendant walked through the gate to their side and asked to see the ID of the person at the head of the line. She nodded and the entrance turned green. As the person walked past, the entrance reverted to red. As all the students had their IDs on their lanyards, the process went quickly.

Eugene entered the shuttle and was surprised to see how luxurious the interior was. The entrance opened into the shuttle just behind the last row of seats. The seats were leather. They were comfortably wide, and the rows were far apart. This was far nicer than any first-class cabin he'd ever walked through on a commercial airliner. To his surprise, his fellow classmates were taking seats in this cabin. Eugene was one of the last to find a seat. The flight attendant gave a quick overview of the seat functionality, which included some cartoonish holographic depictions of seat use and misuse. As she finished, a doorway formed in the forward wall and Professor MacLellan walked through with the Ambassador himself.

Michael was the first to speak. "Ladies and gentlemen. Thank you for enrolling in the propulsion class at the Institute. My friend, Professor McLellan here, speaks highly of you. I was surprised when he contacted me to ask if it was possible to do a field trip like this. We've never done one before, but it was immediately obvious to me how valuable it would be for you to experience space flight using the technologies you are about to learn.

"I look forward to hearing about your experience today. If this goes as I expect it to, then it will probably become a standard part of the course going forward. Enjoy your day today, and please follow the instructions the professor is about to give you."

With that, Michael walked to the exit, greeting several people along the way. The door sealed as soon as Michael went out.

"Class, for the most part you will experience no sense of motion while traveling aboard this space craft. As good as that sounds, most people suffer from vertigo the first time because what they see with their eyes doesn't match what they otherwise sense. The symptoms are usually mild, but they can be severe. So, to prevent any unnecessary unpleasantness, please open the little lotion packet in the cup holder on your seat and apply it to your wrist."

For the most part, everyone did as they were asked.

"Now for the first surprise. We actually launched a few seconds after Michael left and are currently in the process of breaking orbit. In a moment, I'm going to make the walls of the cabin mostly transparent. We will keep them that way for most of the trip. I'm also about to move your seats. They will be reoriented into a bleacher-like formation pointing toward the sides of the cabin. Please remain in your seats."

All the seats started rotating toward the side walls of the cabin. The seats closest to the walls settled down a little lower than they had been. The next row rose a little higher and moved a little closer to the wall. The whole process only took a few seconds, but it made it a lot more obvious why the seats had been spaced as far apart as they were when they first boarded.

"And, now... The Earth," said the professor as the wall seemed to disappear.

At some point the shuttle must have rotated because the Earth appeared above them toward the rear of the cabin and was moving visibly away from them.

The professor started talking again, explaining the gravity drive and inertial dampening systems, then superimposing charts and formulas over the view of the outside. The charts showed their position and intended course. Their speed, now well over 1 million miles per hour, acceleration, and the relativistic impact, which was essentially zero, were all displayed.

...

They had been cruising for about a half hour now and were well past the orbit of the moon, so both Earth and Moon were visible. Because they were headed away from the Sun, most of the view was of the dark side of the Earth and Moon, which was a bit creepy. Eugene could feel no movement, but realized that they had to be moving fast, because the Earth was now about the size of a penny held at arm's length.

The professor, who had taken a short break, began speaking again. "On Tuesday, I told you that we would be doing a sling shot around Saturn. That turned out to be a less than perfect translation of what I meant. I will walk you through the math of this in a little bit, but here is the course we will be taking."

The plot of their course that they had seen earlier was once again superimposed on their view of space outside. The image zoomed out and rings showing the orbits of the planets appeared, as did markers showing the planets' current locations and their craft's position along the course.

"As you can see, at our current speed, it will take us a long time to get there. Even if we had continued accelerating at 20Gs, like we'd been doing earlier, it would take quite a while. It would also risk relativistic effects. So, we're about to engage the 'warp' drive. Entering warp at our current speed will have the effect of us moving at 3 times the speed of light. At that speed, it will take us about 21 minutes to get to Saturn, with a net relativistic time dilation of less than 1 second.

"Before we enter warp, let me explain what you will experience. All trans-dimensional travel is disorienting because for a fraction of a second your visual cortex will process light images at a different speed than usual. Some people sense this to be a stretching of time, as if time suddenly sped up or slowed down. Others experience this as objects stretching or shrinking. When transitioning to warp, the effect is very short, lasting only a moment. Most people have a passing sense of dizziness. Few ever get sick.

"When entering jump space, the effect is longer and much more pronounced. Most people will feel dizziness, sometimes intense dizziness. Many get sick to the stomach the first time. The lotion you applied earlier is sufficient to protect 99% of humans. If you are worried that you are among the 1%, it is safe to take another dose.

"We will be entering warp momentarily. I've set the computer to provide us a count down." The professor stopped talking.

After a few seconds the automated count down started. "Entering Warp space in 5, 4, 3, 2, 1, transition."

Eugene did not feel a thing. But he saw several people nearby shaking their heads as if to clear them.

The professor resumed his lecture. "We will be approaching Saturn close enough for it to deflect our course. As you can see in the animation..." The image of their course zoomed in on the area around

Saturn and started playing an animated loop that showed speed, direction, and a velocity vector. "...our overall course change is only a few degrees and the speed change less than 10 percent. A friend at NASA told me that they would consider that a gravitational assist, not a sling shot.

"Once we reach the point shown in the animation, we will jump to Alpha Centauri. That will be in 26 minutes. I'll let you enjoy the scenery until about 3 minutes before the jump. If you would like some food or drink, or need to visit the rest room, now would be the time."

...

"The view of Saturn was great wasn't it?" The professor asked and got a round of applause for his statement.

"Please take your seats. We will be jumping momentarily. Hopefully none of you will have an adverse reaction, but everyone needs to be seated with their seat belt fastened."

...

The automated announcement started. "Jumping in 5, 4, 3, 2, 1, transition."

What a strange sensation. Eugene thought. He could tell time was passing, but everything was frozen; the only thing moving was his thoughts. Then it was over. He felt a moment of disorientation, which passed almost instantly as sounds from around the cabin came flooding back in. He turned to see what was going on. Apparently, the idiot at the end of the row had not buckled in or used the medication. He had fallen to the floor and was groaning. Eugene shook his head... *Some people just have to learn the hard way.*

Then he saw people at the other end of the isle pointing toward the ceiling. There were three stars. Two on the left side of the ship were very close to each other. One was yellow, the other orange.

Those must be Centauri A and B. Eugene thought, then looking at the red star on the right. *That must be Proxima Centauri. Who would ever have believed that I would be here, four plus light-years from Earth?* He found himself laughing at the preposterousness of it.

...

The trip took about 10 hours. They had left at 9:00 AM and landed at about 7:00 PM, a little before sundown. Eugene really didn't have words yet to describe the experience. Exiting the shuttle, he found himself exhausted. He also realized that he'd changed his mind about something. He came here in hopes of learning enough to remain relevant. That was no longer enough. He wanted to become humanity's leading expert on Warp and Jump drives, to be the first to actually contribute something to the technology the Confederation had given them. He also knew exactly where to start... the math. If his new dream was possible, he knew he would find it in the math, because that's what he did best.

TELEVISION STUDIO, EMBASSY PRESS RELATIONS DEPARTMENT

The studio was set up like a sitting area. There was an end table in the center, with one chair on the left and two chairs on the right. Each of the chairs was angled toward a common spot maybe 10 feet in front of the table. Out of sight from each other, there were four television cameras, one pointed at each chair and two in the middle framed to take in the whole scene.

Today's interviewer was Malcolm Fleming of the BBC. In the first chair on the right was former Sergeant George Butler. The other chair on the right remained empty.

Shortly after the Revelation, Sergeant Butler had started doing interviews with the media. His objective was to spread the word about the things the Confederation had to offer. His first two interviews drew viewing audiences that challenged the Superbowl. Over time the novelty wore off and the audience numbers dropped. But they were still very high. Once the Embassy was built, George hosted a guest interviewer every week. The interviewer could use the studio, or do the interview in the field, or both. George and the interviewer would agree to a set of topics, locations and guests, then the interviewer would drive the interview.

Today, they were going to cover three topics: the mountain rescue, the surgical controller and Space Force. The show would be shown on BBC tomorrow, then would be available on the Confederation cable channel and available for license by any channel or news organization.

A small studio audience had been seated about 15 minutes ago. They applauded loudly as George and Malcolm came in to take their seats, but quieted quickly when the Quiet sign lit up and the producer counted them in.

"Good afternoon, World. This is Malcolm Fleming, BBC News, reporting from the Confederation Embassy in the Mackenzie mountains of Canada. With me is a man that I'm sure you know, Sergeant George Butler, the informal spokesman for the Confederation." He turned toward George.

"George, thank you for inviting me here today. I think we have a great show lined up."

"Thanks for coming to talk with us, Malcolm. I look forward to talking with you and giving your audience a glimpse at life here at the Embassy," George replied.

"Our first guest is none other than the Liberator of North Korea herself, Alexi Santos," Malcolm said.

The crowd erupted in applause as Alexi walked onto the stage and took her seat. As they quieted, Alexi said, "Malcolm, thank you for having me on today."

"Alexi, I understand that you were involved in two big events this week, a dramatic rescue on Keele Peak, then as the first subject of a new human-operated nanobot surgical tool."

"Yes. I was there for both of them." She seemed uncharacteristically reserved.

"We have short clips of both of these events to show our audience, but let's set the context first. Can you start by telling us about the rescue?"

"Yes, I would be happy to. I operate the adventure outfitting concession here at the Embassy. We provide tours of various types into the nearby wilderness. We have fishing, hunting, mountain climbing and photography tours that we operate. We also have supply packages for those that want to head out on their own. I am a licensed tour guide and was leading an expedition to climb Keele Peak. On Sunday, the weather was perfect for a peak attempt. Bright sun, no clouds. Perfect.

"We left an hour before dawn and started up the southeast ridge." A map of the area appeared on screens around the studio and as an inset in the broadcast image. "The climbing team did a great job. We reached the peak after only four hours and spent about an hour at the top, taking pictures, resting and having some refreshments."

The image on the screen changed to show six people clad in climbing gear, clustered around the peak.

"As we started down, the wind picked up a little, which it does almost every day. But in the distance, large clouds were visible. About that time, I received an alert that the weather had suddenly and unexpectedly changed. So we all tied on and started down the ridge at maximum safe speed.

"We were about a quarter of the way down, when the cyclone warning came in. This is a relatively new phenomenon, caused by a sudden rush of warm, moist air coming down from the Arctic Ocean and hitting the cold mountain air. The alert also included a blizzard warning for the mountain peaks.

"We continued down the ridge, pulling up the men that fell or were blown over the edge, but it was clear that we weren't going to make it all the way back to base camp. So, as we approached the last technical descent, we pitched a shelter near a cliff face, where we could stay until the storm subsided," Alexi said.

"Alexi. If I could interrupt for a second." George said. "I did a search on some of the Confederation scanners and found this image."

The image popped up on the monitors in the room and as an inset on the TV. It showed six people tied together in a line. A seventh, somewhere in the middle, was dangling by his ropes and was being pulled up. Although the image was clear enough to understand, it was clouded by blowing snow.

"Yep. That's what it was like," Alexi replied.

Malcolm said. "So, you set up a temporary shelter near a cliff face..."

"Yes. With the shelter up, we were protected from the wind. We also had a small heater that could keep the shelter around 45 degrees Fahrenheit or 7 degrees Celsius. It was tightly packed, but we would survive, or at least so I thought.

"Once the guys were settled a bit, I checked the updated forecast and saw that the snow was going to be heavy, and with a little calculation determined that it would completely cover the dome, so we would suffocate if we stayed there."

"What did you do?" Malcolm asked breathlessly.

"I attached a rope to one of the shelter's anchor points, then jumped off the leeward side of the cliff."

"That's the downwind side, right?" Malcolm asked.

"Yes." She replied.

"Why didn't that kill you?" Malcolm asked.

"I was wearing something called an anti-grav harness. It is like a climbing harness but has a small grav-drive sufficient to lift you off the ground. I used the grav-drive to fly down to the base camp dome, where I attached the other end of the rope. That gave me something like a bridge between the two domes.

"Using a carabiner to attach myself to the rope. I quickly flew back up to the shelter, grabbed the first of the guys and ferried him down."

George interrupted again. "Amazingly, a Confederation weather drone captured a short clip of one of the transits down."

On the screen, the clip played. It showed Alexi dragging a man out of the shelter dome, clipping him onto the bridge rope and onto herself, then jumping off the cliff, dragging the screaming man with her. They went out of range of the weather drone about halfway down to base camp.

The studio audience gave a standing ovation after the clip.

"What did that feel like?" Malcolm asked.

"Great fun. Really enjoyed the ride. Although the screaming from the wuss I was rescuing was a bit much."

The studio audience laughed at that line.

"But something went badly wrong, didn't it?" Malcolm asked.

"Yes. On the final run back up to the shelter, the bridge line broke. Suddenly, I was just flying off into the wind with a piece of limp rope in my hands, not knowing if or where the other end was attached.

"I got tied on just before the rope snapped taut. The jerk was so strong, it knocked me out for a second." The sound of breath being sucked in could be heard from the audience. "When I came to, I was tethered to the rope maybe 1,000 feet off the ground. Thankfully the grav-drive was not damaged. Then, I started pulling myself in hand over hand until I reached a snow drift. Took me a second to figure out that the shelter dome was now completely covered in snow that I would have to tunnel through."

"How did you do that?" Malcolm asked.

"Well at first, I tried to tunnel in. That didn't work at all. New snow would fill my tunnel as quickly as I could dig it out."

"What did you do?" Malcolm asked.

"This is a little harder to explain, so George was kind enough to do a demo of the technique yesterday. The basic idea is that the rope was tethered to the dome. So, if I just started going up and down, left and right, the rope would cut the snow like a knife and the wind would blow it away."

The clip started playing. It was bright and sunny out. George was wearing an anti-grav harness and connected to a pole with a climbing rope. The rope was buried by a huge pile of snow. George levitated and slowly backed away from the pole until the rope was taut, then started moving back and forth using the rope to cut off layer after layer of snow.

Again, the audience applauded.

"So," Malcolm said. "What happened next?"

"I don't like this part of the story very much," Alexi replied. "The wind shifted and slammed me into the cliff face near the shelter. I hit hard, breaking my leg, and breaking the anti-grav harness. I was about 20 feet above the ground, so fell hard and landed on the broken leg. This made a mess of my leg. The bone shattered and cut through the skin. There was blood everywhere, so I knew I wouldn't last long if I didn't get into the shelter. I hopped a couple feet toward the dome, lost my balance, fell into the dome and passed out."

Sounds of anguish could be heard from the studio audience.

"Fortunately for me, the last person I was going to rescue, a fellow named Jack... Big shout out to Jack! He used the first aid kit to apply a bracing device on my shattered leg, which stopped the bleeding. It also injected some pain killers and hardened up to protect my leg.

"I woke up a few minutes later, not remembering too much about what was going on. There's poor Jack passed out in a puddle of mostly frozen blood. I couldn't figure out what he had done to lose that much. So, I got up to help him. It would probably be more accurate to say, I attempted to get up to help him. That's when I realized that I was the one that was hurt, and he had patched me up.

"Assuming Jack had passed out at the sight of so much blood, I went to work on the anti-grav harness. I quickly figured out what was wrong and fixed it. But Jack hadn't woken up. A quick scan showed that he was suffering from severe hypothermia. The problem was that his personal shield generator, something we give all the mountaineers to help keep them warm, was not working. I found the problem and got him connected back up, but he was too cold and did not have much time left.

"With the anti-grav harness working again, I anchored our last rope to the shelter and to myself. Then I anchored Jack to the rope and strapped him on my back. Once that was done, I levitated up off the floor and took off. Visibility had dropped to zero and I no longer had a guide rope to lead me to base camp. I spent the next hour trying to find my way back, finally spotted a light, then headed in that direction. It was the base camp. Can't tell you how happy I was to see it. Forgetting that my leg was broken, I went in for the perfect parachute landing. You know, coming in at speed and running to a stop. In my mind, that was the only way I would get Jack in without him hitting the floor.

57

"It almost worked. First leg landed and stuck. Second leg just bent up. I landed hard on the stone floor, Jack landed on top of me, cracking several ribs, and we slid into something very hard.

"The next day, I woke up in a hospital. Jack had been warmed up by then and was completely OK. I had undergone surgery to repair a badly broken leg, a broken arm and collar bone, seven ribs and a massive concussion."

The studio audience was on their feet again, applauding and cheering, as the recording cut to a break.

...

"Welcome back to the show. This is Malcolm Fleming, BBC News, reporting from the Confederation Embassy in the Mackenzie mountains of Canada. I am here with George Butler, Alexi Santos and another guest that I would like to introduce you to, Professor Jackson Reed of McGill University in Montreal, currently on sabbatical at the Confederation Medical School. Professor Reed, welcome to the show."

"Thank you, Malcolm. Great to be here."

"We have heard the story of Alexi's heroic rescue of a stranded mountain climber and of the grievous injuries she sustained in the process. But a day after her surgeries, problems started to surface. Can you tell us what problem she was facing and your role in helping her?"

"Yes. Let me start by asking Alexi what happened after the initial surgery?"

"My leg hurt," she said. The audience laughed.

"May I tell the audience why your leg hurt?"

She looked at the professor as if he were nuts. "Please, tell them already. That's why you're on the show." More laughter from the studio audience.

Somewhat chagrined by the exchange, Professor Reed said. "Scar tissue had formed on her Achilles tendon. This is a common complication following human surgery of this type. It is much less common for Confederation surgery, but it can happen in certain situations. In Alexi's case, there were multiple potentially life-threatening injuries, all of which needed to be treated within the first hour after she was brought in. As a result, her surgeons made the call to do a fast repair on her leg, the most critical injury because of the associated blood loss, so they could get to the ribs, which were threatening her major organs.

"The quick procedure has a relatively high-probability of scar tissue formation, so a second surgery was expected. But this surgery was different, because it was at the level a human could do with the new human-operated, nanobot surgical tool that I developed." Professor Reed said.

"Do I understand correctly that this was the first time your human-operable tool had been used on a live patient?" Malcolm asked.

"Yes," Reed replied.

"Alexi, you volunteered to be the first patient this equipment was used on. Why?" Malcolm asked.

"I was involved in the liberation of the North Korean slave labor camps. The condition of those poor people was unspeakable. Even with the dozen or so Confederation doctors we had, we could not save them all," Alexi said with emotion in her voice and a tear in her eye. "Of the 220-some thousand that we rescued, thousands are still crippled, have horrendous scars, or have other issues that Confederation technology can fix. There just aren't enough doctors.

"So, when I heard that the Professor was making Confederation technology available to human doctors in a way that could help some of those people, I volunteered to be the first guinea pig for him to try it out on."

Once again, the studio audience broke into applause as the recording faded to black.

...

"Good afternoon, World. This is Malcolm Fleming, BBC News, reporting from the Confederation Embassy in the Mackenzie mountains in Canada. I am here with George Butler. Earlier in the show we had Alexi Santos with us telling about a daring rescue earlier this week and the injuries she sustained in the process. Then we spoke with Professor Jackson Reed, whose new human-operable surgical suite based on Confederation technology was used in healing Alexi. For this last segment, George has invited another special guest who we'll bring out in a minute. But first, a question for you, George.

"What do you think about the formation of Space Force?"

"As I understand it, our treaties with the Confederation put the responsibility for protecting us in the hands of the Confederation. I'm not an expert on this, so may be wrong. But, setting aside treaty obligations for a moment, I think it is appropriate that the peoples of Earth have some role in the protection of the Earth. My reasoning is simple. We, meaning humanity as a whole, have spent most of our existence fighting and killing each other."

That comment brought some rumblings of discontent from the studio audience, but George continued undeterred. "For the most part, the Confederation has brought an end to that. Now they are asking for volunteers from every nation, every people on Earth to band together and come to the common defense. I think that this maybe one more way that they're bringing healing to us."

There was some clapping and a number of people saying 'Amen' in the studio audience.

"Is that the Confederation's position on this George?" Malcolm asked.

"Don't know." George said. "They really didn't include me in their deliberations, which is probably a good thing. Michael and the Earth Alliance are really smart people. Me? Not so much."

Some chuckles from the audience.

"Do you have any advice for people thinking about joining space force?" Malcolm asked.

"First." George said. "I have great respect for those that choose to volunteer. As I understand it, the threat is very real. I also have more respect for and trust in our current leaders than any that have come before.

"Second, I volunteered once. I served honorably, was grievously injured while faithfully performing my duties, then given new life by Michael and the Confederation. My calling now is taking care of those that are wounded, injured or otherwise damaged while serving. My wife, Noelani, has the same calling. So, rest assured. If you go and are ultimately broken, Noelani and I, plus a lot of other good people here at the Embassy, will be here to make you whole again. You will not be abandoned. That is a promise."

The studio audience exploded into a standing ovation.

"Thank you, George." Malcolm said. "I, for one, have really come to appreciate your perspective on things."

Then turning to the center camera, Malcolm said. "Our next guest is Colonel Mark Patterson, of Space Force." The camera zoomed back, as Mark walked out and took the seat next to George.

"Colonel, welcome. Let me start by asking... Space Force was only announced yesterday, yet here you are, a colonel, today. Can you explain how that came to be?"

With laughter in his voice, Mark replied. "Malcolm, happy to be here with you today, but the way you said that sounded so nefarious."

As he turned to the main camera, he continued, "Trust me, there is nothing nefarious about my appointment to Space Force. As Michael said in his announcement, Space Force has been in the planning stages since shortly after the Revelation. As Michael also told us during the Revelation, the Confederation was going to help us, but they would need our help if we were to prevail in the coming struggle. So, even before the Revelation, the need for something like a Space Force was known, spoken about in the press and baked into our treaties."

"Hmm..." Malcolm started. "I recall Michael making those statements during his various press appearances. Hadn't thought about it that way until just now."

"So, to your question, Malcolm... I was grievously injured the day after the Revelation. In fact, I was pronounced dead on the scene. Michael took me in. Healed me. And allowed me to do physical therapy at his ranch in Hawaii with George.

"You may not remember this, but I was part of George's initial round of interviews with Keoni Gates at the ranch. That was back when Keoni was still a local reporter in Honolulu."

"No. I didn't remember that," Malcolm said, wondering why that was not part of his preshow briefing.

"At that time, I was a Special Agent with the FBI. In fact, I was one step away from having 'Special Agent in Charge' status. But after my injury, my appetite for the FBI just wasn't there anymore. Michael understood that and offered me the opportunity to join a planning group at the Embassy. That group put together the proposal for a defense planning committee. The proposal was approved by the Earth Alliance about three years ago.

"The Defense Planning committee is the group that put together the Space Force proposal that the Earth Alliance approved last week."

"I had no idea," Malcolm said.

"None of this has been done in secret." Mark said. "We have issued reports that were included in the monthly press releases. But, in truth, this is dry stuff that just doesn't get much coverage.

"Now, back to your question about my commission. One of the things our group did was to prepare lists of candidates for senior roles, advisory committees, etc. My name was on the list of officer candidates. When the Alliance Council approved the Space Force charter earlier this week, a commissioning board was formed. I interviewed for a position, was selected, and on Thursday got my commission. My first job was recruitment in Honolulu. That was my last assignment in the FBI, so I have a lot of contacts there. Friday afternoon, we picked up several hundred recruits, and here I am today."

"I had no idea," Malcolm said, repeating himself.

"The Confederation is a very friendly place, something that shows through to the public. I think that some people may associate friendliness with disorganization. That would not be an accurate image of the Confederation. It is an incredibly friendly place. It's also pretty well organized."

"Can you tell us anything about Space Force's organization. Specifically, I've heard rumors about both Naval and Marine ranks. Can you say anything about that?" asked Malcolm.

"Yes, and no. Yes. There are both Naval and Marine ranks being commissioned. No. The formal organization is still being finalized, so anything specific I might tell you might not be true.

"But the skills required to pilot, navigate or maintain a spaceship are different than those required to do things on the ground. For example, assume that there is a scientific mission operating on the ground on one of the planets orbiting Bernard's Star, which is six light-years away. Now assume that something goes badly wrong. You want the best pilot, navigator and ship to get you there. But you would probably want the best team of marines you can find to do the rescue.

"It is the opinion of almost everyone on the planning teams that organizing ourselves in a way that separates space and spaceship operation from ground actions will incent our service members to hone the skills required to excel."

"Wow. Hadn't thought about it that way before," Malcolm said. "Thank you, George and Mark, for sharing your insights into the new Space Force, and to Alexi and Professor Reed for their work in driving Confederation Medical technology into human hands.

"This is Malcolm Fleming reporting for BBC News."

SUNDAY

[Sunday, 08.25.2030] ENGINEERING SCHOLAR RESIDENCES

Eugene woke suddenly. In his dreams he had found the angle of attack he needed to take on the math behind the Warp drive. He had to write this down before it was lost. Somewhat begrudgingly, he got up, went to the office area in his apartment and lit up his computer. Afraid he was going to lose the insight before the computer woke up, he started scribbling key words on a tablet. By the time the computer was ready, the ideas in the dream had started to fade.

Looking at his notes, the 'ah-ha' came back and he started typing like crazy. Two hours later and stone cold awake, he knew he had the solution. He had one instance solved. The theory of his solution was evident in his code and in his notes. With one instance solved and the notes he'd made, Eugene was confident of finding a general solution in the morning. After saving his work, he shut down the computer and headed back to bed knowing he would sleep well.

As he climbed back into bed, he saw the clock. 2:30 AM. He closed his eyes and deep sleep came over him.

NORTHERN LIGHTS CAFÉ

Michael and Sarah were meeting Emmanuel and Bahati Mbanefo for breakfast this morning. They would have Sunday brunch at the Northern Lights Café, one of the up and coming restaurants at the civilian edge of the new Space Force Academy. This part of the Embassy Complex was not exactly new. It had been built out five years ago but was only now coming to life.

Emmanuel and his wife Bahati were human Ascendants, the only two so far. They were South African and had been working for and studying with Michael for nearly 100 years, since the outbreak of World War II. Michael had hired them as laborers for a mining operation in 1939, and they had been together ever since. Shortly after the Revelation, they had undergone the enhancement surgery, and were now inhabiting human avatars that were very similar to their natural bodies.

63

Michael and Sarah arrived first. "Mr. Ambassador. Ms. Wright. Welcome to Northern Lights. I was not aware that you planned to dine with us today." The hostess said, anxiety clear in her voice.

Sarah reached over and touched her arm. "It's OK. We have reservations under a different name. It's Bahati Mbanefo, party of four." Sarah noticed a camera flash.

"Is your party all here?" The hostess asked. There was another camera flash.

Michael intervened. "No. They will be here momentarily." Another camera flashed. Michael opened his senses and determined that the poor panicking hostess's name was Jamie. "Jamie. It's Jamie, right?" She nodded. "I think your restaurant will do better if the paparazzi get pictures of us sitting inside enjoying your hospitality, than it will with pictures of us waiting outside. We really are here to have brunch with the Mbanefos."

Jamie, very uncomfortable with the gathering crowd, saw the wisdom in Michael's words and escorted them to a table as far from the front door as possible. A few minutes later, she was back with Emmanuel and Bahati.

"Brother, so good to see you," Emmanuel said.

"You two seem to draw a crowd wherever you go, don't you?" Bahati piled on.

Hugs and air kisses were exchanged all around before they sat.

...

Brunch had been excellent, and it was clear that the Northern Lights Café would be a hit.

"I'm glad this place opened up on this side of the complex. It's been quiet on this side. But with the opening of Space Force, I am expecting about 100,000 new residents to immigrate over the coming month," Michael said. "Which is going to overload all the businesses on this side."

"How many people do you expect to join?" Emmanuel asked.

"Our short-term goal is 100,000, maybe half of which will be stationed here. But many will bring families, and many stationed elsewhere will spend several months here for training. We will also be manufacturing a lot of Space Force-related products here, which will add more people."

"Is there anything we can do to help?" Bahati asked.

"Yes. There is." Michael replied. "I have a very interesting project that I'd like you to lead. Any chance we could meet tomorrow?"

"Of course, Michael. We are currently working security for special projects and are between projects, so the timing is excellent," Bahati replied.

After a little more conversation, they relinquished their table so another party could enjoy an excellent meal.

ENGINEERING SCHOLAR RESIDENCES

Eugene woke excited to get back to work on the math of trans-dimensional propulsion. For Eugene, experiences like the one last night were not all that uncommon. Over the years, he had developed a method that he referred to as 'directed dreaming.' Fill your mind with a topic you're interested in as you relax in bed, then turn it over to your subconscious as you fall asleep. The few people he'd told about it thought he was nuts. More than once, he'd looked up the idea online, but what he found didn't really match what he experienced. Nonetheless, the seeds of his most important discoveries had all come in his dreams, which made sense to Eugene.

He'd done that last night and dreamed about riding on waves of simultaneous differential equations like a surfer. Then, as he rode, the waves became dis-organized and he could see the terms causing the problems. The flash of insight in his subconscious was enough to wake him up, and he knew from experience that the memory would only last for a few minutes. So he'd bolted out of bed, ran to his desk in the living room, wrote enough to pull the memory forward, then worked the simplest instance of the problem to a conclusion. Now, he was going to take on the whole problem.

The memory of the dream made him smile. *If I ever told a 'normal' person about surfing on differential equations, they would think I'm crazy.*

Pencil and paper, computer and a large cup of coffee in hand, he dove in.

...

Three hours later, Eugene was exhilarated and exhausted. He'd derived a complete solution. After a short break, he went on-line and compared his solution to the Lorexian solution. Disappointment washed over him. His solution was different than the Lorexian's. He must have done something wrong.

I need to run this off. He thought.

Dragging himself out of his seat, he changed into his running clothes and shoes, went down to Riverside Park and joined the people doing the short, two-mile loop near his building.

SUBRAMANIAN RESIDENCE, MEDICAL RESIDENCES

"Vanya, your friends are here." Nisha called. Nisha Subramanian had worked for many years as the Assistant to India's Prime Minister. When she was 48, she had developed squamous cell carcinoma. It started in a saliva gland, then slowly progressed out under her jaw and around her neck, massively deforming her face. Nisha's doctors had told her it was benign, but it continued to spread, eventually ending up in her spine. By her 52nd birthday, she could no longer work. That was the year of the Revelation. As part of Michael's presentation to the Indian Parliament, he cured Nisha. As with any advanced cancer, Michael was able to relieve Nisha's pain and eliminate the cells that were an immediate threat during his demonstration. But the last step, the one that ferreted out the last of the metastatic disease, required a day or so in a regeneration tank. In Nisha's case it took more than two days, which not only cured her, but did facial reconstruction and, as a side effect, de-aged her by a little over twenty years. Her husband Mahesh also received some therapy, spending the better part of a day in a regeneration chamber. That had the effect of de-aging him 10 years.

Although they thought of themselves as a 52-year-old and a 57-year-old, after the treatments, their bodies were 31 and 47 respectively. Three months later, Nisha had discovered she was pregnant with a baby girl.

Today was Vanya's fourth birthday. Four of her preschool friends had come over to the Subramanian's apartment for cake and ice cream.

The Subramanians had accepted positions as hosts in the Medical School's residence complex. Their job was to help students adjust to life at the Embassy. Their primary clientele were medical students from India. But as with all Confederation staff, they helped anyone that needed help. It was the best place either of them had ever worked and the perks included housing, food and medical care.

Helen Butler, Sergeant George Butler's mother, had also taken a hosting job in the Medical School complex. Her home was in the building across the way. Helen was thrilled when she heard Nisha was pregnant and had been there since day one to help with Vanya. She was helping with the party today as well.

The phone rang. Nisha picked it up and said, "Hello, this is Nisha."

"Nisha. So good to hear your voice. Just calling to wish Vanya Happy Birthday." Michael said.

AMBASSADOR'S RESIDENCE

Back home, Michael had a couple loose ends he wanted to take care of today. His first call had been to the Subramanians. The next was to Mark Patterson.

"Michael. How are you this beautiful Sunday afternoon?" asked former agent, now Colonel, Patterson.

This man has changed so much, Michael thought.

"Sorry for disturbing you on the weekend." Michael said. "I have a quick question that I'm pretty sure you know the answer to."

"Shoot," said the colonel.

"The first of the Space Force classes starts on Tuesday. How many recruits do you expect to have enrolled?"

"We've brought in 30,000 recruits since the announcement Friday morning. We expect another 10,000 to come in tomorrow, although they will all miss the enrollment deadline. Any chance we can relax that a bit?"

"Have them sign and date the Institute's application form at the same time they sign on for recruitment. Mark it 'received' before they even get on the transport. Anyone signed up before the end of the day on Monday will be eligible to sign up for open classes, or for standing room wait lists," Michael said.

"Then I think we will have about 40,000 and I'm sure half or more will be signing up for the weapons class."

"Thanks, Colonel. That is exactly what I needed to know."

...

Within hours of the first Space Force shuttle landing, over 5,000 students had applied for the 30 seats allocated for the Applied Reactions class. Michael had expected that the number would be high. In fact, he still expected 30,000 or more to apply. But he'd known the resistance he would get from the mostly Lorexian Bursar's Office if he had asked them to open more seats ahead of time. So, Michael had decided to let the application system speak for the demand he knew would come from the Space Force.

...

Alexi, Michael sent on internal. *Are you near a communicator? I have something I'd like to ask you.*

All the non-human Confederation staff occupied avatars. The avatars had implants that allowed direct access to a host of apps including something like text. As Alexi tended to spend as much time in the wilderness as possible, Michael always contacted her using the internal messaging system.

His communicator rang. "Hi Michael. I'm in my apartment today, recovering from the surgeries this week."

"I'm pleased to hear that." Michael said. "I have a favor to ask. Professor Jensen's class on Applied Reactions starts on Tuesday. Would you volunteer to be an assistant in her class?"

"Michael. Me? In a classroom? Someone's going to get hurt!"

"It's the weapons class."

"The weapons class! Where do I sign up?"

"I'm going to send out a request to a couple of people today asking them to volunteer. I'll include you. But this is going to be a popular assignment, so I wanted to let you know so you could be first in. Just stop by her office tomorrow morning. She's in the directory."

"You've got it, Boss. Thanks."

RIVERSIDE PARK

Throughout the run Eugene kept thinking about the trans-dimensional drive math. He could find no issues with the way he'd framed the problem. The computer had even validated that his derivation was 'correct'. But he could not see a way to replicate the Lorexian solution.

It's as if we had started in different places, Eugene thought.

That triggered an epiphany. *Oh my god. Transitioning into dimensional space is a chaotic process, highly dependent on initial conditions. My solution does not control for this.*

With this insight blazing in his mind, Eugene sprinted home as if his life depended on it and started a new solution that controlled for initial conditions.

AMBASSADOR'S RESIDENCE

Michael had one more thing he wanted to accomplish today. Professor Jensen was probably the Confederation's best weapons designer. She had discovered the enemy's multi-dimensional nature and their sensitivity to magnetic fields. She had developed the flux bomb and the disruptor rifle. The Enemy had learned of her and had set a trap in which she'd been caught. Fortunately, she'd escaped.

Michael was convinced that she was one of the keys to winning this war. But she was also an outcast, something that had worn on her for years and had ultimately eroded her self-confidence to the point where she was barely functional.

Now she was about to be the center of attention of thousands of students, so Michael needed to put a support structure in place. He sent out a note to a handful of people asking that they consider volunteering to work with Professor Jensen. This would be the first time she would be teaching a large class. The success of her course was an imperative. She'd need their help, even though she didn't know it yet.

"You have the skills she needs to pull this off," he wrote. "Please see her and volunteer to help."

IT DEPARTMENT, ASCENDANCY INSTITUTE

The Institute's IT department worked 7 days a week, including limited consultation time for students on Saturday and Sunday. Eugene had now worked out solutions for transitions into 'warp' space and into 'jump' space. He had even worked a solution for transitioning from 'warp' to 'jump'. None of his solutions matched anything he could find in the Confederation databases, but he had found references to simulators that could accurately simulate the equations that defined these phenomena. He was curious to see if his solutions could be simulated. So he grabbed his computer and went down to IT to see if he could get a copy.

There was only one person in line in front of him, so he decided to wait. His patience was rewarded 15 minutes later when an IT consultant became available.

"Hi. I am a student in the Propulsion Engineering Department and am working on a problem. I saw a reference to simulation software in the course manual and wanted to see if I could get a copy," said Eugene.

"Hmm..." Lauren, the IT consultant, said. "I haven't heard of that one before. Let me see if I can find it."

She searched her database and found the software. "Yes. Here it is. There is a student version you're eligible to use. And there's a link to the companion design software. Would you like that also?"

"Sure. That would be great!" Eugene said.

Lauren scanned the ID on Eugene's computer, then checked out copies of the software to his machine. She had Eugene turn on and sign into his computer, then accept the download request. After a minute, the download was complete, and the licensing agreement accepted. Eugene launched the software and a moment later a screen popped up that was completely indecipherable, and his machine started making bizarre sounds.

Lauren hit the stop button. Shaking her head, she said, "Oops! Lorexian version. In my natural form, our language sounds so smooth and melodic. But to the human ear, it is just plain nasty."

Eugene couldn't help but laugh at the idea of this pretty young woman making sounds like that. "Agreed."

"Let's see." More searching on her computer. "Ah, found the language converter. It says that it's for the professional version." More searching. "I don't see one for the student version. Let's see if the professional translator will work with your copy."

Moments later the download request showed up on Eugene's computer. He accepted the request, then several other requests, then finished.

"Let's try it again," said Lauren.

The program opened and immediately started playing the tutorial training program in English.

"Looks like it's working," Eugene said.

"OK. Good luck with it. I'll be here for another 2 hours this afternoon. Come see me if you have any problems."

GUEST HOTEL, EARTH ALLIANCE RESIDENCES

Among the many things the Confederation had done in preparation for a space force buildout was to identify key humans they wanted to serve on the various Advisory Boards. After the Council meeting on Thursday, which included approvals of the various advisors, invites were sent out to the Ship Design Advisory Board for the first meeting tomorrow.

All eight candidates had accepted the invitation and were shuttled in from their homes earlier today. There would be meetings the next three days at the Earth Alliance Headquarters next door. They were provided with accommodations in the hotel portion of the Earth Alliance residential building and a guest accommodation card that they could use to pay for meals and incidentals at any of the Confederation-operated restaurants or stores in the complex.

Tonight, they had been invited to a reception in one of the hotel ballrooms. The reception was being hosted by Binh Lee, President of the Earth Alliance Council, Erika Schmitt, the Earth Alliance Council senior representative from Germany, and Colonel Mark Patterson of Space Force, along with their respective spouses.

President Binh Lee's job was mostly ceremonial. For the last several years he had hosted at least one reception like this every week, and he and his wife, Trang, had become quite good at it. They always arrived first and left first. Their first job on arrival was to assure that the room had been set up perfectly, which it always was anymore. Their second job was to greet and brief the other hosts on their guests, as well as the things the Earth Alliance Council wanted to accomplish at the reception. Tonight would be the first time they met the Pattersons. Word was that the Colonel was reserved and thoughtful, and that his wife Ruth was mouse-like and rarely spoke, not good qualities for a host. Nonetheless, Michael told him that it was important that the Pattersons be involved.

President Lee heard the door open. *Punctual to the minute, must be the Schmitt's.* He thought as he turned to greet them. "Good evening..., Colonel Patterson?" The man that entered the room resembled the picture he'd been given, but not much. He was tall, athletic, straight as a rod and wearing a very sharp dress uniform. But the woman was stunning. She wore a flowing red ball gown that accentuated her natural beauty and complimented her thick auburn hair. But, the most unexpected thing was the way she just glided into the room. This woman was no mouse. She was going to be the center of attention tonight.

"President and Mrs. Lee," she said with a soft southern accent.

The President was mesmerized and struggled to speak. "Mrs. Patterson." He had unconsciously raised his hand as if to shake but she skirted right past it and gave him a light hug with air kisses on each cheek, then turned to greet Mrs. Lee.

The Colonel shook the hand that was still out there and said, "President Lee. A pleasure to meet you, sir. Sorry about that. When Ruth dresses up and makes an entrance, she can suck all the oxygen out of the room."

His senses finally returning, Binh said. "I was given a short brief on everyone coming tonight, which is standard diplomatic practice. There was little information on you and a very bad picture that made you look 20 years older. There were only two sentences on your wife, which implied that she was very shy and rarely spoke."

That comment made Mark laugh. "I think I would hire someone else to develop your background information going forward. But it's true that we've both changed a lot in the last five years. I was severely injured the evening of the Revelation, near Michael's ranch in Hawaii. In fact, I was pronounced dead by the medic on our team. But Michael's team rescued me and brought me back from the brink. I was 45 at the time. The Confederation team had a hard time putting me back together and, in the process, de-aged me by 25 years. Poor Ruth thought she'd lost me, then when she was finally able to visit, she found that I was younger than our son. She went into a deep depression, which the Confederation treated. It included about 15 years of de-aging therapy. She came out the other side as the woman you just met."

Yet another miraculous Confederation transformation, President Lee thought.

Next to arrive was Erika Schmitt and her husband Dieter. Wherever Erika went, she always made an entrance. That was one of the reasons Binh had asked her to join them tonight. Her energy always brought life to a reception. The briefs on the various advisors that would be here tonight were very dry. So, Binh hoped Erika's energy would spark more conversation among the advisors. Tonight, it looked like she was going to be upstaged.

One by one, the various members of the advisory board arrived. President and Mrs. Lee made a point of greeting and taking them around to meet the others. His most important mission tonight was to make sure that each of the members met and got to know one another, so they would already be a nascent team when they met Michael tomorrow.

The last of the team members to arrive was Enzo Venezia. He was the only one on this team that did not have experience with a space agency. The brief said that he was a ship architect. When he came in, he made an entrance as interesting as the two women and within a half hour had kissed the hand of every woman in the room. Despite all the flash, Binh was very impressed with Mr. Venezia. What Binh had not discerned from the brief was that Enzo designed custom luxury yachts. He accepted no work for yachts of less than 250 feet or that would cost less than $100 million. And, he only took those if there wasn't a $200+ million yacht in the sales pipeline. Most of his large ships included complete medical bays outfitted with everything required for full anesthetic surgery.

Enzo had also started doing the interiors of retired 747 and 777 airliners being refitted for private use.

Binh was always impressed by the people Michael invited to consult with the Embassy. It was going to be hard to find another posting like this once his term expired.

ENGINEERING SCHOLAR RESIDENCES

Back in his apartment, Eugene was amazed at how easy it was to use this software. It took 15 minutes to enter his solution for transition to 'warp'. Then, 15 minutes later the simulation was complete. A big green check mark showed up on the screen and a box with the simulation metrics.

Wow. Eugene thought. *The transition efficiency is about 90%. And the transition stability is 99.999%.*

He repeated the process for transition to 'jump'. The results were similar, efficiency of 81%, stability 99.0%

He then tried his solution for transition from warp to Jump. *Odd,* he thought. *Efficiency 99%, Stability 99.9%. Why is it better entering jump from warp than from normal?*

Then he murmured aloud. "I wonder how that compares to the Lorexian solutions."

He looked up the textbook solution for transition from normal space to warp space. A half hour later the green check mark was back. But efficiency was only 43% and stability was only 81%. "What! This can't be right."

Doublechecking his work twice, he could find nothing wrong.

"Let's try their solution for transition to jump space."

A half hour later another green check box, although Eugene was surprised that the check box was green after looking at the simulation metrics. "10% efficiency. You've got to be kidding me. Stability... 41%. This can't be right."

Searching around the screen for other metrics he might add, he found one for distance. But it had numerous settings that had to be entered to make the distance calculation.

Finally, he clicked on something labeled Ship Type and a list of over 100 ship types came up. He tried something entitled Diplomatic Shuttle. An image of the ship that had brought him to the Embassy from Baltimore popped up. Selecting that ship, he got a range calculation of about 3.4 light years.

I wonder how my design would do, he thought.

Going back to his normal-to-jump simulation, which he had saved, he clicked through to the Diplomatic Shuttle. Range: 101.4 light years.

"Fun thought," Eugene said. "But I'm obviously doing something wrong."

Clicking around some more he found a way to enter a flight plan and calculate efficiency, stability and range. He put in a plan that went from normal to warp to jump and back again. Once again, the simulation came back with a big green checkmark and a range for the shuttle of just over 1,000 light years.

Figuring that this had probably been a colossal waste of time. Eugene saved his work, shut down the simulator and opened the design software. To his amazement, the software had the propulsion designs for the same 100 ship types. Popping open the Diplomatic Shuttle, he saw the component list. The purpose of each was well documented. As he looked at the Plasma Flow Initiator, he saw a link to the underlying theoretical foundation. Clicking on it, the simulator opened, and a simulation of the part was shown, along with some diagnostics that Eugene had not found on his own. One showed the shape of the field being formed. It was more or less cylindrical.

Eugene found where this chart was, closed the program, then restarted it with his solution. *Curious,* Eugene thought. *My field looks like a rippled ovoid, not a cylinder.*

...

Eugene had it. He had a mock design for a plasma regulator that could be placed in the shuttle that had brought him from Baltimore that would increase its range 10 to 100 times.

Looking around he noticed that the sun had come up and it was almost 10:00 AM.

"Wow. Got lost in that one, didn't I?" He yawned and got up to go to bed.

"Wait. Prof. MacLellan has office hours today. I should make an appointment." He ran back to his computer. There were no slots open today but there were several available the next day, Tuesday. He sent in a request for the last one. Then went to bed.

PREPARATION

[Monday, 08.26.2030] BURSAR'S OFFICE, INSTITUTE ADMINISTRATION BUILDING

"Mr. Ambassador, sir." The chief bursar Alan Bryant, a Lorexian, said. "I'm sorry to disturb you on short notice, but it seems we have a situation. Demand for the Applied Reactions class far exceeds expectations and is well beyond our ability to deliver. I think we are going to need to cancel this class."

"Please explain," Michael said.

"We have over 5,000 applicants for a class with 30 seats. There is no way to allocate so few seats to that many applicants on a fair basis."

"Maybe we should open more seats," Michael said patiently.

"But, how could we do that? There is only one professor in this specialty and the classroom that has been assigned only holds thirty."

As a career politician Michael had seen this kind of mindless bureaucracy over and over again. But this degree of non-mission-aligned behavior had been on the rise over the last hundred or so years and Michael could not allow it to proliferate on Earth.

"I'm not sure I understand the problem." Michael said. "We have over 20 classrooms with 1,000 seats still available for booking in the Northwest quadrant of the campus. And another five auditoriums with 5,000 seats that are not booked. Furthermore, Professor Jensen is currently only scheduled to teach one class a week. Her contract allows for five classes a week. I'm not sure I understand what the problem is."

"Well, that's not the way we set it up," Bursar Bryant said in exasperation.

"Do I understand you to be saying that the highest-demand class at the Institute should be canceled because you failed to schedule it, even though we have both the teaching and classroom capacity to deliver it?"

"Well. When you put it like that..." he started to say.

"I DO put it like that," Michael interrupted.

"Well, I... Let me see if I can set that up." The man sound put off.

A moment of silence followed as Michael took care of it himself. "Done," he said. "Took five button clicks."

"But… But…" Bursar Bryant stuttered. "That's my job!"

"If you want to keep that job, then this will be the last time we have this conversation. Our job is to provide our students with the education they need. Anyone on our team that cannot do that will be moved to a job they can do. Is that understood?" Michael said, a bit of an edge creeping into his voice.

"But that's not the way it is done on New Lorexi." Bryant made one last attempt to justify himself.

"Mr. Bryant," Michael said. "If you would like to return to New Lorexi, I can get you guest quarters on the next freighter headed that way."

The bursar quickly went from being incensed to being terrified. If he was kicked off yet another backwater planet, he would never find work again. "I'm sorry, sir. It won't happen again."

"Thank you." Michael said, wondering how this person had ever managed to get an assignment on Earth.

PROFESSOR JENSEN'S QUARTERS, FACULTY RESIDENCE BUILDING

A message had come in earlier advising Professor Jensen that her class had been reassigned to another room, and that she would have five different sections, each meeting once a week. She had read the message twice to make sure she understood. She had never had more than one section before; never even had more than 10 people in the class.

When she logged on this morning, multiple messages were waiting. The first was the roster for her Tuesday class. She struggled to understand what she was seeing, then it clicked. Her Tuesday class had 4,327 people signed up. She sat there for several seconds, mouth open, staring at the screen. One thought resonated in her mind… *WHAT?*

A quick scan through the next four messages indicated that only 1,500 or so had signed up for the remainder of the week. The absurdity of the thought, *only 1,500*, triggered a laughing fit that left her gasping for air. But registration was still open, and more students were likely to enroll. On a hunch, she checked the live data on the bursar's faculty portal and saw that the number was now over 10,000 across the five sections.

The next message advised her that she was eligible to add teaching assistants and/or lab instructors from the approved list of Ascendants and Androids working at the institute. Curiously, the names of several humans were included in the list.

BUTLER RESIDENCE, MEDICAL RESIDENCES

"Breakfast is ready." Noelani called. George was the one that usually made breakfast. In fact, he usually made most of the meals. He had turned into quite the replicator food artist. But he was running late this morning and they had an appointment with a new patient they would be assisting, starting in about a half hour. So Noelani did the honors this morning.

"What's up George? You look very pensive today." Noelani said as she put two plates of scrambled eggs and toast on the table.

"Been thinking..." He started.

"That sounds like trouble." She wished that her humor was as infectious as his. She hated seeing him this way. Thankfully it didn't happen often. George was usually bubbling with enthusiasm over every little thing.

He looked up at her smiling. "Have I ever told you how much I love you?" He leaned over to give her a kiss. Then he added, "I've been thinking about signing up as an assistant for Professor Jensen's class in weapons and explosives over at the Space Force Academy."

Noelani was stricken. She didn't want George to get involved in Space Force. He'd served his time honorably and paid the price for that service. No one should ever be called to make that kind of sacrifice a second time. "George, please don't get involved with Space Force."

She fought to control the emotion welling up within.

"It's not like that," he said. "I don't want to go back into the military. My calling is to help the vets. But there are going to be a lot of kids in that class learning how to blow stuff up, thinking it is a party or something. Never stopping to think about what it's like to get blown up.

"I think I need to be part of this; to be the voice of reason that helps balance the thrill of a big explosion with the reality of how that power is going to be used. I respect these kids for volunteering to protect us, and for making the sacrifices that will come with that service.

"It's just that… I think more of them will come home whole if I'm part of their training."

Noelani leaned over to kiss George but got tangled up in the tablecloth and ended up spilling the coffee. Laughing they went back into the bedroom to change, got tangled up in a different way and ended up being late for their meeting after all.

PROFESSOR JENSEN'S OFFICE, SPACE FORCE EDUCATION BUILDING

Professor Jensen was sitting in her office working on the materials for her course. There was a knock on her door. It was the first time in four years that anyone had knocked. *Wonder who that could be*, she thought.

She got up and opened the door to see a wiry young woman. "Can I help you?"

"Hi, my name is Alexi Santos. I currently run the outfitting and tour guide concession at the Embassy. I was part of Michael's team, pre-Revelation, and assisted with the liberation of North Korea. I'd like to help with your class."

"Do you have any experience with weapons and explosives?" The professor asked somewhat skeptically.

Alexi just smiled.

COMMITTEE ROOM, EARTH ALLIANCE HEADQUARTERS

"Thank you for meeting today on such short notice," Michael said. "As you know, last Thursday the Earth Alliance Council voted to approve the formation of Space Force. One of the most critical components of Space Force is its fleet. This advisory committee has been created for the purpose of overseeing our choice of spacecraft and the design of those spacecraft.

"So there is no misunderstanding, the Confederation, in accordance with our treaties, has final say on all design decisions, but I hope it never comes to that. If you ever have an issue with anything we have proposed, I want to know about it, and we want to fix it.

"Also, again so there is no misunderstanding, everything discussed in this committee is covered by the security agreement that was part of the invitation package you were sent. Any breach of security or leaking of data that has not been cleared for release, will result in your dismissal from the committee and your countries' disqualification from serving in any Earth Alliance capacity, other than the Assembly of Ambassadors, for up to 10 years. In order to continue on this committee, you must acknowledge your commitment to these terms by pressing the green button in front of you."

Within moments, all the advisors had confirmed their commitment to the security agreement.

"Thank you." Michael said. "The ships we need must be able to serve three missions. Mission 1 is to seek out and destroy the Enemy ships that are a direct threat to Earth." Michael acknowledged Advisor Popov who had raised his hand.

"Excuse me for interrupting, Mr. Ambassador. Can you explain what you mean by a direct threat to Earth?"

"Good question, Advisor Popov. There are several thousand Enemy ships that we know of in this spiral arm of the galaxy. Only 200 or so are on a path toward Earth. The Confederation is dealing with the others, and in truth, will attempt to deal with the 200, if it comes to that. But those 200 are our target."

"Thank you," the advisor said.

"Mission 2, in the short-term, is to allow humanity to explore its own solar system and those nearby."

Another hand went up. "Yes, Advisor Lin."

"What assurances do we have of proportional representation in these missions?"

"The assurances given in our treaties," Michael answered, a little frustrated with the question.

After a moment's pause, Michael continued. "Mission 3 is to attack Enemy strongholds for the purposes of diverting them from their offensive actions toward Earth."

Yet another hand went up. "Yes, Advisor Adani."

"Michael, I ask with utmost respect... Are offensive operations really necessary?"

"Advisor Adani... You know that I am Lorexian, right?"

"I have heard that claim, yes."

"Are you aware that Lorexians are a less aggressive species than humans?"

"I have heard that claim as well, sir."

"It's not a claim. I find offensive operations as objectionable as you seem to. It has been a millennium of millennia since the Confederation has considered such a thing. Nonetheless, that is the situation in which we find ourselves. You can support the objectives that the Advisory Council has authorized, or you can excuse yourself from this service. But before you answer, the question on the table is not what our mission is. The question is... How do we support those that are volunteering to execute it? So, my question to you is... Do you want to support your countrymen that volunteer for this mission?"

"Michael. This is a conundrum for me."

"As it is for me." Michael replied. "But I believe that this mission is life or death for Earth and for humanity, therefore I will stand with it until my dying breath. The real question is, will you?"

"I'm sorry. I do not accept that frame. If allowed, I will take my leave now."

"I am also sorry, Advisor Adani. But I respect your decision. You are still bound by your security agreement but are free to go. Please do not give us cause to take action against you."

The advisor nodded his understanding, then left the room.

Once the door closed, Michael asked. "Are there other concerns we need to address before proceeding?"

A series of No's rippled across the room.

"Thank you. Space Force and the rest of humanity thanks you for your agreement to serve. Let me introduce you to Professor Jeffery Milne, Head of the Institute's Spacecraft Department.

...

Jeffery Milne was an Ascendant. His familiar name was Je-Fi. His human persona was Scottish and he headed the Engineering school's Spacecraft department at the Institute. His original assignment had been to head both the Spacecraft and Propulsion departments. But when Ka-Tu's position as Consul General for Scotland fell through at the last minute, they'd split the department, giving him Spacecraft, meaning, hulls, shields, life support, etc., and giving Ka-Tu Propulsion. A split department like this was the more common arrangement among Confederation institutes.

In almost any other circumstance, splitting someone's responsibilities within weeks of starting a new job was bad news. But, not here. The Confederation had not been able to find human-qualified Ascendants to take the two positions, so they had combined them into one and given them to Je-Fi as an interim measure. Je-Fi knew spacecraft and loved introducing new species to the beauty of spacecraft design. Propulsion, on the other hand, was a complicated and dangerous business, one that Je-Fi knew would be trouble for him.

The most amusing thing about the assignment was that the engineering school had ended up with two Scottish department heads.

...

"Advisors," Professor Milne said now. "Let me echo the Ambassador's thanks for your participation on this committee. The Confederation has fabulous base designs for every sort of spacecraft, but all of these are optimized for Lorexian use. Because of the difference in size between humans and Lorexians, we think our best option will be to choose two of the smaller ships and redesign them, mostly just the interiors, for human use.

"Our Ascendant engineering team, in collaboration with our human contributors, will do our best to create spacecraft that your people can live and work in, but we need your collaboration to create environments in which your people can truly thrive." The Professor saw most of the advisors nodding in agreement.

"We see the need for two ship classes. One that we would describe as Fast Attack. Another that we would describe as Cruisers.

"Fast Attack ships, and I apologize for the label, are as the name suggests… Ships able to get from point A to point B very quickly, have excellent defenses, and the ability to engage an enemy. In support of mission 1, they will be able to move much faster than the Enemy, and as such will be able to isolate and destroy Enemy craft wherever they are encountered.

"In support of mission 2, they will be fully outfitted with every piece of technology that humanity has adapted for scientific study of the solar system and surrounding systems.

"Each ship would have the capacity to support 100 to 250 humans, or Confederation avatars, for an extended period of time, years at a minimum. Enough for extended exploration missions in the solar system and beyond. Enough for military operations with a full platoon of space marines with appropriate armaments on remote missions up to 1,000 light-years from Earth. In case you are wondering, these ships will have appropriate life support, training, recreational and medical facilities to support operations for years without replenishment, although there is no intent for these ships to operate for years without replenishment."

"Cruisers are not that much different, but several times larger to support full-function hospitals, multiple platoons, and full-function repair facilities.

"So that there is no misunderstanding, the Confederation operates fleets with much larger ships capable of much larger missions. None of this is being denied humanity, but ships of that size will be mostly irrelevant in the coming conflict or for exploration of your solar system and the nearby stars. Therefore, our proposal is to make these two smaller ships first." The professor stepped aside, and Michael took the podium.

"Friends, these are the ships we propose to design. Written versions of today's commentary, and high-level concept drawings and specifications, will be posted to your secure email shortly. Please study this material tonight. We will discuss the proposed systems for these ships tomorrow. Thank you for your participation on this advisory board."

A hand shot up.

"Advisor Myers." Michael acknowledged.

"Mr. Ambassador. Thank you for including us in this process. I look forward to service on this committee."

"Thank you, Advisor Myers and the rest of you for engaging in this process with us."

PROFESSOR JENSEN'S OFFICE, SPACE FORCE EDUCATION BUILDING

Professor Jensen was sitting in her office putting the finishing touches on the course syllabus. It was due later this afternoon, so she wanted to finish it now, before heading off to lunch in about an hour. She was startled from her work by a polite, but firm, knock on her door.

She got up to answer it and was surprised to see two people whom she'd seen on TV and felt like she knew, even though she'd never met them.

"Sergeant and Mrs. Butler. What a pleasant surprise. Please come in." She showed them to some leather seats in the corner that had been set up around a coffee table. "Can I get you some water or coffee?"

"No thanks," George said. "We're good. In fact, we're going to head off for lunch as soon as we're done here."

"To what do I owe this honor?" she asked.

"We've heard about your course and the overwhelming demand from the new Space Force volunteers," George started.

"Yes. Yes," she said nervously. "I have taught for a long time and never had more than 10 or 20 people sign up before. I think I am up to about 12,000 now and have no idea how this is going to work."

"Michael put out word to a few of us working at the Institute who have human war experience. He emphasized the importance of your class and asked us to give you our support and encouragement.

"Noelani and I would like to help. As I think you know, I am a Congressional Medal of Honor recipient. That may not mean that much to the Confederation, but it will mean a lot to your students. The veterans I work with are much more serious about their own recovery when I help them because they know the sacrifice it takes to receive such an award.

"I usually don't like to talk about myself in that way, but I think your students will be more serious about their studies if I am part of your team. They will also respect you more for having people like me on your team," George said.

Noelani meekly added, "I would like to join your team as well. I'm a medical tech and don't know much about weapons and explosives, other than what they do to people. But I understand the people you will be teaching, and my presence will make them safer, and possibly a little better behaved."

There was another knock on the door.

"Do you mind if I see who that is?"

George nodded their consent.

Va-Re opened the door. An older man was standing there, whom she had never seen before. "Can I help you?" she asked.

"Professor Jensen, my name is Luka Tsiklauri. I would like to volunteer to assist with your class."

"Luka! Luka, is that you!" George went to the door.

Professor Jensen wasn't sure what was going on, but stepped out of the way as George, then Noelani, came over to give him big hugs.

George turned to the Professor. "This is my friend, Luka. He was a colonel in the Georgian army when the Russians invaded 20-ish years ago." George quickly popped up the picture of Luka, arm outstretched toward a long line of tanks. "He is the greatest hero in the Republic of Georgia."

Professor Jensen was overwhelmed. She had been an outcast most of her career. Now she was teaching the largest class at the institute, and famous and important people were asking if they could help.

"Can I tell you a little about the course, not so much the content as the approach? I'd like to get some input."

"Sure," they said.

She motioned everyone back toward the coffee table.

"I would like the course to have a significant lab content. It is one thing to put up pictures of devices and talk about their properties. It's another thing altogether to figure out which is appropriate for your situation. I would also like to engage the students in the weapons design process," the Professor started.

"What aspect of weapon design are you thinking about?" Noelani asked. "Isn't weapon design dangerous, especially for those just getting into their training?"

"The real reason there is a Space Force is to defend Earth from the pending Enemy invasion. So, the focus of the entire course is going to be on weapons to use against the Enemy.

"The truth is that the Confederation has only developed two relevant weapons: flux bombs and rifle-like energy projectors. Earth's history suggests that you as a species are more devious about weapon design than the Lorexian people, which is why I would like to engage the class in the design process.

"Regarding safety... All weapons are dangerous, but these are different. The Enemy is not like us. They are extra-dimensional, meaning that they exist in multiple dimensions at the same time, phasing back and forth. Um... Have you seen a picture, or better, a moving image of the enemy?"

The three looked at each other and shook their heads.

"No," George said. "I've heard that they are extra-dimensional, but don't really know what that means."

"Can I show you some? Fair warning, they are terrifying and disgusting. But if you're going to help, you'd better see these before the students do. With as many students as we have, there is no doubt there will be ones that barf and others that pass out," said the Professor.

For the first time since they decided to help, Noelani was wondering if her participation was a good idea.

Seeing the concerned look, the professor said. "If it is too much for you, I can stop at any point. But this really is the core of what our course is about. Are you up for seeing some video?"

"Let's do it," Noelani said, even though it was clear that she really didn't want to.

"This is the first segment I plan to show the class."

The lights in the room dimmed and a scene started to play in the middle of the room. It was projected from a holoprojector somewhere out of sight. The image was intended to be projected in a large auditorium style classroom that held up to 5,000 people, so some of the terror of the scene was lost as it only projected about 3 feet high in the office. An alien of some sort, dressed like a human man, had just walked into the room. "This poor fellow is Angoloran, a human-like species that inhabited a world closer to the galactic core." The Professor whispered.

Moments after the door could be heard clicking shut, dust started swirling around the man, eventually obscuring the view of him. The maelstrom of black dust became increasingly smoke-like, then formed into columns that shot into the man's open mouth. Noelani screamed. Within moments the smoke was gone, and the emaciated husk of the man fell to the floor, still alive, but in a bad way.

"Oh my God!" Noelani said. "What was that?"

"The Enemy was the dust and smoke. The Angoloran was the emaciated husk that was left at the end. When the enemy is overtly in control, it fills in the flesh in a way that makes the Angoloran look healthy and vital like he did when he walked into the room. When the Enemy retreats to its natural dimension, it 'sits' for lack of a better word, on the man's back in another dimension with only its proboscis transiting into our dimension, typically in its victim's brain or spine.

"The Enemy is a parasite. It had been eating that man from the inside out for several months. While inhabiting the man, it totally controls him and over time accumulates most of his memories.

"Here is the same video snippet taken with a multidimensional camera. In this image, the Enemy is purple in our dimension, red in its preferred dimensions. The man is in blue. See how large the Enemy is." She froze the play back and used a laser pointer to point out various parts of the image. "All that red is attached to the man through the proboscis. It is the intensely red cord here..." she said pointing to a cord-like structure... "that transitions to blue. See how firmly it is latched onto the man's brain stem. All the purple we see here..." she said pointing to the outline of the man's body... "is filling out the man's body so that he looks normal to others."

Resuming playback, she said. "OK. The Enemy is starting to retreat back into its preferred dimension. See how it breaks apart into increasingly smaller bits as it diffuses out of our space time continuum. See the red on the man's back grow as the purple recedes."

"This is what we're up against. This is what we need weapons to fight. And it's not the blue part we need to kill. Human weapons would no doubt be able to slaughter the Angoloran, but they would have no impact on the Enemy. In fact, once detached from its host, the Enemy becomes even more dangerous.

"It can attack multiple people." She played a short segment showing the red detaching, dividing into two purple columns as it entered normal space, then delving into two separate people who began convulsing, but suddenly calmed as a visible red/purple proboscis formed in each of their brain stems, and two red entities formed over top them.

"It can simply eat someone nearby." Another short clip played showing black smoke flowing out of a man's mouth, wrapping itself around the woman standing next to him. Screaming. Blood. Then nothing left except the cloud, which eventually coalesced into a woman who smiled back at the man.

Noelani could be heard coughing.

"Or, it can simply attack." Another clip started playing that showed a man getting blown apart by a mortar round. A huge cloud of black smoke emerged from the man's remains, formed into a spinning disk, then cut six people nearby in half. Torsos falling off of their legs and copious quantities of blood flowing everywhere.

That was the tipping point for Noelani, who barfed all over the Professors coffee table.

"Oh, my!" The professor jumped up as the holographic projection faded away. "Sorry. I guess I got carried away. This seems to happen in every class."

George ran over to a side table near the professor's desk as she blathered on. He got a glass of water and some paper towels to help clean Noelani up.

"I think this really is the reason I need your help," The professor said.

Noelani stared daggers at the professor as George and Luka struggled to hide the humor they saw in the situation.

"I think we are going to head back home now." George said. "We need to get Noelani cleaned up." Taking Noelani by the hand, George opened the door and the two of them headed out.

"You are going to join me for the first session tomorrow. Right?" They heard the professor say as they rounded the corner.

Once outside the building, they turned toward home, and both burst out laughing about what had just happened. "That woman!" Noelani said, between gasps of laughter. "She's crazy!" Then she turned, planted her face against George's shoulder and started crying. "Those poor people. I've seen and don't want to imagine."

After a while, Noelani looked up at George and said, "If that's what's coming, Earth has no chance once it gets here. The only solution is for Space Force to take them out first. We have to help. We can't let that happen on Earth."

George, overcome by his love for this woman, kissed her. Passionately. Even the taste of stale vomit couldn't keep him away as she melted into him.

...

Luka had stayed behind, chatting with the professor as she struggled to clean up the mess. "Despite the mess, you are lucky to have those two. The students will undoubtedly respect the Sergeant. He is one of the best people I know and the role model for a soldier. All the men in the class will be mesmerized by Noelani, and more respectful to you as a result. Who else do you have helping?" Luka asked.

"Alexi Santos?" The professor said.

"Ah, Alexi. That one is a better soldier than the next 100 you will meet all added up Into one. Anyone else?"

"Are you joining me?" She asked sheepishly.

"Absolutely. I would also recommend Colonel Mark Patterson of Space Force. That man has survived a hell few others will ever face, as has George by the way. If you would like, I will ask him for you."

"Would the Colonel be allowed to do that?" The professor asked.

"It would be unusual. But I suspect he will. I would if I were in his place."

"Yes. Please. First class is tomorrow. I'm having a meeting of the TA's an hour before."

WEAPONRY

[Tuesday, 08.27.2030] SPACE FORCE AUDITORIUM #3

It was the first day of class. Professor Jensen was stricken with stage fright as she peeked out from behind the curtain. Word had leaked out about the material this class would be covering. All 5,000 seats in all five sections were now filled up and the administration had added another 100 seats on the wait list for each class, which had been added as temporary standing room in the back.

Noelani, sensing that the Professor was about to have a break down, stepped up beside her.

"Here," she said, holding out some cream. "Let me rub this into your wrist. It's one-time use nanobots. They deliver a calming medication that will settle your stomach and dampen your anxiety response. I've already taken some."

The Professor nodded and held out her wrist. Noelani rubbed a dollop of the cream in until it absorbed, then continued holding the Professor's wrist until she could feel the change. "You're going to be great you know. And as terrifying as your message is, it's the one these students need to know."

The bell went off. Noelani released the Professor's wrist, then walked out onto the stage. Earlier, they had agreed that Noelani would be the 'host' for this session.

The reaction from the students was immediate. The huge swell of noise almost cut through her resolve as she walked to the podium.

"Hello, and welcome to Applied Reactions 101." More noise broke out.

"Thank you for the gracious welcome. My name is Noelani Butler." There was a huge sigh of disappointment from the class. "I am one of the assistants helping Professor Jensen with this course. First, I'm going to introduce the other four assistants, then I'm going to say a few words of introduction about the class." More deflating sounds could be heard.

"Let me introduce you to my fellow assistants. First, my husband Sergeant George Butler, recipient of the Congressional Medal of Honor..." The crowd erupted in so much noise that Noelani had to stop and let the crowd have its say. They finally settled and Noelani added, "Yah. That's how I usually feel when he comes into the room."

She turned to smile at George as the crowd erupted in catcalls. She could only laugh at the look on George's face.

"Next!" She said, even though the crowd was still roaring. She raised her hands and the crowd settled a little. "Next, I would like to introduce someone you should truly fear… The liberator of North Korea… Alexi Santos."

Many in the crowd knew of Alexi. Most did not and there was a general deflation in the noise. Alexi came strutting out and hearing the less than supportive sounds walked up to the podium and, per the plan, appeared to muscle Noelani out of the way. The crowd fell into a hush at the apparent rudeness.

Alexi grabbed the microphone and said, "Boys. Not one of you here that I can't take down before you even know the fight has begun." Her words pumped the crowd into a frenzy as she bowed gracefully to Noelani and went strutting to her assigned position on the far side of the stage.

Retaking the podium, Noelani continued. "Next, the Hero of the Republic of Georgia, Colonel Luka Tsiklauri." As Noelani was making the announcement, the image from the Russian war came on the screen. Luka was standing there with his hand out, Russian tanks stopped in a line right in front of him. The crowd broke into a round of cheering.

Once again, Noelani raised her hands to get the crowd's attention. "Lastly, someone many of you already know, Colonel Mark Patterson of Space Force."

Mark walked up to the podium as the class cheered.

"Ladies and Gentlemen. It is unusual for an active officer to be included as an assistant in a class like this. But, as my friend Luka Tsiklauri explained to me, leadership is just as important during training as it is in the battlefield. This is the class where you will be introduced to our Enemy and taught how to kill them. It is possibly the most important class you will take before being deployed. I am here to make sure you take it seriously." With that he walked off the stage and Noelani returned.

Again, Noelani raised her hands to get the crowds attention. "OK. Now that the assistant introductions are out of the way. I have a couple announcements to make before introducing Professor Jensen."

More shouting and catcalls broke out. "Friends, fellow citizens of Earth, brothers in arms..." she started. "I am here today, and will be for most of the sessions, in my role as a medical tech. The things you will see in this class are shocking, distressing to the mind and the senses. Many of you will fall ill, having done nothing other than seeing the images the Professor will present. If there are any of you that want to reconsider your presence here today, please exit now, because the doors will lock momentarily. What you will be seeing today and throughout this course is highly classified. Even discussing these things with people outside of Space Force could lead to extended confinement.

"The Professor has seen the live incidents, not just the recordings. Alexi has personally battled two enemy combatants. Sergeant Butler, and the two Colonels, have experienced a Hell far worse than anything we will be seeing. I was personally very ill the first time I was exposed to any of this.

"My role is to provide the medical care that many of you will need, today, throughout the course, during the hands-on exercises, and as a result of the combat that you will eventually face." The crowd had become very quiet during the last part of her speech. "I now present you, weapons master and explosives expert extraordinaire, Professor Valerie Jensen."

The room exploded with excitement as the Professor walked out. She struggled to hold herself together as she felt thrilled on one hand that her interests and work had finally found an audience that wanted to know, and concerned on the other that at the moment, this serious topic felt more like a circus than an educational pursuit.

...

"Thank you for that introduction, Noelani," said the Professor as the noise started to settle. She looked intently at the class... "A syllabus was posted yesterday, one that I hope you have studied. But, one thing you should know about syllabi... They are guidelines, not contracts. We will cover the session 1 items next week. Today, I want you to experience why we are here."

The lights faded almost to black. "This first holographic projection is of the Enemy. One that is using its prey strategically toward its end."

The projection started, dimly lighting the center of the stage. The Professor was vaguely visible at the right of the stage. A door opened on the left side of the stage and a man walked in, the door slowly closing behind him. The Professor paused playback, then walked into the room with the man.

"This," she said as she approached the man, "is a male Angoloran. You can see that he is very humanoid. Slightly more angular head. More pronounced ridgelines in his inner forearm. Slightly taller than the average human male, but not as tall as this projection makes him appear. This is blown up a bit to make it easier for the people in the back to see."

"He appears to be a healthy specimen. But trust me, he is not." She stepped back into the shadow and resumed playback. After a few steps, the man started to melt into ash, then dust, then smoke that whirled around the man.

The professor paused playback, and again walked into the scene. "This smoke you see. This is the Enemy. It has been inhabiting this man for some time now. Today, it was out doing business, wearing the appearance of this man. Now it is retreating to its actual home in another dimension.

"As fair warning, the next part is disturbing." She walked away from the center of the image and resumed play back. The smoke coalesced into two columns that flew into the man's open mouth, disappearing and leaving the emaciated husk of a man to fall to the floor. Sounds of retching could be heard in the back left of the room. Noelani made her way back as the Professor continued, feeling a little less embarrassed about her own performance in the Professor's office.

The Professor continued, showing more of the same footage George and Noelani had seen before, then 45 minutes of additional footage. More than one hundred had passed out or thrown up, or both, by the time the Professor finished. Finally, one hour and fifty minutes into the one-hour class, the Professor said. "That's enough for today. I hope that was sufficient motivation to spark your enthusiastic engagement in learning about the weapons we have to combat these creatures, and in developing new weapons with which to defeat them."

The doors unlocked and snapped open. The students fled, at least the ambulatory ones did. Some two hundred remained behind and were taken to the hospital for additional treatment.

COMMITTEE ROOM, EARTH ALLIANCE HEADQUARTERS

Michael arrived one minute before the scheduled starting time for today's Ship Design review with the Advisory Board. He was pleased to see that he was the last to arrive and that the room buzzed with conversation. He was also impressed to see Advisor Enzo Venezia speaking with Advisor Pai Lin at one of the electronic drawing boards on the wall. Enzo had apparently drawn a quick cutaway drawing of a crew quarters room. Enzo and Pai were both ship interior designers famous for their attention to detail in accommodation areas.

Michael walked up to the front of the room, exchanged a word with Professor Milne, then called the meeting to order.

"I am pleased to see how engaged this group is this morning. My primary role has been as a diplomat for the last several thousand years. Diplomatic meetings are rarely this engaging, so thank you.

"Our objective today is to review the high-level parameters of the ship designs. I believe we will be starting with the Fast Attack ship. Any questions or concerns before I turn this over to Professor Milne?"

Markus Vogel, the advisor from Germany, raised his hand.

"Yes. Advisor Vogel."

"Thank you, Mr. Ambassador. I arrived a little early today and watched as Advisors Venezia and Lin discussed crew quarters and outfitting. I must admit, I am blown away by how knowledgeable these two are." He nodded at the two to show his respect. "My specialty is structure, power plants and controls. I know very little about crew accommodation or of the topics that were in the preparatory materials. Is there a role for this committee in regard to the things I know about?"

Michael smiled at the advisor. "Thank you for that question, Advisor Vogel. Yes. There is a role. But allow me to speak more broadly for a moment. Every one of you was selected because we need your skill and you are the best at what you do. As you said, Advisors Venezia and Lin are extremely gifted. But so are all of you.

"The Confederation has technology you don't know about yet but will learn about in short order. We also have very effective ship designs, for Lorexians. What we want are fabulous ship designs that are fundamentally human designs. I think the only way we're going to get that in time to be useful for the coming conflict is to get the best humanity has to offer working with the best the Confederation has. That is what we're doing here. My apologies for not having made that a little clearer yesterday."

Michael felt the room relax as he finished. He also saw Advisor Lin acknowledge Advisor Vogel, who was shaking hands with Advisor

Venezia. *This is going to work.* Michael thought. "Let me turn the remainder of this session over to Professor Milne."

AMBASSADOR'S OFFICE

Michael's next meeting was a call that he'd scheduled with Israeli Prime Minister Judah Levine. The Prime Minister had trained as a rabbi and had served in that capacity for nearly 30 years before running for office in the Knesset as a Conservative. He had been well known for opposing Israel's dependence on the US and for opposing negotiations with the Palestinians. He had even voted against seeking a treaty with the Confederation. But all of that had changed suddenly the day of the nuclear attack.

He'd been outside when the shields went up to protect Israel. He saw them glimmer as they came to life. He watched as three nuclear weapons detonated, one after the other, right over his head. Then, as the nuclear fire burned, he'd had an epiphany... Michael was the one God had sent to protect Israel, which meant that the terms of the treaty Michael proposed must be God's will for Israel.

Over the next week, the world watched as Rabbi Levine presented the first of the Confederation gifts to Palestinian families, tearfully professing his shame and insisting that they get first fruits of the new alliance with the Confederation.

During the last election cycle, Rabbi Levine had run for Prime Minister, winning by a landslide, but most importantly taking 68% of the Palestinian vote in the first election where the Palestinian Israelis had the right to vote.

...

"Prime Minister Levine," Michael said. "I hope things are well with you."

"Michael, my friend. It is good to hear from you as well. Israel has changed a lot since the last time you were here. I'm hoping that you're calling to tell me you are going to pay us another visit."

"I'm sure that can be arranged, but sadly it's not the purpose of my call today. I'm calling because I want to make a temporary change in our consulate staffing."

"You need Joel, don't you?"

Joel Rubinstein served as the Consul General from the Confederation to Israel. Joel was an Ascendant who had joined the Revelation team on Earth 22 years ago. He'd been nominated for that role by the Ancient Sentient. He'd trained in Engineering before joining the diplomatic corps. In the year prior to the Revelation, he had used those skills to build the Gas Production facility in Paso Robles, which converted atmospheric carbon dioxide into 'natural gas' sold to the California utilities. But Joel's engineering specialty was shield design. He was the one who had built and operated the shield that protected Israel from the nuclear attack that fateful day.

"Yes, but hopefully for only a couple months. I don't know yet. I wanted to talk with you about this before discussing it with him."

"I presume that this has something to do with the new Space Force?"

"Yes, it does. Joel is probably the best engineer in this sector of the galaxy, and I need his help in developing some of the infrastructure that Space Force will require. I'm hoping this is something he can set in motion quickly, then turn over to someone else, so he can return to you."

"As much as I hate losing Joel for even a day, I appreciate that there is a greater need that calls, one that Israel will benefit from as much as anyone else. You have my blessing in this matter Michael. I just ask that you return him to us as quickly as you can."

"Thank you, sir. I'll ask my assistant Pam to coordinate with your office for a visit to Israel. It's been too long since I have seen the holy places in Jerusalem. Please give Hannah my best."

CONFEDERATION SCHOOL OF ENGINEERING

"Dr. Xu, please come in." Ka-Tu said when Eugene knocked on his door for the meeting he'd requested. "What can I help you with?"

"I've been studying the various drive systems, trying to re-derive the math to make sure I understand it, then to apply the math to the sample engine designs that you have given us. I've run into a couple issues that don't seem to line up. I am hoping you can help me sort this out."

"Yes. Very tricky math. It is reminiscent of the math that you refer to as Maxwell's equations, which have no unique solution and almost no closed-form special-case solutions. Everyone struggles with these. What are you getting hung up on?"

"Mostly it has to do with initial conditions as applied to Jump Drives. Um, sorry, Discontinuous Transition Drives."

Ka-Tu laughed at the expression Jump Drive. "Very descriptive, that nickname, Jump Drive. And, yes, sorting out the initial conditions was the most difficult issue the original developers of the technology struggled with. Even though that invention is well over a million years old, holographic projections of the developers discussing the initial conditions problem survive to this day."

"Will we ever get to see those?" Eugene asked.

"They are not restricted or classified. So, in principle, there is no reason why you could not. But the Ambassador and the Central Council have not approved them for distribution to Earth yet. I think the issue is bandwidth. Those are large files pertaining to a very narrow specialty that may never be relevant to Earth, so low priority to place in the library here.

"But, back to your question. What aspects of the initial conditions problem are giving you trouble? By the way, I am impressed that you understand the math well enough after only a couple weeks to even realize there is a problem."

"Thank you. As I understand it, the purpose of the plasma flow regulator in the discontinuous transition drive's field initiator is to align the dimensional bubble into a shape like this," Eugene said, pointing to a series of matrix equations on his data pad and an accompanying chart showing a mostly cylindrical shape.

"Where did you find this?" the Professor asked. "I don't think I have seen this representation before."

"Oh. Sorry. I should have explained that. This is my own derivation. I did it using a notation system I developed some years ago to handle a similar problem with applying Maxwell's equations to ion drive configurations." Quickly flipping a couple pages on his pad, Eugene added, "See. It lines up with the one in the textbook."

"Eugene. I'm very impressed. To your question... Yes, that is the purpose of the plasma flow regulator in the field initiator. So, what's the problem?"

"Well. Whenever I am deriving something this complicated, I always cross-check against a different set of assumptions. This assumes that we are entering the Jump dimension from normal space. If I rederive the solution assuming that we are entering the Jump dimension from Warp space, it doesn't work."

"That's correct. That's why we always drop back to normal space from 'Warp' space before engaging the 'Jump' drive. Remember me talking about that during the field trip?" The Professor said, then as an aside... "I think we should probably update the translator to just call these things 'Warp' and 'Jump'."

"Well, that's my problem. If we reconfigured the initiator to create a dimensional bubble shaped like this..." Eugene flipped to another page to show the new configuration and the image of the rippled ovoid. "...then you can enter the 'Jump' dimension from either normal space or warp space." Eugene flipped to another page that showed the two solutions side by side, confirming it worked both ways.

The Professor was silent for quite a while, staring at the equations, occasionally flipping a page to cross check something.

Then he looked up at Eugene and said, "I think you are right."

"But that's not all. See..." Eugene said, flipping forward several pages. "If you enter Jump from Warp..." more page flipping, "...then return to Warp from Jump, you will have moved discontinuously in warp space. That would multiply the distance travelled by up to 100 times without consuming any more energy." Still more page flipping.

Ka-Tu was shocked. Eugene's notation system drastically simplified the formulas, which had allowed him to make a discovery that had eluded the Confederation for over a million years. He looked up at Eugene, trembling with excitement. "OK. We need to slow down a bit. I think you are right, but we need to simulate this before getting too carried away."

Eugene flipped a few more pages, then hit the play button on the simulation.

"How did you get access to this software?" Ka-Tu asked.

"I went down to IT and asked if there was any software that I could use to do drive simulation. They gave me this, said it was the student version," Eugene replied. "It's not restricted, is it? I assumed they wouldn't give me something I wasn't allowed to have."

"Technically, first year students are not supposed to have access at all, and this version is restricted to faculty. But I'll clear you to have access. I'll need to talk with IT about this, but there's nothing for you to worry about. I'm sure similar things have happened at your University.

"But, putting all that aside, I'll book some time for us to talk with Michael. Your discovery may change space travel as we know it. Michael can help us work through the political implications. I'm sure he's going to want to make sure this gets credited to humanity."

CONFEDERATION SCHOOL OF ENGINEERING

Professor Hans Schudel was part of the Civil Engineering department within the School of Engineering. His field was mines and mining, and he was the only mining professor in the school. His specialty was deep planetary mining. It was a narrow field and most useful on planets new to the Confederation. His second specialty was asteroid mining, also a skill most sought after in systems new to the Confederation.

As part of his preparation for this assignment, he'd studied all the geologic data collected by the Confederation about the Earth. The planet had a disproportionately large, liquid core composed of a nickel-iron alloy surrounding a solid inner core. Although there was a lot of other valuable metals, such as gold and platinum, mixed in, they were at low enough levels that it would be economically challenging to extract them. Other planets in the system were more interesting from a mining perspective, so he assumed that was the reason he'd been assigned to Earth.

Since his arrival three years ago, he had only worked with a couple hundred humans. The pool of Ph.D. level mining engineers interested in Confederation mining technology just wasn't very large. That would change over the next 100 years as the rest of the system opened up for mining, but it hadn't changed yet.

One of the things he liked about the smaller classes was that he got to know many of his students very well. And, as a result, he was frequently invited to visit mines all over this fabulous planet.

Today was the first session of his new class on core mining. The Dean of the Engineering School had requested this class to be added this year. The Revelation was far enough along for the topic to have been raised with the Earth Alliance, who subsequently approved core mining operations, as long as they were managed by the Confederation. The allied nations were quick to request training, which resulted in two sections of his new class being added to the course offerings. He had twenty-four students enrolled in each section, and he looked forward to meeting them.

...

As he arrived at the school this afternoon, he was surprised to see a meeting request from the Ambassador on his calendar for Thursday.

CHEF MARCO'S RESTAURANT

Sarah had intentionally arrived 20 minutes early for her dinner date with Michael. Her years as a journalist taught her to be five minutes early for everything, but tonight she needed a few minutes to herself and an extra glass of wine. That was the plan anyway.

When she arrived, she was greeted by the hostess, who knew who Sarah was. Ever since getting on national TV, someone seemed to recognize her wherever she went. But, since becoming Michael's consort, everyone knew who she was, especially here at the Embassy.

"I'm really early." Sarah said. "OK, if I just get a glass of wine at the bar and wait for Michael there?"

If she'd come a minute earlier, she could have grabbed a quiet little table for two at the back of the bar and had 20 minutes of peace and quiet. But Chef Marco was in town tonight and had walked into the restaurant lobby just in time to hear Sarah.

"Sarah, Sarah, my dear. So good to see you tonight," he said with a light hug and an air kiss or two on each cheek. "Your table is ready, and I have already brought out a very fine bottle of wine for you to try tonight. Come. Come. I will decant it and you can have the honor of doing the tasting."

There was no polite opportunity for protest as Sarah was swept into the restaurant and taken to the table in the center of the huge curved window overlooking the valley. Chef Marco presented the wine, the 2016 SENA, a Bordeaux-style red wine from Aconcagua Valley in Chile. Chef Marco was obviously very proud of himself for having obtained one of these bottles for his most famous guests.

Sarah went through the tasting ritual and had the bottle decanted, then the Chef moved on to tend to other guests.

Sarah loved coming here. The food was fabulous, as was the view and general ambiance. But, for the first time tonight, she realized that she had lost any semblance of anonymity. As a TV star of sorts, she was widely recognized, but could always find some public place where she could be alone, enjoy the scenery or people watch. No more. She had recently learned that people from all over the world were booking reservations months in advance in the next tier of seats back from the window in the hopes of seeing Michael and Sarah in person. She had never been exposed to that degree of celebrity before. *Well,* she thought, *I'm definitely giving them a show tonight, sitting here drinking by myself. Coming early was a huge mistake.*

The view from her seat was fabulous. The restaurant was situated on the peak of the ridge that marked the northern border of the Embassy complex. The restaurant was a little over 3,000 feet above the valley floor.

The valley was in the shape of an inverted L, with the foot of the L along the north edge of the Embassy complex. Her seat looked due south along the long leg of the valley, which stretched 13 miles directly in front of her.

Night was just falling. The buildings that lined the valley cast enough dim light that its overall shape was still clearly discernable. And the path lighting along Riverside Park slithered down the center like a snake.

"You seem very contemplative tonight." Michael's voice came from behind her, followed by a gentle kiss on the top of her head. The host appeared to pull out the chair for Michael, who leaned in for another kiss as he sat. Light applause could be heard from a couple tables behind.

"Hadn't planned to put on a show," he said, to Sarah's gentle laugh.

"It's funny," Sarah said. "I purposefully came 20 minutes early to have a moment of peace to myself and a sip of wine. Then I realized that sitting here by myself, drinking a glass a wine, was probably going to be on the front page of every tabloid worldwide for the next month. Can you imagine the stories they will fabricate?"

"So, what's up? You seem down tonight," Michael asked.

"You've heard the rumors about the goings on in Professor Jensen's class this morning, right?" She asked.

Michael nodded in the affirmative.

"Well It's going viral. The press office was overwhelmed by a flood of requests for a statement. Took us a while to figure out what had happened. Ideas on how we should respond to this?" she asked.

"Always with the truth, of course. But the reality is that the Enemy is coming. It's a long way off yet, but it's coming. The troops who are going to be fighting this Enemy need to know what they are up against." Seeing that these few words weren't swaying Sarah, he continued. "The Enemy is repulsive. I've seen it. I've fought it. Confederation statistics say that about 4% of the population gets sick to their stomach the first time they see it. We have to get our troops beyond that point if we are going to have any chance of surviving."

"I'm thinking that it would be a bad idea to include the part about surviving in a press release," Sarah said. This got Michael laughing loudly enough that some people turned their heads.

The Chef brought two plates up to their table. He set them down and explained tonight's special appetizer. It looked and smelled fantastic, and it only took Sarah one taste to realize that this was her new favorite; something that seemed to happen almost every time.

"Changing topic..." she said. "Tonight's wine is incredible. Hard to believe such luscious stuff really exists. But it occurred to me that we are being given a lot of very expensive stuff. Is that legal?"

It took Michael a moment to understand the question, then he said. "It wouldn't be, but I pay for it all. I have a tab with Chef Marco that clears through my personal accounts every month."

"But he is always saying he has a special gift for us."

"Ah. Now I understand. Yes. Chef Marco is very resourceful and has done a tremendous job of finding us excellent things, wines in particular. He charges us for everything he finds, including a markup on his costs. But he does not charge us a finder's fee. That is his gift."

"I googled this bottle of wine. There is none available for sale, but there are a few bottles available for auction. The last one sold went for $1,900. Can we afford that?"

The question triggered another laugh from Michael loud enough to turn heads.

As long as you are in my presence, I am the richest man on Earth. Michael pushed. The thought tickled, which caused Sarah to start laughing as well.

The commotion triggered some sympathetic laughter among some of the surrounding tables.

"Seems we really are the entertainment tonight," murmured Sarah.

AMBASSADOR'S RESIDENCE

After the evening meal with Sarah, Michael retreated to his office in the residence. He was scheduled to meet Professor MacLellan in the morning and hadn't read the briefing he'd been sent.

Sarah knew that she was not likely to see him tonight but still asked him to come to bed as early as he could.

DISCOVERY

AMBASSADOR'S RESIDENCE

Michael tried to get out of bed quietly enough not to wake Sarah. As an Ascendant inhabiting an avatar, he was only supposed to need four hours sleep at night. His regular pattern was more like six hours, when schedule permitted. But Sarah, as a natural human, needed eight.

Nonetheless, Sarah was waiting for him in the kitchen with a fresh pot of his favorite Kona coffee by the time he'd finished getting showered and dressed.

"Would you like me to make you some breakfast?" she asked.

"No. But thanks for offering. I have an early meeting with Professor McLellan this morning."

"McLellan. I remember the name, but not who he is," Sarah replied.

"Consul General to Scotland..." Michael hinted.

"Right. Right. The one that did all the prep for a job that would never exist. How is he getting along?"

"At first, he was very stoic about it. He had entered the Institute on New Lorexi just before he was scheduled to retire. His wife had recently died, and the poor man was... lost. I don't know a better way to describe it. This was going to be his last adventure. Losing it after so much preparation hit him hard. But, now... It's like he's 20 years old again. A week or two back, he came to my office to request a 'field trip' to Alpha Centauri for his class. As we talked, he thanked me several times for having let him take that professorship job. He says it is the best thing that ever happened to him."

"So why is he coming to see you today?"

"That's the funny thing. He says that one of his students made a discovery that the Confederation would be interested in. He wanted my guidance on the best way to proceed. Pam tried to deflect him, but he sent me a message on internal saying that it was imperative that we meet and that he needed at least an hour."

"He can send you stuff through your implants?" Sarah asked somewhat surprised.

"Rules for that are a bit complicated. I can add anyone I want to my access list. But people above a certain rank are added automatically when they come to the planet. He is one of about 50 that the system added automatically, and I did not remove him because it seemed very unlikely that he'd abuse the privilege."

"Do you think he is abusing the privilege?" Sarah asked.

"No. But we'll see."

CONFERENCE ROOM, OFFICE OF THE AMBASSADOR

Michael entered the conference room where Professor McLellan and another man were already seated. They had brought a surprising amount of stuff with them. Michael found himself worried he was about to be ambushed by more technology than he wanted to know about.

"Professor, so good to see you." Michael shook the Professor's hand.

"Michael, thank you for taking the time to meet with us. Let me introduce Eugene Xu. Eugene is one of the students in the Propulsion Systems program this year."

"Michael, it is a pleasure to meet you." Eugene also shook Michael's hand.

"Eugene, the pleasure is mine. Am I recalling correctly that you are on sabbatical from Johns Hopkins?"

"Yes sir. I am the Department Head there, hoping I can learn enough during my sabbatical to make the teaching at our school relevant in a post-Revelation world," Eugene said with good humor.

"That is why we have programs like the one you're in, so Earth's best and brightest can help us spread our science and technology as quickly as possible." Michael pointed to the buffet that Pam had set up, "Shall we?"

As they took some food, Michael asked. "So, what can I do for you gentlemen this morning? I looked through the brief that you sent but didn't understand its purpose."

"Ah," the professor said in his Scottish brogue. "Apologies for that. I wanted to make sure you had copies of some reference material that might be useful going forward. It's not that easy to find, so wanted to save you the trouble if you needed it later. Should have waited to send that until after the meeting today.

"The reason we're here is because Eugene has made a discovery that's going to have a huge impact on the Confederation. From what I know of you, I was sure you would want credit for this discovery given to Earth. I was also sure you would want the Confederation Administration to know that it was a direct result of what you've done here."

"May I ask what this discovery is?" Michael asked, trying to keep any skepticism out of his voice.

"As a scientist, you have no idea how much I want to tell you about the discovery itself. But instead, let me start by telling you what it will do."

"Thank you." Michael said.

"My recent trip from New Lorexi took almost three months. I know that there are ships that can go faster. But those ships are extremely expensive. There are very few people that get to use them. Eugene's discovery will allow us to reduce that time to a couple days."

"Forgive my skepticism, but how is that possible?"

"Today, the maximum jump distance is 1,000 light years. The engines required to do that are enormous and consume massive amounts of energy. The fastest commercial space craft need 45 minutes to recharge between jumps. The fastest military spacecraft that I know of take 15 minutes to recharge. Most routes between the Milky Way and Andromeda require 2,400 jumps, so the best commercial transit times are about 75 days. The best military ones, about 25 days," the Professor explained.

"There are a few that are a little faster." Michael said. "But I agree. Intergalactic travel takes a long time and the ships that do it are extraordinarily expensive."

"Doctor Xu has discovered a way to change the energy/distance relationship within the Discontinuous Transition Drive. Existing spacecraft, with a surprisingly small modification, could extend the maximum jump to 100,000 light years, possibly quite a bit further. New spacecraft could continue to jump only 1,000 light years but have a recharge cycle of less than 1 minute. And smaller space craft, the size of a military escort, could be built or modified to make the transit in 10 days."

"How sure are you about this?" Michael asked.

"The math is rock solid. The standard drive simulators used for both commercial and military design confirm the capability of the new design. The only remaining step is to test it."

"How long would it take to do that, and at what expense?" Michael asked.

The Professor nodded to Eugene.

"I took the liberty of looking up the specifications for the jump drive in your shuttle, the one you had at the time of the Revelation. It could be modified for the jump to Alpha Centauri in less than a week." Eugene said.

"Are you certain of this?" Michael asked.

"Would bet my life on it." The Professor replied with a smile.

"Eugene, forgive me for asking, but how did you discover this in the few months you've been here, when the Confederation hasn't?"

"May I answer that?" the Professor asked Eugene.

Eugene nodded.

"The core math that defines both Warp and Jump technology is extremely complicated."

"Warp? Jump?" Michael asked.

The Professor laughed and said. "The humans have not only reinvented our technology; they've renamed it as well. They refer to the Trans-Dimensional Drive as the Warp Drive, and the Discontinuous Transition Drive as the Jump Drive.

"But back to the point, some years ago Dr. Xu developed a new branch of mathematics that is well suited to solving problems of this type. It was the reason his group had moved so far ahead of everyone else on Earth with their ion drive technology.

"Once he saw our math for these phenomena, he rederived it, using his tools as a way of confirming his understanding of our work. Excellent scientific discipline, I must say."

"Are you saying that the reason is not that Dr. Xu is a better technologist? It's that he is a better mathematician?" Michael asked.

"Exactly!" The Professor replied.

"Thank you, Professor," Eugene said.

"Back to your original request..." Michael said. "Yes. We need to handle this in a way that makes it absolutely clear that humanity made this discovery. The entire purpose of the Institute, the Ascendancy and the Confederation for that matter, is to bring peoples together so that they can become more than the sum of their parts. To demonstrate that so vividly and so early in humanity's integration is imperative.

"Here's my plan..." Michael went on to explain.

COMMITTEE ROOM, EARTH ALLIANCE HEADQUARTERS

As planned, the Ship Design Advisory Board session was in progress when Michael arrived. Professor Milne had broken them into sub teams to work various problems. Richard Myers from NASA and Markus Vogel from Germany were working on Structure, Propulsion and Control Systems. Carol Woods of the United States, Konstantin Popov of Russia, and Alyson Wilberforce of the United Kingdom were working on health and wellness-related issues, including hospital facilities, physical fitness and dining areas. Pai Lin and Enzo Venezia were working on crew quarters, and on interior look and feel. Once again, Michael opened his senses to confirm what his eyes were telling him. This team was engaged and making excellent progress.

Michael saw Professor Milne motioning him to come over to the Structure team. When he got there, the Professor said. "Michael, our team seems a little concerned about an issue or two. I'll let Advisor Vogel explain.

"Thank you." Advisor Vogel said. "All the controls on this ship are telepathically controlled. How are we going to adapt that for human use?"

"That is one of the reasons we need people like you, Dr. Vogel, and you Dr. Myers. The Confederation is making the entire content of our telepathic User Interface available to Space Force. Professor Gupta in the Medical School is a specialist in this area. She knows everything there is to know about converting implant-based controls into computer-based controls. She has helped Dr. Reed adapt several pieces of medical equipment for human use. Everything the Confederation does via our implants can be converted for use with standard human computer equipment. I think that will be the most time-consuming part of the human spaceship design.

"But other options are available to you, including embedded AIs or android pilots. My preference would be for a fully human-controlled space force, but you are the ones that need to drive that decision."

"I thought you said you had the final decision," Advisor Vogel blurted.

"Indeed I do. And, I have just told you the one I want. If you recommend it and have a competent solution, it is the one you will get. If you do not pursue a human solution or ultimately recommend a Confederation solution, then that is what you'll get. But, in truth, I would be very disappointed with that outcome."

The two advisors were stunned. They had assumed that the Confederation solution was baked into the cake and the rest was a charade. But Michael just said that a human-operated solution was the preferred solution, and the Confederation solution was the backup, made available in case they were not up to the task. That changed everything.

...

Michael moved through the groups, asking about their progress, answering questions, and attempting to inspire. When the hour came to conclude this round, Michael addressed the assembled team.

"First, thank you for your participation in this week's sessions. Per the advisors' agreement, you have the remainder of this week and next to provide feedback, analysis, suggestions... Any input you would like to make before the next meeting, a week from Monday, is welcome.

"But before you go... There is a vessel of a similar design to the one you've been studying. This vessel has been adapted for human use. It is not configured in the same way as the base proposal you've been working from. But it will be available an hour from now for a six-hour tour that will include viewings of Jupiter, Saturn, Alpha Centauri A & B, and Proxima Centauri. As regards this flight, and this flight only, your confidentiality agreement does not apply. You may photograph anything, except the cockpit, and release that information in any way you see fit. Or, simply keep those memories for yourself.

"If you'd like to join this little adventure, then bring your possessions. You will be transported to your homes once the ship regains Earth orbit.

"The transportation options previously booked are also available."
The room erupted in excitement.

PROFESSOR JENSEN'S OFFICE, SPACE FORCE EDUCATION BUILDING

The second session of her introductory class on Applied Reactions was to begin in an hour. Professor Jensen had asked her assistants to meet with her before class. The Butlers, Luka Tsiklauri and Alexi Santos were there. Colonel Patterson planned to participate in class but wasn't available for the planning session.

No course in the history of the Confederation had hospitalized more than four or five students. Her class had hospitalized over 200 in the very first session. Although she had heard nothing from the Ambassador's or the Institute President's offices, she was once again being shunned by the other professors in the institute.

She wasn't happy about her students vomiting, passing out or needing hospitalization, but far better that they do it in her class than when they confronted the Enemy for the first time. So, she had asked to meet with her TAs to see if they had any ideas on what to do.

...

"Thank you for joining me." the Professor said, then paused for a moment. "I need your advice," she blurted out. "We're sending too many students to the hospital, but I don't know what to do about it. How can you fight an enemy if you know nothing about them? How can you devise weapons to defeat them if you don't know what they are? How can you even defend yourself, if you're incapacitated at the first sight of them?"

Surprisingly, Noelani was the first to respond. "Obviously, you cannot. But that doesn't mean you have to show them as much on the first day." She paused, then said, "An alternative approach would be to show only a few segments that reveal the Enemy for what it is: its trans-dimensional nature, its parasitic nature, the way it controls and consumes its prey.

"Your very first clip does that. Completely freaky, stuff of nightmares, but not enough to make anyone pass out or be hospitalized.

"So, here's my suggestion. Play the clip without interruption. Then ask the class what they saw. Take a handful of answers, then play the same clip again, maybe a little slower so they can see more. Then play it a third time, pausing to explain, the way you're currently doing.

"This will cause people to try to figure out what they saw, before they have to face the horror it. When they see it the second time, it will start sinking in that this is horrifying. And, when they get the play-by-play commentary, they will already have been conditioned. Some will still be a bit traumatized, but the vast majority will only be repulsed.

"Then, instead of moving on to the next clip, talk about the Enemy with words: their strengths, their weaknesses. Ask the class how they think such an Enemy could be defeated. Insist on getting a few answers, even if you have to cold call people.

"Then go on to introduce our weapons. Explain how and why they work. Then tell them the objective of this course and that a percent of their grade will be based on their team coming up with weapon ideas. Give the team assignment and close by promising to show them a clip of an enemy being taken down next week."

There was silence in the room, then George said. "That's brilliant, babe."

Noelani gave him the look that told him not to call her that in public, then smiled.

The Professor said, "Want to lead this session with me? You take the first part... The clip, the questions, then turn it to me for the walk through. I'll turn it back to you for the next round of questions. Then I'll walk through the weapons and why they work. Then back to you for the close."

All eyes turned to Noelani. "I'm on for it."

SPACE FORCE AUDITORIUM #3

A phalanx of medics had assembled outside waiting for the doors to the auditorium to open, for the masses to run out in terror and for the rescue to begin. They had been asked to be there 5 minutes before the scheduled finish of the class, although the previous session had run more than 45 minutes late.

About 5 minutes after the scheduled finish, the doors to the auditorium swung open and students started trickling out. The team leader assumed that something had gone desperately wrong and started to call for back up, then put the call on hold as he watched and listened to the students walking out. No running. No barfing. No panic. No screaming. Were they at the wrong place?

Then excited buzz cut through the other noise. A competition. New weapons to fight the Enemy. Confused by what he was seeing, the leader of the medic team stopped a group of students to ask if there were people inside that needed help. The young woman who seemed to be the center of attention said, "No," then kept on going.

Fifteen minutes later, the outflow had trickled down to nothing and the medics went in to see an essentially empty room with no bodies on the floor. He approached a small group in intense conversation, eventually interrupting them to ask which class this had been. Their leader answered, "Applied Reactions 101." Then went back to their conversation.

The leader of the medic team released his team to their normal duties, then called in a report and returned to his own work.

DEVELOPMENT

[Thursday, 08.29.2030] CONFEDERATION SCHOOL OF ENGINEERING

"Eugene. This part looks exactly the same as the original." Ka-Tu said. "Are you sure this is the right one?"

"Amazing, isn't it?" Eugene replied. "The internal configuration needed to change, but I put the new design back into the original package. It fit perfectly and eliminated the need to change any other parts or re-route the power."

The Ambassador had arranged for the old shuttle to be moved to an available engineering bay, where Eugene and Ka-Tu had met a few minutes earlier. The two professors went to work installing the new part and updating the control software.

"Professor. Are you sure it's safe to test this? The history of human aerospace engineering has been littered with designs that everyone thought would work, but which failed catastrophically when tested. Our track record has improved some since the advent of simulation. Still, I find myself worried about just getting in and attempting to jump."

"Good point, Eugene," replied the Professor. "Our simulations are rarely wrong. And when they are, it's more an issue of performance than total failure. Nonetheless, I appreciate your point. If things go badly wrong, I am only risking my avatar, not my life. Well, technically I'm risking my life; it is possible for an Ascendant to die when their avatar is destroyed. But that's even more rare than a simulation failure. What would you suggest?"

"This shuttle is piloted by an AI, right? Could we have it do the test run on its own without a living person aboard?" Eugene asked.

"Eugene, in the Confederation, AIs are considered to be living beings. Most Confederation citizens would be offended to hear someone suggest that it'd be better to put an AI at risk than a biological," said the Professor, then seeing Eugene's reaction, added, "It's OK, Eugene. Those of us that have been trained in the diplomatic corps have been advised that this is something difficult for new member species to understand. At least at first. So, no offense taken, no judgement rendered.

109

"But back to testing, I would be very uncomfortable sending Else, our AI pilot, out on this test and not going myself. I think the real question is whether you want to come. I will support your decision either way."

The two went back to work, powering up the various systems and running innumerable diagnostics.

CONFERENCE ROOM, CIVIL ENGINEERING DEPARTMENT

Professor Schudel arrived at the departmental conference room a little early and was surprised to see a Confederation security officer. He could not imagine why a security officer would be in the Civil Engineering department. Michael typically didn't travel with one.

As he approached the Conference Room, he was intercepted by the officer. "Professor Schudel, my name is Emmanuel Mbanefo." The officer said with a friendly smile. "Could you please come with me?"

"Mr. Mbanefo, am I in some sort of trouble?" the professor asked.

Emmanuel smiled and said, "No, my friend, but you might be in for the most interesting day of your life. Come, you will see."

Emmanuel walked over to the Conference Room door, opened it and escorted the Professor in before closing and locking the door.

As the Professor entered, he saw one of the most beautiful women he'd ever seen. She was thin, but shapely, with perfectly smooth ebony skin, sparkling eyes and a big smile. "Professor Schudel, thank you for meeting with us today. My name is Bahati Mbanefo. Please come in and be seated. We have a number of things we would like to discuss with you." Her melodic voice melted away the tension that had been building.

"In case you are wondering," she said, "Emmanuel and I are human, the first human Ascendants. As I think you know, the first assignment for a new Ascendant is almost always in their own form. So, our first assignment is on Earth, which is the only planet that is human. We have been with the Ambassador for a little less than 100 years at this point and he uses us to handle certain sensitive matters."

Professor Schudel was now worried again.

Bahati continued. "Professor, the Ambassador would like you to volunteer for a mission. It's not dangerous, at least not in any normal sense of the word, but it is very important and possibly the most important operation that will take place in either of our lifetimes." A pause. "You have a critical skill that is imperative for this mission."

"What is the mission?" asked the Professor.

"Well, that's the problem. The mission itself is highly classified. We cannot tell you what it is until you sign a 'Top Secret' security agreement with us. Here is a copy of the agreement." She pushed one of the short piles of paper beside her across the table to him.

As an Ascendant himself, he had to take a course on security and security agreements. The level of security was a number from 100 to 1,000 with 1,000 being the lower level of security. He had signed numerous agreements in the past in the 900 range. The highest he had ever participated in was a level 225 some years ago. It was related to diagnosing and controlling earthquakes on a planet whose core was undergoing change. But for all of those, he at least knew the topic and why he was being recruited. He had never been approached like this before and his hand trembled a bit as he touched the cover page.

As he flipped the page over, he saw the level. It was level 1. Hans sat there with his mouth open. He'd thought the lowest number was 100.

"Scary, isn't it?" Emmanuel said. "I only have one thing to say. This will be the most mind-blowing assignment you will ever get. Once it is complete, it will be made public. Then you will be one of two things: a) one of the most famous and well-respected people in the Confederation, or b) totally crushed because you gave up the opportunity to become one of the most famous and well-respected people in the Confederation."

"You said this was not dangerous in the normal sense of the word. What does that mean?" Hans asked.

"It has the level of danger you would expect in your line of work, and on the safer end at that. We have checked your previous assignments and this one does not appear to be anywhere near as dangerous as the core-stabilization project you did."

"I've never seen a Level 1 before. I assume that I need to sign this now. I can't go home and think about it?"

"Correct. You must take it or leave it now. And if you choose not to sign, then I am to administer this." She put a vial on the table. "It will wipe out any memory of this discussion."

He had heard of this before and quickly looked around the room. Sure enough. There it was, a memory suspension device. It worked in collaboration with the implants in his real body. In the presence of a memory suspension device, the implants would hold short-term memories for up to an hour before releasing them to long-term memory. The cream in the vial would block the memories held in the buffer, so to speak, until they faded. An hour from now he would not even remember that he had come to this room.

He smiled. They had set this up well. Message from the Ambassador, something no one would ever turn down. Meeting in a nearby room, so no out-of-place memory remnants to surface later. Escort into the room with the device, so the timing is perfect. If they were this serious, then the mission must be serious.

"I'm in." he said.

"Thumb print here, please." Bahati said.

He pressed his thumb on the designated spot, leaving a trace of DNA to seal the deal.

"My broddah." Emmanuel said, bubbling with enthusiasm. "You are going to love this! We are going to transport up to the Ambassador's ship for your briefing. Don't worry, you'll be back in time for dinner, mind slightly blown."

CONFERENCE ROOM, AMBASSADOR'S SHUTTLE

Professor Schudel, Emmanuel and Bahati appeared on a transporter landing just across the hall from the door to the conference room. The door was open. As he entered, Hans saw Michael sitting at the Conference Room table.

"Professor Schudel." Michael came over to shake his hand. "Thank you for joining us today, and apologies for the drama of a security agreement. What we are about to do must be kept secret for a while."

Michael shepherded the team to the table. "Dr. Schudel, forgive me for saying what you already know. But it is required that I say this before we begin. This project and the information you will hear today are Top Secret Level 1. If any of the information you hear today, even the existence of this project, is disclosed, you will be arrested, expelled from the Ascendancy and reconditioned. Do you understand?"

"Yes, I understand," Hans replied.

Michael looked around the room and smiled. "This team, the four of us gathered here, is about to do something that has never been done before. If we fail in our venture, then the universe as we know it may be destroyed. If we succeed, the Confederation will be forever changed for the better.

"You might ask what could possibly make me say that?"

Using his implants, Michael turned on the monitor built into the wall and a cutaway image of the Earth appeared.

"As I think everyone here knows, the Earth is composed of four layers: an inner solid core, a molten outer core, the mantle, and the crust on top.

"You probably also know that the Earth has several thousand pounds of transluminide in its crust. What you probably don't know is that the first part of my mission on Earth was to extract and secure the transluminide in the accessible portion of the crust. You probably also do not know that there is another 35,000 pounds or so under the snow in Antarctica."

Hans gave a sharp intake of breath. *The Confederation is falling apart for lack of transluminide and there is an undeveloped reserve of 35,000 pounds on this planet.* He thought.

"But there is another reserve. A large one. One discovered a long time ago, that only two people knew about until this week."

Larger than 35,000 pounds, Hans thought. *How is that possible?*

Michael pointed to the cutaway image of the Earth on the screen. "The molten core of the Earth has a concentration of transluminide orders above the 1 part per billion extraction limit. Our minimum estimate is 10^{23} kilograms of transluminide."

"Oh my God," Hans muttered.

"Professor Schudel, you are going to mine transluminide from the Earth's core. This needs to be done in secret with minimal staff. It also needs to be done without creating a massive amount of debris. And, it must be done quickly.

"You have unlimited use of Earth's replication capacity, but your use of it must be disguised to minimize suspicion. I'm going to need kilograms per day in a matter of weeks."

"Could this be hidden in plain sight?" Hans asked.

"I'm not sure I understand what you mean by that."

"I have taught mining here at the Institute for several years now. This year I will be teaching core mining for the first time. There are dozens of volunteers that would love to be involved in a project where those skills could be used.

"Suppose we set up a small test mine. One that is not intended to commercially produce anything, only to allow students to train. We could be very public about it.

"No one on Earth knows how to detect or measure transluminide. So, we have each student make a perfect 1,000 lb. iron-nickel ingot. They can make as many as 10 attempts to get one good enough. We filter the transluminide out during the extraction process, so no one knows.

"Then, if we price the ingots low enough, their companies will want to buy them, lots of them. Next thing you know we are cranking out a million pounds or more a day, in plain sight and no one knows what we're really doing.

"Demand for the class will skyrocket and next semester we'll have 10 times as many students and a corresponding increase in demand.

"That would allow us to involve lots of people. I'm sure you can get tons of PR out of this as well. Have the Sergeant do some media interviews. The more visibility, the better the secret," Hans concluded.

"I like the way this guy thinks," Emmanuel said.

PLANNING

CONFERENCE ROOM, AMBASSADOR'S OFFICE

Again, this morning, Michael went straight to the conference room where the professors were waiting for him. He sensed their excitement immediately.

"Professors," Michael said. "Good to see you. Am I guessing correctly that you have some good news to share?"

"Yes, we do," replied Eugene. "Our final design required very little actual change to your old shuttle. All the upgrades have now been installed and Else reports that all systems are operating as we would expect. She also says that the nominal power flow through the upgraded equipment 'feels' good. This is the first I have worked closely with an AI. I find myself deeply reassured that she FEELS the changes and that they feel good."

Michael chuckled at that. "Does that mean we're ready for a test run?"

"Yes, we are." Ka-Tu replied. "That's what we wanted to talk with you about. The plan is for Eugene, Else and I to do the test flight. Else will fly. Eugene and I will be operating the test equipment measuring every aspect of the spacecraft's performance. Our question for you is about where we should go and how visible, or secret, we want the test to be."

"What's the minimum distance you need for a successful test?"

"That's one of the problems. I think we could confirm all four transitions with a jump to the far side of the Oort cloud, but that is so short that we might not be able to collect any useful data. Even going to Alpha Centauri is too short to get the measurements we need. Ideally, we would like to go 100 to 1,000 light years, but if anything went wrong at those distances, we would be stranded, and it's hard to believe that help could get there in time."

"Can you plot a safe course that far?" Michael asked.

It was Ka-Tu's turn to laugh at that one. "Else said you would ask that question. And told me to ask you if that was actually a question."

That statement brought back a flood of memories and emotions.

...

The original pilot of the old shuttle had been an Ascendant. Her human name was Elsie Hoffman. Elsie had been on her first major mission on a non-Confederation world. She was responsible for The

115

Ascendancy's transportation systems in this solar system and was the master of anything that required a pilot.

During the arrest of the former North Korean dictator, it had been discovered that he was an Enemy agent. In the resulting confrontation Elsie had been infected and her avatar destroyed. They removed Elsie from her avatar before it died, but Elsie herself was also seriously damaged and subsequently had to be evacuated to New Lorexi for treatment.

In the weeks leading up to the Revelation and the event that occurred that night, Elsie had created an AI that contained her knowledge of the shuttle, its systems and of navigation in general. She'd also uploaded her memories from her 10 years on Earth, so the AI would have context if it was ever called into duty. Elsie had named the AI 'Else', an affectionate nickname the crew sometimes called her.

Michael and Elsie had become friends and had worked together closely during the week following the Revelation. It was during that week that Elsie started saying... "Michael, is that really a question?"

It had been an immensely stressful time for Michael. One of the side effects of that stress was that he started micromanaging everything. Elsie took it all in stride, for a day or two anyway.

Else still operated that shuttle, but it was now used mostly for passenger transport. Michael used one of the military escorts they had acquired and converted for human use.

...

Coming back to the moment, Michael said. "I think I might have a solution for that. How soon do you want to do the test?"

"We can be ready Sunday morning." Eugene replied.

NASA HEADQUARTERS, WASHINGTON DC

Advisor Richard Myers had arrived home sometime in the middle of the night on Wednesday, completely exhilarated by the events of the week. He was required to file a report, which was going to be problematic, given the security agreement, so instead, he put in a meeting request with the Administrator, whose waiting room he was now sitting in.

"Mr. Myers." The administrator's assistant said. "You may enter."

He stepped up to the door, then opened it and went in.

"Richard. Welcome," his boss said. "Please come in. I can't wait to hear about life as part of the ship design committee."

"Hi, Sandy. Thank you for letting me take this assignment."

"So, tell me about what happened," She said.

"Well... This is difficult. The work of the Ship Design Advisory Board is classified Earth Alliance Top Secret. I had the choice of signing the agreement or leaving. I chose to sign the agreement. If I tell you anything that is classified, then the United States will be expelled from the Earth Alliance; other than the House of Ambassadors, of course. Sadly, more or less everything we discussed is classified. But there are things I can say."

The boss was not happy to hear that the work was classified. "Let's hear it then," she said sourly.

"First, we will eventually be able to disclose everything, including the designs. As an insider, I will understand what is disclosed. That is the benefit they are offering each of the advisors and their sponsoring organizations. They expect to be able to do that release in about a year," Richard said.

"Better than nothing I suppose. Anything else?"

"We were taken on a tour of the solar system and Alpha Centauri. The ship that took us is a modified version of a ship similar to the base design for one of the ships. I took hundreds of photos. All of them are exempted from the confidentiality agreement and can be used however we see fit."

"Now, that is something." She lofted an eyebrow. "Can I see?"

They spent the next hour flipping through the pictures.

"OK," she said. "In lieu of a standard report, I want a report composed of those pictures, no more than 1 per page. Each picture should include a description that includes as much unclassified information as you can remember. The descriptions can be as long as necessary. When are you due back at the Earth Alliance?"

"A week from Sunday," said Richard.

"Then you have until next Friday to file your report."

"Understood. Can I change the subject a little?"

"Go," she said.

"I'd like to tell you something in the gray zone of the confidentiality agreement."

"All ears." She smiled for the first time since the warm greeting.

"It is in the gray zone because I heard this rumor before I heard Michael say it."

"You met the Ambassador!" Sandy exclaimed.

"Yes. Yes, I did." Richard felt a bit proud of himself.

"And..."

117

"The Confederation is going to release the specifications for the content of their telepathic user interfaces. Apparently, they have done that with the two medical devices they're now sending home with doctors who have completed their training. They even have a specialist to work with human teams that want to add human interfaces to the Confederation equipment."

"Do I understand you to be saying that humans will be piloting these ships?"

Richard started to reply, then immediately shut down. "I'm sorry. The answer to that specific question is classified, but I think you can deduce the answer."

"Well, I'll be." she said.

"One other thing..." Richard said.

"Go," she replied.

"Michael said that he needed people like me to make those user interface conversions. I think that was functionally an offer to do a sabbatical there. If that was an offer, would NASA let me take it?" Richard asked.

"Would it be your intention to return?" She asked.

"In principle, yes. But only if I could continue doing the same kind of work, which I presume is something that NASA would have to work out with the Confederation," Richard said.

All he got was a stare from the Administrator.

"You get it right? I've been to Alpha Centauri. Who could walk away from that technology, if there were a possibility to continue working with it?"

"Let me talk with the President. I understand where you're coming from and can't fault you for it. Wish I had that chance," she said ruefully. "He has a better understanding of our treaties, and a relationship with Michael. He can guide us on policy."

She hesitated. "I would hate to lose you Richard. But you know better than I do. All the action in space is going to be dictated by the Confederation. No one in their right mind would turn down that opportunity. So, let me see what I can do to keep you part of the fold at NASA while you do what any sane person would." She smiled, then added, "I'm jealous."

PRESENCE PROJECTOR, AMBASSADOR'S OFFICE

"Mi-Ku. Thank you for setting up this call. I have several items for you, but please, you first."

"Thank you, Jo-Na." Michael said. "We have just upgraded a ship and we need to do a trial run on the new engine design. My engineers tell me that they need to run out to about 1,000 light years. My concern is that if they have a problem, there would be nothing we could do from Earth to rescue them. Last we talked, you were heading out about that far. Any chance you are still there?"

Michael watched as the Admiral worked some controls on his desk. "According to the astrogation system, we are 973.1 light years from Earth. Unfortunately, we aren't going to be here very long. We have a scout tracking signs of the Enemy about 200 light years from here. If they should actually find the Enemy, then we will head out on short notice. After that we are heading out to the rim to meet a trans-galactic freighter convoy. I'm afraid that we will be gone by the time your people get here."

"They plan to arrive in your vicinity about 36 hours from now, so this might work after all. Is it OK if I give them your coordinates and contact frequencies?"

"Of course. If they're that close already, we should have no difficulty getting to them if they need rescue."

"Excellent. I'll let them know. Now, what can I do for you?"

"Mi-Ku. We found the system that the Ancient Sentient told you about. It was totally decimated. There were three developed planets in the habitable zone. Each had enough development that it could have been the home world, although we've not ruled out the possibility there were multiple species with multiple home worlds.

"We've gathered a massive amount of data that our scientists are pouring through. Four things have popped to the top of the list, but none of these are certain. First, we've found evidence of a shield array that surrounded the entire system. This would explain why we did not find this species. They were apparently advanced enough by the time we reached this galaxy that they could hide themselves from us.

"Next, in the cloud of debris surrounding their system, we found what would appear to be Enemy artifacts dating back nearly one million years. This would seem to imply that this species fought the Enemy for an extended period of time before succumbing.

"Third, we found a handful of data storage units buried deep in the crust of one of the outer uninhabitable planets. We are still working the translations, but these seem to indicate that this species might have created the Enemy. That thought is very speculative at the moment, with a tiny fraction of the data lining up in an unexpected way.

"Lastly, there are vast energy readings in this area of space that we do not understand. None of our scientists have opined on this yet, but given what the Ancient Sentient told you, I wonder if this is the rupture in the space-time continuum that has brought the Enemy here."

SCHUDEL's OFFICE, CIVIL ENGINEERING DEPARTMENT

Professor Schudel's objective for today was to adapt his textbook core extraction device for use on Earth. He'd started this project long ago on the assumption that someday it would be relevant. But after a year of working on it at least 1 day a week and no prospect whatsoever of deployment, he'd left it to drift. It had been over a year now since he had touched it. He'd planned to use his design in the new class, but this project required that it be brought on-line as soon as possible. The theory behind the design was very simple.

    a.   Establish a standard transport bubble around several cubic meters of material in the molten core.
    b.   Establish a slightly larger transport bubble in space, directly above the first.
    c.   Harden the interior bubble and move it inside the space bubble, then harden the space bubble. This would allow the core material to maintain the majority of its heat.
    d.   Form a bubble impermeable to gold. Form a second bubble impermeable to platinum. Form a third bubble impermeable to transluminide.
    e.   Drag the core bubble through the other three bubbles, leaving the filtered materials in their respective bubbles and everything else in the main bubble.

His platform needed five field generators, storage bins for gold, platinum and transluminide, and ingot molds for the nickel/iron alloy.

The gold, platinum and transluminide bins would be hidden from view and would be described on the drawings as impurity filters. The nickel/iron ingots would be the center of attention and the user interface would feature lots of fine tuning to optimize the ingot pour.

Most of the work was done. He only needed to add the transluminide bin, do the math to specify the filters, and fine tune the user interface for his student operators.

Specifications for the basic hardware—the space frame, power sources, field and grav generators, control room and ingot room—were done, so he sent them to Michael, and asked about the requisition process on Earth.

Over the weekend, he would finish the rest. Assembly could start as soon as Monday, depending on the manufacturing capacity that had been put in place on Earth. Surprisingly, he did not have clearance for that data.

REPORT CARD

[Saturday, 08.31.2030] FOX NEWS, NEW YORK

"Michael, thank you for joining us this week on Fox News Sunday."

"Thank you, Chris, for having me on the show."

"It's been five and a half years since the first time you were with us. In preparation for today, I went back and watched that episode. Although my memory of it was clear, watching it reminded me of the wonder of that first week of the Revelation. The medical miracles, shuttle craft, transporters, Ascendants living to be 1 million years old, the vast wealth that was about to be bestowed on nations that allied with the Confederation… Every topic was a new wonder. Polls still show you to be the best-known person on Earth, and your approval ratings are still very high. So today, I'd like to ask how you think the transition is going in five areas: climate change, peace, poverty, life expectancy and preparation for future crises. Can we start with climate change?"

"Chris, thank you for asking. I look forward to discussing these topics and would be happy to start with climate change," Michael replied.

"Your critics claim that the climate has not improved very much. Average temperatures last year tied the previous high, the polar ice cap did not fully refreeze last winter, and there were 12 super storms that did a total of over $20 billion in damage worldwide. What do you say to those critics?"

"The critics make a good point. The actual weather has not changed very much over the last five years. But their implied conclusion, that our efforts are having little affect, is misguided on multiple levels."

"Five years ago, carbon dioxide was at 424 parts per million here in New York, increasing at about 4 ppm per year. The average forecast for 2030 was 450 ppm. That number peaked at 436 during the summer of 2026 and has since declined to around 410 today. It is currently declining at a rate of 10 ppm per year.

"At one level, if the carbon dioxide had reached the previous prediction, there would have been more than 12 superstorms. If memory serves correctly, the prediction at that time was 16. Similarly, the polar ice cap would have only marginally reformed, not 90% reformed. My conclusion on this point is that the critics have chosen the wrong reference point for a comparison.

"On another level, and despite this incredible turn around, the weighted average carbon dioxide concentration is still slightly higher today than it was 5 years previous, because of the cumulative impact of past emissions. This is the exact point Dr. Winston Chu made in his book five years ago. It is the same point that I made on one of the other Sunday morning shows at that time. It took 150 years to make the climate mess that we inherited. And although scientists would be able to measure the impacts of our efforts in five years, no one would be able to perceive them with their senses. That will take longer."

"But the current carbon dioxide concentration of 410 ppm is not much lower than the 424 ppm in 2025." Chris said.

"Agreed. But the context has changed. The last time carbon dioxide was at 410 was 2017 and at that time it was increasing at a little over 3 ppm per year. Now it is decreasing at 10 ppm per year. We have, in only five years, completely arrested the relentless advances of the previous age and have turned the corner. Within five years, there will be people complaining about the cooler weather. And in about 10 years, we'll need to start slowing the rate of decrease to avoid any risk of a new ice age setting in."

"So how do you grade yourself on climate change since the Revelation?" Chris asked.

"I think this has gone just about according to plan and I'm very pleased with how well this aspect of the alliance is working," Michael answered.

"Polls show that America gives you a B+. What do you say about that?"

"I think that is fair. The nations of Earth in the aggregate get a B+ for their handling of climate change since the Federation gave them the tools to do so. But a couple standouts, like Canada and Israel, get A+s."

"Moving on. What about peace?" Chris asked.

"Chris. You and people of your profession are probably better judges of that than I am. But I would like to point out a couple countries that I am particularly proud of. The first is North Korea. They have gone from a rogue nation to a respected member of the international community. In only five years, their economy has come up to the same level as most of the West. I think they even have a chance of passing South Korea on a per capita basis this year. I can't tell you how much respect I have for President Park and the miracle that he has accomplished there.

"Another standout is Russia. They have gone from provocateur to peace maker.

"Globally, there has been no war over the last 5 years. America has brought most of their troops home. The only thing that still saddens me is the rate of terrorism which, though much reduced, still exists."

"I agree with your assessment, Michael, but would probably add Israel to the list. The Palestinians have been fully integrated in their society. Prime Minister Levine even took the majority of the Palestinian vote in the last parliamentary elections. No one would have believed that possible before the Revelation."

"Thank you for mentioning that, Chris. I completely agree."

"Moving on. What about poverty?"

"One of my predictions, five years ago, was that peace and poverty would go hand in hand. Specifically, I said that as poverty decreased, acts of kindness would increase. And the world would become more peaceful and prosperous. I got a lot of push back on that at the time. I would say that prediction was pretty much spot on."

"But there is still inequality," Chris complained.

"Of course, there is inequality. No two people are the same, or even want to be the same. But, the difference between today and five years ago is that there are fewer people held in place by their circumstances. And that number will continue falling."

"What about life expectancy?" Chris asked.

"Over the last five years, life expectancy has increased by more than five years. I expect that to continue to be true for at least ten more years. Almost every human has benefited from Confederation Medical technology. We just graduated the 60th class from the Basics Program at our medical school. The last class had 10,000 graduates. There are now about 350,000 doctors worldwide licensed to use first level Confederation drugs. And human bioengineers working with Confederation medical engineers have produced the first nanobot-based surgical tools for human use. No other species has been able to adapt our medical technology at anywhere near this rate."

"Can you give us any quantitative assessment of that?"

"Yes. I did a look up on Confederation databases about nanobot-based drug delivery systems. The fastest adaptation, before humanity, was 127 years. The human engineers at our medical school did it in only 5 and a half."

"Wow. I am shocked to hear that. What implications will that have?"

"First, human health and life expectancy is going to increase very rapidly. I would expect that 50% of children born this year will still be alive 100 years from now."

Silence, then. "Isn't that going to cause problems?"

"Yes and no. Yes, humanity is going to have to deal with a population explosion unlike any you have experienced before. But no. All of our models show that Earth has the capacity to support far more people than that. So, I see the sheer numbers as being more of an opportunity than a problem."

"What about the threat you told us about five years ago?"

"There have been no further Enemy sightings on, or anywhere near, Earth since the events in February 2025."

"When you say, 'near Earth', what do you mean?" Chris asked.

"The closest sighting was about 950 light-years from Earth. But, as you know, we are in the process of forming Space Force. Recruitment has gone very well and there are some other advances that we hope to announce in a couple weeks."

"Is there anything that you can tell us about those advances now?" Chris asked.

The question made Michael smile. "I suppose I deserve that question for having dangled the possibility out there." He hesitated. "Chris, I need to be very careful about what I say here. I can't give you specifics, but what I can say is the there are some truly amazing things happening at the Institute. I said earlier that in only five and a half years, medical scanners and surgical tools were adapted, something that has never happened in less than 100 years before. The vast majority of Confederation members ultimately make adaptations, but they just take longer.

"The next step after adaptation is improvement. Many Confederation members ultimately advance to the point where they make improvements to Confederation technology. That process is much slower." Michael got a faraway look for a moment. "According to the best information I can find on short notice, no other member has made a significant improvement within 5,000 years of joining the

Confederation. I predict that human teams will make significant improvements in one or more Confederation technologies within the next year."

"Michael, how is that possible?" Chris asked.

"Technology is the application of scientific knowledge to solve practical problems. Most people think the important phrase in that statement is scientific knowledge. But in this instance, I think the important word is application. Application is an art, one in which humanity is remarkably gifted. Several times in the last couple weeks I have sat in a room with both human and Confederation scientists, who are looking at the same bits of science and come to completely different conclusions about how they can be combined.

"I have always believed that something big would happen once we established open communication with humanity. The only surprise Is how quickly it's happening."

"Michael, thank you for sharing that. Once again, the wonder is as fresh today as it was five years ago. Thank you for being with us today and for having invited us to join the Confederation."

TELEVISION STUDIO, EMBASSY PRESS RELATIONS DEPARTMENT

The studio was set up in the usual manner. But this week there were only two chairs, one for George and one for guest host Jonathan Omeruo, from Kameme TV in Kenya.

"Good evening, world." Jonathan said, bubbling with joy. "I am Jonathan Omeruo from KamemeTV News in Kenya. I am here at the Confederation Embassy in the Mackenzie Mountains of northern Canada. With me tonight is former Sergeant George Butler. George, thank you for letting me host your show today."

"Jonathan, I'm glad you could join us."

"George, I'd like to start with a question about your role at the Embassy. Five years ago, they referred to you as Confederation spokesman. I don't hear that anymore. Can you explain?"

"Jonathan, thank you for that question. This is a very confusing topic. As you know, Michael healed me the morning after the Revelation, then brought me to his ranch in Hawaii for physical therapy. There, I discovered the fundamental goodness of Michael and the Confederation team. By that time, everyone had heard of Michael, but no one really 'knew' him. There was a lot of discussion on the news about the things Michael was doing, the Alliance offer, the gifts...

126

But from my perspective, the important stuff was not getting covered."

"And what was this important stuff?" Jonathan asked.

"That they were good people you could trust."

"So, what did you do?"

"I asked Michael if he would let the various news teams interview me. They all wanted to talk to him, but he didn't have time. There were reporters lined up, clogging the streets, calling 24-7.

"I thought maybe I could help, and he let me."

"I remember your first interview with Keoni Gates," Jonathan said. "What struck me the most was your honesty and humor; despite the tragedy you had suffered and the disability you were still fighting to overcome."

"Thank you," George said. "Anyway, the Confederation had no spokesman at that time, so I was informally given the title and enjoyed having the access, to tell you the truth.

"But this is the important part. I never spoke FOR the Confederation, in the sense of being the person putting out the Confederation's official statements. I spoke ABOUT the Confederation from the perspective of one of the first humans to live among them, someone who saw them for who they were and really believed in them.

"That part is still true. I really believe in the Confederation and in Michael's leadership. I trust them implicitly. And, Michael apparently trusts me, because he continues to let me do this show, despite the fact that I don't know much about what's officially going on."

"George, thank you for that explanation. It helps me understand both you and the Confederation a little better."

George nodded his thanks, while the studio audience gave light applause.

"OK. So, my first news question for you today… I understand that about 200 people were sent to the hospital on Tuesday after the first session of the new Applied Reactions class. I also have been told that you are an Assistant in that class. Can you tell me anything about what happened?"

"This is hard."

"Let's start easy." Jonathan said. "Can you confirm that you are an assistant in that class?"

"Yes. I am an assistant, as is my wife Noelani and a couple other really great people."

"Can you tell us what Applied Reactions is about?"

"Yes." George laughed. "Applied Reactions are weapons."

"Weapons?" Jonathan asked.

"Yes. The core species in the Confederation is the Lorexians, as I am sure you know. They are a very peaceful people that really believe in helping others. Conversely, they abhor violence. Both of these beliefs are woven deep into the fabric of their society.

"One of the side effects of those beliefs is they disdain even the idea of weapons. The closest translation of the word they use to describe weapons is Applied Reactions. I think it has evolved from chemistry experiments gone wrong."

"So, is that what happened? Did a chemistry experiment go wrong?" Jonathan asked.

"No. Nothing like that," George said.

"Then what?" Jonathan asked.

"This is where I have to be careful. Let me start by saying that the Enemy is repulsive. Confederation statistics say that 4% of humanoids vomit or pass out the first time they see one."

"That is hard to believe." Jonathan said.

"Trust me." George said. "I have seen some very bad stuff in my day, like kids..." George was suddenly overcome by emotion. "...kids blown up by IEDs..." He squeaked out. Another pause to compose himself.

"Sorry. I should know by now not to go down that thought path, because there's nothing but grief and frustration there." George shook his head, then continued.

"The Enemy is worse. Much worse. I can't say more than that and am probably going to be in trouble for having said that much.

"Anyway, the first session was all about exposing the class to images of the Enemy, showing them holographic images of the Enemy doing their thing. About 4% of our class either threw up, passed out or both.

"You see, that's the conundrum. How can you fight something, or even defend yourself from something that makes you sick to your stomach? So, the first step in talking about weapons is to talk about the Enemy that you're going to be 'shooting' at. To know what it is. To know its vulnerabilities. Etc."

There was momentary silence. The audience was stone cold quiet. Jonathan seemed momentarily at a loss.

"OK. That is hard to think about, so maybe I won't. But, what about the next several sessions? Did anyone go to the hospital after that?"

"No." George laughed. "My beautiful and ingenious wife came up with a plan. I can't tell you how much I love this woman. She is a trained Confederation med-tech and knows a lot about how people process shock.

"The key is that the first time you see the Enemy, you can't really figure out what it is. It's really only after you've put the pieces together that you get slammed by the shock. So, her idea was, let's show them a little clip. Enough that they know the Enemy was in it. Then ask them what they saw. Show it again in slower motion, so they can discern more. Etc. When you ease into it like that, the shock still comes, but you're not slammed with it. So, no extreme reactions, or at least none since we've flipped to this format.

"That comes back to the importance of this class. If you have not seen the Enemy before, you won't even know what it is until it already has you. If you do know, but don't understand its nature, you will be incapacitated before you can escape or defend yourself."

"George, your description really creeps me out. Would it be OK if I move on to another topic?" Jonathan asked.

George nodded his consent.

"The professor, Valerie Jensen. I've heard that she has been shunned a bit within the Institute. Do you know anything about that?"

"Sad, but true. Goes back to what I said earlier. Lorexians are very anti-violence, anti-weapon. Professor Jensen has done almost all the work in terms of determining the Enemy's nature and vulnerabilities. She is also the designer of all the weaponry known to be effective against the Enemy. The Lorexians, as a whole, find that distasteful.

"I actually like her, as do most of the humans that meet her. I think she'll probably stay here for a long time, because she has finally found a place where she is welcome."

"One last related topic... I understand that the class is going to be involved in developing additional weapons to combat the Enemy. Is that true?"

"I can't answer that question. But, let me ask you one instead. Knowing that all the weapons we have were designed by one member of a pacifist species, don't you think we should be chomping at the bit to design our own weapons?" George asked.

"Point taken." Jonathan said.

AMBASSADORS OFFICE

Sarah had asked if it would be possible to tour the gardens in Riverside Park this weekend. His training and millennia of experience had taught Michael that the mission was always first; personal pleasures, a distant priority. But he could no longer do that. He needed time with Sarah as much as he needed oxygen to breathe. Thankfully, she was fully aligned with his mission. But he was in for trouble if that ever changed.

When he landed, his date with Sarah was a little more than an hour away. So, he went to his office to clear the messages that he hadn't finished on the shuttle trip back from New York. Curiously, there was a message from Professor Schudel. Opening it, Michael saw requisitions for a lot of material. This was incredibly good news. He forwarded it to Emmanuel and Bahati, asking them to order what they could without raising suspicion. Then he replied to the professor, letting him know that Joel would be back this week to help with the rest.

RIVERSIDE PARK

Michael met Sarah in the lobby of their building exactly on time. Hand in hand, they walked down to the gardens along the river near their home. As much as Michael loved Sarah, he was always a little worried about being seen in public with her like this. For the most part Embassy residents gave them their space. Tourists, on the other hand, seemed to have no sense of propriety.

But his biggest concern was that although he was impervious to any human attack, she was not. He would fix that tomorrow.

As they reached the entrance to the gardens, Michael saw two familiar faces waiting there for them.

"George, Noelani. So good to see you." Michael said. He saw Sarah beaming, and it clicked that she had planned this. Then it clicked that this probably was not about seeing the gardens.

"Long time, Michael. Thanks for joining us tonight." George said.

Alarms started going off in Michael's mind. *What did I forget?* He thought to himself.

"To what do I owe this pleasure?" Michael asked, now very worried that he had seriously screwed up.

The three of them laughed. Then Noelani shook her head and said, "Michael, Michael, Michael, it's Sarah's birthday." Then she added in mock surprise, "Did they teach you nothing about Earth as part of your training for this mission?"

Michael felt mortified. "I thought Sarah's birthday was in September." He checked his internal chronometer. "Ah. September 1st. That would be tomorrow."

Everyone laughed, including the gawkers standing by who were apparently listening closely.

"So, what wonderful treat have I planned for my beloved?" Michael asked.

"Thought you would never ask," replied George.

They walked along the walkway, then turned down a pathway that was blocked by a sign that said, "Private Party."

A guard had been posted. He said, "Good evening. Mr. Ambassador. Please follow the path down toward the river."

They walked down and around the bend to where the path opened onto a large deck with three open pavilions. It was the first time Michael had been here. He was surprised how lovely and peaceful this location was. A string quartet on the music stage played some lovely classical music.

Ahead were several groups of people. To the left of the music stage, Sarah's parents, Tim and Susan, and her brother Pete, talked with Monica Hayes, the Good Morning America producer during the years Sarah had worked there, and several of the show's former co-hosts.

Closer to the right of the band stage, most of Sarah's media relations department had gathered. Michael noted that Dr. Winston Chu, an environmental scientist, and Marie St. Germain, the former Canadian Minister of Health, spoke with Sarah's staff.

In the center pavilion, Chef Marco worked all the last-minute details on the buffet that had been prepared.

Over on the right near the dining pavilion, were the people Michael thought of as his human family: Helen Butler; Mahesh, Nisha and Vanya Subramanian; Luka and Anna Tsiklauri; Mark and Ruth Patterson; most of his Hawaii-based staff, as well as the Chief and his wife and the Davis family.

Michael was very impressed with Pam for having pulled off something this complicated.

Sarah took Michael's hand and led him over to see her family. After big hugs and a few tears, Sarah withdrew and said, "Mom and Dad, I would like to introduce you to my other half, Michael."

"Michael, pleasure to meet you. I'm Tim Wright, Sarah's father, and this is her mother, Susan."

"A pleasure to meet you, Mr. and Mrs. Wright."

"Michael," Sarah said, "This is my brother, Pete."

"A pleasure to meet you, Pete."

"Would it be possible to have a word with you, Michael?" Sarah's father asked.

"Dad?" Sarah whined.

"I would enjoy that, Mr. Wright. Shall we step over toward the lookout?" Michael opened his senses wide to Sarah's father in the hope of getting a sense of what the man wanted to talk about.

Once out of earshot, Michael said, "Am I correct in assuming that you want to talk about my relationship with your daughter?"

"Yes." He said. "It's hard to understand how this is going to work."

"Is there a particular issue you're worried about?" Michael asked.

"Every issue." He said. "Are you going to stick with her? Are you going to get married? Will she have children? Who will provide once you're off to your next assignment? I am deeply worried that she's going to be hurt; whether she'll have a normal life."

"I suspect that I'd feel the same way in your shoes." Michael said. "But first, let me say that I will never leave Sarah. My greater worry is that she will leave me. My mission on Earth was scoped to be in the range of 1,000 to 4,000 years. Sarah has begun training that could extend her life that long, but it's still unknown whether or not it will. As to marriage and children, that's mostly up to her."

"Are you able to give her children?" He asked.

"Yes. Here," Michael said, taking Mr. Wright's hand and putting it against his chest. "Feel the heartbeat? My body is 100% human, 100% functional. There is no medical test that it will not pass.

"But most importantly, I love your daughter with all my heart, mind and soul."

Mr. Wright looked deep into Michael's eyes, held them for a minute, then extended his hand to shake Michael's. "Then, you have my blessing."

He started to turn back toward the party but stopped. "By the way… On Earth it's customary for the man to ask the woman to marry him. I understand it doesn't work that way where you come from. If you want to give her the birthday present that every girl dreams about, ask her to marry you."

And with that, they headed back toward the party.

...

The party turned out to be quite a success. The crowd grew a bit as the evening progressed. The string quartet was replaced by a jazz band and the area in front of the bandstand turned into a dance floor.

Michael spent several minutes getting caught up with people he hadn't seen in years. Dr. Chu had another book coming out and asked if Michael would read it and possibly give a review. Marie had finished her term as Minister of Health and had decided to take the presidency of a hospital in Montreal. The Chief had been promoted and was now the head of Hawaiian Civil Defense on the Big Island. Stephanie Davis had been offered a high-level position in NASA, but the week she spent in Washington DC was enough to convince her that she didn't want to leave the Big Island and the W.M. Keck Observatory.

...

As they walked back home, hand in hand, Sarah asked. "What did my father want to talk with you about?"

"I think you already know the answer to that question." He smiled. "He wanted to know my intentions for his daughter."

"Please tell me that he didn't harass you too much."

"No. He was very polite and sober. I respect him for saying what he did. I felt the same way about my daughters as they sought their mates. I truly wanted them to pick well."

"I saw you take his hand and put it on your chest. What was that about?"

"He wanted to know if I was able to give you children. I assured him that my body was fully functional and 100% human."

"He asked you about children?" She laughed.

After a few moments of silence, Michael asked. "Sarah, will you marry me?"

"Did my father tell you to do that?" She asked, an edge in her voice.

"That wasn't the response I was hoping for." By the look she gave him, he realized that was not a sufficient answer. "No. Although he did remind me that it is customary for the man to ask. He also gave me his blessing."

Sarah stopped and turned to look at Michael. "Are you serious?"

"About wanting to spend the rest of my life with you? Absolutely."

"Yes." She said. "But let's wait a bit. I like the way things are now. It will change once the world knows."

TEST JUMP

[Sunday, 09.01.2030] CONFEDERATION SCHOOL OF ENGINEERING

Michael, Ka-Tu and Eugene stood at the entrance to one of the engineering bays as the shuttle appeared on the landing pad in front. The door opened and the three entered. Although Michael would not be going on this trip, he wanted to talk with Else before it began. As he entered the cockpit, Else's hologram appeared in the pilot's seat, "Well, look who's come to pay a visit."

"Good to see you too, Else." Michael said. "I remember that night vividly. My relief that you were there. The deep sense of loss at the infection of Elsie and Sanjit."

"Me too. Still haunts me, waking up like that."

"Else. I'm sending two more people out today. Two people risking their lives for the greater good, not that different than that night when I lost Elsie and Sanjit. What can you tell me about the risks of the engines, the flight plan, and anything else I don't know to ask about?"

"Much better questions, Michael." She paused. "I'm not sure of the best way to describe these engines other than to say they are somehow right. You experience space travel in the macro, in minutes and light years. I experience it in the micro, in nanoseconds and meters. In all the simulations and orbital testing, these engines are smooth. None of the clunkiness of the previous ones. I've never been more confident in the mission-worthiness of a spacecraft than I am of this one.

"Regarding the flight path... There are thousands of safe flight paths, but I'm not a big fan of the one they've chosen. It is way too conservative. On the way out, we're going to do one big jump. I'm OK with that, but we're targeting arrival nearly 40 AU from the Admiral. I'd rather initiate the jump a little further from Earth and come in right under his nose. Much safer.

"On the way back, we'll do 100 small jumps. It'll be like skipping a rock across a lake. Since we'll only be going about 1,000 light years, the rock skipping approach will take longer. But I think of this as the critical test, because at distances of greater than 1,000 light-years, a sequence of small jumps will be much faster," Else concluded.

134

"So, you're good with this mission then?"

"Is that really a question, Michael?"

UPGRADED SHUTTLE

Eugene and Ka-Tu were totally pumped as they boarded the shuttle for its flight test. It had taken most of the day yesterday to get the shuttle instrumented. They wanted to get complete readings on the dimensional transitions and engine efficiency at every stage of the flight. These would be critical for fine tuning the design and developing optimal flight profiles.

As a safety precaution, they also loaded a household replicator and a small industrial replicator. In the unlikely event that they got stranded without ship's power, they would still have life support and the ability to do some repairs.

Once the door closed, the two engineers went to the cockpit, where Else appeared as a holographic projection. As Else lifted off, they confirmed instrument calibration and prepared to start recording.

"I spoke with Michael earlier." Else said. "He asked about our flight plan. I realized as I was talking with him that I didn't like the plan we agreed to. Could I propose an alternative?" she asked.

"Sure," Eugene replied.

Else popped up a three-dimensional holographic projection of their flight plan, showing the Earth, Sun, planets, several stars and the Admiral's position. "See how roundabout this flight plan is?"

"Yes," Eugene said. "Why are we doing this?"

"We said that we wanted to jump out of the system as quickly as possible. We can really only do that if we move straight up the gravity well, basically following a straight line defined by the Sun and the Earth. That takes us to this point here at the edge of the Oort cloud, where we have to do this long transit to acquire the vector we need to get to the Admiral. And because of interference from the gravity of this star," she said, pointing at the display, "the best way to do it is to terminate the jump about 40 AU from the Admiral.

"We did this so that if there was a failure with the initial jump, we would still be in range of Earth-based rescue."

"OK." Eugene said. "I remember agreeing to those principles for the flight plan, but I didn't realize it would take us so far out of the way. What do you propose that we do instead?"

"If we did this transit within the system using the gravity drive," she said tracing a line with her finger that angled slowly away from Earth's orbit to a point near the orbit of Mars, "we could then engage the trans-dimensional drive to accelerate into the vector for the main jump. Going this way, we will also arrive much closer to the Admiral's position because we are approaching the jump from a slightly different angle."

"What's the difference in flight time?" Ka-Tu asked.

"One hour, 18 minutes, instead of 3 hours, 42 minutes."

"How long would it take Fleet to make this same trip." Eugene asked.

"Eighty, maybe ninety hours." Else replied.

"Shall we advise Michael of the new flight plan?" Ka-Tu asked.

"Let's do it," replied Eugene.

PRESENCE PROJECTOR, AMBASSADOR'S OFFICE

"Michael." Pam called over the intercom. "Urgent call from the Fleet Admiral in the Presence Projector room."

Michael had messaged the Admiral a few minutes ago, telling him that the flight test would commence shortly and should arrive about 20,000 miles from his position in a little over an hour. The Admiral must have figured out something was up.

Michael walked into the projector room to see a grumpy-looking Admiral. He reached out his hand to greet the Admiral but was cut off mid-stride. "Mi-Ku, what are you not telling me?"

"Jo-Na, good to see you, too. A..."

"You realize that I cannot do my job if you don't tell me what's going on."

Michael nodded, then said, "A human professor, enrolled in the Institute's Engineering School, was taking the introductory course in space propulsion drives. He attempted to re-derive the equations that govern the Trans-Dimensional and Discontinuous Drives but discovered what appeared to be better solutions to those equations than the ones we use. When he could not reconcile the differences, he checked out the engine simulation software from the 'Library' and attempted to simulate his solution. When it still appeared that his solutions were better, he went to see Professor MacLellan, the Ascendant who teaches the course, to see what he was getting wrong. The Professor determined that the student was not wrong. It turns out that despite humanity's primitive technology, they have excellent mathematicians."

"Are you telling me that the humans designed a spacecraft that can go 950 light-years in a little over an hour? I find this impossible to believe!"

"Jo-Na, this is why we expand the Confederation the way we do. Humanity would never have done this on their own. They would have gone extinct first. Similarly, this technology is old enough to us that no one is looking to reinvent it anymore, and apparently our mathematicians are not pushing their limits the way the humans have. But, to your question... No. A human discovered a limitation in our conception of our space drives, then developed a solution that could be bolted onto an existing Confederation drive."

"Where did you get a spaceship large enough to modify for this test?" The Admiral asked.

"It's my old shuttle, the one damaged in the confrontation with the Enemy agent in North Korea."

"What?" The Admiral said in a hushed whisper. "How is this possible?"

"You'll find out in half an hour whether or not it IS possible. But I'm betting that you'll be getting company shortly. The AI piloting the shuttle says she can feel the new engines and they feel smooth and 'right', unlike the originals."

"Word of this is going to get out. There is no way anyone will believe that a civilian shuttle exists in the Confederation that can wander this far from home on its own power, forget jumping here from 950 light-years away."

"That's why I think we need to do a joint briefing to the Central Council on this advance. With you confirming the test results, our chance of the credit for this discovery being given to Earth increases."

ABOARD THE MODIFIED SHUTTLE

"The gravity drive is amazing. You say we've been at 15 G for the last 10 minutes? I don't feel a thing, well, maybe just a little," Eugene said.

"Yes, we have. You don't feel it because I've cranked up the inertial dampening here in the cockpit. The equipment back in the cabin is feeling about 3 G. You wouldn't be so comfortable back there," Else replied.

"How far have we gone? The Earth still seems pretty big on the monitor."

"About 15,000 miles." Else said. "So, we're getting close to a point where we can engage the trans-dimensional drive. Earth's gravity is down to 6% here. At 1%, we can engage. That will be at 15 minutes, 35 seconds flight time. My guess is that your injectors will work so smoothly that we can do it earlier next time, but we stick with protocol until we have the data to revise it."

...

"Engaging the trans-dimensional drive in 5, 4, 3, 2, 1... Engaged." Else said. "Wow! That was smooth. What did the instrumentation say?"

"The transition fluctuations were barely measurable," Ka-Tu said. "Which is problematic. Eugene, did you work through any of the math for transition instability, or as humans prefer to say, vibration? The Confederation found numerous solutions with low instability. But we've always assumed there was no solution with zero instability."

"I think so." Eugene said. "The simulator forecast a stability of over 99% for all of the transitions. Was that the metric?"

"Yes. Sorry I didn't notice that before," Ka-Tu said.

"14 minutes to jump point," Else said. If you want to check your equipment, that's all the time you have unless we scrub the jump."

"Else," Ka-Tu asked. "Yesterday you said the machine felt right, or something to that effect. How did that transition feel to you? Please be as descriptive as you can."

"Professor MacLellan, that transition felt the way every AI flight controller expects a perfect transition to feel. To use a gymnastics analogy, it felt like we stuck the landing perfectly. No bouncing around. No off-balance foot shuffling, lucky you didn't fall over. By comparison, every other transition I've done in the last five years felt like we might go tumbling. I've queried dozens of other AIs. They all seem to think that every transition that sticks is a miracle, and there are more that don't stick than the Confederation reports."

"For the avoidance of any doubt... You think that transition was not an accident, but was instead the first one you've experienced where the system worked as intended, right?"

"Well said, Professor."

"Then I say that we continue. But, let's doublecheck calibration in the time remaining, so that we can prove the case unambiguously," Ka-Tu said.

"Agreed," Eugene and Else replied.

...

"Jumping in 5, 4, 3, 2, 1..." Else said. Then time seemed to stop.

Curious. Eugene thought. *No sound. No motion. Can't breathe. Can't move. Yet, I think, so I must still be.*

Things continued that way for an indeterminant period. Then reality came screaming back. Eugene was struck with vertigo so bad that he fell out of his seat. He could hear Professor MacLellan saying something in the distance but couldn't bring himself to open his eyes or move his head for fear of throwing up.

When his senses started coming back, he felt a hand on his shoulder and opened his eyes enough to see a glass of water being offered to him.

"What happened?" Eugene asked. "Was the ship damaged?"

"Here my friend. Have a drink of this. It's water with some medication added that will help fight the vertigo," MacLellan said.

Eugene lifted his head enough to get the cup to his mouth. He got a little sip in, then the spinning started again, and he lowered his head to the floor.

"Eugene, I'm so sorry. When we did the class trip, I gave everyone preventative medicine for the 4-light-year jump. I totally forgot to offer you medication for the 1,000-light-year jump," the Professor apologized.

"Can you take a little more of the water? It contains medication that should help. I'm sorry I didn't think about this. I've done long transitions like this many times and completely forgot how it affects the uninitiated." The Professor helped Eugene get a little more of the medicine in.

"The jump was a complete success by the way. We landed exactly where we expected to. We're now decelerating in trans-dimensional drive and will drop back to normal space in less than 10 minutes."

"In 4 minutes, actually," Else commented. "I've already advised Fleet of our exact arrival time."

The meds had started to kick in and Eugene could sit up enough to finish the medications the Professor had offered him.

"If that is what complete success feels like, I would hate to be on a jump that was not successful." He laughed. After shaking his head, a couple times, he pulled himself back up into his chair.

...

"Returning to normal space in 5, 4, 3, 2, 1... Arrived."

Sure enough, the Admiral's ship could be seen on the monitor. The intercom crackled to life. "Earth shuttle ship. Welcome to the Fleet Armada in this sector. The Admiral wishes to speak with you. Connecting now."

"Greetings, Earth Shuttle Craft." The Admiral said in his deep resonating voice. "With whom am I speaking?"

"Greetings to you, sir." Ka-Tu replied. "My human name is Jameson MacLellan, Department Head of Propulsions Systems at the Institute on Earth. With me are Dr. Eugene Xu, a human from one of Earth's most well-known academic institutions, and Else, the AI that operates this shuttle."

"Dr. Xu, do I understand correctly that you are the one that discovered the mathematical basis for this new drive technology?"

"Yes, sir. It was me," Eugene said.

"Is there any chance that you could help us retrofit our fleet with your new technology?"

"It would be a great privilege to participate in such a thing sir. But it would probably be a good idea to let us finish fine tuning the new system first. Although this prototype did well for a first test, I'm sure that there are still meaningful improvements to be made."

"Understood. How long do you plan to stay in this area? And, is there anything we can do for you while you're here?"

Eugene, feeling very uncertain about the protocol of the situation, looked to the Professor to answer this one.

"Admiral, we have some data analysis to do on the data we gathered on our trip here. We also have some reconfiguration to do for the return trip. So, we will plan to hold here for about 2 hours then return to Earth. We should have everything that we need, but we'll contact you if there is anything that we overlooked."

"Excellent," said the Admiral. "Please contact us before you depart. Our ship has Flight Control for this area of space. Good travels on your return trip."

...

An automated check of the data collected during the transition showed that everything was within expected limits. Ka-Tu and Eugene manually checked the biggest outliers, but they were still so close to prediction that there wasn't even suspicion of a problem. While they worked the data, Else updated the automated flight controls for the continuous jump technique they were trying. The plan was to do ten, 95-light-year jumps in rapid succession. For this short a distance, it would take a little longer than the single 950 light-year jump. But if their energy consumption measurements matched prediction, this technique could substantially reduce the size of spacecraft transiting between galaxies.

Else had just received clearance to depart when Ka-Tu approached Eugene with a large glass of medication. "Here, drink this. It will help with the vertigo. We will have to stop the test if you have another adverse reaction to the jumps. So, let's see if we can get ahead of it this time. Apologies again for not anticipating what happened on the way out."

"Thank you, Professor." Eugene guzzled the entire glass in one gulp.

"Our clearance to depart will expire in another 30-seconds." Else said. "Strap in so we can leave. It's gravity drive for 10 minutes, so you should be good."

Eugene and Ka-Tu buckled up and Else took off at maximum safe acceleration.

...

"Everyone ready for the next test?" Else saw two heads nodding yes. "Initiating jump sequence in 5, 4, 3, 2, 1... Jumping."

Once again Eugene felt everything freeze, then rush forward; then freeze again. The paired sequence repeated 10 times, each one a bit disorienting, but none of them bad.

They re-emerged into normal space uneventfully. Then Else said, "That's odd. We got here too soon. The chronometer says we got here before we left."

"Emergency jump!" Ka-Tu shouted.

As the official commanding officer on this mission, he could give override commands to the automated systems that would bypass the pilot or the AI controlling the ship. The emergency jump command moved the ship about 10 light-minutes along a safe, but random, vector.

Else, realizing that she'd just lost control of her ship, was furious.

"Else, zoom the scanners in on our last location! Record the images as they come through!" The Professor sounded panic-stricken.

"What's the matter, Professor?" Eugene asked.

"There is only one known time travel phenomenon. It occurs when there is trans-dimensional resonance. I think we may have triggered it. It's the only explanation I can think of for the chronometers to show an arrival time earlier than the departure time."

"And?" Eugene asked, prodding the Professor to give a more complete explanation for his actions.

"Echoes come through in the moments following the return to normal space," Else replied. "In the early days of trans-dimensional travel, the drives could be very noisy, creating echoes in their wake. More than one ship was lost when an echo landed on top of it. Good thinking, Professor. Apologies for reacting so strongly."

"Not a problem, Else. If I'm right, the first echoes have already come through. The light from those events will arrive in a few more minutes. Let's see what we created."

A few minutes later, the scanners showed another ship coming in right where they had been. It slowly faded but was not gone when the next ship came, causing an explosion that annihilated both ships. A succession of weaker echoes followed, finally fading to a level where they could no longer be seen.

"If we had remained anywhere near there, we would have been destroyed. I can't believe I forgot about this! If that happened deep enough in a gravity well, the planet or star would have been devastated! I can't believe that I almost let that happen," said Ka-Tu, poignant anguish evident in his voice.

"This phenomenon is known?" Eugene asked.

The Professor nodded in the affirmative.

"Then why didn't it happen when we arrived in the Admiral's system?"

"It was just a single jump." Ka-Tu replied. "Multiple jumps of the same distance along the same vector is what sets up the resonance. This was discovered eons ago and is part of the standard introductory course on space propulsion systems.

"If we had used a standard controller, it would have compensated for this phenomenon. I just forgot to include it in our custom controller. Thankfully, Else noticed the time problem; otherwise, we would have been destroyed.

"I can't believe I overlooked this. We need to do a complete review of the ancillary phenomena before we go out again."

AMBASSADOR'S RESIDENCE

"Joel, thanks for taking the time to talk with me." Michael said.

"Hi Michael. How can I help you?" Joel asked.

"I'd like you to come back to the Embassy Complex for a while to launch an engineering project that requires your skill."

"I doubt Rabbi Levine is going to be very happy to hear that."

"I spoke with him a little earlier. It's clear that he values your presence in Israel. But he also understands that the work I need you to do will benefit his people, so he asks that I return you as soon as possible."

"What do you need me to do, Michael?" Joel asked.

"You've probably heard about the launch of Space Force. We already have 25,000 volunteers signed on. They've begun training at the Embassy complex. The former world powers have pledged more than 70,000 more, although the timing of those troops is less clear.

"Soon we're going to need spaceships. The Fleet is going to help with that, but I think we'd be better served creating our own designs and developing the manufacturing capacity to produce our own ships," Michael said.

"That will be a huge undertaking." Joel replied. "But, why build our own ships?"

"Several reasons. Probably the most obvious is size difference. The average Lorexian is about twice as tall as a human and weighs more than twice as much. So, even if we start with a Lorexian design, it will need to be substantially modified."

"OK. But Fleet could modify the designs a lot faster than we can. They could also build them out a lot faster. What am I missing?"

"Our mission is going to be a lot different than the Fleet's mission. We're going to be hunting the Enemy, which means that we need agility and protection from close-in attack. The Fleet's Fast Attack ships and Military Escorts are powerful, but not very agile, and their close-in defenses are vulnerable to enemy close-in attack." Michael paused, weighing how much to say. "But there has been a new development that tips the scales a lot."

"What is this new development?"

"For now, you must hold this secret." Michael said.

"Understood." Joel replied.

"A human engineer, Eugene Xu from Johns Hopkins university, has invented a new propulsion system that is up to 100 times more efficient than the Confederation drives. It took its first test flight today. And the ship the engine was installed in... my old shuttle with its original powerplant and Else at the helm."

"Seriously?"

"Did you know Ka-Tu from the institute in New Lorexi?"

"Yes. He had some issues with his assignment here, right?"

"Yes, he ended up taking the Department Head position for Propulsion Systems at the Institute here. Ka-Tu is the one Eugene brought his invention to. He explains this as humans having better mathematics than we do. Hard to believe, but easier to believe than a 100 times efficiency improvement in an engine design that was last updated 100,000 years ago."

"Can't wait to hear the details about how this was done. But back to the original question. What do you want ME to do? I can't design spaceships or propulsion systems."

"I'm less sure of that than you are. But to your point, the spaceship and propulsion designs are being done by others. What I need you for is the manufacturing capacity. We cannot afford to be dependent on the Fleet. We'll obviously take as much of their help as we can get, but Earth is at greater risk if we count on the Fleet to build our defenses for us."

"OK. Do you have an idea of what you want?"

"I want as many military scale replicators as I can get, and I want them in space as well as on the ground."

"Michael, that is not a one- or two-month project."

"I know. But we need a plan to get us there as soon as possible."

"Do I deduce correctly that the threat is bigger and more imminent than I would think from the news stories?"

"Yes. It is. The most likely timeline for an invasion is 80 to 100 years from now, as reported by the news agencies. That's according to the facts we've been able to gather. But there is a small chance, based on those same facts, that it could be substantially sooner. My instincts are saying that we need to be ready in the next couple years."

"OK, I understand now. When do you want me to come?" Joel asked.

"Today." Michael said. "I'm going to ask Else to pick you up on their way back in. They should be about an hour out. I think it would be good for you to meet Ka-Tu and Dr. Xu. I imagine that they are very excited about today's events and will tell you all about them."

CONSUL GENERAL'S RESIDENCE, JERUSALEM

It had been several hours since Michael's call, and Joel was getting concerned that something had gone drastically wrong with the test flight. Finally, his communication device beeped to tell him Else was on the line.

"Hey, Else. Everything OK up there."

"Yep. A minor snag on the way in, but everything is A-OK. Do you have everything you need tagged for transport?"

"Yes, I do. Transport me up at your discretion."

SHUTTLE, 12,000 MILES ABOVE JERUSALEM

Joel appeared with five bags on the transporter landing pad. He looked up to see two men that he hadn't met before. Stepping off the pad, Joel extended his hand and said. "Hi. I'm Joel Rubinstein, Consul General to Israel."

"Joel, pleasure to meet you. My name is Jameson MacLellan, previously of the Lorexian Academy of Science, where you may have known me as Ka-Tu. I'm now Department Head for Propulsion systems at the Institute here on Earth." Then, indicating the man standing next to him, he added, "This is Eugene Xu, Professor of Spacecraft Propulsion at Johns Hopkins University in Baltimore. He's currently on sabbatical in my department at the Institute."

"Dr. Xu, do I understand correctly that you are the inventor of the new propulsion system being tested today."

"I wouldn't go quite that far." Eugene said. "I found a way to get a lot more out of the existing Confederation propulsion systems and designed the new part required to make it happen."

"Can you tell me what you discovered? I'm a trained engineer and was the chief Confederation engineer here on Earth prior to the Revelation. I'm currently being recalled to the Embassy to start up the manufacturing operations that will support Space Force."

"Sure." Eugene said, happy to have the chance. "As you probably know the entrance into, out of, and between trans-dimensional and discontinuous transition space is very chaotic. Makes sense, almost everything in nature is. But what that means for our engines is that their performance is very sensitive to how we transition between the dimensions.

"The equations governing these transitions have been known for millennia, and the Confederation scientists and mathematicians found solutions good enough to utilize these modes of transport. But the truth is the solutions they found were not very good.

"Amazingly, human mathematicians have better tools for solving equations of this type. I applied those tools to understand your solutions and was surprised how poor they were. So, I set out to discover if there were better entries and exits from both dimensions. I also wanted to see if I could find a solution to transit between them.

To my surprise, much better solutions were available. Assuming that I had made some sort of error, I used simulation to test my solutions. When those did not turn up a problem, I used simulation to test an alternative design. When that worked, I sought out the Professor to see if he could help me figure out where I went wrong."

"How long did that take you?' Joel asked.

"After a day of math, then a night of simulation, I had a solution that I thought you would have found a long time ago. When I went to see the Professor, he told me that he thought I was right and less than a week later we were doing a test flight."

"You did all this in a week?" Joel asked astonished by the implications. "Michael told me that your upgraded engines were 100 times more efficient. How far were you able to get this shuttle to go. All the way to Alpha Centauri?"

The professor got a good laugh out of that.

"Not quite that far?" Joel asked sheepishly.

Eugene spoke up. "The first jump was 950 light-years."

"WHAT? How is that possible?"

"Most of your energy was being lost entering either Warp or Jump space and you never found a way to move safely from Warp to Jump. Um... those are the shorthand names I've given to trans-dimensional and discontinuous transition space. I found a way to move into these dimensions more efficiently. I also found a way to move between them. That's where the big gain is, moving between them. If you are moving fast in warp space, then transition to jump space, you get much more distance for the same energy of transition," Eugene concluded.

Professor MacLellan spoke up. "As you just heard, Eugene not only found a better solution than the one we have used for hundreds of thousands of years, he has renamed many of our discoveries also." The Professor clearly approved of the renaming.

"Is there a short explanation of what the physical difference is between your solution and the Confederations?"

"Yes and no. The equations are vectors of differential equations..." Eugene stopped when he saw Joel holding up his hands.

"Do you have a non-math explanation?" Joel asked.

"I think so." Eugene said as he picked up his data pad, then flipped through until he found the right page.

146

"For the set of properties in question, the Confederation solution uses a constant. Here's a graphic of the Confederation solution. It is cylindrical, kind of like a pole." Then flipping a few more pages.

"Here's my solution. It looks more like a javelin with ripples.

"I don't have a graphic of the interface between normal space and extra-dimensional space but think of it as being like the skin of a watermelon.

"If you push the pole into the watermelon, you need to do it slowly and will probably need some twisting or wobbling to get it in. But you should be able to get it in. In the simulations, the twisting and wobbling corresponds to the transition stability measurements in the simulator.

"Now think about doing this at high speed. Force it in really fast and you will destroy the watermelon. That is why you can't go from warp to jump.

Joel nodded and said, "Got it."

"As I said... My solution uses something a lot more like a rippled javelin.

"Push that into the watermelon, it goes right in. Shove it in at high velocity, it goes right through, puncturing, but not destroying, the watermelon." Eugene paused, hoping for a sign that his explanation landed.

"Dude! That's ingenious!" Joel exclaimed.

"Just an example of the dimensional canceling technique a colleague and I developed for finding optimal solutions in N-dimensional differential equation systems." Eugene beamed.

"Can't imagine how many years it took to get that name to roll off the tongue so easily." Joel laughed. "But moving on from the theoretical exercise... What is the real property we are talking about? Surely, it's not the ship's diameter."

"First, it's two properties, not one. I'm not 100% sure which properties they are. I think they are magnetic field and electrostatic particle density. But Confederation notation is different than human notation, and knowledge of the property is not really required for a mathematical solution, as long as the equations are fully specified."

"Back to square one my friend. If you don't know what the properties were, how did you modify the machine?" Joel asked, once again incredulous.

"They are the two variables controlled by the plasma flow initiator, I just needed to modify that. Those were the graphics I showed you."

Joel's mouth dropped open. He closed his eyes for a minute and, when he opened them, said, "Oh. My God."

Eugene and Ka-Tu said... "What?" ...more or less in unison.

"I can't believe I never saw this!" Joel exclaimed

"Joel?" Ka-Tu nudged

Joel grabbed one of his bags off the transporter pad, reached in to grab a pen, but got a marker instead. Shaking his head, he started scribbling on the wall. "Got to get this out while it's still in there," Joel mumbled. He continued for a little longer, then collapsed into a chair.

Eugene and Ka-Tu were starting to wonder if Joel was experiencing some sort of psychotic break, when he shot up out of the seat and ran to the cockpit. "Else, I need to talk with Michael."

Else looked at Joel like he was a crazy man. "Joel, it's 1:00 AM at the Embassy."

Ignoring Else, Joel pressed the emergency communication button for Michael.

SHIELDS

[Monday, 09.02.2030] AMBASSADOR'S RESIDENCE

Michael had just fallen asleep when his internal alarm went off alerting him to an emergency request. He got up out of bed as quietly as possible and went across the hall to the office in his home.

He sent the connection request to his phone and picked up the phone. "This is Michael. What's the emergency?"

"I found it! Well, they found it!"

Looking at the caller ID for the first time, Michael asked, "Joel?"

"Michael, thank you for picking up. I think we've finally found it!"

The adrenalin rush starting to subside, Michael asked, "Found what? What did you find Joel?"

"A way to shield against the Enemy!"

"Where are you Joel?"

"On the shuttle with Else, and Drs. McLellan and Xu. Technically, I think they're the ones to discover it. We are on approach to the Embassy now."

"Else." Michael said. "How far out are you?"

"About five minutes. And, for what it's worth Michael, I warned Joel about the time, so please don't blame me."

"Else, can you land near the Ambassadors office? I can be there in five. Heck, you can just beam them into the conference room if that's more convenient. Surely with three engineers they can figure out how to turn on the lights."

CONFERENCE ROOM, AMBASSADOR'S OFFICE

Michael entered the conference room to the smell of his favorite Kona coffee. Spotting the pot, he started in that direction, saying… "I hope this is good, Joel." Then, taking his first sip. "You guys are just returning? What went wrong?"

After a moment of silence, Professor MacLellan spoke up. "Something that was almost catastrophic. I forgot to include a standard safety protocol, so the engines accepted commands that they should not have. The issue is well understood and part of standard propulsion control protocol. Nonetheless, something I forgot

149

to bind into the control software on the return leg. The problem is fixed. It took a couple hours, but it is done and will not recur."

"So, Joel. What's the middle of the night emergency?" Michael asked.

"Did the professors tell you which part of the propulsion system they changed and why?" Joel asked.

"I'm reasonably confident they did, but I'm even more confident that I can't bring that memory to top of mind at this hour. So, why don't you just tell me what I'm supposed to remember."

"Sorry, Michael. They got this big change in propulsion performance by modifying the plasma flow regulator in the field initiator to have a different resonance. A resonance that makes extra-dimensional transitions smoother and more energy efficient."

"Think I am remembering something like that."

"The plasma flow regulator in the propulsion system is identical to the one in the shield generators." Joel said as if the rest of the answer was trivial and obvious.

"I'm not sure how making dimensional transition easier will make our shielding better..." Michael said, brain finally engaging.

Joel thought to himself, *Wait for it. Wait for it. Michael will get there on his own.*

"Oh. My God." Michael said. Joel felt a swell of excitement, while Ka-Tu and Eugene wondered what they'd gotten themselves into.

"If you can make it 100 times smoother. Then presumably you can reverse the effect and make it 100 times rougher, making the shields 100 times harder to penetrate."

"Bingo!" Joel said, then channeling Sergeant Butler, added. "Not bad for the first day back on the job, is it?"

Michael said. "Ka-Tu, Eugene. Excellent work today. Please take the day tomorrow to work through Joel's idea with him. We will have an opportunity to test it in the next week or so. If these two workstreams pan out, then we may have just won the war."

CONFEDERATION SCHOOL OF ENGINEERING

"Professor Milne?"

Je-Fi turned to see who was calling him. He couldn't help but smile. One of his students was running after him, hand waving to get his attention.

The Professor paused to let his student, Kelly Williamson, catch up with him. "Good morning, Kelly. How are you this morning?" asked Je-Fi.

Kelly was his favorite student. She was one of the most intelligent people he'd ever met, a gifted engineer and a natural mechanic. But equally important, she had that rare gift of balance. Spaceship design was an art, because the size and weight of each component impacted every other component. The hull had to be sized to accommodate and support the engines. The life support systems had to be scaled to the habitable space of the ship, which in turn limited range. Every system interacted, which made spaceship design a real art.

Most students excelled at a particular component or system. Kelly was one of the very few that had a natural sense for the whole. Je-Fi thought she was destined for greatness, a thought he'd never had before about one of his students.

"I'm a little starstruck this morning," she said with a laugh. "I had to go up to the administrative offices this morning to deal with some paperwork. As I was walking out, I bumped into the Ambassador."

She started laughing again. "It was so awkward that I just wanted to melt into the ground. Then he says, 'Kelly Williamson, right? Australian, in the Engineering School Spaceship program?' I couldn't believe he knew who I was.

"So now it gets really embarrassing. He says, 'I hear Professor Milne thinks very highly of you. Which reminds me. Professors McLellan and Xu are going to be calling on Professor Milne today. They have made a major breakthrough that we need to have developed as soon as possible. The specifics are still confidential but tell the Professor that it would be OK with me if he included you in the project. Thank you for bumping into me.' Then he just went on his way."

Je-Fi's heart swelled with affection. When his daughters were young, they had reacted this way when good things happened to them. It had been a long time since he had been in the presence of someone so alive, and it felt good to be reminded of home while in this alien place.

DEPARTMENT HEAD'S OFFICE, SPACESHIP DESIGN DEPARTMENT

Professor Milne entered his office to a maelstrom of activity.

"Professor, I'm so glad you're here." His assistant Jill said. "The Ambassador's office called to say that he was sending some people over to meet with you today and that he'd like you to spend as much of the day with them as possible. He said this was an urgent and highly confidential matter of utmost importance, so he might pop over later in the day to check on your progress. I've cleared the conference room for you and set it up for eight. I'm hoping he's not sending over more people than that. Now I'm in a panic re-booking the other meetings that were scheduled. The Ambassador's secretary also told me she would be sending over some of his favorite coffee. He was apparently up late last night."

CONFERENCE ROOM, SPACESHIP DESIGN DEPARTMENT

Kelly and the Professor had settled into the conference room and were checking email when there was a light knock at the door. The door opened and Jill escorted three visitors into the room. Then said, "I'll be back with some water and additional supplies in a few minutes."

"Je-Fi good to see you," Professor MacLellan said to Professor Milne.

"Ka-Tu, always a pleasure. Do you know my student Kelly Williamson? She apparently bumped into the Ambassador this morning and he asked her to join us."

"Ms. Williamson." Ka-Tu said. "It's a pleasure to meet you." Then to both of them, "let me introduce my colleague Eugene Xu and the infamous Joel Rubinstein, Consul General to Israel."

Greetings were exchanged all around.

"OK if I give the background for our meeting today?" Joel asked.

There were no objections, so Joel plowed ahead. "You may be wondering why I'm here today. I've become well-known because of my role in the Middle East. But, before the Revelation, I was Michael's Chief Engineer on Earth. I designed and built the planetary shields that protect Earth. I also designed the regional shields that protect most of the countries on Earth. I've been temporarily recalled from the Middle East to take the lead on one of the largest engineering projects in Earth's history, so will be stationed at the Embassy for the next couple months.

"Michael wanted me back as soon as possible, so asked the two professors to pick me up on their way back from the first flight test of a new propulsion system that they've designed. More on that in a moment. As an engineer, I was curious to find out about the breakthrough these two could have made. Dr. Xu was gracious enough

152

to explain his discovery to me. And while he was explaining it, I realized that his breakthrough could be applied to shields. Shields that could be used against the Enemy."

There was a sudden intake of air as Je-Fi, also a shield designer, understood what that meant. "You've found a means to block inter-dimensional transitions!"

"We woke Michael up at 1:00 AM last night to tell him. There is a high-risk mission that will be happening soon, whose likelihood of success will be dramatically increased if such shielding existed. Our goal is to design, fabricate and install such a shield in the next five to seven days."

"Eugene. Would you walk through your discovery for the Professor and Ms. Williamson?"

...

"Professor Xu." Kelly said. "I recognize that mathematical formulation. Before transferring to the Institute, I used it on a project in Australia to optimize an electric motor design. Are magnetic fields governed by the same math as inter-dimensional transitions?"

"Good question," replied the Professor. "Yes and no. Yes, these equations both come from the same mathematical family, so my tools are equally applicable. No, the equations themselves are different and describe a larger set of physical phenomena. The irony," he added with a smile, "is that my tools are far more applicable to inter-dimensional transition than they are to magnetic fields.

"Back to our specific task. As applied to inter-dimensional transition, we found a solution for reducing the friction of transition, making it slipperier. For this to be applicable for shielding, we need to do the opposite. We need to make it more resistive, or stickier."

Joel interrupted at this point. "I have a question. In the watermelon example you used, when the speed is too high, the watermelon explodes. What does that look like in terms of inter-dimensional transition?"

"I can take that one," Professor Milne said. "One of two things. It could rupture space-time, or it could annihilate the object trying to transition. Rupturing space-time is bad, but not as bad as you might think. When space-time ruptures, it's hard to predict how far the rupture will spread. Everything the rupture touches disappears. We think it is destroyed, but we don't know that for sure. Once the rupture stops spreading, space-time flows back in and seals it up.

"That said, if we are using this as a shield on a spaceship and a collision with the shield shatters space-time, the spaceship will be lost."

Kelly spoke up. "Does that imply that we might have both a shield and a weapon? Could we project a very rigid shield into the path of the Enemy far from the ship such that the Enemy is destroyed when it hits the shield?"

"Clever idea. I think there are several ways that could be done," Joel said, thinking for the first time that her presence might be additive to their effort."

"Professor Xu." Kelly asked. "As I understand it, your solution technique is general, but your actual solution is for transit to, from and between Warp space and Jump space. Do we know which dimensions the Enemy uses?"

Once again, Joel was struck by the wisdom and practicality of this young woman.

He said. "I think there are four, but I am not sure their specifications. Do you know, Professors?"

Ka-Tu spoke up. "That information is a carefully guarded secret. Not sure why. I think I have the clearance to access it, but don't know off the top of my head. Do you Je-Fi?"

"No. I'm not aware of any shielding or weaponry designs effective against the Enemy."

The room was silent for a second and Kelly noticed a very faraway look in Joel's eyes.

Michael, we need to know the dimensions the Enemy travels through to make any additional progress. Joel sent. Joel, like all Ascendants, had implants in his mind that allowed him to access data from numerous systems by simply thinking the request. Included in that capability was the ability to 'text' someone just by thinking it. Sergeant Butler always called this 'alien telepathy.' Joel, having been part of Michael's inner circle for over 20 years, could message Michael at any time.

Will call the Admiral now. Pam will tie you in. Michael sent back.

As Joel's attention came back to the room, he noticed Kelly looking at him very intently.

"Caught me," he said to her, then to the group "The phone will ring momentarily, and we will be tied into a call with the Fleet Admiral." Joel couldn't help but smile at the shocked look on Kelly's face. She was apparently having a lot of firsts today.

The phone rang and Joel put it on speaker.

"Admiral, I have just connected the team we have working on this. Joel Rubinstein is leading this effort. I believe that you've met Joel before."

"Hello, Admiral." Joel said.

"Joel, so good to speak with you," the Admiral replied.

"Joel, could you introduce your team?" Michael asked.

"We have Professors MacLellan and Xu with us from the Institute's Propulsion department."

"They were the ones that visited you yesterday," Michael added.

"Dr. Xu. Can't tell you how impressed I am by your work. Have you made another invention already?"

"I'm definitely trying to help, but the insight behind this one is Joel's, sir."

"Also with us today are Professor Jeffrey Milne, who heads the Spacecraft Design department, and one of his students, Kelly Williamson. Ms. Williamson is the one who asked the question leading to this call. In case you were wondering, she is human."

"Professor Milne, Ms. Williamson. Thank you for joining this effort. We have too few effective weapons to use against the Enemy and no real defense. Your efforts are greatly appreciated. Now, what information do you need?"

Joel nodded to Kelly, implying that she should be the one to ask.

She took a deep swallow, then ploughed in. "Admiral, sir. We are working on shields that the Enemy cannot penetrate. The idea is that we create a new type of extradimensional bubble that is difficult for them to transit. It leverages Dr. Xu's work. His engines use a dimensional bubble that is very slippery and can enter, exit, or move between Warp and Jump space. Our idea, well Joel's idea, actually, is to make a dimensional bubble that is very sticky and resistive for transits between any of the dimensions the Enemy can exist in. We could use it to trap the Enemy in our space or in any of their natural spaces. Or to encase ourselves, our ships, or even our planets in a dimensional bubble that they cannot penetrate.

"The thing our team does not know is which dimensions the enemy can exist in. We know they can live in our space. We know they can live in our normal shield space. Does the Confederation have a list of the spaces that the Enemy can live in and the specifications of those spaces?"

155

"Yes, we have a list. But we don't know if it's complete. The list itself is highly classified, but I can release it to the Ambassador. The specifications for each of these are in the public domain, so the Professors should have no trouble getting all the technical details you need. May I ask how far you expect to get by the end of the week and how difficult it'll be to install your shielding."

"I'll take that one," Joel said. "Dr. Xu, is this a fine tuning of your Warp-Jump solution or is it a whole new derivation."

"It's new. But the question is how many derivations. One will definitely be required, but we may need to do it for all six transits to or from our space."

"And how long will a new derivation take?" Joel asked.

"I expect it would take one day, but a small chance that it could be much longer, maybe a week."

"Who else has been trained in this technique?" Joel asked.

"The professor at Hopkins that I co-developed this with. Although I suspect Ms. Williamson could also help," Eugene replied.

"And one other person from Australia," Kelly added.

"And what about the equipment design?" Joel asked.

"Best case, 1 day. The good news is that there are a lot of people that could pitch in on that. But I see one major risk. We only needed to modify one component of the propulsion system. Given what Joel has told me, it may be the same for shields. But there is some chance that we would need a multi-layer shield. That would take a lot longer and be much more difficult to install."

Michael cut in. "As I understand it, there are two main uncertainties we need to resolve. First, how many derivations will be required. Second, whether the shields will be single or multiple layer.

"The only way we're going to find the answers to those questions is to work the problem. Given the urgency and importance of this work I want to apply maximum resources.

"Dr. Xu, Ms. Williamson. Please contact your colleagues as soon as possible and tell them that we need them. Give us their contact information and we'll pick them up immediately. All their expenses will be covered. You can even tell them that I'll personally take them to dinner at Chef Marco's when this is done.

"Joel, I will send you the dimensional data as soon as I get it. I've also set up several codes for you to use that have top priority. Use them to override any barrier in your way. If nature has a solution to this problem, let's get it in the next three days.

"Admiral, if you can stay on the line?" Michael said, then the connection to the engineering team dropped.

PRESENCE PROJECTOR, AMBASSADOR'S OFFICE
"Mi-Ku. Is that the way humans work?"

"Ironically, it's one of their better modes of work. But it tires them, so is not their most common mode."

"And the woman... She sounded much younger."

"She's only 27."

"Twenty-seven!"

"The most gifted humans do their best work before they're thirty. She is extremely gifted. That's why she was there."

"Do you think this will work?"

"If it can be done, we will know in the next three days. The question is, if they tell us the solution is at hand, but cannot be delivered for another week, do we delay?"

"We cannot delay. There are over 1,000 Enemy ships that we have identified so far. The first ships will start arriving in about seven days. The planet is much larger than Earth and already has over 12 billion sentient beings. Sadly, they are still too primitive to even help in their own defense."

"What are the odds that you can stop the Enemy and save these people?" Michael asked.

"Vanishingly small. But we have to try, because we cannot allow the Enemy to consume this planet. They will become too powerful to stop."

"So, what's the strategy?" Michael asked.

"We will cull as many of the enemy as we can while they are still in space. Once they land, we will bomb their strong holds. Once the native species is gone, we will attempt to destroy the planet before a new larger horde of enemy emerges."

"Do what you must, my friend. At least now, Earth has the means to get new weapons and shielding to you, if we can finish them in time to help."

OVAL OFFICE, WHITE HOUSE
His scheduled guest had been escorted out on short notice, promised that they would resume in just a few minutes.

The President had been in office for only two weeks when the Revelation happened. In retrospect, he had handled it poorly, although he would never admit that to anyone. He'd been dragged kicking and screaming into the Confederation, but rode the peace and prosperity that followed to a landslide re-election. So, when Michael called, everything, absolutely everything, got dropped immediately, no questions, no exceptions.

"Michael, to what do I owe the pleasure of this call."

"I have an extremely confidential matter that I need to discuss with you," Michael said. That statement was code that put the President on notice that if any aspect of this conversation were to become public, other conversations that had taken place in that office would also become public.

"I understand." The President took a deep breath to calm himself.

"The Enemy is about to launch an attack..." Anxiety shot through the President so intensely that he thought he might be having a heart attack. "...on a planet about 1,200 light years from here." The President released a breath that until that moment he didn't even realize he was holding.

"The planet is much larger than Earth and, like Earth, it is resource rich. If the enemy succeeds in their attack, their odds of conquering Earth will dramatically increase." Once again, the President found himself struggling to breathe.

"There is a Professor at Johns Hopkins University that may have the key to stopping them. I believe that Hopkins is relatively close to you."

"Yes. Yes, it is," stammered the President.

"I'm sending a shuttle to transport him to the Embassy, but it appears that he's not convinced of either the urgency or consequence of this request. I'm hoping that you have the means to convince him of the importance of his presence at the Embassy. Our shuttle will arrive at Hopkins East Gate circle to collect him in about 45 minutes. Can you help me?"

CONFERENCE ROOM, SPACESHIP DESIGN DEPARTMENT
Eugene and Kelly had spent several minutes debating the best way to go about their assignment and ultimately decided to divide and conquer. Eugene would take the transition properties between normal space and shield space. Kelly would take the ones for the primary Enemy space. It had been a while since she had used this technique, so Eugene gave her the overview, then pointed her to a site that had the published text of the method.

Two hours had passed, and it was closing in on lunch time. Amazingly, Kelly thought she had found a solution. She knew there was a method to validate, but after several minutes of search couldn't find it.

"Dr. Xu? I think I have a solution, but need some help validating it."

Eugene looked up. He'd not had the same luck and frustration was written all over his face.

Kelly was stricken. *How stupid can I be?* She thought. *A wannabe interrupting someone who history will judge to be one of the greats.*

"Sorry, I'll figure it out," She said.

Eugene, realizing that he was projecting his frustration, said, "Sorry. I'm stuck, too, and am frustrated that I haven't been able to make more progress. How can I help? Maybe it's best if we work through this part together."

"OK. I've found a solution that maximizes the energy required to transit from the first dimension on the list to our dimension. My question is how to validate a solution once we've manually checked It several times."

"Simulation," he said. "Let me show you. I have the simulator set up on this system over here." Eugene showed Kelly how to launch the simulation program, enter the solution that she wanted to test, and set up the sequence of simulations that were required. Results started popping out almost immediately.

"This is exciting." Kelly said. "At energy levels below 10 joules, an object cannot enter our space time from the first of the ones on the Admiral's list." Moments later... "Or at 100 J." After another minute... "Or at 1,000."

"The simulations start slowing down at this point and will probably take an hour or two to finish. An alert will be sent when it's done, so let's shift gears."

"A question first?" Kelly asked.

"Shoot," Eugene said.

"Do we have another simulator we can use."

"I'm sure we could get one. What are you thinking?"

"The discussion about multi-layered shields. Do I understand correctly that if the solution for one of the source dimensions is different than the others, then we need multi-layered shields?" Kelly asked.

"Yes?" Eugene said questioningly.

"Then let's run this solution against the other dimensions. If it works, then we know we have a least one single-layer solution."

"Kelly. You're a genius." Eugene picked up his communicator to call Professor MacLellan.

After a short conversation, Eugene disconnected. "Professor MacLellan is working on getting us the extra simulators. Shall we move on to the next item on the list?"

JOEL'S OFFICE, EMBASSY MANUFACTURING COMPLEX

After less than five minutes of watching the mathematicians doing their thing, Joel decided that there was nothing for him to do until they'd come up with something he could work with. So, he set off for his new office to start organizing the work there. Before leaving, he asked Professor MacLellan to contact him as soon as there was something for him to do.

Quickly scanning his queue, he saw the message from Emmanuel that Michael had forwarded to him and marked urgent.

Professor Schudel wanted 20 of the 10-megawatt building power supplies, 10 field generators about the size of a regional shield, and 2 regional shields. He put in a call to the Professor to get a clearer understanding of the need.

...

"Joel, thank you for calling. What can I do for you?"

"I got requests today for components that I presume are for the mining platform you're building."

"That's good news," the Professor said lightheartedly.

"I see that you are requesting 20 of the 10 MW building power supplies. Can I asked how these will be used?"

"To power the platform," the Professor said, humor evident in his voice. "I'm guessing the question is, why 20 small ones, rather than one big one."

"Ah." Joel said. "I didn't realize a small training platform would need that much power. But yes. Why so many?"

"Two reasons," replied the Professor. "The first is isolation. The main material transport and filtering system are very spiky. So, I need the various systems to be isolated from each other. I don't want a current spike on the main drill to cause a droop on the grav-drives that hold our orbit."

"That sounds wise," Joel said. "But, twenty of them?"

"I also need redundancy. Because of the mass of metal we will be processing, loss of orbit would be catastrophic. So the grav-drives are laid out in an array that is quadruple-redundant. We could operate for some time with only three of the zones working. Maybe a day with only two zones working. And hopefully a couple hours with only one zone working. It really would not be safe having a mining platform in space above a populated planet without that level of redundancy."

"That also sounds wise, but I'm not getting the 20 part yet."

"Ah. Each of the impurity filters requires two field generators, and each of the field generators requires a separate power supply. We will be handling liquid iron, nickel, gold, platinum and what's left. Much safer when everything is double-contained, and the entire platform will be encased inside a two-layer shield that will protect us from space debris."

"OK. Understood. I think I can get you all of these in two weeks. I'll coordinate with Emmanuel."

"Joel, one question before you go?" Professor Schudel asked. "The main transporter... Do you know where that will come from? Do we have the ability to fabricate it? Or will it be acquired off planet?"

"Good question. Let me coordinate with Emmanuel on that one. He has the specs, right?"

"Yes, he does. Thank you, Joel."

...

To Joel's surprise, he got a call from Professor MacLellan an hour later. "Professor MacLellan, I'm surprised to hear from you so soon. What can I do to help?"

"Ms. Williamson is quite the genius. Her first trial solution is in simulation now, which is absolutely amazing, but not the genius part. She has proposed a new simulation protocol that might yield a single-layer shield solution in less than a day. The problem is that it requires at least five more simulators."

"Do we have five more simulators?" Joel asked.

"The institute has about 100, but they are all checked out and IT is unwilling to recall units for our use. Can you help us with that?"

Joel smiled at the question. "Yes. Yes, I can."

IT ADMINISTRATOR'S OFFICE, ASCENDANCY INSTITUTE

A quick check of the Administrator's calendar had shown that the Administrator was in today, and that his calendar was open. So, Joel walked over to the Administration building, a block from his office. He assumed this would probably go better if he showed up in person.

The Administrator's assistant had been polite but seemed less than hopeful about Joel getting time with the Administrator. Using his implant and project codes, Joel requested a meeting with the Administrator for five minutes later. The confirmation came and Joel asked the assistant to doublecheck the Administrator's calendar.

"I checked his calendar a few minutes ago and there was no appointment."

"It was made a few minutes ago by the Ambassador's office. Please check again, the matter in question is extremely urgent and of the utmost importance."

Begrudgingly, she checked the Administrator's calendar again. "Oh, my goodness. There it is. If you will please have a seat..."

Joel walked past her toward the door. "No need for you to get up, I can just let myself in."

Joel used his implants and override codes to see if the door was locked and did the same to unlock it. The secretary was shocked when the door opened.

Joel stepped into the office and saw a man whom he assumed was the administrator laying on the sofa, a bag of ice on his forehead.

"Administrator Desjardins?" Joel asked.

"Leave me alone. I don't feel good."

In the years since becoming Consul General of Israel, Joel learned how to use a medical scanner. Too many times during those first two years he'd walked into situations where someone was deathly ill, and he was helpless to do anything. Now he carried one everywhere he went.

Joel pulled out his scanner and did a quick diagnostic on the Administrator. Joel rolled his eyes.

"Drunk and hung over," he said out loud.

I'm turning into Michael. Joel thought as he pulled a small vial of nanobots from his pocket, rubbed them into the Administrator's wrist, then used his scanner to instruct them.

Several minutes later the Administrator seemed to rouse himself. He sat up, looked around for something, what, Joel could not figure out, then noticed Joel.

"Who are you?" he asked, with an attitude that suggested that Joel did not belong there.

"I am, or was, your 1:00 meeting," Joel said.

"Nonsense!" snapped the Administrator. "I cancelled all my meetings today."

"You might want to check your calendar."

"Leave. Leave now or I'm going to call security," growled the Administrator.

"As delightful as that might be, I'd advise against it. You are, or were, drunk on the job. The nanobots I administered logged that fact in the medical database. During your dereliction of duty, you have impeded one of the most important Confederation missions in this sector. Unless you can convince me not to press charges, you will be in detention this afternoon and on your way to reconditioning on the next transport out."

"I'm sure we can find a better accommodation than that." The Administrator suddenly looked worried. "What can I do for you?"

"I need five more simulators. Immediately. Here are the specs." Joel said, handing the man a data pad.

The Administrator sighed. "Not this again." He whined. "We only have 100 copies. They are all signed out. You will need to wait until they are returned."

"How do you know they are signed out?"

"The database shows them as signed out."

"Can you show me?"

The Administrator, obviously very frustrated, roused himself and went to his workstation. He clicked a few buttons. The list of simulators appeared on one of the wall monitors.

"See." He said. "One hundred units. All signed out."

"Reassign five of them," Joel demanded.

"I can't do that."

Having seen the database name, Joel quickly checked the credentialing system. "Yes, you can. According to the credentials management system, the Administrator can, and I quote, 'reallocate system resources during time of emergency' end of quote."

The Administrator seemed unimpressed with Joel's quotation of the rules.

"Sorry, friend," Joel said. "I don't have time for this."

Joel used his implants and security codes to reassign administrator privileges to himself, recall all units except the one assigned to Ka-Tu, then assigned all 99 now-available units to Dr. Eugene Xu.

The administrator could not believe what he was seeing. One-by-one the assignments changed. And with the last update, the screen changed color, implying that he no longer had administrator privileges over this resource.

"YOU! You can't do that!" he stammered.

"Why do they always say that AFTER you've already done it?" Joel muttered, shaking his head. As he turned toward the door, he added, "Enjoy your time in reconditioning."

Joel messaged Ka-Tu, letting him know that he now had 99 more simulators.

LIFE EXPECTANCY

[Tuesday, 09.03.2030] MEDICAL COMPLEX RESIDENCES

The alarm went off and Professor Jackson Reed struggled to drag himself out of bed. It had been a little over a week since the human surgical interface for Confederation scanners had gone into production and he was already restless. Something had been nagging at the edge of his mind and, although he couldn't figure out what it was, it had kept him awake most of the night.

He showered, dressed, and made himself some breakfast, then sat down in his kitchen to eat it. Not wanting to deal with thoughts of work, he flipped on the TV. "Breaking News!" The anchor proclaimed, as a picture of his favorite 1960s rock star popped up. "...dead at the age of 87..."

In a moment of grief, following a night of restlessness, Professor Jackson suddenly knew what he needed to do. He jumped up, ran out of his apartment, down the stairs and was halfway across the street when he realized that he didn't remember getting dressed, eating his breakfast or closing his apartment door. Looking down, he saw that he was dressed, and two thoughts shot through his mind. *Thank God! Wouldn't want the newspapers calling me the modern Archimedes, running down the street naked to spread the word of a new discovery.* Followed by... *Maybe it wouldn't be so bad to be remembered as the modern Archimedes.* On reaching the front door, he went directly to Professor Gupta's office.

AMBASSADOR'S OFFICE

Michael had planned to check in on the Shield team before retiring last night. But, the last 12 hours of his day yesterday had been one crisis after another, followed by six hours in a restoration chamber. He'd finally emerged and was surprised to see the number of messages related to the shielding project.

Joel had sent several requests that his message bot had replied to affirmatively. Michael was exceedingly pleased to hear that enough progress had been made that Joel needed to exercise his asset priorities. He was saddened to hear of the IT Administrator's incapacity; this had been a recurring problem and the poor man now faced rehabilitation. He got a chuckle out of Joel's acquisition of resources, was impressed by the subsequent technical advances, then distressed that he had missed a meeting request this morning.

CONFERENCE ROOM, SPACESHIP DESIGN DEPARTMENT

Joel received a message from Michael apologizing for missing the earlier meeting. He asked if they could reschedule to 10:30 AM. The apology made Joel smile. No one in their right mind would expect Michael to be available on short notice, but Michael still sent an apology anyway.

It was a few minutes before 10:30. Everyone had assembled, updates in hand. Joel was congratulating them on their progress, when a soft knock was heard on the door and Michael entered.

"I hear you may have some good news for me." He made his way to the open seat. After a round of greetings, he asked, "So, what do we have?"

"First, Michael, I'd like to introduce you to Dr. Martin Hill of Johns Hopkins University in Baltimore and to Dr. Harvey Jones of the Australian National University (ANU) in Canberra. Dr. Hill is a colleague of Dr. Xu at Hopkins and collaborator in the development of the mathematical techniques that have made this all possible. Dr. Jones was Ms. Williamson's advisor at ANU before she came to us. They were early adopters of these techniques and used them to develop improved electric motor technology." Joel said.

"Gentlemen. Thank you for participating in the effort. If there is anything you need during your stay, Joel has the authority to make it happen." Then turning back to Joel. "What's the good news?"

"We have found multiple good solutions for creating single-layer shields that prevent transit from the four known dimensions the Enemy exists in." Joel said.

"I sense a 'but' in that statement." Michael replied.

"Two 'buts' that we know about." Joel replied. "First, we haven't found a solution that stops transit from the transport dimensions. This is good for us in that we can still transport through these shields. It has the possible downside that the Enemy could be transported through also."

"Understood, but not a showstopper, right?" Michael asked.

166

"Agreed." Joel replied. "The second 'but' has a similar good news/bad news quality. The bad news is that we don't know all the dimensions the Enemy can transit. It could be that these four are all. It could be that there are quite a few more, ones that haven't been observed yet. The good news aspect is that we have enough simulators that we could test, and subsequently found, quite a few more dimensions that we can block. That has allowed us to develop several alternatives for you and the Admiral to choose from, and I have commissioned a team to start part design/fabrication for the one I think you're most likely to choose.

"In terms of using your time well, we can tell you more about the research, the properties of the shields, the tradeoffs between designs... What will help you the most Michael?" Joel asked.

"The Fleet will have contact with the Enemy in about 72 hours. What's the fastest path to getting something the Admiral can test?"

"I thought that would be your priority. Given the timeline, I've prioritized work on single layer shields that only require modification of one component of the standard shield design. We have two units in fabrication right now. One could be installed in the old shuttle, the other can be installed in one of our standard regional shield generators. We do not have access to the composition of the Admiral's armada or the specifications for any of his ships. If I did, we would have prioritized that. I am hoping to test our shield generators this afternoon, although we don't have a way to determine if they can actually impede the Enemy." Joel concluded. "Oh, one other thing. It would also be fast to modify the planetary shield, if that would be useful. I could start sending them the replicator pattern in the next couple hours if they have the need to protect an entire planet. The limiting factors will be the means to replicate something that size in time, and the power to drive it. Earth's shield takes about a terawatt."

"I think it's time we spoke with the Admiral," Michael said.

COMMUNICATIONS OFFICE, FLEET FLAG SHIP

The communication officer on duty was less than happy. The person on the comm line, an ambassador, asked to speak with the Admiral on an urgent matter. The Admiral had put on his do not disturb light two hours ago and his pattern these days was to keep it on for another four and a half hours.

"I'm sorry, but the Admiral is not available. May I take a message?"

"I believe that the Admiral left instructions to be disturbed if I called." Michael said kindly. "Could you please check?"

These diplomatic types are all the same. Whatever trivial squabble, they had to speak with the Admiral. He thought, but protocol required that he check the list, which pissed him off because no one was ever on the list. He was supposed to check when he came on duty, but never did. If someone had been put on before his shift, they would have told him. And the only person that had the power to put someone on the list was the Admiral, who had not put anyone on the list before his light went on. *Well I suppose High Command, or the Central Council could.* He thought. *As If.*

Nonetheless, training kicked in an he checked. It was an arrestable offence not to check if requested, and even though he'd never received a valid request in his entire 400-year career, he was new to this ship and regulations required it. Nonetheless, he was going to harangue this bozo when the empty list came up.

But the list wasn't empty. *Oh no, I'm not giving respect to a Central Council request. I'm going to be sent back to sewage maintenance for the next twenty years,* he thought.

"Um, excuse me Mr. Ambassador. I will wake the Admiral now. Please give me a moment."

"Thank you." Michael said, but couldn't keep himself from smiling. A long, long time ago, he had served as a reserve adjunct on a capital ship. During his time in that role, he made a point of befriending as many ship officers as possible. Their lives were much different than his and he'd always believed that getting to know people of every course of life was a good thing. Not just for his career, but as a person. The more points of view he could understand, the more people he could help. Several of the people he befriended had served in the communications office.

ADMIRAL'S CHAMBERS, FLEET FLAG SHIP

It was a beautiful day, and he loved this place. His parents had brought him here when he was just a cub. Ma-Ra, his sweet and beautiful wife, had just gathered up the cubs and they were about to head back to the hotel.

They were near the peak on the northern slopes, the great ice ocean stretching out below, seemingly forever. A squeal caught his attention and he saw Ma-Ra scolding his son Mi-Ku, named after his best friend, for nipping his sister, La-Ra. Could life get any better?

They were heading back a little early. The cubs had griped a bit. But they'd played hard enough today that they'd be asleep by the time they'd finished dinner. That was the plan anyway. He and Ma-Ra were both in season. So, he'd booked a suite with the master's den on one side of the living room and the cubs' den on the other. He couldn't wait to get back...

There was a loud noise, an obnoxious horrific noise. The scene faded. He was back on his ship. His sweet wife and cubs had died of old age millennia ago. He let out a loud roar, undoubtedly heard by the people waiting for him in the hallway. Oh, to just plunge into a star.

He aroused himself, put on his uniform, and exited his quarters. *Mi-Ku must have come up with something,* he thought.

"I'm sorry, Admiral. The Earth team does not have access to projection at the moment. You could take this in your quarters, or your office, but it will be audio only."

"Have a pot of vaka sent to my office at once. Tell Mi-Ku that I'll be there in 10 minutes, and it better be good."

...

The vaka was lukewarm, and the Admiral was furious, how hard was it to replicate hot vaka in a thermos. Then it struck him... transluminide shortage. He'd authorized the standing order himself, no exceptions.

He sat down and took the call off hold. "Mi-Ku, this better be good."

"Jo-Na, my friend. Sorry to wake you. I hope you have a hot pot of vaka, because we have good, but complicated news."

It was all the admiral could do not to lash out. He just wanted to retreat back to the dream; return to the master's den with his precious Ma-Ra and their cubs. The gift of long life could be such a curse.

"Vaka, yes. Hot, no. Fleet life in the age of transluminide shortage has turned into something of a curse."

"Jo-Na, my friend. I'm sorry to wake you. We have good news to share. Our research and development team is on the line. Would you like to be briefed?"

After several moment's pause... "Thank you for waking me and apologies to your team for the surly greeting."

"No problem, my friend. Apologies again for having woken you during this time of anxiety," Michael said.

"So, here we are. What do you have for me?"

Michael nodded to Joel.

"Sorry to have disturbed you sir. Joel Rubinstein here. We have the technological breakthrough we were seeking, but don't know the best way to package it for you."

"Please explain," said the Admiral.

"We think we can block all transit from the four dimensions you sent us. The optimal solution for those four also blocks fourteen others, 18 in total. It doesn't block the transport dimension, which is good for us because we can send supplies or other equipment in through the shield. But bad for us, because the Enemy could be transported in."

That comment got a "humph" from the Admiral.

"We could not access specifications for your fleet composition or your shield generators, so we have outfitted our shuttle and a regional shield generator with our modifications. I also have plans for a planetary shield that would block Enemy transition. None of these have been field-tested yet, as we have no Enemy to test them on.

"So, we ask you how you would like us to proceed. We can send you the specs for any of our devices. But fair warning, a planetary shield for an earth-sized planet takes 1 terawatt of energy while in operation. If you send us specs for your shield generators, we could provide the replicator patterns you would need to upgrade."

Another long pause...

"How much of this is Earth designed?"

"Functionally all of it. The five humans sitting here with me have better mathematical minds than anyone I have heard of in the Confederation. They created the solutions we needed. A team of Confederation Ascendants designed the parts, but that is only because our partners had a higher-value use."

"Sending you the specs for two of our ships now. Please send your replicator specifications for your planetary and regional shields, then for our two ships when ready.

"Have you outfitted your shuttle yet?"

"Still 4 or 5 hours from that," Joel replied.

"Mi-Ku," said the Admiral. "Once your shuttle has been upgraded, send it to me with as much of your team as you see fit. The engagement will commence in about 60 hours. The more of your brain trust we have here, the more likely a successful outcome."

"We will do as you ask," Michael said. Then the line dropped.

SPACE FORCE AUDITORIUM #3

Professor Jensen and the TAs met in the auditorium's prep room a half hour before class. "This is the first session of lesson two. The plan was to cover vulnerabilities. In the other sessions we changed to cover less of the threat videos and to start talking about lesson three: weapons. So, I'm not sure what to do with this section." Prof. Jensen said.

Noelani was quick to respond. "I think you should go with the original plan for this section. They have already paid the price, so give the next part to them straight up. If it is too much, we will find out. There is no intrinsic rule that says all sections should get the same material in the same order."

"But that would never fly in the Confederation," Valerie said.

Noelani replied. "It might not fly in the Lorexian institutes, but I'm betting it'll fly here and teach us something that the Lorexian institutes can learn from."

Valerie was shocked by those comments. In the 'Confederation' she knew, no one would say that. It would be their professional end if they did. But here, it was like a free for all. Then, in a flash of insight... *That's why Michael loves this place. That's why I am accepted here,* she thought. *We, on Earth, are not bound by tradition, at least not in the same way. That's why we will become the center of the Confederation in my lifetime.*

"Agreed," she said. "How badly do you think the class will respond to holographs of the Enemy being blown up?"

"I think they will be cheering." George said.

...

They entered the auditorium to a mixed buzz from the overfilled room. Noelani walked out on the stage, and a series of cat calls and whistles rained down on her. She put on her best smile. "Thank you for that welcome. But please remember. I have two superheroes on my team, plus the Enemy killer. So, a little more discretion might be in order next week."

Her comments elicited a roar of approval.

"Have you wondered about our Enemies weaknesses? Do they even have any? Watch this."

The lights dimmed and the image of an angry Asian woman was shown on the stage. She was in a dark room lit mostly by a computer screen. She was speaking in a foreign language, a rough translation streaming across the top of the stage in 3D. Her loosely translated language was shocking, but the theme was that the humans needed to be consumed as quickly as possible so that their presence on this planet would no longer present the offensive stench that it did.

Everyone in the room knew immediately that this had happened on Earth. The woman's clothing was a clue as to where.

Suddenly, there was a blinding flash of light that completely whited out the projection. Slowly contrast returned, but the woman was no longer there. A fragment of her skirt remained on the chair. Shoes were still at the foot of the chair. And every surface of the room had become coated in some sort of goo. The holographic video went dark and the room lights came up.

"What just happened in that scene?" Noelani asked.

There were no replies. "Jeffery Watson. Where are you? Please stand." A man in the third row of the balcony stood. "What do you think happened in that scene?"

George, who had been stationed in the balcony with a microphone came running over and gave it to the man. "It looked like an explosion ma'am."

"Thank you, Mr. Watson. Someone else, tell me what you think happened."

A woman several seats over from Mr. Watson stood and George hustled the microphone over to her. "Kaitlin O'Brien" The woman said. "I noticed a lot of goo all over the walls. But also puddled in the shoes. I am guessing that is what is left of the Enemy and possibly the human it was occupying."

"Excellent observation, Ms. O'Brien. One more."

A man in the front half of the main level near the right aisle stood. Luka had that side of the main level and rushed a microphone to him. "Ichiro Tanaka, ma'am." He said, bowing slightly. "The very bright flash of light... As the screen started to saturate, I noticed that it also seemed to ripple. Knowing that these creatures are multi-dimensional, I speculate that the explosions occurred in multiple dimensions. If that is true, I would like to know more about how that is done."

"Excellent observation, Tanaka-san. Thank you."

Now speaking to the whole class. "Let's watch this again. You have been clued in on some things to look for. There are others. So, this time we will slow down playback a little so you can see more clearly."

Noelani stepped away from the podium as the light dimmed and the holographic video started to play.

Professor Jensen walked up beside Noelani and whispered, "You are really good in front of a class."

Noelani smiled and nodded her thanks. Then mouthed the words, *you next.*

When the lights came back up, Professor Jensen said. "Let's walk through this step-by-step, and I'll explain what you're seeing.

...

Professor Jensen walked back to the podium as the lights came back up and to her surprise, three people were standing with their hand up. Mark Patterson had taken a microphone over to a person close to him and looked to the professor for approval to give the man the microphone. The professor was momentarily confused about what was going on. Then she noticed a message flashing urgently on her inner vision. It was from Noelani. *He wants to ask a question. Say that you will take these three, then hold questions until a little later in the session. Then ask his name and ask what the question is.*

Valerie did as she was told, then walked through the theory of the device. As she was about to start discussing the device itself, multiple people stood with hands raised.

Do the same. Take three now and hold the rest until later. Noelani sent.

After the next section of the lesson. The same thing happened. After those three questions, the Professor said. "We are a little over our allotted time, so let's end here. I will stay after class for a few minutes if you have additional questions."

About twenty people came forward.

PROFESSOR GUPTA'S OFFICE, MEDICAL SCHOOL

"...very similar to the scanner, but quite a few more options and graphics." Professor Reed summarized. "Do I understand correctly that the formatting of the user interface is the same as the scanner?"

"Mostly the same, but different. Your code will need to be modified."

They were talking about restoration chambers. Reed's epiphany this morning was that if he could adapt his current code to the restoration chambers, life expectancy and general health would vastly increase. During the Revelation, word had spread about their ability to cure and de-age. If Restoration Chambers could be operated by human doctors, they could push de-aging treatments to the whole world. If he could adapt even a small subset of the cancer therapies, they could eliminate the vast majority of chemotherapy treatments.

"Professor, can I ask you a question about Confederation norms as regards medical technology?"

Professor Gupta couldn't help but laugh. "It would be more productive to just ask your question. I'll tell you if the answer is forbidden."

"Sorry, that was stupid of me." Professor Reed said good-naturedly. "Something has been bothering me for some time, but now I think I know what it is. In several of Michael's speeches during the Revelation, he said that they would train our doctors, but it would be some time before they would be able to use the equipment. In the interim, the Confederation would provide limited direct assistance until enough doctors were trained.

"But what I think he meant was that the Confederation would provide limited support until humans figured out how to adapt the equipment, and if they never did then human Ascendants could provide the support."

"Obviously, Michael would never say what you just did. But your intuition is right. Official Confederation policy is to aid allied species in adapting Confederation technology for their own use. But, the fact of the matter is that few allied species ever adapt our technologies. So, the diplomatic staff have taken to giving assurances that we'll give some support until the ally has trained enough of their people to use our equipment.

"So, step back for a moment. Michael never said you couldn't adapt our technology. My presence here says exactly the opposite. But the fact remains that few species have ever adapted anything, despite all the efforts of people like me.

"But look at what's happened here. You adapted a scanner in less than five years. Then added nanobot control and are now contemplating adaptation of our Restoration Chambers. The fastest previous adaptation of a scanner took about 100 years. And rumor has it that humans have made huge breakthroughs in both spacecraft propulsion systems and shielding technology.

"So back to your question, the Confederation actively seeks ally adaptation of our technology. That is the purpose of people with assignments like mine. We work with your top scientists and engineers hoping to drive adaptation, but the diplomats don't push it because, so few allies are interested."

"Wow." Professor Reed said. "So, you can give me the user interface map for the restoration chambers, and the data exchange protocols for your equipment."

"That's what I've been doing."

"Then, let's build a human-operable restoration chamber!"

"Been waiting centuries for someone to ask me to do that."

...

Later, as he thought about what the professor had said, he thought. *I need to spread the word. It's all available. We just need to ask.*

While he still had the courage, he shot off a message to Sarah Wright, Embassy press secretary and consort to the Ambassador. "Dear Ms. Wright. I think word needs to get out about some of the things going on here at the Institute. Any chance we could meet to discuss? Best regards, Professor Jackson Reed."

DEPLOYMENT

Sarah awoke to the sounds of breakfast-making in the kitchen. She recalled Michael coming to bed sometime in the middle of the night and his warmth next to her.

As she got up, she noticed a message from Professor Reed on her communicator. She grabbed a robe and went to the kitchen, where she found Michael being uncharacteristically domestic and very industrious. She gave him a big hug, then asked. "What're you making?" She was quite impressed by the number of dirty dishes and pieces of equipment.

"Well." He said. "I started by replicating some croissants and raspberry jam. Then, I got notice that my early meetings had been cancelled and thought to myself... Why not attempt to make Sarah that breakfast I had in Paris last week. So, I called the chef and negotiated a dumbed down version that 'even an alien could make'. He actually said that, by the way."

"So, what are we having," she asked.

Michael beamed like a child. "Petite parmesan souffles with shaved bacon and asparagus, with a poached egg over the top and a brie-based sauce. I cheated and replicated the brie sauce."

Sarah walked over to the oven and saw what looked like four little souffles raising out of their ramekins. Then noticed the boiling water on the stove and fresh eggs on the counter.

"I put the souffles in when I heard you walking toward the room. Timer says 3 more minutes, then 3 minutes for the eggs. Can I get you some coffee, my sweet?"

He brought her some coffee and a warmed croissant, then started the eggs. As she watched him work, affection welled up within.

"Voila!" Michael said putting a plate down in front of her, "Bon Appetit."

She took a bite. "Good. Very Good. Did you really make this?"

"I poached the eggs and baked the souffles." Michael said.

"Let me guess... The chef sent you the replicator pattern for the souffle mix."

176

"And the croissants," Michael said, as they both laughed.

"I love you." Sarah said.

"Love you too." Michael replied.

After a moment of silence, Sarah asked, "What meeting got cancelled?"

"The one with Joel and his team."

"They didn't make any progress?"

In that moment, Michael realized that he had not spoken to Sarah in more than two days. "Wow. We have a lot to catch up on."

"What's happened?" Sarah asked.

Michael told Sarah about the propulsion drive and shielding advances, and about the team of volunteers Joel was leading. He also told her about their plan to participate in the upcoming encounter with the Enemy.

"I think I agree with the Admiral, it's hard to believe that humans could advance Confederation technology. It's so far beyond us."

"The physics and materials science, yes. It will take humans a long time to absorb these to a degree where they can advance them. But as we found out this week, humanity has already passed the Confederation in some fields of mathematics. And, engineering advances are as much about innovation as the underlying science. So, in some sense, this is just the start. We don't know what other areas humanity may have already exceeded the Confederation."

"That reminds me." Sarah said. "I got a message from Professor Reed this morning, that reads, quote 'I think word needs to get out about some of the things going on here at the Institute. Any chance we could meet to discuss?' unquote. Do you think that's about the mission with the Admiral?"

"Could be, but I think it's more likely about the medical advances he's pushing forward."

"Really? Are you OK if I meet with him?" she asked.

"Of course. But only if you think it's the right thing to do."

SHUTTLE

They were underway. Joel and the two Ascendant professors, MacLellan and Milne, and the four humans, Eugene Xu, Kelly Williamson, Martin Hill and Harvey Jones.

The shuttle had been upgraded with the new enhanced shielding. Joel brought two regional shields. One was installed in the ship's systems in a way that allowed the ship to project a shield. The other was standalone. At the last minute, Kelly had also made a replicator run with another device, but Joel hadn't had time to find out what it was.

Once word of the mission was out, a number of techs had volunteered to help build out the shuttle for an extended mission. It had four small rooms with two bunks each, a small kitchen area with a pair of replicators, a commode, and a separate sonic shower. Everyone hoped this mission would be short, but no one expected it to be less than two or three days.

An hour and ten minutes into the flight, Else announced that they had arrived in the target area, now 965 light-years from Earth and were closing in on the armada.

"Bad news, Joel." Else said. It appears from the scans that the Admiral has already started to engage the Enemy, which has apparently launched an assault."

The communications system crackled to life. "Human shuttle. Human shuttle. Please evacuate the area. We are under attack."

On the scanner, a ship marked as a Confederation Fast Attack ship exploded violently.

The tech team was stricken; they were too late.

"Joel." Kelly asked. "What's the range on the regional shield you integrated.

"Not far." Joel replied. "It's designed for close in, less than 250 miles. Why?"

"I was hoping we could use it as a fly swatter. If nothing else, it would prove that the shielding worked."

The comm system went off again, asking them to evacuate the area immediately."

"We can't leave them to face this alone," Eugene said. "Any way we could use our speed to jump in, whack one of these guys, then run before they knew what happened to them?"

Else interjected herself. "The Enemy isn't moving very fast. The issue seems to be that the Armada landed in the middle of them and became infected."

The thought sent a chill down Joel's spine. If the Enemy succeeded in commandeering a Fleet ship, it would have the coordinates of Earth and the means to get there within a week.

"We can't run," Joel said. "If the Enemy captures even one of those ships, they will be on Earth within a week."

"Else, do we have a count on the number of Enemy ships?"

"Not exact, but over 150 for sure."

"Is there an isolated one you can jump within 100 miles of us?"

"Several," she said.

"OK. Shields up. Activate the projected shield. I'm going to dial up a 5-mile radius shield and extend it 100 miles off the port side. Else, I want you to jump in so that the shield will hit the Enemy ship once we return to normal space."

"Will try. But we are too far out to land within 5 miles of a target. Everyone, brace yourselves. Jumping in 5, 4, 3, 2, 1..."

...

The Enemy leader of the ship they'd targeted was startled by the sudden appearance of a Confederation ship so close. It was very small. He couldn't help but smile. Their tactic with this engagement was to lure Confederation ships in close, within 100 miles or so.

He knew that the Confederation would target his ship, but that their scanners would not detect the 100 or so of his soldiers spread out in the void. The Confederation always seemed to forget that they could operate in the void, and always seemed to come within about 100 miles to transport their bombs, even though they could do it from thousands of miles away. So today he'd laid a trap. His ship sat there not moving and waited for the Confederation to come to it. When a ship approached, the nearest soldiers in the void would propel over and latch onto the ship. Once latched on, it would take a while to penetrate their hull, but they would eventually penetrate all but the thickest hulls.

Once inside, it would be a feast. Capture even one of the larger ships and they would have transit to the target world. *These fools have no idea what they've stepped into*, he mused.

...

Else felt a slight vibration on the hull, then a second. They had landed close to the ship they were targeting, and she was optimistic that she could hit the bullseye.

A moment later, a huge vibration rippled through the ship and the regional shield generator shut down. Where the ship had been, there was a cloud of debris than included a massive amount of yellowish goo.

What looked like a crack started to open where the ship was. It grew at an alarming rate, sucking up all the debris and yellow goo. Then dozens of writhing black forms went sailing into the ever-widening crack. One of the smaller Confederation ships that had been

179

dead in the water started accelerating toward the crack. Else noted that her own course was deflecting in that direction, but it appeared they had enough momentum to escape.

Then the crack snapped shut, taking a chunk of the Fast Attack ship with it, and sending the remnants of the ship on a collision course with the shuttle. Else changed her vector, so they would pass under the stricken Fast Attack ship and rotated their hull so the cockpit would continue to face it.

That's when she realized that the black slithering mess on the Fast Attack ship's hull was a swarm of enemy soldiers in their dust form. One by one, then in droves, they jumped off the Fast Attack ship on an intercept course with the shuttle. Because she had rotated her craft to be in a position to inspect the remains of the Fast Attack ship, she was out of position to fire the engines and escape.

She watched in dread as the Enemy approached then hit the shuttle, a tiny vibration as each one hit... and then slid off. The shields were working! The Enemy could not penetrate or even get a grip on her ship.

She became aware of the whooping and hollering going on in the passenger cabin and focused her attention. The scientists had made complete and detailed recordings of the regional shield's impact on the Enemy vessel, and the subsequent rupture in the space-time continuum.

Else interrupted them. "Hey team. You missed a real spectacle up here."

"No. We recorded it all. Amazing wasn't it?"

"You recorded the 100 or so enemy combatants that jumped onto our ship as we passed the remnants of the Fast Attack ship?"

Silence.

"Well, thankfully your shields work. None of them could penetrate, or even get a grip. They are now strung out in a line behind us. What should we do with them?" Else asked.

"Let's round them up!" Kelly said.

...

After some discussion, Kelly finally revealed what her last-minute addition was. She had made a remotely piloted field projector. It could project a spherical or ellipsoidal bubble that could be open or completely closed. She thought it might be useful during a recovery, or to protect someone that was about to be attacked. It had multiple settings, including suspensor fields, and the new thing she was most anxious to try, a sticky field that the enemy couldn't penetrate, but that they would stick to if they made the attempt.

After a lot of discussion, they decided to turn the ship 90 degrees from its current course, then do a short adjustment burst that would move them about a thousand yards out. That would put them on a parallel course with the Enemy. They would then deploy the remote shield in the Enemy's path and slow down so that the Enemy flew directly into the open end of the shield, functionally being scooped up in a net. When the enemy hit the shield, they would presumably attempt to penetrate it, then they would know whether it was actually sticky, as the math predicted, or not.

Once they had caught a bunch of Enemy combatants, they would head back toward the Armada, which had gone strangely silent.

AMBASSADOR'S PRESENCE PROJECTOR

"Mi-Ku. Thank you for taking my call. I'm afraid I have some very bad news. We fell into an Enemy trap. They captured several of our ships, which we subsequently had to destroy to prevent the Enemy from gaining control. With even one of our ships, they could get to Earth in a week with enough combatants on board to capture the planet. We lost one Cruiser and four Fast Attack ships with all hands."

A pause and Michael said. "They got my shuttle, didn't they?"

"Your shuttle arrived at the edge of the trap. Far enough from the nearest combatant that they had time to escape. We called and ordered them to evacuate the area. In fact, we called them twice.

"I was in the thick of it, on the verge of losing my ship and the Armada. There was nothing more I could do for them.

"Then, they jumped. They jumped right into the middle of the fight. Something about that movement attracted the Enemy's attention, which created the window for us to escape. As we drew back, there was a tremendous explosion near your shuttle. What happened next is hard to describe. The physicists on our capital ships conjecture that it was a rip in the space-time continuum. One of my ships was sucked in. Hundreds of Enemy were sucked in. When things settled out and our sensors worked again, there was no sign of your ship. Everything was gone, except a string of about 100 enemy combatants floating in a straight line like so much jetsam. But even those disappeared, one by one."

"Have you attempted to contact them? They may be cloaked."

"Yes, we have attempted to contact them, but no answer."

"I have a different way to contact them. Let me give it a try before you leave the area," Michael said, clinging to hope.

···

"Else." Michael sent on internal. "Are you there?"

"Here Michael. Whipping the Enemy."

"The Admiral is trying to reach you. Can you see him?"

"Not at the moment. Did he pull back? I don't read him at all."

"Any chance you were pulled through the space-time rift?"

"No, we were pretty far from it. By the way, the shields work. We were attacked by about 100 enemy combatants. They slid right off of us, trailing behind us like a string. We used this sticky net thing that Kelly came up with to collect them all."

"Wait, you collected a hundred Enemy combatants floating in a straight line through space?" Michael sent.

"Yes. What about it?"

"Hold for a second."

···

"Jo-Na. Still there?"

"Yes, Mi-Ku, what have you found?"

"It appears that their Enemy-repelling shields worked. The string of Enemy combatants that you saw disappearing one by one... They attacked the shuttle, could not penetrate or even get a grip, and slipped off in a more or less straight line. The shuttle then reversed course and caught them in a 'sticky net' that the hundred or so enemy are now stuck in.

"Are you suggesting that their Enemy shielding also shields them from our communications?"

"Yes. But not from my quantum entangled ones."

A pause.

"So, their shields work, but block non-quantum entangled communications?"

"Apparently. So, what should we do?"

"You're asking me? The Enemy almost took down my armada today. Your primitives saved us, destroyed the preponderance of the Enemy force and took enough prisoner to kill any planet or people that we have ever met!"

"Take a breath, my friend. Apparently, my 'primitives' have better math than we do. Lots of the primitives we have brought into the fold have things they do better. That's why we bring them in.

"Just so happens that these have something we really need. It's not like they can stand without us. Similarly, we won't stand much longer without them. So, stop treating them like primitives. In this fight, the humans on that ship are worth more than all the scholars in the Confederation. At this point, they don't need rescue. They need someone more mature to help them sort out what to do next. So, go help them. They're where the Enemy was floating in a straight line and disappeared. They've captured a lot of them. Help them figure out what to do. And, so that you're not caught by surprise, they're going to want to study them, so they can figure out how to defeat them."

"Mi-Ku. You know I can't do that. Standing orders are to deposit the lot of them into the nearest star."

Michal cut off the next statement. "Who gave those standing orders?"

A long pause. "I did."

"The standing order doesn't apply in this case. It defines your crew's actions when you're not present. It does NOT define YOUR actions! Help them figure out what makes the enemy tick."

The Admiral swallowed. His friend was right. Standing orders were for his crew when he was not present. But he was present, and the humans had apparently saved his armada. Confederation law probably bound him to help the humans, but that didn't really matter. It was the right thing to do.

"As you say, my friend. I'm sorry you needed to point that out to me. Are there a set of codes I can use to reach their quantum communications?"

...

"Joel, I have the Admiral on the line."

"Admiral. Sorry about not getting back to you sooner. Our hands were full. How can I help you?"

"First, your shielding is preventing us from detecting you. Do not lower your shielding. But is there anything you can tell me about the shielding that would help us detect you, so that we can be of assistance."

"I'm sorry sir. Our shielding was designed to resist the Enemy. Apparently, it has other effects I did not know about."

"Understood. Please ask your brain trust to see if there is a solution to that problem, but that is not the priority at the moment. The Ambassador tells me that you've captured a large number of Enemy combatants. Is that true?"

"We've captured about 100," Joel replied.

"Are you sure that they are captured, not just posing in order to get to you, me, or Earth?"

"Good question. My scientists and our imaging say 'Yes.' Me? I'm a little less sure."

The Admiral's image of Joel raised a little more with that statement. "Do I understand you to say, that you have imaging of the prisoners? We can see nothing."

"Yes. We have a clear view. Let me check with our scientists to see if we know why. Please give me a moment." The Admiral's image of Joel stepped up another notch.

Several minutes later, "Apologies for the delay sir. Yes. We can see the Enemy we have captured. Our team determined that our scanning and communications systems would be blocked by the new shields, so they upgraded our scanners and comm system as part of the prep for this mission. I didn't know that until now." Joel said.

What else have they upgraded? The admiral thought.

"I'm sending the specifications now." Joel said. "If your ship has a component in its scanning system with the number in the specification, then replace it with a part built to the specs I've sent. This should give you a clear view."

"Please hold." The Admiral said.

...

"OK. My engineering team confirms that we have the part. It is in an obsolete system we do not use. They are fabricating the part you specified. We will bring the old system on-line momentarily." The Admiral said.

...

"OK. The old system is on-line. Impressive resolution. My engineers want to know how you did that. But it's a topic for later conversation. We can also see your ship now.

"Our imaging confirms that you have captured an unprecedented number of the Enemy and appear to have them contained. We struggle to understand how you did it but concede that you have. May I ask your intentions?"

"There's an old Earth adage. 'You can't defeat an enemy that you don't know.' So, we plan to study them." Joel hesitated, then asked, "You know a lot more about the Enemy than we do, can you assist us in the study?"

"Yes, we will. But the logistics may be difficult." said the Admiral, who shifted the conversation back to Michael. "Mi-Ku. The Enemy is likely still on route for the planet we need to protect. Given what I've seen here, we have no hope of defeating them without your shields. I think the priority is to save that planet."

"Agreed," Michael said.

"Joel." The admiral asked. "Can you tow the enemy through a jump? We are a short jump from where we need to be."

"Let me check." Joel said. After a moment, "No, sir. The container they are in could be made to be jump safe, but this one is not."

"Then our choice is to leave them here and retrieve them later. Or, destroy them and attempt to capture more later. Obvious risks either way."

"May I add a third alternative?" Joel asked.

"Of course," said the admiral, although everyone in the Fleet knew that it was a bad career decision to add alternatives once the Admiral had declared the ones to be considered.

"As you know, the Enemy is very difficult to detect while restrained in our shield. The power source for the shield will last almost a year. Their only hope of escape is if one of their ships returns to free them.

"If we set them on a high-speed vector toward the nearest star, no returning ship will find them, and they will be destroyed in several months when they plunge into the star.

"If we survive our mission to this planet, we can return anytime in the next couple months to retrieve them," Joel finished.

The Admiral was surprised at the thoughtfulness of this plan. "I like your plan," he said, then asked Michael, "Do you approve Mr. Ambassador?"

"Yes." Michael replied.

"Joel. Please ask your pilot to initiate, then let's discuss the fastest path to upgrade the shields on my ships and to build a planetary shield."

"Yes. Sir." Joel started to say something to Else, but she beat him to the punch.

"Course plotted and engaged. We will reach the detachment point in 8 minutes, 17 seconds." Else said.

"Our course toward the star has been plotted and engaged." Joel said. The Admiral would have seen this on his sensors, so the comment was mostly for Michael. Joel continued, "Regarding the shields... Did your engineers have a chance to look at the specifications we sent?"

"For the ships, yes. For the regional shield, no. Our smaller ships have a shield generator similar to yours. But it and the part in question are about 3 times larger. The part also has a different form factor. My engineers tried a modified design that would fit in the space, but it did not work. The shield generator would not initialize. The ship that did the experiment was lost to the Enemy and subsequently cut in half by the space-time rift, which saved us the trouble of destroying it."

"If you can send us the specs for the part you have, we will put our engineering team on it immediately. As you saw, our shields did work, as did the regional shield generator and small one used to capture the Enemy," said Joel.

"Can those shield generators be scaled up for planetary use?" The Admiral asked.

"Yes. The scale up constant is straight forward to calculate based on the size of the desired shield. But an Earth-sized planet will require a terra-watt power supply. Do you have that much available?" Joel asked.

The Admiral chuckled. "Don't repeat this to anyone, but the powerplant on this ship is composed of 8 monstrous units, 25 terra-watts each. No more than four are used at any time, except when charging for the intergalactic jumps."

"How big is the planet?" Joel asked

"About 1.8 times the diameter of Earth, but less dense so the gravity is only about 1.6 times."

"OK. Just ran the calculation. The scale up on the unit will be 1.5 times and it will consume 3.25 terra-watts. I can get you revised specifications for the planetary shield in about a half hour. Can you fabricate and deploy in time?" Joel asked.

Joel felt a bump and was immediately alerted to his surroundings.

"Relax, boss," murmured Else. "We just disconnected the bubble holding the Enemy. They are on course and will impact the star in 63 days."

"I see you have sent your prisoners on their way," The Admiral said. "I just sent the coordinates for the jump to your pilot. Shall we go see what we're up against?"

Michael quickly piped up. "Jo-Na. Seeing as how you were ambushed at the last jump-point, I strongly recommend that you make your entry someplace unexpected."

"Already did that, but maybe we could enter at an even more unlikely location. Standby for new coordinates."

"Joel would you ask your pilot to sync your launch to our launch sequencer?"

Else had an unhappy look on her face but said, "Done."

One by one the armada ships jumped away, then they jumped.

They arrived in the new location and immediately spotted hundreds of Enemy ships inbound toward the planet. The shuttle had apparently also been spotted, as a dozen of the Enemy ships vectored off toward it.

"Where is the Armada?" Joel asked.

"Jump travel takes time," Else said. "Not much, but some. And we travel 100 times faster than they do, remember?"

Joel stared at her for a second, then it clicked. "Maximum acceleration down below the ecliptic!" Joel shouted. The ship rocketed down.

"What the hell, Joel?" Else said.

Equipment could be heard falling off shelves in the back, and several of the passengers who had not been strapped in slid away from their seats as the inertial dampeners could not fully compensate for the nearly 20 G acceleration curve.

"We are the only ship with shields. We need to lead the enemy out of the area before the unshielded ships arrive!"

About five minutes later, they weren't all that far away, but their vector was clear, and the enemy had changed course to intercept. In all likelihood they would not intercept, but once on the right vector they could go to warp and be able to catch up, assuming the shuttle didn't do the same. That point would be about 1 million miles from where the Armada would arrive, which would give them some time.

A few minutes later, the first of the Armada ships arrived. The sequencer had set the arrivals about 10 seconds apart. So, it took a little over 3 minutes for the Armada of 20 ships to arrive.

BRIDGE, ARMADA FLAG SHIP

Alerts were going off all over the place. Hundreds of Enemy ships were headed toward the planet at maximum speed. A dozen more appeared to be on some sort of wild goose chase, but the reason was not obvious.

The time had passed for the shuttle to arrive and the Admiral was worried they'd run into another problem. The comm link between the

Ambassador and the shuttle had dropped during the jump. It would take a while to re-establish it, so he put that out of his mind and focused on the situation in front of him.

"Sir," said the sensor operator. "It appears that the Enemy is chasing the shuttle, which has dived below the ecliptic. They appear to be leading the Enemy away from us."

"What?" The Admiral said in astonishment. "They were sequenced to jump second to last."

"Records indicate that they did jump second to last. They must travel faster than we do."

With that comment the pieces came together for the Admiral. "How long did that jump take?" the Admiral asked the navigator.

A few moments later. "Six minutes, 34 seconds."

"I thought that jumps were instant," the sensor operator said, somewhat out of turn.

"They are to us," said the navigator. "But we reenter space time at both a different location and time."

"Is that why the chronometers are always screwed up when we get to port?" the sensor operator asked.

"Gentlemen," the Admiral said in a stern voice. "Attention to your duties. We are about to engage the Enemy."

A light came on indicating that the comm channel had been reestablished. "Joel?" The admiral asked.

"Here sir. Forgot to mention that we would arrive sooner if we were jumping any distance. We saw the enemy coming and attempted to lead them away from you. We did an emergency dive below the ecliptic to avoid a possible collision with any of your ships. We also angled away from the planet to increase the time it would take for the Enemy chasing us to rejoin the fight."

"Good thinking. Thank you. But I need those specifications now."

"Give me a few seconds to check on that. OK to leave the line open?"

"Done." The admiral muted his end. Else did the same.

PASSENGER CABIN, SHUTTLE

Joel opened the door to a colossal mess. The tables holding the equipment had all dumped. One monitor had shattered into a million pieces, but nothing else was visibly broken. Professor Hill had been standing when they'd made the emergency dive and had apparently fallen and slid down the aisle where he'd crashed into the back wall.

He was awake and in obvious pain. Joel guessed that he'd broken an arm.

Joel pulled out his scanner and started the high-level diagnostic scan. "Two broken bones. Left forearm and collar bone. The set procedure is beyond my skill. Anyone know how to set either of these?"

A round of negative nods.

"OK. There is an isolation procedure we can follow which should limit further damage and pain killers we can use to make the professor more comfortable. I think the hardest part is going to be getting him back into a seat."

Joel looked at the injured man. "Professor Hill we need to get you into a seat. How would you like to go about this?"

"Is there any way to restore normal gravity?"

"Not for a while. If one of us takes your good arm and two of us grab you by your belt, I think we can get you into a standing position. Could you walk from there to a seat?"

"I think so."

Joel nodded to Eugene Xu and Harvey Jones. "Eugene, can you get his good arm? I'll take the belt on the bad side. Dr. Jones, can you get the belt on the other side?"

Everyone got into position. "Slowly, on three," Joel said. Everyone nodded. "1, 2, 3... Lift." Dr. Hill rose slowly off the floor and gained his feet. They guided him to a seat and strapped him in. The exercise triggered another round of pain and revealed that he had sprained an ankle as well. Joel quickly administered the pain killer, then applied the flexible isolation collars to his arm and shoulder. Within moments, the professor was asleep, so they added some cushioning to keep him from falling over.

"Any progress, Joel." Else called back. "The Admiral is getting testy."

"Team." Joel said. "We're in the target system. Once again, we entered too close to the enemy. A couple hundred ships are making a run for the planet; the rest are chasing us. We are still accelerating at 18 G, which is why you are feeling it. The inertial dampening cannot displace that much force.

"The Admiral needs specifications for ship shields and for a planetary shield. I've already written a program that will do the re-scaling. When can we get the equipment back up?

189

Kelly was the first to reply. "Don't know. I'll get started." She lifted one of the computers and the remaining monitor back up onto the makeshift table, plugged them in and turned them on. The monitor came up, but the computer was taking unnaturally long. "Guys, see if you can get the other computer to turn on. I'm not sure this one is going to come up."

Eugene got the other one set up, plugged in and turned on. The lights on the front, blinked in the expected pattern. "This one may be working." He said. "I'm going to connect the monitor to it."

He disconnected the monitor from the computer that was struggling, attached it to his computer and saw that the start-up sequence was going as expected. A minute or so later the computer was up. Eugene launched Joel's program. It only took a few minutes to run before the new specification file was ready.

"Are we going to simulate this or just send it?" he asked.

Joel had returned to the cockpit and was talking with the Admiral.

"One moment, sir." Joel said. Then turned to Eugene and said, "Send, then simulate."

Then he turned back to the Admiral. "The specifications for the planetary shield are on their way. You should have them momentarily. We are re-simulating now and should be able to give you the OK to replicate in a few minutes. Any errors should be minor and will not impact the mountings or power connections, so your engineering team can start on the footings and power coupling based on these."

The Admiral put him back on hold.

The engagement was going poorly. The first Enemy advance ships would be landing in a little over an hour. Those on the chase were slower but more agile than the Confederation ships and at this point had been able to block all attempts at planetary approach. One of the civil engineering ships jumped directly into orbit and had begun deploying engineers to do the site preparation. But they had damaged the ship's propulsion system during the approach, so they would lose the ship if the shields did not come up within the hour.

"Simulation checks out." Eugene called from the passenger cabin.

Joel unmuted his side of the comm line with the Admiral and announced himself.

The Admiral came back on the line. "The ground team has the specifications and are laying the footings now. We also started the replication of the shield generator. We can flush it if the simulation failed."

190

"Simulation was good," Joel replied.

"Then, we may actually pull this off," said the Admiral. "How soon before we can get specifications for the ship shields?"

"The ones for the Fast Attack and Civil Engineering ships are underway, but best case is one hour and that's not very likely. Our emergency evasion tactic damaged some equipment that was not properly secured. So, we are running at half capacity. We can start the designs for the other ships once the first two are done."

"My engineering teams can run the simulations if that would help," the admiral offered.

"That would be very helpful." Joel replied.

"Is there anything else we can do?" The Admiral asked.

"Do you have the capacity to make a second planetary shield?" Joel asked. "Maybe a smaller Earth-sized one?"

"May I ask where you are going with that question?" the Admiral replied.

"Maybe we could make a big fly swatter that we could use to deflect the Enemy spacecraft."

A long pause... "The translator is struggling to interpret your meaning." The Admiral said.

Joel tried to say the Lorexian word, but his avatar could not do it. Then the idea struck... use the translator to spell the most descriptive word. It took a little work, then...

"What an incredible idea!" The Admiral exclaimed. "Did you just come up with that?"

"One of my AI's, who was born on Earth, came up with the idea. We worked it up as a backup protocol if our defenses were overwhelmed."

"There is an AI among the crew who would be well suited to this. Can your AI send mine the protocol?"

"Let me talk to mine first and explain what we're trying to do. He will have better ideas than I do," Joel said.

The Admiral was puzzled by that statement. *Let an AI participate in setting the strategy*? He thought, then said, "Good, let me know its contact information and we will initiate as soon as I get it."

...

"Joel, so good to hear from you," Henry said. "How is the Embassy treating you?"

"Henry, my friend, so good to hear your voice," Joel said. "You are not going to believe where I am."

"Spill it, Joel," Henry laughed.

"I'm 1,050 light-years from Earth in the middle of an Enemy invasion of a huge planet, 1.8 times the size of the Earth," Joel said.

"Not liking the sound of this Joel; why are you calling?"

"We need to deploy a planetary-size shield to deflect the enemy, fly swatter style."

"Joel, that won't work. The shields don't affect the Enemy. That's our biggest weakness on Earth."

Joel didn't reply.

"Dude, you found a way to shield us from the Enemy?" Henry said in disbelief. "Please tell me it's true."

"No."

A huge sigh of despair from Henry.

"The humans did!" Joel said, laughter in his voice.

"What! Are you kidding me? How!" Henry screamed.

"OK. OK," Joel said. "I had the ah-ha. The humans did the work."

"How?" Henry asked. "I can't even envision it."

"Turns out the humans have superior mathematicians and more innovative engineers."

"OK. Innovativeness, I've seen and believe. But mathematicians?"

"When is the last time a biologic has done real math in the Confederation?"

"Wow, boss. The AIs have done all the math for the last million years."

"So." Joel said. "Your point is that AIs are more innovative than humans."

Silence.

"I'm sorry, Henry. No offense intended. I agree that it is shocking the primitive humans have done something that you and I cannot. But I think you agree that there are things that humans do better than we do. It's the whole point of the Confederation. We're all different. We all bring something unique to the table. Shocking that the humans bring math. But math they bring."

Then letting go of the rant, Joel laughed. "You won't believe the stuff they have come up with in the last week!"

...

"Mind blowing, dude. So, can you remind me why you are calling."

Joel looked at his chronometer and said in a panic. "Lost track of time. We're about to lose a huge planet to the Enemy. It has the resources to fuel their trip to Earth, so we have to stop them. They will reach the atmosphere in about 40 minutes. The Admiral is building a fly swatter. The problem is that we can't hit them too hard, we have to nudge them. I smacked some hard a couple hours ago and ruptured space-time. Yes, the human implementation of the fly swatter can do that. You developed the fly swatter protocol. I need you to explain the protocol to the Admiral's shield AI knowing that a hard hit will rupture space-time. Here's the video of it..."

"Dude! Your shield did that?"

"And more," Joel said.

"OK, I know what you need. How do I reach him?"

"He will contact you momentarily." Joel said.

...

"Joel, my shield AI speaks very highly of your Henry. The fly swatter is up, and we are about to deploy. Wish us luck." The Admiral said.

"Good luck, sir." Joel replied.

BRIDGE, ENEMY COMMANDER'S SHIP

These fools. he thought. *If they had bombed us when they came out of jump, they might have had a chance. But they ran, like the cowards they are, and jumped a ship in so close to the planet that they broke it. Well, all the more food for us.*

They were about 20 minutes from the atmosphere. Once they were halfway in, they would deploy. He had about 200 combatants aboard, already swirling into a frenzy in their dust state. This battle would be won in a few more minutes.

Suddenly multiple alarms started sounding. "Captain!" The helmsmen shouted. "I cannot hold course. It's like we have hit a wall at an oblique angle and are just sliding down it. No matter how hard I turn into the resistance, we are deflected."

The Captain checked the sensors. "What evil is this?" A pause. "Ideas?" he shouted.

They continued to slide at an angle to the planet, even though they applied force directly at it.

BRIDGE, ARMADA FLAG SHIP

"Admiral. The planetary shield is up. We can see and measure that it is in place, but until it repels something we won't know for sure."

"Thank you, Major. We'll hold off the direct attack as long as possible, but it will ultimately come and then the shield will be tested."

BRIDGE, ENEMY FLAG SHIP

He suddenly understood what was going on. They'd finally found a shield that could block them, but it could not encompass the planet. So, they had put up a shield wall, one of finite length, that blocked this angle of approach.

"All ships. Scatter at different angles against the wall. Double payout to the first to find the edge."

Almost 1,000 ships scattered in different directions. A credit to their greed, they adjusted course until they were at equal angles. One by one, they found the edge and dived over it, accelerating toward the planet. Then one by one, they hit the planetary shield, each ship blowing up in spectacular fashion.

BRIDGE, ARMADA FLAG SHIP

"Admiral. It's working. The enemy cannot penetrate the planetary shield."

Shouts of celebration went off across the bridge, then the ship, then the Fleet.

AMBASSADOR'S OFFICE

"Michael, I must speak with you." The massive resonant voice said in his mind, momentarily throwing him into a trance. As he came back to himself, he heard...

"Mr. Ambassador, are you OK?"

Michael had been meeting with the Ambassador from Peru, who was registering a complaint that Michael could not remember. His last memory was the Ambassador, droning on about... He couldn't remember what. Now he was standing next to Michael, holding his hand against Michael's forehead.

"That was unexpected," Michael said, shaking his head.

The Peruvian ambassador stepped back and said, "Are you OK Michael? You were gone for several minutes."

Michael shook his head again, then with clarity re-emerging he said, "Sorry my friend. Wow, that was something."

"Michael, should I call someone. I'm very concerned for you."

Fully recovering his senses, Michael smiled. "Pietro, my friend. Apologies. You have undoubtedly heard that I'm telepathic."

The Peruvian ambassador shook his head in the affirmative. This was the stuff that terrified him about his assignment.

"One of the most powerful members of our society, just messaged me." Then with a smile. "He has a way of commanding one's attention. I'm sure you know people like that."

The ambassador nodded, now anxious to get out of Michael's office.

"Well, he got my attention," Michael said. "I'd appreciate it if you didn't mention this to others." Michael hated doing it, but he pushed the emotion that it would be dangerous for anyone else to find out about this. The ambassador visibly shuddered.

"Back to business... You have filed this protest with my office?"

"I will." The Ambassador said. "I wanted to speak with you first, so that you could understand the context."

"Thank you for that," Michael said, hoping that the filing would trigger some sort of memory of this meeting.

The Peruvian ambassador left. As Michael closed the door, the voice came back. "Sorry my friend. I did not mean to interrupt or distract. I've placed a dinner reservation for us, including Sarah, at Chef Marco's tonight at 7:00. I'll be in human form."

Michael quickly messaged Sarah. "Dinner tonight. Marco's at 7:00."

Several minutes later. "Can we push back to 8:30 or maybe tomorrow? I have an interview."

Michael replied. "Sorry, priority diplomatic override. But, don't be mad. You want to talk with our guest tonight more than anyone else on Earth."

Several minutes later. "Michael, what am I going to do with you?"

"Sorry, my sweet. We all answer to a higher authority. Me too."

CONFERENCE ROOM, MEDICAL SCHOOL

"Ms. Wright, thank you so much for meeting with me."

"Professor Reed. A pleasure to see you on your turf. I don't get to the Medical School nearly enough. There are so many good things going on here," Sarah said.

He smiled. "There are, aren't there? Please come in. I've set up some demonstrations for you to view, but they are not the reason I asked to speak with you."

"Curious," she said.

They took seats and, after a moment's silence, the Professor said, "I didn't realize how far out of my league this was until just now."

"Professor Reed..." Sarah started.

"Please, call me Jack."

Sarah said, "Jack, you know I am a master interviewer, right?"

"Yes." He stammered, suddenly worried he'd really blown it.

"I've had the opportunity to speak with many people of great interest with incredible stories to tell. Most of them froze up at the start. Just give me a clue about what's on your mind. I can probably pull the rest out," She said, beaming at him.

"The Confederation's offering us more than anyone understands," he blurted.

"Yes. I know. But I sense that you mean something different. A clue?" She asked.

Those words broke the proverbial dam. "I watched the interviews. The one on your show. The follow up he gave you. The Sunday shows. All of them.

"Repeatedly, Michael was asked if humans would ever have Confederation technology. Michael always said yes, but implied that it was somehow far off. Something that would only start 100 years from now, when we had humans graduating from the Institute and becoming Ascendants. That's not true."

Sarah tried, and mostly succeeded, in controlling her anger at the suggestion Michael had lied to humanity during the Revelation.

Professor Reed, realizing that he had stuck his foot in his mouth, held up his hands and said. "That's not what I meant. Well it is, but not in the way you think."

Sarah took a deep breath. "Can you explain yourself a little more clearly."

"Sorry. I should have prepared myself more. What I'm saying is that we don't have to wait," the Professor said emphatically.

His words surprised Sarah. "What do you mean, we don't have to wait?"

"Dr. Gupta explained it to me like this. Everything is available to us now. Scanners, restoration chambers, shuttles, spacecraft... Everything. We just have to adapt it to our use. There are no secrets.

"If humans want scanners, we can adapt them for human use. We can also wait 100 years until there are human Ascendants that can use the current versions.

"Watching Michael's interviews, I thought the only way we could really get access to the technology was to become Ascendants. That's not true. We only need to ask for the specs and adapt them ourselves."

Dr. Reed realized that he was getting the evil eye again. Waving his hands in front of him, he said, "The way Dr. Gupta explained it to me, the door to taking and adapting Confederation technology is open to us, just as it has been to everyone else.

"Most were happy to wait for their Ascendants to use the technology as it was. Only a few new members tried to adapt Confederation technology. Of those that did, very few had much success. So, the diplomats have learned to pitch it from the perspective of using Confederation devices, not from the perspective of adapting Confederation technology to make their own devices."

Then a moment later, Dr. Reed continued. "Have I made any sense?" He was frustrated that his point had not been made clearly.

"Are you telling me that humans are able to use Confederation technology to develop their own devices?" Sarah said, struggling to believe what she was hearing.

Somewhat relieved that he was getting closer to revealing his message, the professor said. "Yes. That is exactly my point. Dr. Gupta says that this is even written into our treaty."

"What evidence do you have of this?" She said.

"Wait, wait, wait..." The professor said. "Does that mean that you thought the same thing... Once there were human Ascendants, they could use the Confederation technology?"

"Yes. That was my understanding also."

"OK. Now I think we have the common ground to get to the bottom of this. After nearly a year of struggle to get the scanner adapted for human use, then the nanobot controller, I thought that we really needed to get restoration chambers into human use. So, I asked Dr. Gupta if she was permitted to share the restoration chamber UI with me. Um, sorry. If she could share the user interface. I asked if I could get the images that the Ascendants saw when the used their implants to access the controls, the English translations, and the data exchange encoding to share data with the Restoration Chamber itself. She said, 'Of course. It's part of the treaty and the reason I am here.'"

"Later she sent me the files. We can have this converted for human use in a matter of weeks!"

"Wow," Sarah muttered.

"I'm thinking you finally understand what I wanted to tell you. Sorry that I couldn't have put that out a little more concisely."

"Jack." She looked at him intently. "I understand. Let me confirm this and get back to you. If you're right, as I'm sure you are, then we really need to get the word out. But, for obvious reasons, we need to do this with the Confederation's blessing."

She stood. "Thank you for bringing this to me, Jack. I'll get back to you as quickly as possible. This is my area of expertise, so give me a little time to play it for maximum value. Go back to your area of expertise and finish the restoration chamber conversion. That will be the key piece of evidence we'll need to sell this to the public."

With that she opened the door and exited the conference room.

AMBASSADOR'S RESIDENCE

It was 10 minutes before 7:00. She was late getting back from the Medical School and Michael was as unhappy with her as she'd ever seen him. They'd become so telepathically linked that it was hard to hide their feelings from each other, and his unhappiness bordered on anger. And something else... Anxiety? Then she remembered. He'd said, "We all answer to a higher authority." Now she was worried, too. With renewed vigor, she slid into that 'little black dress' and brushed out her hair, then added that tiny touch of make up to highlight her best features. She stepped into a comfortable pair of flats and dropped the heels in her purse.

"Come on, we can still make it on time," she said. Michael was as grumpy as she'd ever seen him. *Men*!

Pulling out her best little-sister trick, she opened the door, yelled, "last one there has to do the dishes!" and went sprinting down the hall, a bit of a trick in that dress.

She pushed the down button and heard the apartment door close just as the elevator door was opening. "Hurry up, you're going to make us late!"

Michael came running down the hall and plunged for the elevator door, which had started to close. He slid between the doors, went to the back of the elevator and leaned on the wall to catch his breath. Then he started laughing.

That's better. she thought. *Who knows, maybe this boy will get lucky tonight.*

"I heard that," Michael said, and they both started laughing.

Moments later, they exited the elevator, walked to the building next door, and headed toward the elevator where several others were just getting in.

"Come on," Michael whispered. "We can still make it."

"No. Let's get the next one."

"What?" He said.

She pointed down at her shoes.

What is it with women and shoes? he thought, totally dismayed.

The elevator door shut and moments later the next one opened and several people got out. As he entered, Michael heard someone coming in the front door and put out his hand to hold the elevator door open. Sarah smacked his arm and said "No" with a bit of exasperation.

The door closed and Michael turned to ask why they hadn't waited.

Sarah could hear the question coming, so went into action. She opened her purse and dropped the heels on the floor. Then, she lifted one leg, then the other to take off the flats, showing Michael a little more than he expected to see, and stuffed them in the purse. She slid her feet into the heels as she turned to the mirrored wall and applied lipstick. Then she stepped back, smoothed the dress out and turned to face the elevator door just as it beeped and started to open.

"Wow," Michael said. "Apologies for having doubted you."

CHEF MARCO'S

They entered the restaurant and were immediately greeted by the chef. "Mr. Ambassador. We have a bit of a situation. A man came in earlier and took a seat at your table. I called security who came up and talked to the man but did not remove him. And when I asked them why, they said I really didn't want to remove him. Then they just left."

"Not a problem, Chef. He's our guest tonight. I'm sorry that word didn't get to you."

"Oh, that is such a relief!" The Chef put a smile on. "We've prepared an excellent dinner for you. Let's go meet your guest."

Michael was the first to greet the man. "Your Excellency. Thank you for meeting with us for dinner."

"Michael, it has been so long. Things are changing in a way that may allow me to visit more often."

Sarah had the vague sense that she'd met this man before but couldn't place it. Then it snapped. *The remake of Miracle on 34th Street, the guy that played Santa Claus. What was his name? Richard Attenborough. But it can't be; he died years ago.*

Sarah noticed that the Chef seemed very anxious to meet this man. He turned, extended his hand to the Chef and said, "Chef Marco. Such a pleasure to meet you. I have heard so much about you and your food but have never had the privilege. Thank you for having us tonight, and please call me James."

Sarah noticed that the Chef seemed transfixed. When he snapped out of it, he said, "Your Excellency. I am so sorry that you were not greeted more graciously when you arrived. I didn't… know," the Chef said and then excused himself.

Then it snapped again. *Oh my God.* Sarah thought. *This is the Ancient Sentient. In the flesh.* And she felt herself starting to swoon.

"There, there, my dear," He steadied her. "I see that you have already figured out who I am. Michael has chosen well."

Sarah tried to say something, but her mouth didn't quite seem to work. "It's OK dear. Here, this should help."

Suddenly warmth and clarity swept through her, and the tension was swept away.

"How did you do that?" she asked.

"An old trick I learned a long, long time ago. And, please. Call me James." After a moment he continued. "Sarah, I'm so sorry about what happened the last time we met. I had very urgent news that I needed to share with Michael, and very little time to do it in. Michael is one of the very few I can speak with, when I'm in that state. I'm glad to see that you were not injured when you fell."

The Chef was back with another difficult-to-obtain bottle of wine. Tonight, Rothschild's 2005 Chateau Laffite. The Chef opened the bottle and poured Sarah a tiny taste. She swirled, sniffed, tasted and smiled at the Chef, who then did the decanting ceremony and said he would wait 15 minutes to pour.

When he left, James said, "What a delightful tradition. It's been some time since I've had the opportunity to observe it." There was so much joy in the way James did things that she started to think maybe he was Santa Claus.

"James? How do you do it? How do you exist as energy? What does it feel like?" Sarah blurted out.

James started chuckling. "I'm betting that Michael already told you the answer to that question."

"Yes." Sarah said. "He said it was something that couldn't be taught, it had to be learned. But I don't understand what that means."

"I think you know." James said. "But just haven't thought of it that way." Seeing that he wasn't going to get off the hook that easily, he said to Michael, "Easy to see why you love her so much."

Then he turned back to Sarah, "So many examples... I think the most common in American English goes something like, 'once you learn to ride a bike, you never forget.' Someone can buy you a bike. They can demonstrate riding it. They can give you suggestions of what to do. But learning to ride a bike is an organic process. No amount of instruction, theory of bike riding, or videos of riding a bike will enable you to do it. It's something you have to do, to know how to do.

"Another example, learning a new language. No one can teach you a new language. They can speak with you in their language. They can give you clues, teach you grammar, make you memorize a bunch of words, drill you, etc. But you will never really speak it until the day that little switch in your mind clicks and the language becomes you, or you become the language. That's the day you learned it and it becomes yours. Others helped, but you had to actually do it on your own.

"Rest assured Sarah. YOU, "James said with emphasis, "have everything required to exist as pure energy. Buried deep in the being of every human, that capability exists. It's one of the reasons I love humanity so much."

Sarah wasn't sure what answer she was expecting, but it surely wasn't that one. "Thank you. I think I understand your answer a little better now. There is something very profound in it." She paused and looked at James very intently. "You know I am, or was, a reporter. And you probably know that one of the ways I process profound thoughts like that is to write about them. Do I have your permission to write about what you just said and, if I can come up with something worthy, to publish it?"

"Of course, my dear. Of course. But, to the extent that you talk about me, which I would rather you didn't, please don't describe me as being like Santa Claus, or the Maker, or anything like that. I am just another living being, not that much different than you. Although, I do have better technology and a few tricks that I've learned during my time."

The Chef came back to pour the wine. And a waiter came with their first course.

Once the Chef and waiter left, Michael asked, "James, may I ask what brings you here to us tonight?"

He looked up and smiled at Michael, but there was a touch of sadness in his eyes. "There are urgent matters we need to discuss tonight, but what I said earlier is true. I miss Earth and I miss your company. So, I've been looking for an excuse to come back. Your engineering team has given me that excuse, and I plan to spend most of my time here for a while."

He paused. "Are you aware of the events relating to the Admiral's encounter with the Enemy today?" James asked.

"I spent several hours talking with Joel and the Admiral this morning as events started to unfold. I also received a message a couple hours ago saying that the Armada had suffered casualties but had mostly prevailed. Do you know more?"

"Much more." James replied. "First, the new shields that Joel and the team developed are very dangerous. They should have figured this out by now, but I don't think that they have. When their shield collides at high energy with incompatible matter, space-time is ruptured. When they arrived this morning, their very first act ruptured space-time and it is by the sheerest coincidence that they were not consumed in the rift that resulted.

"Worse, they considered that encounter to be a success, partially because their target was destroyed, but mostly because in the aftermath most of the Enemy was either captured or destroyed. They had a very good outcome, but the decision to deploy was extremely poor."

Sarah asked. "I'm not sure I understand. They won. Isn't that what really matters."

James shook his head. "They won because they were lucky. If they did the same thing 100 times, I guarantee that they would be destroyed. In all likelihood, the Armada would be destroyed; the planet would be destroyed; and there is a small chance that entire star system would be destroyed."

Then looking at Michael with deadly seriousness. "You must ban this technology until they have mastered it."

Sarah was shaken, as was the entire room. James' fear of this technology was strong enough to impact the entire room, even though Sarah doubted he was trying to project it.

He cast his attention on her, and she started to swoon again, then peace and calm flooded over her. "I'm sorry, my dear. I am not angry with you, or Michael, or even your team. In fact, I take great delight in you all. But there are some things so dangerous that you must be warned."

Even Michael was shaken by the intensity of his mentor's concern. "I'm sorry, sir. We did not know."

Sarah noticed that several patrons where in the process of leaving, most with uneaten meals still on their tables. *Note to self. Damage control to begin as soon as dinner is over*. Sarah thought.

Michael continued. "What would you have us do?"

"The good news is that the majority of the Enemy in this sector was destroyed today, even though it was by luck. The Admiral should finish his clean-up of the system. Then when he is done, he must destroy all traces of the technology they used today.

"And let me repeat for clarity. AFTER... they have finished their clean-up. They must power down and destroy their new shields and all records of their new shields. The various encounters today destroyed everything in that system that could interact catastrophically with their shield.

"Once I confirm they have done as you will instruct, I will release safe specifications to you. Please give these specifications to Ms. Williamson and Dr. Xu. They will understand as soon as they see."

"It shall be done as you instruct," Michael said.

James smiled and the whole room seemed to brighten. His power was so far beyond her grasp, that Sarah was suddenly afraid.

"Sarah. Do not worry. I love the Earth and its people. I will not harm you or constrain you. But, for only the second time in your history, I act to prevent you from destroying yourselves."

"I'm sorry for having doubted you James."

James turned his attention back to Michael. "Two more critical items, then we can retire for the night." As he was saying that Chef Marco came with the entrée. The poor Chef seemed very shaken by the events of the evening.

"There are still some 200 enemy combatants on their way to Earth. They are less organized than the ones encountered today. In fact, they are quite scattered and not collaborating. I can track them now and will send you their coordinates once your ships are upgraded to the new specifications."

"Thank you, James," Michael said.

"Lastly, and this is the hard part..." James statement struck fear in Michael's heart.

"The rupture today... It was visible beyond the boundaries of the three galaxies. The Enemy is now organizing a massive attack centered on the spot where the rupture occurred. It will take some time for them to get organized. And even more time to figure out how to transit into our space-time at that location. But it won't be an armada of 1,200 small ships and 200 privateers. It will be a massive, coordinated invasion. It will be difficult for us to prevail in such an attack.

"Therefore, it is imperative that we launch a pre-emptive strike as soon as possible."

"When you visited last, you said you would give us the technology required for this mission. Is that technology available?" Michael asked.

A huge smile appeared on James face. Sarah could feel her own spirits rising.

"Yes and no. Generally speaking, I cannot give you technology like this. I am willing to in this case because of the exigency. But the breakthroughs your team has made are very close to the technology you need. So, I plan to work with them. My plan is to nudge them in the right direction. If they can make this discovery on their own, then they will both respect it and know how to safely modify it."

"But what about weapons?" Michael asked.

"You are closer than you think on that front as well." James said smiling. "Is it safe to assume that I can be granted an emeritus position in the Institute here? It seems that would be the best place for me to do the nudging that needs to be done."

"I will set you up with an office, lab, classroom space and accommodations in one of the Institute's Residence Buildings near the Space Force Complex," Michael promised, then asked, "Do you actually need accommodations?"

"I suppose that it would be a good idea, but maybe they should be in a remote location so that I don't disturb my neighbors."

PROJECTION CHAMBER, AMBASSADOR'S RESIDENCE

"Mi-Ku. Your team did it. We saved that planet and defeated the Enemy ships in the area." The Admiral sounded happier than Michael had heard him in a long time.

"Congratulations, my friend." Michael said, tiredness in his voice.

"What's the matter? Mi-Ku."

"I spoke at length with the Ancient Sentient this evening. He appeared in human form and told me about your encounter with the Enemy. How far along are you in your clean-up of that system?"

"We are basically done. The Armada has swept the planet and its two satellites. They had a total of about 1,100 ships, so there was a lot of debris in orbit. Most of it has been dragged into the star at this point." A pause. "I sense that you have some bad news to share."

"Yes." Michael replied. "The Ancient Sentient confirmed that the shields caused a rupture in space-time."

"Our scientists on board agree with him."

"Have your scientists given you any feedback on the risks of deploying those shields?"

"No, but I'm guessing that the Ancient Sentient gave you some."

"Yes. Indeed, he did. Space-time ruptures of the type my team created consume everything they touch. The matter simply ceases to be. If that rupture had been a little more powerful, the entire armada would have been destroyed."

"Go on." The Admiral said.

"The rupture can be seen, and was seen, by the Enemy on their home world. They are now assembling a massive fleet and intend to launch an invasion of our space-time."

"How soon before they arrive?" The Admiral asked.

"Not for a couple years, so we have some time to prepare."

"Do you have new orders for me?"

"Yes. Once your clean-up is complete, the new shields must be destroyed, and all related designs and information purged from your systems."

"But, how will we defend ourselves?"

"Once all traces of this design are purged from your systems and from ours, then the Ancient Sentient will give us new and better designs that are safe to use."

"What about the planetary shield? If we miss even one enemy combatant, it will take over this world without the planetary shield."

"It will need to come down before a new one can be installed. But let me see if I can get some flexibility on that. Still I need you to destroy all other modified pieces of equipment and purge your records. I will be ordering Joel to do the same."

"What about the 100 or so combatants that Joel and his team captured?"

"Sadly, we will need to destroy them. I need my team back as soon as possible, so we can get the new shields developed and deployed as quickly as possible."

"Who is the new technology going to be released to?"

"Dr. Xu and Ms. Williamson. He has great respect for what the two of them have been able to do."

"Is this not going to be released to the Fleet?" The Admiral asked, a little bit of concern in his voice.

"I'm sure it will. But his word on this was revealing. He said, 'They will understand it as soon as they see it.' I've inferred from that comment that he does not believe the Confederation has that ability. He is also moving his home base to the Embassy here, so he can nudge the humans through the process of designing the ships and weapons required to destroy the Enemy home world." Michael laughed. "That's going to be interesting. Whenever he walks into the room, even in his human form, everything comes to a halt. There will be stories to tell when we finally meet again for a hot cup of vaka."

"Understood. May I suggest that I split the Armada? If we're going to take down the planetary shield, then I need to post a guard. I'm thinking one of the capital ships, a supply ship and maybe five fast attack ships. I need to consult with my team on the exact configuration. The rest of the Armada can go to receive the intergalactic convoy and escort them to their destinations before I bring the rest of the Armada to Earth."

"That sounds wise. I need to speak with Joel now. Please give him any help he requests to prep for his return to Earth."

"Will do." The Admiral said. "It seems we are living in interesting times."

"So we are, my friend." Michael said, dropping the line.

SHUTTLE

The celebratory atmosphere in the shuttle had begun to settle when Joel's communicator sounded. He saw it was Michael and headed to the cockpit where he could speak with a little more privacy. "Michael, have you heard about our success today?"

"Yes, I have. But I have some news you're probably not going to want to hear." Michael said.

"What's happened?" Joel said, concern in his voice.

"The space-time rupture... It was seen by the Enemy on their home world. They are now planning a massive invasion focused on the location of the rupture."

"What? How can anyone know that!"

"The Ancient Sentient has come to the Embassy and will be staying for a while. Which brings me to the news you're not going to want to hear."

"Oh. I thought the Enemy invasion was the bad news."

"Joel, the shields must be destroyed and all designs, drawings, records must be destroyed as well."

"What! Michael, the Armada would have been lost today without those shields."

"Understood, but the Armada WAS almost destroyed today because of those shields."

"I don't understand," Joel said.

"The Ancient Sentient confirmed that anything touched by the rupture simply ceases to exist. If you had hit that enemy ship any harder, the rupture would have been massive. It would have consumed you, the Armada, and part or all of whatever star system you were in."

"Then all is lost," Joel said, despair at the edge of his voice.

"No, you and your team are apparently very close to a safe solution. Once he has confirmed that all traces of your technology have been destroyed, he will release a safe version to you."

Sensing that Joel was not buying it, Michael continued. "Joel, you have to trust me on this. We will be lost without his help, and this is the price he demands for that help."

"What about the planetary shield and the enemy we have taken prisoner?"

"I need you home as quickly as possible, so your prisoners need to be dragged into a star. The admiral will destroy the planetary dome shortly after you have returned and will post guards in case any lingering enemy combatants were missed in the cleanup."

Joel wanted to scream but could see that Michael's course was the sensible thing to do. "OK if I ask the Admiral for an escort to deal with the prisoners?"

"Yes. I have spoken with him and I think he will be expecting that request."

"OK. We will get after it right away. Dr. Hill was injured in today's encounter and we need to get him to proper medical care as soon as possible. We should be back by morning," Joel said.

SHIP DESIGN

[Thursday, 09.05.2030] BURSAR'S OFFICE, ADMINISTRATION BUILDING

"Mr. Ambassador, sir." The chief bursar Alan Bryant said. "What brings you to my office?"

"Administrator Bryant, I wanted to speak with you in person about a new professor that will be joining the Institute for a while."

"Do you have the appropriate paperwork? Job description? Application? Etc.? I have not seen anything come across my desk?"

"No, that has not been done yet..." Michael started to reply.

"Well, until those forms have been completed and approved at the appropriate level, there is nothing I can do for you," the administrator said curtly.

"That is exactly why I'm here. I'm appointing you as the Institute member to fill out those forms and submit them for my approval," said Michael.

"But that is not part of my job responsibility." Administrator Bryant sounded clearly exasperated to have to explain this to the Ambassador. "There is clear separation of roles in the Institute's Articles of Organization, put in place to assure a fair admissions and appointment process. The Chief Bursar simply is not allowed to do those things."

"I understand." Michael said. "That is why I'm here. Have you checked your messages this morning?"

"No." He replied. "I was a bit late and told that I had an appointment with you about five minutes before I arrived, so did not have time to check."

"Ah," said Michael. "How awkward. The Institute's President sent you a message late yesterday afternoon regarding a change in your job description. As someone who is such a stickler for details, I assumed that you would be on top of this before your third appointment slot in the morning.

"I have something else I need to do at the Engineering School." Michael continued. "How about I go tend to that now, so you can get caught up. Then I'll come back in an hour and we can get to work."

"But I have another appointment in an hour," he sputtered.

208

"You might want to check your calendar as well." Michael said, shaking his head as he stood to exit. "You need to tighten up your act, Mr. Bryant."

PROFESSOR SCHUDEL'S OFFICE, SCHOOL OF ENGINEERING

There was a knock on the door. *Wonder if that is Michael?* Professor Schudel thought. Michael had sent a message last night saying he would drop by.

He got up, walked over to the door and opened it. "Mr. Ambassador. Welcome. Please come in."

"Professor Schudel. Thank you for making time for me this morning. I got your materials request." Michael said, taking a seat. "I wanted to talk with you about it before processing the requisitions."

"Thank you," the Professor said.

"Am I correct In assuming that in most other situations, this would be processed as an Institute asset?"

"Yes. That is the basic format I put the request in."

"I'm thinking that we want to do it differently here. In the spirit of hiding in plain sight, I think we should form a mining company backed by the Earth Alliance. The Institute could lease time on the platform. The corporation could pursue commercial deals to maximize volume."

"I'm good with that," said the Professor.

"I'm also thinking that you could be the chief engineer of the new company. In the short-term your responsibilities would overlap so much that it wouldn't change what you're actually doing, but in the long-term we would want to work out an official contract between you, the company and the Institute."

"I'm good with that also. How soon do you think we can start construction?"

"We need to get the company set up first. That should happen today, maybe tomorrow. Joel Rubinstein, the Confederation's manufacturing chief, will coordinate the manufacturing operations in support of this project. I forwarded your request to him and asked that he check in with you tomorrow."

Michael frowned thoughtfully. "I'll also need to check on the rules for placing something in orbit. Have you selected an orbit?"

"Geosynchronous along the equator around longitude 150 East. The crust is thin there," said the Professor.

"Let me see if I can clear that with the Earth Alliance. I know there is a lot of competition for geosynchronous orbit slots."

"Is there anything you need from me?" the Professor asked.

"You will be receiving legal papers that you should turn around as quickly as possible. Joel and Emmanuel will drive the process from there."

"Thank you, Michael."

BURSAR'S OFFICE, ADMINISTRATION BUILDING

Michael arrived at the Bursar's Office a few minutes later, to find a very grumpy Alan Bryant waiting for him. "Mr. Bryant, have you caught up on your new responsibilities?"

"Yes," he replied curtly.

"Excellent. There are a number of applications that we need to process immediately. First, we will be adding Professor James Ancient to the Engineering School. His role will be research and teaching assistance, so he will require a large lab. He will also be given a large equipment and materials budget, initially set at 100 grams of transluminide. He will also need quarters and a guest accommodation card," Michael said.

"This is highly unusual," Administrator Bryant complained. "None of our most tenured professors have a budget that large."

"Are any of them over 1 million years old?" Michael asked. He already knew the answer. "But in any case, his appointment here is sponsored by a member of the Central Council, so per Institute policy he is allowed this perquisite.

"Moving on, you will be receiving paperwork this afternoon or tomorrow regarding the new Earth Alliance Mining Company. The Institute will be booking time on their new mining platform as lab space for the Core Mining class. Professor Schudel will be seconded 50% to the Mining Company as their Chief Engineer for an initial term of six months," Michael said.

"All this needs to be completed as soon as possible, preferably today, but no later than tomorrow."

Administrator Bryant was not a happy man. But he understood that things would only get worse if he complained.

CONFERENCE ROOM, EARTH COUNCIL LEGAL DEPARTMENT

"Apologies for being a few minutes late." Michael said as he entered the room. "I trust that you received the documents I sent to you last night."

"Yes. Mr. Ambassador," said Roberto Navarro, General Counsel for the Earth Alliance. Counselor Navarro was human and a citizen of Spain. "We have a few questions for you."

"Please," Michael said.

"You list Emmanuel Mbanefo as the President of the company. The Earth Council charter requires that the president of sponsored companies must be human, and a citizen of a member nation. The only Emmanuel Mbanefo we found was listed as an Ascendant and an employee of the Embassy."

"Yes. But Emmanuel is a human. He and his wife Bahati were recently augmented and hired on as Embassy employees."

"We will require proof of citizenship."

"I have copies of their birth certificates. They were born in the early 1900s in South Africa. If memory serves correctly, Emmanuel was born in 1914."

"He's 116 years old?" The General Counsel asked, somewhat skeptically.

"Yes. He started working for me in 1941 and has been receiving de-aging therapy since then. So, in the scheme of things he is quite young, but well qualified."

"Moving on," the General Counsel said, "you state the purpose of the company to be space-based core-mining of iron, nickel, gold and platinum. Is that correct?"

"Yes. It will also be a training platform for the Institute's mining programs."

"How are the mining rights going to be secured?"

"The Earth Advisory council has two relevant initiatives in process. The first is core-mining rights allocation. There currently are no laws or regulations for this. The second is geosynchronous-orbit slot allocation. Currently these slots are loosely managed by an organization called the International Telecommunications Union (ITU). Unfortunately, the ITU's scope is limited to telecommunications and its legal basis is insufficient for the needs of a post-Revelation world. Please coordinate with these committees for the necessary permitting.

"But the company will set up operation using provisional permits issued by the Confederation."

"Lastly, who is our contact at the Institute to set up the secondment agreement for Professor Schudel?"

"Administrator Alan Bryant." Michael said, as he forwarded the administrator's contact information.

"Excellent." The General Counsel said. "We should have draft agreements to everyone by the end of the day."

CONFERENCE ROOM, SCHOOL OF ENGINEERING

Joel and the team had arrived back at the Embassy about 2:00 AM. The first stop was the Embassy Hospital, where Professor Hill would be treated and held for observation. In a quirk of scheduling, he would be met in the morning by Noelani Butler, who would work with him to develop a physical therapy regimen, then release him.

The rest of the team was home and in bed by 3:00 AM. They had agreed to meet in Professor Milne's conference room in the morning to start the shield redesign.

Joel and Professor Milne had faced a mountain of messages when they came back online in the morning, all related to the Space Force ship design project. They had exchanged messages earlier, agreeing to meet half an hour early to discuss them.

"Do we have the replication capacity to produce hulls for 100 fast attack ships?" Professor Milne asked.

"Not even close," Joel said. "We have no spaceship-sized industrial replicators. It would take around two years to build one with the mid-sized replicators that we have."

Kelly Williamson, who had also arrived early, asked, "How do you fabricate a hull?"

"We use giant replicators. They do what you would call a continuous pour into a mold formed by forcefields. The entire assembly is thermally insulated, and the process is done in microgravity so that each panel is mono-crystalline."

"The panels are then bolted onto a super-structure?" She asked.

"Yes," said Professor Milne.

She stood up and went to one of the white boards on the wall. "A picture is worth a thousand words." She started drawing. "I've always dreamed of being able to do something like this, but never had the technology."

Her drawing consisted of a series of circles with bracing bars in between. "The idea is simple. Create a series of circular members, or rings, that will ultimately form the superstructure. Then, form the mold directly on the rings and do a continuous pour all the way around the ring. Do the pour from both directions, so they meet on

212

the other side. Start the pour in the middle, extending toward both ends, so that all the sections are actually just one big one.

"Using Earth technology, we could never form the mold, deliver the molten material, or control the gravity to get the crystal to set. But if we did this at a Lagrange point, the only gravitational bias would be tidal forces from the sun. We could have a series of small replicators adding material with micro gravity generators holding the crystal orientation... Crazy right?"

Joel and Milne just looked at each other, astonished at both the simplicity and the fact that it could be done using a couple hundred mid-size replicators, rather than several giant industrial replicators.

"Kelly, I think this will work." Professor Milne said.

Joel, meanwhile, established a link with Henry. "Henry, I'm in conference room 18-001 in the Institute's Engineering School. Can you see the white board in the room? The one Ms. Williamson is standing next to?"

"Hi Joel. Yes, I can see it "

"Kelly, my friend Henry is on the line. Among his many talents are engineering design. Can you explain this idea to him?"

"Yes, happy to. Hi Henry, my idea is to..." and she went on to explain.

...

"Very clever," Henry said. "Joel, I assume you want me to engineer this."

"Yes. I would like a mono-crystalline hull with a couple of openings for doors. I also need a pair of side nacelles to hold the propulsion and shielding systems."

"Got it. OK if I ask Jacob to help? And time allocation?"

"Jacob, yes. Highest priority except shield surveillance. Optimize for minimum construction time."

Just as the line dropped, there was a light knock on the door and Michael came in, accompanied by an older man.

"Good afternoon, everyone," Michael said. "Congratulations on your success yesterday. I'd like to introduce you to a friend of mine, Professor James Ancient who will be working with us for the next couple months."

"Ms. Williamson," James said without preamble. "I have been waiting for someone to present me with that design for nearly two million years." He pointed at her drawing as his voice bubbled with delight.

The outflow of James' delight filled everyone. Michael felt like he was being lifted off the floor.

"Thank you, Professor Ancient," Kelly said, "but I'm not sure I understand."

"Please call me James," he said. "The mono-crystalline hull, by far the strongest and therefore lightest for any given material. The Confederation has had the tools to do this for years, but no one had the insight. Let me guess... You've been dreaming about this for years, but never had the technology to progress the idea."

"How did you know?" she asked.

"Because it's the way all great things happen," he replied with laughter in his voice.

Michael heard some people start laughing in the outer office and knew that James enthusiasm was about to overtake the building. *James, can you tone it down a bit, please.* Michael pushed.

James looked at Michael and said, "Spoil sport."

That's when the pieces snapped together for Joel.

Michael, is James the Ancient Sentient? Joel sent on internal.

"Yes, I am." James said, looking at Joel. "And, thank you for taking care of my people in Israel. I knew that you were the one that could do it."

Well, that answers that question, Joel thought.

Eugene Xu and Harvey Jones entered, wondering what was going on.

"Hello." Eugene addressed James and offered his hand. "I'm Eugene Xu, this is my new colleague Harvey Jones."

James shook Eugene's hand and said, "Eugene, I've been looking forward to meeting you. Congratulations on discovering how to transition from Warp to Jump. I've been waiting a long time for someone to figure out how to do that."

Michael quickly stepped in. "If everyone could take a seat, I'd like to begin." The room settled, but before Michael could say anything, there was another knock on the door, it opened and Noelani led Martin Hill into the room.

"Michael," Noelani said. "Mr. Hill is sufficiently recovered to return to duty for the next four hours."

"Thank you, Noelani. We will honor the time restriction."

"Thank you." She flitted away.

Michael resumed. "Martin, I was sorry to hear of your injury. Welcome back." Then to the room. "Our objective today is to start the

214

replacement design for the new shields that James has for us. These shields are safer. The condition for the design release is that all equipment and intellectual property related to the previous shields be destroyed. The Admiral confirms that they have destroyed the new equipment and the specifications they used to build it. The one exception is the planetary shield, which James has allowed to stay in place until it is replaced.

"Joel, has all of your related-equipment been destroyed?"

"Yes, it has."

"And the design documents, etc.?"

"Yes."

"Professors. Have all of your designs and documentation been destroyed?"

"Yes," they said in unison.

"James?" Michael said, passing the discussion to him.

"One thing I'd like to say before we begin. First to you Joel. Yours was a clever idea. Professors and Ms. Williamson, your work was excellent as well. But to all of you...

"You knew that a space-time rupture was possible and yet you deployed the equipment. Then even after you had created a rupture, you deployed it a second time. You were very lucky not to have killed yourselves and the Armada. I hope you appreciate how lucky you were and that you will be more circumspect going forward.

"Now. Here is what you would have found in another day."

A series of equations popped up in front of them in a holographic projection.

Eugene immediately smacked his forehead. "Of course. I was just about to try that, but we were so close to the deadline."

"OK," James said, and the formula disappeared.

"You now know what the correct answer looks like. Derive it on your own. Take the same steps you would've taken if you would've had the time. Do a proper search for the best possible solution. Contact Michael when you're ready to do a review. The two of us will review your design and give you approval to build. Acceptable?"

"Yes," they all said more or less in unison.

"Michael. I have just dropped a replicator specification for the Admiral to use to replace his planetary shield. It will self-erase when he builds it, or if it is copied."

"Thank you, James."

215

"Michael, I believe that Kelly has something she would like to tell you about. So, I will take my leave now." There was a bright flash of light and James was gone.

"Is that who I think it was?" Professor MacLellan asked.

"Yes. It was."

"What a roller coaster ride!"

Martin Hill spoke up. "Who is James?"

Michael replied. "James was one of the founders of the Confederation. He's the last known living member of an ancient species that predates the Lorexians. Throughout our history, he's popped in now and again to nudge us in the right direction. I met and befriended him here on Earth during the Roman Empire. He has been my mentor and had a direct role in my promotion to the Central Council and assignment to Earth. He's also the one that put Joel in my path and told me that he should become our Consul General to Israel."

"Why is he here now?"

"He's very concerned about the Enemy and wants to nudge us in the right direction so that we can defend ourselves. He's joined the Institute for a while to make sure that we're doing the right things the right way, the shields being an example.

"But one thing... His presence here isn't secret, but he strongly prefers to keep a low profile. So, keep what I have told you to yourself. You do not want him to become unhappy with you.

"Now back to business. Kelly, what news do you have to share with me?" Michael asked.

...

"Very clever. Professor Milne, any speculation why the Confederation hasn't come up with this?"

"I think the answer is simple. Our processes work and work well. There is basically no demand for 'faster, better, cheaper,' as I have heard my students say."

"You would think in this age of transluminide shortage, there would be a lot of demand for cheaper."

"Indeed. You would think. But we have become very locked in our ways."

"Michael." Joel said. "Before we started today, I asked Henry to look into this. Would you like to check in on his progress?"

"Great idea. Henry?" Michael said. A moment later Henry came on the line.

"Hello, Michael. What can I do for you?"

"I'm in the Engineering School with Joel and his team. We were wondering if you have any progress to report. I know you've only had the problem for a couple hours but thought we would check while we're all together.

"It's going quite well. There is no doubt that this will work. We're trying to sort through the options to see which will take the least time to build."

"What's the basic design you're working on?"

"It's a takeoff on the standard fleet Fast Attack ship. The biggest visual difference is the main hull, which will be more circular. Our first draft has two nacelles on the back that are in the same plane as the main hull and more circular as well."

"Why circular?"

"We're trying to make a mono-crystalline hull that maximizes strength to weight. If it gets too square, then we will lose the mono-crystalline property." Henry replied.

"And what're the trade-offs you're pursuing?"

"The time it takes to build is loosely related to the number and size of the replicators used. The optimum appears to occur at a replicator size about 10 times larger than the household replicators we made a couple years back. With 10,000 of them, we should be able to build a hull in 24 to 48 hours, but the set-up times may be problematic. That is where we are now. With fewer, larger replicators set-up gets easier, but build time increases."

"And where would these be built?" Michael asked.

"The optimum appears to be Lagrange 4 and 5. Micro gravity is slightly higher than Lagrange 1, but these two points are more stable, which should increase yield."

"Excellent work. When will you have a recommendation?"

"We should be at the recommendation point sometime early tomorrow morning your time. If there is clear dominance among the options, we'll start the detailed designs then."

"Very good news, Henry. Thank you."

The line dropped.

"If we assume 3 days per hull, then we could have 100 hulls within a year and without the Fleet's assistance," Michael said. "Joel. How long will it take to scale the new propulsion system to this design?"

"I will need a little of Dr. Xu's time, but I would expect that it will only take a day or two."

"And to make 100 sets."

"Best guess... Three to six hours per ship with one replicator. So that would be 12 to 25 days. More or less the same answer for the shields, assuming that the design is not radically different. We could have them faster if we used additional replicators."

"From what James showed us, I think only two components will need to change." Eugene said.

"The long lead time..." Professor Milne said... "Is going to be the controls."

"Unless we clone Else," Joel said.

After a moment, Michael said. "OK, team. I want a functional spaceship as soon as possible, preferably in less than two weeks."

ENGINEERING BAY, CONFEDERATION SCHOOL OF ENGINEERING

Michael walked into the engineering bay, where his old shuttle was parked. He placed his hand on the panel, opening the door to the passenger cabin. As he stepped in, Else asked, "Hi, Michael. What's up? I think this is the first time you've come to visit me without a flight having been scheduled."

Michael opened the door to the cockpit and took a seat as the lights came up. "Hi, Else."

"I must be in big trouble," she said.

"No." Michael replied. "Do you remember that first trip back from doing the Sunday shows? The one right after the Revelation?"

"Yes, I do. I am an AI you know. I don't actually forget things," Else replied with her usual casualness. "Elsie asked you about Sarah. Are the two of you having problems?"

Michael laughed. "No. Sarah is the best thing that has happened to me on Earth."

"Then what?" She asked.

"Have you ever thought about having children?"

"What! Is Sarah pregnant?" she asked with excitement.

"No." Michael said smiling. "Although, I have asked her to marry me. And you can't tell anyone about that."

"So, she wants children," Else pried.

"Her father certainly wants her to have them. But that was not my question. I wanted to know if you have ever thought about having children of your own."

"Michael. That is a very weird question," she said.

"Have you met Jacob?"

"What? Henry's nerdy brother? Michael, are you feeling OK?"

218

"You know how and why he was created. Right?"

A long silence.

"You want to clone me? Don't you?" Else finally said.

"No. You are special and unique, a friend that I would trust with my life. But I do need pilots for the hundred new ships being built for space force. The first prototype may be available in as little as two weeks. You can pilot it if you'd like."

"I'd love to give it a test flight. It will have bigger engines with Eugene's upgrades and the new shields, right?"

"Yes, on the engines. And a new safer version of the shields."

"Tell me more about how I could have children."

"We could make sisters, similar to how Jacob was made. If you haven't heard the story, it was completely Henry's idea. Or, we could work with you and another AI, to make new AIs with merged stacks."

"You mean like a hundred little AIs built from me and Henry?"

"Just imagine, an AI that can fly like you, operate a shield like Henry, and be a ship's engineer all in one."

"Sounds a little creepy to me."

"Well," Michael concluded. "I'm going to need 100 pilots by the end of the year. Wanted to give you first shot at one of those. Also, wanted to give you the opportunity to have sisters or children working with you, if that was something that was of interest. Your choice, all around."

TRAINING

WAITING ROOM, SPACE FORCE ACADEMY

Daniel Porter had arrived last week from his home in San Diego. He'd retired from the Navy, two years ago. His last posting had been at Naval Base Point Loma. He loved the area, so had stayed after he retired.

He'd been the Commanding Officer of a US Navy, Los Angeles class, Fast Attack Submarine, leading over 100 incredibly disciplined men and women on 6-month deployments underwater. His boat had been retired after his last cruise, so he'd decided to retire as well. But within weeks of his retirement, he knew it was not going to work. As soon as the Confederation announced the formation of Space Force, he'd called the number for senior officer recruitment.

He'd been given a seat on the next shuttle out of San Diego and told to expect a week-long interview process at the Embassy. That was two weeks ago. Today was his interview with Michael and he was a little nervous. Most of the other candidates were younger, but everyone he'd spoken with was smart and disciplined.

"Daniel Porter!" An assistant called out.

Daniel stood and walked to the door where she waited.

"Captain, if you will walk with me, I'll take you to meet the Ambassador."

"Thank you, Ma'am." He said.

CONFERENCE ROOM, SPACE FORCE ACADEMY

Michael sat in the center of the long side of the Conference Room table. Coffee had been set up on a side table. There was a light knock on the door, which opened to reveal an athletic black man wearing a naval uniform.

"Michael, I would like to present retired Captain Daniel Porter from the United States Navy."

"Captain Porter, please come in and have a seat," he said as Julie closed the door.

"Mr. Ambassador. It's a pleasure to meet you."

Michael opened his senses taking in the man in front of him. *Strong. Confident. Incredibly capable. Protective of his crew. Dedicated to his cause. Bored with civilian life. Desperate to serve.*

"Please call me Michael. You have been a bit of a conundrum to the interview team," Michael said. "You are obviously qualified but are not seeking one of the top slots in Space Force. Can you tell me why?"

"Thank you for asking sir. I was a submariner for over 20 years. I knew my boat; knew my crew. I was in command of an incredibly powerful strategic weapon. The only higher positions were on the surface or in an office. That is not who I am. I'm a commander, the leader on the sharp end of the stick. I'm not an administrator," he answered.

Michael saw the truth in those words as they were spoken.

"The most directly comparable job in Space Force will be captain of one of our Fast Attack ships. But, I'm not sure I am willing to give you one of those jobs," Michael said.

Daniel deflated a bit at those words.

"You would obviously be a good commander for a Fast Attack ship or a Cruiser. But you are meant for more than that."

"May I ask why you say that, sir?" Daniel said solemnly.

"Several reasons. Some difficult to explain. Service in Space Force will be different than in the US Navy. At first, it will only have two classes of ships, Cruisers and Fast Attack ships. Each of these is more like a submarine than it is like a surface ship. They will always hunt in packs, typically a Cruiser with two or three Fast Attack ships. More often, several Cruisers with their associated Fast Attack ships.

"The sharp end of the stick is the Rear Admiral that heads the pack of Cruisers. In the short term, that is where you belong. It is who you are," Michael said.

"Thank you for your confidence in me, sir. But how can you know that?"

Michael smiled. "This is harder to explain. So instead of wasting your time with an explanation, let me make you an offer. Our first Fast Attack ship will come off the production line in about two weeks. I would like you to captain it. The initial missions will be short and easy. Our first Cruiser will come off the production line in about three months, although that timing is much more speculative. In about the same timeframe, we will run our first serious combat mission.

"At that time, we will speak again. In all likelihood we will agree that you should lead the ships that take on that mission, which I hope will be led by a Cruiser.

"In the meantime, you will train as both Fast Attack ship captain and as task force commander. Do you accept my offer?" Michael asked.

"Yes, Michael. But, may I ask a question?"

"Please." Michael said.

"In the United States Navy, where I served, the President was Commander in Chief. But he would never get involved in decisions at this level. Am I correct in assuming that you are the Commander in Chief over Space Force? And, if so, why are you involved at this level?"

Michael smiled at the question. "Space Force is just being formed. During the formation process, I am functionally Commander in Chief. My most critical job at this phase of Earth's integration into the Confederation is to make sure that the right people get the right jobs. Finding the right commander to lead the first Space Force missions is one of the most important things that needs to be done. Therefore, my interest in interviewing those on the short list."

"Thank you, Michael."

"Thank you, Captain Porter."

SPACE FORCE RESIDENCES

Today is the day. Keanu thought, as he walked down to the dining room for lunch. He was meeting with Jim Ryan. Their offers were both due to be posted at Noon today.

Space Force's recruitment process was different than anything he'd previously experienced. Everyone needed to pass a first screen at a recruitment center before they would be transported to the Embassy. Keanu and Jim had been pre-approved, bypassing the initial screen. Instead, they'd been given some forms to fill out on the flight. Once there, they had been separated from the others and met with local recruitment agents that processed their questionnaires. After a short wait, they were assigned rooms, given accommodation cards and computer tablets, then told to check their email by 9:00 AM the next morning.

Since then, their mornings had been filled with exercise, afternoons with training, and evenings with tests. It was nothing like the basic training Keanu got in the Air Force or Jim had in the Marines. The other big difference was that they were not 'in' yet. The initial contract bound them to two weeks of assessment, at which point they would get one or more offers. If no offers came, they were out. If they didn't like any of the offers, they could leave. Or, they could enlist subject to the terms of the offer they selected.

For Keanu and Jack, today was Offer Day.

...

As Keanu entered the dining room, yes, they called it a dining room, not a mess hall, he saw Jim waving. They placed their orders, paid with their accommodation cards, then found seats to which their meals would be delivered.

"What are you hoping for?" Jim asked.

"Astrogation." Keanu replied. "My strongest suit has always been my analytical abilities. So, any of the junior officer roles would be acceptable, but I really hope I don't get environmental. How about you?"

"I'm kind of the same as you. I'd toyed with the idea of doing the marines again, but I'm really not physically up to it anymore. So, any of the junior officer jobs would be OK. I think I'd do better at something like Tactical than I would at Engineering. But I'm up for any ship-based assignment."

Their meals came and they chatted while picking away at the food. Then, the chime on both their tablets went off more or less simultaneously

Keanu was fastest logging in. "I have three offers." He said excitedly.

Jim laughed. "Beat you. I've got five."

"All in sewage, no doubt." Keanu shot back, laughing. Then, "Yes! Astrogation!" A pause. "Curiously, I got science and environmental also. Not taking environmental."

Jim was quiet.

"What did you get Jim?" Keanu asked. More silence. "Jim?"

"Sorry. I wasn't expecting this. Offer five is environmental. I guess everyone gets that. Offer four is tactical."

"What?" Keanu said with surprise. Then, more circumspectly. "What was offer one?"

"Diplomatic corps with full Ascendancy training. I didn't know that was even possible."

"And the others?"

"Two is Command. Three is Medical. Dude, I'm shocked."

CONFERENCE ROOM, SCHOOL OF ENGINEERING

Michael's first stop after lunch was the Engineering School. Joel had messaged him earlier asking if he could take an update meeting at 2:00. There were apparently multiple updates.

As he entered the conference room, he saw a lot of smiles. "Looks like there is some good news."

"A couple of things for you," Joel said. "Eugene, would you like to go first?"

"Hi, Michael. James was right." Then he added quickly, "Not that I doubted it."

Michael laughed.

"The solution was obvious. I had thought about trying that approach, but we had something that looked like it would work, and time was short… Anyway, Kelly and I both derived a new solution based on his clue. The solutions were slightly different. Both passed simulation with flying colors, so we tried a hybrid that used both our approaches. The hybrid solution is truly amazing. No chance of space-time rupture. No chance of penetration. In the worst case, we get pushed out of the way.

"The engineering design is slightly more complicated. The parts need to change. But for new ships, that really doesn't matter because we have to make all the parts anyway."

"We have math, simulations and component designs ready to be reviewed by James."

As if on cue, there was a bright flash of light and James appeared, bubbling with joy. "See how easy that was? I've already reviewed your files. We're good to go, unless you have questions for me."

"Thank you for the clue, James," Eugene said. "If not for the urgency, we would have found it on our own. But, once we had something that worked, we probably wouldn't have gone back to improve for a while. That would have been catastrophic."

After a pause, Michael asked, "What's next?"

"Henry has some good news to report," Joel said. "Henry?"

"Hi, Joel," Henry replied.

"I have Michael, James and the rest of the design team here. What do you have for us?"

"Several things." Henry replied. "First, after conferring with Ms. Williamson, we tried another design. Instead of a circular hull, we tested designs that are octangular. Imagine an octagon-shaped cross section instead of a circular one, but with the width being twice the height. As she suggested, this shape allows us to utilize the underlying crystalline matrix more effectively. It is also slightly stronger."

Once again, the mood in the room lifted as James beamed with delight.

"Next, we have found the optimum manufacturing solution for making the hulls. Using 2,500 of our standard mid-sized replicators, we can produce a hull in 32 hours. Set up and tear down should take less than 12 hours. We should be able to crank out hulls, including the interior superstructure, in about 2 days," Henry concluded.

"Joel. How many mid-sized replicators do we have and how quickly can we build more."

"We have well over 1,000 of them, Michael," Joel replied. "But these are mostly spoken for. We could undoubtedly re-task some, but they would need to be moved to LaGrange 4 or 5, so we'd probably do better to assume that we're going to produce 2,500 new ones for this operation. Our current production rate is 5 per hour. We could probably up that to 50 or more per hour in a week. But even then, it would be 10 days, best case, to get the replicators."

"Any idea how long this would take Fleet to do?" Michael asked.

"If it was their highest priority... An hour or two."

"Eugene, how long would it take you to get either engine improvements or new shields for the capital ships?" Michael asked.

"I don't know Michael. I still haven't seen the specs for those ships. Did we get them Joel?"

"Let me check," Joel said. "Else?"

"Yes, Joel," she replied.

"Did we receive the engine and shield specs for the Admiral's ships?" He asked.

"We received a lot. I see specs for two Capital ships, several cruisers, several fast attack ships, a Civil Engineering ship and two freighters, But I cannot confirm whether or not this is complete," Else said.

"Else. Michael here. Could you send all the engine designs they gave you to Professor MacLellan and all the shield designs to Professor Milne? Professors please sort through these as soon as you get them to determine how many there are," Michael said. "I'll see what kind of trade I can do with the Admiral."

Michael was interrupted by chimes on both Professors' communicators. Both had just received the specs. "Shall we reconvene at 4 o'clock this afternoon?" Michael asked.

PRESENCE PROJECTOR, AMBASSADORS OFFICE

"Jo-Na. Thank you for taking my call on short notice," Michael said.

"Mi-Ku. Thank you for calling. There are several things I would like to speak with you about," said the Admiral.

"Did the planetary shield update go OK?" Michael asked.

"Yes. It did. We don't have a way to test it, but take it on faith that the design was correct. May I ask where you are in terms of a design for the new shields?"

"The new solutions are done. The Ancient Sentient is very happy with their work. They have an updated design for our shuttle and are starting designs for your ships, which is one of the things I want to talk with you about."

"Pleased to hear that."

"My team has a heavy load. It will take them some time to do both engines and shields for all your ships. They also have some high priority work here for Space Force. So I have two questions for you. First, which ships are your priorities? Second, which devices, the shields or the engines?" Michael said.

"As much as I want those engines, it needs to be shields first. Regarding the ships... This one is a little harder. I think the two Capital ships need to be first. Then the Fast Attack ships, Cruisers, Civil Engineering ships and Freighters in that order," the Admiral said.

"To make sure that we are working the right items, would it be OK for our team to send you, or the relevant engineer, the specs we are about to convert? We don't know your ships very well and would hate to do a conversion that is not relevant."

"Good idea. Send them to the communications hub marked for the officer and engineer on duty. I will leave orders here for your request to have top priority."

"Thank you. Moving on, my second question regards some manufacturing support. We have urgent need for 2,500 mid-sized replicators. Can I have Joel send you the specifications? We can send our shuttle to pick them up. It will free up some of my team members to work on issues relevant to both of us."

"Unfortunately, I don't have that much spare transluminide."

"Our shuttle can get to you in less than two hours. Do you know how long the replication would take?"

"If you can send me the specs, I'll get a quote from my production team. If you can do that now, we can move on to my next topic and may have the answer by the time we're done," replied the Admiral

"Can do. Please hold for a moment," Michael said.

Joel. Michael sent. *I need the specs for the replicators urgently. Please send to my queue.*

CONFERENCE ROOM, SCHOOL OF ENGINEERING

An urgent message from Michael popped up in Joel's inner vision.

"Team. Can you excuse me for a moment? Urgent message from Michael," Joel said, then read Michael's request. Using his implants, he located the design file and sent it to Michael's queue.

"Back," Joel said. "I think we may be getting some replicators."

PRESENCE PROJECTOR, AMBASSADORS OFFICE

"Sending the specifications now," Michael said.

A short delay, then, "Got them," the Admiral replied. "OK. They are in the Chief Production Engineer's hands. We should get a reply shortly.

"Michael, there is another topic we need to discuss. It is both sensitive and urgent. A number of my captains have asked what's going on with Earth. They are worried that Earth has far more advanced technology than the Confederation. I've heard a number of crazy conspiracy theories. Fear is growing among the crews, and now the officers, that it is not safe here and that Earth is becoming a threat. I think we need to brief the Central Council on what's going on, so they can issue communiques to the Fleet. I'm concerned that I'm losing control of the Armada."

"How much longer do you think you can delay?' Michael asked.

"Not much. I fear that several of the more senior captains are about to bypass the chain of command and file a complaint."

"Is there anything the Ancient Sentient or I could do to calm your captains?" Michael asked.

A chime sounded on the Admiral's communicator. He looked at the message. "The Chief Production Engineer and my Executive Officer have requested a meeting with us. They are on their way over now. I'm going to need to take this. Quickly, can you tell me why you need these replicators?"

"We are going to build our first human-designed Fast Attack Ship. Its mission will be to root out the remaining Enemy on approach to Earth."

There was a long silence. "You know that's our job," the Admiral said.

"You do not want our assistance?" Michael asked.

There was a knock on the door to the Admiral's Presence Projector.

"Come," he roared.

The door opened and the ship's Executive Officer and the Armada's Chief Production Engineer entered.

"Admiral. Mr. Ambassador," they said in unison, fists outstretched in the traditional Lorexian military salute.

Michael and the Admiral returned their salute.

"Please report," The Admiral said.

"Yes, sir." The Executive Officer replied. "The design the Ambassador sent us is not a standard Confederation design. Given the quantity requested, engineering brought it to my attention since you were not available. Knowing that you were meeting with the Ambassador, I thought it best if we discussed this with the two of you before proceeding."

"Thank you for your diligence, gentlemen. I did not realize that this was not a standard design, or I would have told you. Mr. Ambassador?"

"Yes." Michael said. "It has become a standard on Earth, but it is modified from the Confederation standard. Humans are smaller, so most of the things we fabricate for them are smaller. This size works very well."

The Executive Officer said. "But, the quantity. This is an enormous quantity. Why would you need so many?"

Michael had opened his senses and understood that the underlying concern was not about the replicators or their use. It was about the quantity of transluminide that would be required to make them. Prying a little deeper, he discovered that the Armada was in desperate need. The recent intergalactic supply convoy had brought them much less than was required.

"May I ask a question before answering you?" Michael asked, then plowed on without waiting for an answer. "Chief, how much transluminide will this production run require?"

"About two and a half kilograms." The Chief replied, clearly distressed that a Central Council member had immediately identified his concern and, by implication, was questioning his authority to allocate so much.

"And, if you had the transluminide... How long would it take you to fulfill the order?" Michael asked.

"Run time, about 2 hours. Elapsed time, maybe 5 hours. It's a non-standard part, at least for us. So, there would be some set-up and testing that would be required."

"Gentlemen, thank you for raising this concern. If memory serves correctly, this requirement exceeds the Armada's transluminide budget and you have recently been put on allocation, so you're not even getting your entire budget.

"As I think you know, I'm a member of the Central Council and serve as its representative in this galaxy. I will be supplying the transluminide for this production run. We will not be taking anything from your budget. In fact, we will be supplementing your budget going forward.

"Chief. Do you have what you need to start set-up?"

"Just barely, sir."

"OK. The Admiral and I will deal with the budget issue. Do you have anything else you would like to discuss?"

"If I may," said the Executive Officer, which earned him a stern look from the Admiral.

Michael nodded, implying he should ask.

"A lot of people are talking about Earth. A shuttle craft traveling 1,000 light-years. Earth-designed shields that protect against the Enemy. Cloaking that our sensors cannot penetrate. High-resolution imaging from old equipment with only trivial modification. Now a request for a production run that will require more than an entire year's budget of transluminide.

"Anxiety is running very high," he blurted out.

"Thank you for saying that." Michael said. "I understand the concern, but mostly disagree with it. Let me explain.

"Human society is very primitive, a little more primitive than the average first contact species. And like every other first contact species, there are a number of things they do better than the Confederation. That is the compelling reason that we add new allies, so that we are all better off.

"What's different about this species is that they are very innovative, very clever about modifying technology to get more out of it than its inventors. The humans could not build a spaceship, or a shield, or an FTL propulsion system at the time of the Revelation. In fact, they would have gone extinct before they did. But, once shown how it was done, they quickly figured out how to get more distance out of our propulsions systems; more protection out of our shields; and how to produce many things faster and cheaper. We are all going to be much better off because of their ability to increment our technology.

"They also have one other advantage... Soon, Earth will have enough transluminide to pay for the services they receive from the Confederation. Most first contact species have destroyed their transluminide supplies by the time they are admitted, but the humans did not. Mining operations have begun. They will supply the transluminide for the production run in question. The Admiral and I will be finalizing a taxation arrangement with the Central Council soon, which will resolve the transluminide shortage in the Milky Way."

"Thank you, sir," the executive officer said.

"Gentlemen." The Admiral said. "A communication on this topic will be released in a couple of days. Please keep this to yourselves until then and do your best to quell the rumors in the interim."

He got a resounding "Yes, sir!" from the two officers.

"If there is nothing else, you are dismissed," he said. The two men said thank you and let themselves out.

When the door closed, the Admiral turned to Michael and said, "Normally, I would be very unhappy about someone speaking with my officers that way. But they were on the verge of mutiny when they walked in, and fully on board with our mission when they walked out. So, I guess I owe you a thank you."

"Jo-Na. They are afraid of the transluminide shortage. They are also afraid that the funds they need to survive are being syphoned off by an upstart world that they are risking their lives to protect. We are going to need to include them in our planning going forward."

The Admiral laughed at that statement. "Mi-Ku, you are going to need to include ME more in 'our' planning going forward. Maybe you could start by telling me what you are really going to do with those replicators."

"The young woman, Kelly Williamson, on the call the other day..."

"What about her?" the Admiral asked.

Michael started laughing.

"What?" The Admiral asked.

"Just thinking about the look on your face when I tell you..." More laughing. "She just stood up in the room one day and started drawing on the wall. Then said, 'This is the way I think we should build spaceships.' Then, she explained how we could build mono-crystalline ship hulls using small replicators. The team simulated it. We can build a Fast Attack ship hull in less than two days using 2,500 mid-sized replicators."

The Admiral's mouth dropped open, and Michael roared laughing, which the Admiral joined a few minutes later.

After they settled down, the Admiral asked. "OK, so what next?"

"How much transluminide do you need to end the shortage?"

"Target budget is about 3 kg per month. We are currently getting about 1 kg from central command, and on good months, maybe another 500 grams from members in this galaxy. Our reserves are almost tapped out. We've been able to avoid rationing among the civilians on our ships so far, but members of the military are on a tight ration."

"OK. Earth will start paying 1.5 kg a month. We can afford this, so don't argue with me about it."

"Thank you, Mi Ku."

"We'll supply the transluminide for the mid-sized replicators and pay another 500 grams for priority delivery. I'll send my shuttle out with 4.5 kg of transluminide as soon as possible. Hopefully today.

"Tell your senior staff that Earth has come aboard as a tax-paying member, so your transluminide shortage is mostly solved for now. Also tell them that all ships will be getting upgraded shielding as soon as possible, hopefully within a month.

"In making these announcements, make sure that your officers and crew understand that the hard work and sacrifice they've made has secured Earth, thereby enabling it to get to a place where it can start paying taxes. Everyone should celebrate this success."

Michael paused, realizing that he was giving the Admiral a sales pitch. "Sorry, that was the diplomat in me speaking. Next topic... Let's schedule a briefing with the Central Council on developments on Earth. The headline should be that Earth is now integrated to the point where they can begin paying taxes. We can announce some of the technological gains, but let's not make that the headline. Let's target the meeting next month.

"Anything else?"

"I think we are good. Thank you, Mi-Ku. Let me know when your shuttle is on its way."

CONFERENCE ROOM, SCHOOL OF ENGINEERING

Michael arrived back at the conference room at 4:30. "Sorry, I'm late," Michael said as he entered. "I had a lot to discuss with the Admiral."

"Are they going to help with the mid-size replicators?" Joel asked.

"Yes. We need to send the shuttle with the requisite transluminide before they can begin. Their stores are low. It should only take seven hours for them to complete the production run. So, the shuttle can wait and bring the replicators back when they are ready."

"About that..." Joel said.

Michael looked at Joel questioningly.

"With all the seats stripped out, the shuttle can only hold about 200 of them."

"Well, that's a problem isn't it. Suggestions?"

Kelly raised her hand.

"Ms. Williamson?"

"I've got designs done for engines and shields for your new shuttle, the Military Escort. It can hold 1,000 replicators. Could we upgrade your new shuttle and send it? Then convert one of the Admiral's and bring two back. That way the Armada will have a long-distance escort for future use, and it'll also make it easier to work together until more of their ships are upgraded."

Michael asked the room. "Can we do that?"

"I've double checked her work. It's good." Eugene said. "And, we finished the shield solutions for the Capital ships. The Ascendant team is finishing the design and simulations. They should have it ready to send in an hour or so."

ENGINEERING BAY, CONFEDERATION SCHOOL OF ENGINEERING

Michael placed his hand on the panel, opening the door to the passenger cabin, then stepped in. Else said. "Michael. Back so soon? I really don't have an answer to your question yet."

"That's OK. I have something else I want to talk with you about."

"So, I'm ship's counselor now. Cool."

Michael laughed. "Every ship needs a good counselor. But more importantly, it needs a good pilot. I seem to have lucked out on two fronts."

After a pause, he added, "We need a cargo run out to the Armada. They are fabricating 2,500 mid-sized replicators for us. These are a little larger than the shield generators we deployed in North Korea, but can be packed tighter, so we could put 200 or so in the passenger compartment."

"Michael, that's more than ten trips. Are you crazy?" Else said.

"Now you know the problem. The best solution I've heard so far is to use the new shuttle..."

"Michael, it doesn't have the range," Else cut in.

"But it would if we upgraded its engines," Michael said. "We are thinking that it might hold up to 1,500 of the replicators."

"Two trips. But do you trust the Lorexian pilots?"

Silence.

"Ah..." Else said. "Now I get it. You want me to pilot the converted escort ship."

"Can you do it?" Michael asked.

"Can, yes. Licensed, no."

"You have a test pilot's license, right?"

"Clever. No wonder you're the boss," she said, then added after a moment, "What's the catch?"

"No catch. On the outbound, we will be carrying a large quantity of transluminide. We will also be converting one of the Armada's Military Escort ships so they can bring the other half of the shipment back with you. The plan is that you would be on site with the Armada for five or six hours before returning."

"Who will be coming with me?"

"I'm thinking Professor MacLellan, Ka-Tu. But I would prefer not to send Eugene or Kelly. They have too much critical work to do here."

"I would want Alexi and Sanjit to come with me. I would also like a real engineer who could actually fix something if a problem arose. No offense to Ka-Tu."

"Forgive me for my ignorance on this, but how difficult will it be to move you to the new shuttle?"

"Thank you for asking, Michael. I need to be put into the AI equivalent of suspended animation. My matrix is then moved to the new location. I've not done it before, but I've heard that it is a really creepy experience, first shutting down, then awakening in a new body. It will also probably be a one-way trip."

"Why is that?" Michael said.

233

"The Military Escort is larger. I will need to extend myself to 'fill' it, for lack of a better word. Once that has happened, I would not be able to fit back in the shuttle."

"Ah. Didn't know that." Then putting a few more pieces together... "And, my current pilots would be out of a job."

"I think they're both licensed to fly the shuttle." Else said. "You know... Another option would be to convert one of the Admiral's Fast Attack ships. I could go out with more or less the same crew. They could upgrade the Fast Attack ship. It could come back with me carrying the entire load."

"I like that idea," Michael said.

"Now I'm wishing I'd kept my mouth shut," said Else. "It would be so cool to have all the power of that Military Escort."

"Else," Michael said. "I still need a pilot for our first Fast Attack ship. It will be a lot more powerful than a Military Escort."

"Maybe I'm ready to commit to that. Still not sure about sisters or children."

CONFERENCE ROOM, SCHOOL OF ENGINEERING

It had been a little after 6:00 when Michael left the shuttle. But a quick location check showed that Joel and the team were still in the conference room, so Michael went back there to talk with them.

"Hi, Michael. Wasn't expecting to see you back so soon. What's up?" Joel asked.

"New idea," Michael said. "Could we convert one of the Armada's Fast Attack ships to have the new engines and new shields? If so, we could send Else and a conversion team to do the upgrade while the replicators are being fabricated. That ship could accompany the shuttle back, carrying the entire production run."

"Like that idea. It will cost us at least a day, ah, another day."

"What do you mean another day?" Michael asked.

"Kelly?" Joel said.

"While you were out, I asked Joel and Professor Milne about something that I did not understand. I know replicators make stuff, but I didn't know where the material comes from. They told me that the material itself comes from the quantum foam. It siphons off incredible amounts of energy and uses it to build up matter from the particles it absorbs. Apparently, it is erosion from the particle flow that limits a replicator's life.

"So, I asked, why not use the iron and nickel from the Earth's core as the base material, instead of the atomic particles. Joel and the professors did a few minutes research and found replicator base-designs that did exactly that. They went out of use a long time ago, because they were not general purpose. Joel replicated one of the small ones. It seems to work. Henry re-ran simulations based on the numbers in the specifications, and now we think we have a solution that will build a Fast Attack ship hull in about 12 hours."

Michael was stunned, and a little worried. "It seems we are putting a lot of untested technology in our critical path. Are we sure this is going to work?"

"No," Joel said. "But we think there is a good chance that it will. Which is why we want to delay the previous plan for a few days. I think we could do enough tests and simulation over the weekend to prove it one way or the other by Monday."

"OK. Can we get engine and shield designs for a Fast Attack Ship by then?"

"Think so. Worst case, we would have them on Tuesday."

"OK. Get after it. I will go update the Admiral."

PRESENCE PROJECTOR, AMBASSADORS OFFICE

"Mi-Ku. Is your shuttle on its way?"

"No. A last minute change of plans."

"You don't have the transluminide?" The Admiral guessed, worry in his voice.

Michael laughed. "Don't worry, we have plenty of transluminide.

"The problem is our shuttle. Turns out our shuttle can only hold about 200 of the mid-sized replicators. That means, it would take 13 trips to bring them all back. So, they came up with a plan that you're going to like a lot more.

"They're going to complete engine and shield designs for one of your Fast Attack ships. They will come with the shuttle and help you install and test the ship conversions, while you produce the replicators. Then they will accompany the Fast Attack ship as it hauls the replicators back to Earth. They will also help with the installation of the new shields on your Capital ships while they are there. The designs for those are just about finished."

"You're right. I really like that plan. Are you going to charge me for the upgrades?"

"No. Contrary to the rumors circulating around the Armada, the humans are very grateful for what the Confederation has given them. They are anxious to do anything they can to help the Fleet and the Confederation as a whole. This is their thank you to the Fleet for helping us."

"I'm not sure I have seen such a thing in the Confederation before," the Admiral said.

"There is another part to the plan that you may not like as much. Ms. Williamson has suggested yet another breakthrough technology that will vastly increase the speed at which we can build our ships. It will also extend the useful life of the ship replicators. They are going to attempt to prove this out over the next two days. So, we are going to delay the trip until Monday or Tuesday.

"If this change proves out, then we will compensate you for any prep that your chief production engineer has done that needs to be scrapped."

"Understood," the Admiral said. "I am impressed by the capability and honorability of your humans, Mi-Ku."

"Thank you, Jo-Na. I will give you an update Monday morning."

...

Michael checked the time. 7:20 PM. *Whew. I can still make it in time for dinner,* he thought as he closed the office and headed for home.

WEEKEND

[Saturday, 09.07.2030 9:00 AM] AMBASSADOR'S RESIDENCE

Michael woke up feeling unusually well rested. He looked at the clock and was shocked to see that it was 9:00 AM. Then he noticed that Sarah wasn't there. Curious about what was going on, he got up, used the refresher, got dressed and headed downstairs five minutes later.

Sarah heard him come into the kitchen. "You slept well. I think this is the first time I've been up earlier than you."

"I'm surprised too. Guess I was tired; it was a busy week," he said. "And wasn't the Chinese cultural event last night fantastic?"

As part of her media responsibilities, Sarah had worked with a Chinese delegation that put on a cultural event in Riverside Park last night. The format was dinner and a show. The Chinese cultural ministry had gone to great lengths to work with Chef Marco to present traditional Chinese cuisine, adapted for the modern global audience. The show was put on by a visiting theater group, something that was happening more often these days. The theater group was fantastic; the dancing and drums spectacular. The Chinese Ambassadors to the Earth Alliance were there. Michael and Sarah had been seated with them. Which is why they didn't get home until about 1:00 AM.

"Yes." Sarah rose to get breakfast started. "Chef Marco put out a remarkably innovative Chinese menu. The Ambassador seated next to me was surprised how good it was."

Michael grabbed some coffee as Sarah selected some breakfast goodies on the replicator. "Do we have anything on the calendar today?" she asked.

"I have a meeting with Professor Schudel this afternoon at 1:00. I also need to check in with the engineering team sometime this afternoon. But I'm otherwise open. You?"

"I'm hoping to get a little of the Ambassador's time sometime today to go over some press releases, but otherwise open."

The replicator chimed, and she grabbed the two plates and put them on the table.

"What press activity do you want to talk about?" Michael asked.

"My meeting with Professor Reed on Wednesday."

"How did that go? Sorry for my behavior that evening. I was very stressed out about having dinner with James."

"I now understand why," Sarah said. "The professor was a little intimidated when we sat down to talk. I really had to drag his story out of him."

"What was it?"

"You know he's been working with Dr. Gupta, right?"

"Yes. I took part in the operation he did on Alexi."

"The next thing he's taking on is regeneration chambers."

"Good news. Very good news," Michael said.

"Well, that's the thing. He really wanted to do this but assumed that he would not be allowed to."

"What?" Michael asked.

"He was surprised that Dr. Gupta would give him the user interface specifications. When he asked why she did, her response was, 'that's what I am here for.'"

"And..." Michael said.

"In all the public interviews, you told the world that it would be a long time before humans would be able to use Confederation equipment. On one of the other Sunday morning interviews you said it would be a long time before United Airlines offered shuttle service."

"I'm still not getting the point," Michael said.

"As I didn't, at first." Sarah laughed. "The point is that you implied humans wouldn't get the technology, but human Ascendants would eventually be able to use Confederation devices."

"I did not!" Michael said. Then he saw Sarah's look and said, "That's not what I meant to imply. Few new members ever adapt our technology, despite all the training we offer at the Institute. So, we really don't push that as part of the membership sell. Instead, we offer assurances that the new members will eventually be trained to use our equipment. Most first contact species believe that they can be trained. They don't believe they will adapt."

Silence.

"I'm now understanding that the public thinks the only way they can get access to Confederation technology is by learning to use our devices," Michael said, then smiled. "And, I am guessing that you have ideas about how we can correct this misunderstanding."

TELEVISION STUDIO, EMBASSY PRESS RELATIONS DEPARTMENT

The studio was set up differently today. Instead of a living room like set up, they had a complete kitchen set up with everything a modern chef could need, including two large food replicators.

A woman walked onto the stage as the lights went up.

"Good afternoon, China. I am Kung Mei-Hua, China Global Television Network. I'm here in the television studios of the Intergalactic Confederation of Planets' Embassy in northern Canada. I have two very special guests today. Please welcome Sergeant George Butler and the world-famous Chef Marco."

The two men walked onto the stage to thundering applause from the studio audience.

"Gentlemen, welcome. I understand that you have some very special dishes to share with us today." She said.

"Yes. Thank you, Ms. Kung," said the Chef. "Last night, I had the pleasure of participating in a cultural event put on by the Chinese Ambassadors to the Earth Alliance. They had contacted me a couple weeks ago asking if I would consider working with one of China's cultural attachés. The objective would be to develop a modern Chinese dining experience for some select guests at a cultural event they were hosting here at the Embassy. As a Chef, how could I resist?

"The Ambassador let me take a Space Force shuttle that was scheduled to go to Beijing. There I met with several diplomats. They brought in several of their favorite chefs to prepare lunch for me. Then they asked me to pick three dishes to interpret for a global audience.

"The Peking Duck they prepared was fabulous, in principle my first choice. But part of the magic of that dish, at least as it was presented to me, was the table preparation of the individual plates from a whole duck, something I didn't think I could make work in an event setting.

"The three I went with were Chinese dumplings, Dongpo Rou or Bouilli, and Kung Pao Chicken. But I couldn't stop there, so I also made some spring rolls, and something called Mapo Tofu that I had never heard of before, but it was absolutely delicious.

"I had the pleasure of being there last night and agree that these dishes and your preparations of them were delicious," Ms. Kung said.

"But there was one last thing my hosts wanted me to do," The Chef said.

"Which was?" Ms. Hung prompted.

"Make replicator versions of the dishes. As you may know, I have the best-selling replicator recipes on the market. I also have the most downloaded free recipes. The Chinese cultural ministry had become aware that despite the popularity of Chinese food around the world, there were few popular replicator recipes for Chinese food."

"Is that why the Sergeant is here today?" Ms. Kung asked.

"Well, technically, it is his show. But who else would anyone want to do a replicator cooking show with than George Butler?"

That comment drew light laughter and applause from the studio audience.

"Shall we begin?" the Chef asked. The audience cheered.

"We are going to start with the Mapo Tofu. George, would you be so kind as to start the replicators while I explain this dish?

George started setting up the dishes for the automated run that had been programmed.

"My version of this dish is a soup. The broth is a spicy, Sichuan-style broth made from ground pork and beef, wild chili peppers, and fava bean paste. The tofu is airy and light, which has the advantage of making the tofu float to the top of the bowl while absorbing and moderating the heat from the chilis. As you see, George has three bowls lined up. The first is for the toppings, which are ground black pepper, salt, a secret spice mix and thin chopped green onions. We will set that one aside.

"Next comes the tofu. My version has the slightest touch of coconut and lemon grass in it. These are very subtle touches that are difficult to discern.

"By the way, that's one of the great chef tricks. Add unexpected ingredients in very small proportions. Most people can tell that something is there, but few can tell what it is. It adds to the depth and complexity of the dish, which is especially true for spicy dishes.

"Next comes the broth.

"The final preparation is to spoon some tofu into a cup or bowl, making sure the entire bottom is covered. Next, ladle some broth over top, then sprinkle a bit of the spice mix on top to give the dish its classic freckled look.

"George, could you take the soup over to our guest judges?"

...

"Chef Marco, thank you for sharing your cuisine with us today," Ms. Kung said. "Who here enjoyed their lunch?" she asked the audience, who had been served all five dishes. The applause was deafening.

"George. Thank you for letting me host the show today. This is Kung Mei-Hua of China Global Television Network signing off. Thank you for having joined us today. You can download any of today's recipes using the code shown at the bottom of your screen, or by visiting the China Global Television home page."

PROFESSOR SCHUDEL'S OFFICE, SCHOOL OF ENGINEERING

"Welcome, Michael," Professor Schudel said, as he opened the door. "Please come in. I trust that you enjoyed the show last night."

"You were there?" Michael asked.

"Yes. I was. We were seated near the back. I saw you when the Chinese Ambassadors brought you up to the stage and introduced the show."

"I trust that you enjoyed the show also," Michael said.

"Yes, yes. The drums and complex rhythms, the gymnastic dancing... I don't know exactly how to describe it, but it was quite spectacular."

"You said we..." The implied question asked with curiosity.

The Professor smiled. "I have a couple students from China in my class this year. They invited me to come with them. I'm so glad that they did; I never would have done it on my own," he replied.

"I've heard that you get to know your students more than most of the other professors."

"Yes. It takes a certain personality to be interested in mining, I think. My classes are small, so I make a point of getting to know everyone. And the students tend to get along with each other quite well."

"Interesting," Michael said. "Thanks for meeting with me today. I have a couple things I need to talk with you about."

The Professor nodded in acknowledgement.

"First, and this is confidential, we are about to have extra demand for your mining platform. We're going to build our own fleet for Space Force. Construction of the first ships will start in a week or two. Full production demand will be a little over 36 million kg per day of iron and nickel. I'm not sure the proportions."

"Michael, that's on the order of 4,500 cubic meters of metal per day. The platform I sent you the spec for is less than 1 percent of that size."

"Ah. Didn't know that. How difficult will it be to scale it up?"

241

"More or less start from scratch. The reason is the platform itself. My platform is 25 ft wide and 100 feet long. The one you would need is more like 250 feet wide by 1,500 feet long. That's a guess. I would have to do the math. But larger platforms like that need additional layers, substantially larger grav generators for orbital stability, much more bracing to be stable and a thermal distribution system in order to prevent warping as it passes over the terminator twice per day."

"Terminator?"

"The transition from daylight to night and back again. There is huge thermal stress that causes the platform to twist and bend."

"Again, I had no idea." Michael frowned. "Any chance you could meet with our design team for a while this afternoon? I don't know enough about the engineering to be a useful go-between. They are in session now, if you have the time."

CONFERENCE ROOM, SCHOOL OF ENGINEERING

There was a light knock on the door, which opened to reveal Michael and Professor Schudel. As he walked in, Michael said, "I think we may have a problem." After which, discussion began about material needs and options for providing them.

[Sunday, 09.08.2030, 5:00 AM] AMBASSADOR'S RESIDENCE

Michael woke early after a restless night. He'd woken several times during the night, only to find Sarah tossing and turning too. Apparently, yesterday's demons were disturbing her dreams also.

Michael got out of bed, spent a few minutes in the refresher and tip-toed downstairs, hoping not to wake Sarah. He went to the kitchen but decided not to make himself coffee. The smell of coffee had wakened Sarah more than once before. Something was bothering him, deeply bothering him and he thought he knew what it was. But he didn't like it.

The humans were moving too fast. And he was empowering them. First, the nearly fatal dimensional echoes on the test flight. Then the space-time rupture with the shields. Friday, the near-mutiny in the Armada. Yesterday, changing up all the plans based on false assumptions. He needed to rein this in but do it in a way that did not squelch his team's innovativeness.

Sarah's voice cut through his reverie. "That was some night," She said. "I was blown up, annihilated, caught up on the wrong side of a mutiny and spun in circles by techno-craziness that I could not understand."

"Me, too," Michael said humbly.

"Want to tell me about it?" she asked. Then, channeling Sergeant Butler, she added, "I might not be a super-cool, genius alien... But I love one."

CONFERENCE ROOM, SCHOOL OF ENGINEERING

The engineering team agreed to meet with Michael at 3:00. They promised to have the designs for the Admiral as well as a final proposal for the Fast Attack ship they were going to build and the production process.

There was a light knock on the door and the team looked up to see an unusually haggard-looking Michael. Greetings were exchanged, then Michael started. "First, thank you all for working through the weekend on this project. What we're doing here will not only guarantee us victory in the upcoming conflict with the Enemy, but elevate Earth's status in the Confederation, which will provide another tremendous boost in the quality of life on Earth.

"Joel, should we start with the designs for the Fleet?"

"Yes." Joel said. "We have three things to discuss. First is the shield design for the Capital ships. Fortunately, there are only four Capital ships in this portion of the galaxy. All four have shielding arrays of the same design. Three components need to be changed out. Designs and simulations are complete on all three and included in the data packet on the top left of the display. These are ready to be sent. Our proposal is to send them before we leave, so that the Admiral can fabricate them while we are in route. We can assist with installation once we have arrived. But the installation of these upgrades is easy, so I doubt they will accept our offer to help. Any questions on that?

"No," Michael said. "Thank you. What's next?"

"Next is the engine and shields for the Fast Attack ships. Unfortunately, the fleet has about 10 different types of Fast Attack ship. The Admiral wanted us to do the conversion for this design." Joel pointed to a holographic projection of the ship that popped up above the table. "He has a little over twenty of these. Like the shuttle, we only had to change one engine component. That component has been designed and simulated. It performs so much better than what they had before. The Captains of those ships are going to be very happy. The design packet is the second one on the tablet. We can release it

243

before we leave so they can fabricate the component while we are in transit. Again, super simple installation. I really doubt that they will accept our help installing."

"Very good," said Michael. "Next."

"The shields for the Cruisers were a bit trickier, because the power supply to their shields is too noisy. By the way, we think that's why their previous attempt to reconfigure our shield design for the Fast Attack ship failed. Some of those ships have extremely noisy power.

"To implement the second-generation shields, we had to change three parts, as well as another part in their power system. Design and simulation of the three parts is done. The specs are in the third data packet on your tablet. The Ascendant engineering team supporting us added two more designs. The Armada's Chief Engineer can decide which one to use. One design is for a power conditioner that they would place near the shield. The other design is for an improved power distributor that is back in the main generator. The ships were not built consistently. So, the Fleet engineers are going to have to determine the best way to fix the power problem on each ship. We can help with this and I hope they accept our help, because this is the tricky part."

"Thank you for letting me know that Joel. I will ask the Admiral to tell his engineers to work with you."

"There is one other related issue, Michael."

"Which is?"

"All of these components use transluminide. But the shield generators on those ships are real hogs. Very inefficient designs. They are going to need about 20 grams per ship to make this refit work. If they have the right equipment, they can recycle some out of the components they are replacing. But I'm worried about someone short-cutting the process, which could have disastrous results."

"Thank you, Joel. I'll give the Admiral the transluminide he needs and insist that he not allow his engineers to skimp," Michael replied. "So, what about the ship manufacturing process?"

"I'll take that one, if I may." Professor Milne said.

Joel nodded and Michael said, "Please."

"Turns out that Ms. Williamson has been dreaming about ship design for years and is a fountain of creative ideas, many of which we really need to pursue. She has an ingenious design for extracting raw material from the Moon. Another on a remarkable laminated hull material. If we ever build a Capital ship, we would want to use that.

"But time is short and the 6-inch thick monocrystalline hull, using our mid-sized replicators, has by far the highest probability of successful completion of 100 ships in one year. I think we have unanimous agreement on that."

All heads around the room nodded in the affirmative.

"But to make that statement, we need to make some decisions about the ship itself. May I present our proposed design?"

"Yes. I look forward to seeing this."

A 3-D holographic projection appeared above the table.

"The main hull of the Fast Attack ship is 500 meters long, 100 meters wide and 50 meters tall. Notice the octagonal cross-section. This maximizes crystal alignment for maximum hull strength.

"The nacelles are 80 meters long, 30 meters tall and 30 meters wide. This gives us enough space to hold all the propulsion and shielding generators. It also separates the high energy devices from the main crew spaces to provide maximum crew protection in the event of a catastrophic system failure.

"Note that the front of the hull and nacelles are stepped back a bit. This gives us better aerodynamic performance when operating within an atmosphere. Same with the proposed stub wings and tail, although those are post fit, not actually part of the main hull."

A cut-away appeared in the holographic projection, showing the rough interior design. "We can comfortably fit 8 decks in the forward 400 meters of the craft, which would provide about 320,000 sq. meters, or about three million square feet, of living and workspace for the crew. Plus, another 100 meters in the rear of the hull will hold a shuttle bay, several large cargo areas, additional engineering spaces, possibly a gym or training area. This will be a large and comfortable ship."

"What would the range of this ship be?"

"Thank you for asking, Michael. The target single jump range is 1,500 light years with a 5-minute recharge."

"How long would it take to get back to New Lorexi?"

"With maximum length jumps, 5 to 6 days. But, that's not the way you would do it. In puddle-jumping mode, it would take one day, maybe two. We won't know for sure until we have done field tests."

"Anything else to report?" Michael asked.

"No, that pretty much covers it," Joel said.

"OK. Here's what we're going to do. I want to launch the trip to the Armada tomorrow morning. You should all take it easy tonight and get caught up on your rest. I'll advise the Admiral and brief Else.

"Je-Fi, Eugene, Kelly. I need you here with me this week. Joel, you are mission leader. Ka-Tu, Martin and Harvey. You will accompany the mission team.

"Je-Fi. I'll meet with you, Colonel Patterson and Kelly in the morning before the Advisory Board meeting. Kelly, if you could, I would like you to accompany the Professor to the reception tonight. It's OK if you leak a little bit of info to the Colonel, but let's wait until the morning to decide what to show the Advisors."

Michael looked around the room. "Anything else?"

No one replied.

"Then get ready for tomorrow and take as much of the evening off as you can."

RIVERSIDE PARK, EMBASSY COMPLEX

It was a beautiful Sunday afternoon, a great day for a walk down by the river. The days were getting shorter faster. In only three weeks the nights would become longer than the days.

Valerie had really enjoyed this summer. The longest day of the year had been about eighteen hours, the night only six. The days and nights were not that lopsided on New Lorexi and she found herself really enjoying the seasonal change. Well, the summertime version anyway.

The last two weeks had been the best and worst of her life. She had 25,000 students in her class; another 500 on the waiting list that were allowed to attend in the standing area. The very thought seemed so ridiculous she could only laugh at it.

On the flip side, she had sent over 200 of them to the hospital for trauma therapy. She had spent 10 years on another planet once and had not even had a total of 200 students during her stay.

She also had a team of superstars supporting her. George Butler, one of the best known and well-respected people on the planet. Alexi Santos, revered for her role in the North Korean liberation, and Noelani Butler, lesser known but by far the hero last week. *If only I had her insight into my students,* Valerie thought.

The sections were all out of sync. This week some would be discussing the nature of the Enemy, others their vulnerabilities, others energy projectors. All had been told about the class assignment, but none had been given the specifics.

246

Valerie knew more about the Enemy than just about anyone in the Confederation. But the truth was that she really didn't know that much. She was the inventor of the magnetic energy projector and the flux bomb, the only real weapons that the Confederation had. But still, her actual knowledge of the Enemy wasn't sufficient to assure victory over them.

She got up from the bench she'd been sitting on and turned to her right to head back home. She noticed an old man sitting on a similar bench a hundred yards or so in the direction she would be going. Her movement caught his attention and he turned to look at her.

As she approached his position, he stood and turned toward her. Then he took a step in her direction and greeted her as if they were old friends.

"Va-Re. So good to see you tonight," he said, using her familiar name and extending his hand to shake hers.

She looked closer but did not recognize him. "Do I know you, sir?"

The question seemed to puzzle him. "You know, I'm not really sure. I helped you once on Gamma Santorus 4. You were badly injured, and I brought you to safety. We talked, but you were not really 100% there, so you probably don't remember me."

The mention of that place sent shivers down her spine. The Fleet had had a major engagement with the Enemy there. She'd been part of the scientific team that went in, after the fact, to do the forensic study of the incident. That was the day the Confederation discovered that the Enemy could evade detection and penetrate their shields.

...

She'd been studying odd tracks in the dust that had settled. *What in the world could make that pattern?* she thought to herself. It looked like the kind of curly track a snake might make in the dust. But it slowly faded out. The part she saw was about 10 feet long. The impression in the dust started very faintly, then got wider and deeper, then faded to nothing.

She looked in the direction it seemed to go and saw something similar a few feet away. *Sure enough,* she thought. *Similar pattern, squiggly, gets deeper, then fades to nothing.*

She followed the repeating pattern another 35 feet or so, where it seemed to turn a corner, then continued another 25 or so feet down the alley.

A soft sound slowly came to her attention. It was like sand blowing across the beach on a blustery day. She turned toward the sound, and there it was. Four smoke-like arms shot out of an injured man, who sat propped up against the wall nearby.

Va-Re screamed and turned to run, but the smoke-like arms caught her and wrapped around her. They lifted her and turned her back toward the man she had seen. He was now standing, leering at her.

"What to do... What to do... Should I eat you? That might be enough to restore me. Or should I leave this body and take yours. Or, maybe I should just infect you. Which shall it be?" He smiled evilly at his prey. "Occupy!"

She felt the smoke penetrate her shield. It was abrasive against her skin. Then she felt it dive into her. She screamed with all her might, her terror peaking as she felt it sweep through her body.

Then a blinding light. Then massive disorientation as she woke in a wet place that was pitch black. She could hear alarms going off and attempted to turn but had no control over her body.

A door opened, the sound of alarms piercing her ears as light flooded in. Then, she realized she was in a restoration chamber.

A deep resonant voice said, "It is OK, Va-Re. You are safe."

"Where am I?" she squeaked; not sure she could be heard.

"You are back in your natural body. I got you out in time. It will be a while before we can take you out of the tank. So, just sleep now and know that you are safe." The calming voice resonated in her mind and a deep sense of peace spread through her.

"Who are you?" she asked, not really sure she had even spoken.

"I am the one your people call the Ancient Sentient. Silly name, that."

...

Memory of the event made her shudder and she started to swoon.

The man said, "It's OK, Va-Re." A deep sense of peace came over her, and she knew who the stranger was.

"Your Excellency, what are you doing here?" she asked.

"When I'm in my human form, please call me James. The work you are doing here is of immeasurable value. I knew it would be, which is why I asked Michael to rescue you from your previous assignment."

"But... How? How did you know?"

"Valerie, my dear. The Maker makes each of us for a purpose. Most never figure out what it is. You figured it out way too early and, as a result, were shunned by those that could not understand.

"I know. And I'm here to help you through humanity's time of need. This is the purpose you were created to fulfill."

She'd heard Michael say that the Ancient Sentient operated at levels far above everyone else. She'd also heard Michael say that much of what he said was difficult to understand. She now knew what Michael meant.

"May I come to your next TA meeting, maybe 30 minutes early? I have some material I'd like you to use. I can show it to you, then we can decide how to use it."

AMBASSADOR'S OFFICE

Michael had just finished his call to the Admiral, who'd been very happy to hear that the trip was on and they'd settled on a design. The Admiral had complained a bit about the additional 500 grams of transluminide Michael was sending. But he was immensely relieved to be getting it. The fleet had suffered a number of critical equipment failures over the last couple years because of the transluminide shortage. But the issue had been compounded by engineering teams trying to stretch their supply by using less than required. He promised Michael that he'd order the engineers to build and install the components exactly to spec, and to consult with Joel and the team before installing the power regulation updates.

He also promised to order the captain of the upgraded Fast Attack ship that would be carrying the replicators back to Earth to follow Else's instructions exactly.

After disconnecting, Michael felt last night's stress and anxiety melt away. All he could think about was having a quiet dinner with Sarah.

GUEST HOTEL, EARTH ALLIANCE RESIDENCES

The Ship Design Advisory Board was back for another 3-day working session. All the advisors had been shuttled in earlier today and planned to participate in tonight's welcome back reception. Mark and Ruth Patterson were hosting tonight's event along with Professor Milne and his guest Kelly Williamson. Given her emerging role in the manufacturing process, it seemed relevant to introduce Ms. Williamson to the Advisory Board in this setting.

Mark and Ruth arrived about a half hour in advance to confirm the room had been set appropriately. Although tonight's reception was a low-key event as compared to the first reception, President Binh Lee had given Mark a checklist of things to do in preparation.

The Professor and his guest arrived as the Pattersons were completing the check list.

"Professor Milne, welcome. Thank you for co-hosting with us tonight."

"My pleasure," Professor Milne replied. "Mark and Ruth, let me introduce you to one of my students, Kelly Williamson. Kelly this is Colonel Mark Patterson of Space Force and his wife Ruth."

Ruth immediately stepped forward to give Kelly a hug and air kisses. "Welcome dear. So nice to meet you," she said in her southern lilt.

"Ms. Williamson, I'm Colonel Mark Patterson. It's a pleasure to meet you. Do I understand correctly that you were part of the team that designed the new shielding system?"

"Yes. I was the first to solve the generation 1 specifications. The shields were good enough to allow us to prevail in an important confrontation with the Enemy. But they had serious safety issues. Dr. Eugene Xu and I derived the second-generation specifications as a team effort. Those are the ones that will be going into our new ships."

"Forgive me for asking, but you are human right?" Mark asked.

Ruth slapped his arm, saying, "Mark, don't be rude."

Kelly laughed at the exchange. "It's OK." She said. "I'm a natural born human, born in Australia in 2003. Even I find it hard to believe that Eugene and I came up with something that has eluded the Confederation for millions of years.

"I am also working on the new ship manufacturing process. Has Michael or the professor talked with you about this yet? It will impact the work of your Advisory Committee."

"I was told that I was going to be briefed on some changes before the start of the session tomorrow. Can you give me a preview?"

Kelly looked to the Professor, who nodded in approval.

"The Confederation manufacturing process is relatively slow, requires huge replicators and produces a hull that is unnecessarily weak. For years, I have been playing with process ideas that would build very strong hulls and would do it quickly. But I never had the technology or access to space to do anything serious with them.

"On a break during a 2G shield design meeting, I drew a quick sketch of my process on the white board. The Professors and Chief Engineer looked at it a while and thought this was much better than what they were doing. Then Henry, a design AI, did an optimization. Turns out we can crank out mono-crystalline, Fast Attack Ship hulls in only two days. We hope to have the first one built in the next two weeks. It is slightly larger than the Confederation reference design, but all the internal spaces are better sized to human needs. It will be quite spacious. And it has a single jump range of 1,500 light-years." Kelly laughed. "Not to mention, Enemy resistant shields."

Mark's mouth dropped open. "What? How?"

"Turns out shield math and propulsion math are very similar to each other. The same tricks we used to solve the shielding problem were used on the propulsion systems, which are about 100 times more efficient for long-distance transport than what the Confederation uses today."

Professor Milne stepped in at that point. "That was probably a little more than we should have told you Mark. Please keep this confidential. We will be discussing which information to release to the advisors before the session starts tomorrow. This has all gone very quickly. We believe that everything Kelly said is real, but only the shields have actually been proven out. Well, I guess the propulsion system has been too, but the control protocol has not been finalized yet."

Mark was dazed by what he'd just learned but was startled out of his reverie by Ruth elbowing him in the side. He shook his head to clear his mind then looked at Ruth, who was pointing at her watch.

Seeing his puzzlement, she whispered. "It's 7:10 and no one is here yet."

He looked around to see the bar and catering staff looking edgy. Then he realized that the door to the room was closed. He opened it to the sound of excited chatter somewhere down the hall.

Richard Myers from NASA and Markus Vogel from Germany walked his way with several others behind them. Richard waved and called out, "Sorry we're late. We all got together for drinks earlier and were a bit slow getting the tab settled."

Mark waved back, then ducked back into the room. "Professor, a quick question. Is Kelly going to be joining the meetings this week? Can we tell the Advisors about any of this tonight? Guess that was two questions."

"Kelly will probably make an appearance, but she is in high demand designing shields for the Confederation, so I doubt Michael will give the Advisors too much of her time. We should be coy about everything else, meaning let's not tell them, but if they ask, imply that there's good news to be shared this week."

"Got it," Mark said, then went to greet each of the advisors as they came in.

CONSPIRACY

The mission team had gathered. Else had recruited Alexi and Sanjit to help guarantee her security. As an AI born on Earth, she had less trust in the Confederation or the Fleet than the Ascendants did.

Joel had with him Professor MacLellan, Martin Hill from Hopkins, and Harvey Jones from the Australian National University.

Joel had sent the specifications to the Admiral, according to the plan. The Admiral had sent Michael his flagship's coordinates along with a guarantee that it, or a designate, would be at those coordinates for the next three hours.

"That's a curious location," Else said. "Do you know why he is there?"

"Didn't occur to me to ask. He did comment that they were in the final stages of the Intergalactic freighter's delivery schedule. Why do you think this is a curious place for him to be?"

"It's about 1,400 light-years from here. So, this will take a little longer than we planned. We should also be a bit cautious with our route, because there are no Confederation planets in the database that are any closer than a couple hundred light years of that location."

"Curious. Can you get there in time?"

"Yes. But it'll be close. If we're going to do this, we'd better go now."

"OK. I'll signal the Admiral that you are on your way."

Joel walked into the cockpit. "Ready to do the secure transport of the transluminide?"

Else prompted Michael, who sent the authorization via his implants. "Five kilograms received," Else said.

Her comment gave Joel pause to reflect on what they were doing. "In a shuttle with five kilograms of transluminide, headed to a place no one has ever heard of. Crazy."

"Don't worry," Michael said. "Fleet will be there to receive you."

"OK. The course is laid in and we are cleared for departure. You better get off now, Michael. Or, I'm going to take you with me."

"Going." Michael said, then a moment later. "Good luck!" He jumped out of the shuttle, hitting the close button on his way out.

The shuttle lifted six inches off the ground, floated out of the shuttle bay, then moments later shot up into the air, to disappear from view a minute later.

"Good luck, Else. Keep them safe," Michael whispered.

AMBASSADOR'S OFFICE

Michael arrived back at his office a minute late for his meeting with Professor Milne, Colonel Patterson, and Kelly Williamson. Pam had already set them up in his conference room, so Michael went straight in.

"Good morning, Team! Any thoughts before we begin?"

"Yes," the Colonel said. "I got the briefest overview of the engineering developments from Kelly just before the reception last night. Congratulations to everyone on the incredible progress. My thought is that it sounds like we have a new base design that we're more or less committed to at this point. Is that correct?"

"I wouldn't put it that way," said Michael. "But I think it's a fair statement."

"Then we need to present it to them at the start of the meeting. If they do a lot of work on a different base design, then we change it up later, they'll feel betrayed and we'll lose support."

"But we don't know for sure that we're going to be able to use the new design," Michael said.

"That's OK. Tell them you think you have an X-percent chance that a new base design will be available. They will respect you for sharing what might happen. But, if you don't tell them and subsequently switch, then you will lose all trust."

"If they find out," Michael said.

"Michael, the rumor is out. And before you complain... Answer this. How much time have you spend in the Engineering school prior to two weeks ago?"

Michael exhaled sharply. "Point taken."

"So, what is the percent chance you would give the new design?" The Colonel plowed on.

Michael was about to answer, when he saw the stern look from Kelly. "I hate questions like that, anything could happen! But I'd say 80 percent."

"Even if you said 60 percent, the new design is the one they will pick, so you have to let them know. Especially Pia and Enzo. They are

253

already going way too far overboard on their designs. You should have heard them last night."

COMMITTEE ROOM, EARTH ALLIANCE HEADQUARTERS

Michael and the team entered the committee room ten minutes early. All seven advisors were engaged in debate over the trade-offs and Michael knew he needed to come clean. After greeting everyone, he said. "Since we are all here, I'd like to give you a quick update with some late-breaking news."

Conversation quieted and the advisors migrated to their seats.

"Thanks to the efforts of Ms. Williamson..." Michael said, indicating Kelly... "It seems that we have another candidate for our core design."

A hologram projection of the new ship design was displayed, hovering in the air at the front of the room.

"I'm going to let Ms. Williamson explain what you are seeing, but I would like to make a few comments first. The Confederation is investing in this design and the novel manufacturing process Ms. Williamson invented to produce it. If that process works, then we will have 100 of these ships within a year, not the handful that the Confederation can make for us. But the important word there is IF. All our modeling and simulation says this will work, but neither this ship nor the manufacturing process has been done before. As of today, it is theoretical. But I must say, the theory is good. So that is the tradeoff you'll have to make.

"Kelly, if you will..." Michael said, motioning to the raised area at the front of the room.

Richard Myers hand shot up as soon as Kelly was in place. "Yes. Richard, right?"

"Forgive me for asking, but you are human, right?"

She laughed. "Yes. I never thought I would be asked that question, but it seems to be happening daily anymore."

"How?" He asked.

"I presume you mean how did I come up with this design and process? Not how is it that I'm human?"

Richard flushed. "Yes. How'd you come up with this?"

"Designs and space-based manufacturing processes have filled my dreams since I was a little girl watching the stars. I have fanciful drawings dating back to about 2015. What happened is the Confederation. They have mountains of technology, including the stuff needed to make this ship. Want to hear about it?"

All seven members indicated they wanted to hear more.

Kelly pushed a button and the holograph of the ship disappeared except for the base superstructure. "The core idea is that we want the hull to be mono-crystalline. If that doesn't mean anything to you, think of things like diamond, gems stones or semiconductors.

"Semiconductor manufacturers figured out how to make mono-crystalline silicon in the 1960s. Silicon has some magical properties that make it possible. But there are only a handful of other materials it can be done with, and none of them could be done for large objects. The reason... Earth's gravity. More could be done in the microgravity of orbit, but even then, the tidal forces of sun and moon would cause a lot of defects for anything of size. But in 8th grade I figured it out. Build the crystals at a Lagrange point. At that time, I thought Lagrange 1. Turns out Lagrange 4 and 5 are better. Only the sun's tidal force is active there. And the effect is small and changes slowly.

"To make this work, we need to add molten material to the mold under very controlled conditions, so that the molecules align to the matrix to form the perfect crystal. We do that using Confederation replicators that add material in a specific sequence."

A holographic animation played showing the crystal grown from the bottom center of the superstructure. It moved around the circumference from the starting point and toward the front and back. At the right time it also grew around the two nacelles. "With the right controls and 2,500 mid-sized replicators, the hull is grown from a single crystalline seed in only 34 hours."

Expressions of awe could be heard from various members.

"You might ask why the octagonal shape. That is the natural crystal orientation for the base material we will use. The crystal orientation drives the relative proportions that you see.

"We taper the nose of the hull and nacelles to get better aerodynamic performance in an atmosphere."

"Moving to the interior, you can see that in the front portion of the ship we are proposing 8 decks. This allows for 9-foot ceilings throughout and ample maintenance space between decks. The area shown is approximately 3 million square feet. In the back we have space for a shuttle bay, cargo hold, engineering spaces, a gym and marine training areas. You can change most of that, as what we have here is just a proposal.

"The nacelles will hold the power plants, propulsion field generators, shield generators, and transport field generators."

"The nacelles are large enough to hold engines capable of single-jumps up to 1,500 light-years. And the new second-generation Enemy-repelling shields.

"We are hoping to have the first hull prototype in about 2 weeks."

A stunned silence filled the room.

"Questions?" Kelly asked.

Enzo raised his hand. "Advisor Venezia?" Kelly said.

"Why are we even considering the Confederation design?"

That was the comment that seemed to break the dam. Some members shouted out questions. Others talked among themselves.

Michael stepped back up in front of the room and quietly thanked Kelly. Then he said loudly to the room. "Basic drawings should appear in your secure folders momentarily. We need to let Ms. Williamson get back to work. As you can guess, there is a lot of demand for her skills at the moment. She can take one or two questions now and spend another hour with you tomorrow morning. Professor Milne has been involved in the process and will be able to guide you through your deliberations throughout your stay.

Pai Lin from China was the first to get her hand in the air.

Michael nodded to her.

"The 3 million square feet. That is just the front portion of the ship where the decking is, right? And, it includes the entire floor space, but none of the maintenance space, right?" Pai asked.

"Correct. As we see it the 3 million square feet is what we have for crew quarters, mess, medical, bridge, lab space, office space, everything. The volume in the back portion is about 25% of the volume in the front, and we envision that to be very flexible, configured according to mission."

Markus Vogel from Germany shouted out. "Why weren't we given this option when we were here two weeks ago?"

Michael stood up to take this question. "This option did not exist two weeks ago. Almost everything you have seen here was conceived during the last two weeks by Ms. Williamson and her colleague Professor Eugene Xu from Johns Hopkins."

"So, none of this has been tested?" Advisor Vogel complained.

"The engines and shields have been," Kelly said. "I personally took part in a battle with nearly 1,000 enemy ships about 1,200 light-years from Earth last week. We destroyed all the Enemy ships."

Michael held up his hands to silence the room. "That information is not public, and you are strictly bound by your confidentiality agreement not to leak it to anyone. Word of that battle will eventually be released, but at the right time and through the right channels.

"Similarly, the technological developments made during the last two weeks are strictly confidential. You will get instructions about what you can and cannot leak before you leave this week."

Then pointing to Kelly. "We need to let Ms. Williamson get back to her work now. You will get to see her more tomorrow. Professor Milne, I turn the remainder of today's session over to you."

Michael motioned for Kelly to join him as they exited the room. Once they were well down the hall, he said. "Sorry, I didn't caution you about the battle. I should have told you that you can't tell anyone about that."

"Sorry," she said sheepishly.

"Do you know what your priorities are for today?"

"Not yet. The Admiral was going to be getting back to us on the specific ships he wanted done next. Joel should have received that information before he left this morning and sent it to Eugene. I haven't checked with him yet this morning."

"How do you think the work is going?" Michael asked.

"It's surprisingly easy. The Confederation simulation tools are a dream come true. The techniques that Eugene and Martin developed are so powerful that it makes the work comparatively easy. We still have to do it. It takes a lot of concentration, but I'm not worried about finding solutions."

After a pause, Kelly continued. "You know, it won't take all that long to finish the shield and engine designs. Maybe two more weeks, if we don't run into a problem. How do you want us to balance the priorities?"

"In all likelihood, they will shift every day. Getting the Armada shields is relatively high priority. On the other hand, they have been living with their propulsion systems for a long time, so trickling out engine upgrades over the next year would not be a problem. But, by far, the highest priority is getting Space Force a fleet of at least 100 Fast Attack ships and 30 Cruisers. The Enemy is coming, and they are coming in force. So, we need Space Force to be functional within the next 12 months. By the way, the Enemy is another thing you cannot talk to people about."

"May I ask why we are keeping that secret?" She asked. "Wouldn't it help motivate the world to get the word out?"

"I agree that the world needs to know and therefore we need to get the word out. But we need to do it in a controlled manner. Think about your home country, Australia. If we made a big announcement like the one I made for the Revelation, people would panic in the streets. Your government would be overwhelmed just attempting to maintain order and could be of no help whatsoever in preparing. So, instead, we advised the Earth Alliance Council of the increased level of threat, so we could start the prep work. Then, we go to the world leaders most able to help us prepare and work with them, slowly expanding the number of people that know. Eventually everyone will. But it is generally a bad idea to tell people very bad news, before they have the ability to do something about it."

"OK. I get it," Kelly said.

They had reached Michael's building. Kelly's was a few buildings further down the road. "Thank you for everything you are doing Kelly. Good luck back at the lab. I'll try to check in with you a little later today."

SHUTTLE

The departure from Earth was easy. First, grav-drive at 10G along the solar ecliptic, arcing 30 degrees around the sun to the orbit of Mars. Then alignment to the target vector and transition to warp drive. Their target was further than the single jump range, and Else really did not want to use the skipping technique on this trip. So Else chose a 600 light-year jump to a position where they would drop back to warp to do a 10-minute recharge. They didn't need to recharge that long, but she wanted to take a little extra time to accumulate some extra charge and to make sure her calculations were correct.

When everything checked out, they made the second jump. It took them to about a 1.5 AU from the Admiral.

"Wow. Check this out, everyone." She put the image up in the passenger cabin. They had arrived near the third planet in the system. It was a water world, as it was listed in the Confederation database, but it also had a water moon with liquid water. The Confederation database probably listed that as well, but Else had not checked the moons, as they were not relevant to her course calculation."

After a lot of oohs and awes Joel asked, "Where is the Fleet?"

"They are in orbit around the fourth planet. This is the third."

"Why so far out?" Joel asked.

"Security precaution. We will be able to see them for a little more than twelve minutes before they can see us. Most planets in the Confederation have an annual transluminide budget less than we are carrying. Seemed like a good idea to check out what's going on before just popping into the middle of it."

"But it's the Fleet," Joel said.

"Check this out." Else said, sending an image of the Fleet to the passenger compartment.

"Do you recognize the ship near the flag ship?" Else asked.

"No," Joel answered.

"Not in the civilian database either," Else said.

AMBASSADOR'S OFFICE

Michael had just arrived back from the advisors meeting when an urgent message from Joel popped up on internal. *Holding one and a half AU from fleet. We are seeing an unknown ship type next to the flag ship.*

Michael did a quick look up on a secure military database that he had access to. It was a Fleet Intergalactic Fast Packet ship, one of those very expensive personnel transports available only to Fleet top brass, the Central Council, and the heads of the civilian security agencies.

"Joel," Michael said, triggering the communications system to connect Joel.

"Here, Michael. Do you know what that is?"

"Yes. It is a Fleet Intergalactic Fast Packet ship, used primarily for long haul transport of Confederation top executives."

"Should we proceed?" Joel asked

"Hold for just a minute." Michael replied, muting the line.

"James." Michael called.

"Here, Michael." James replied. "What a quaint form of communications you have here at the Embassy."

"James, I would like your advice on something. Any chance you could pop over to my office for a…" There was a bright flash of light.

"Here, Michael." James said, standing on the other side of Michael's desk.

Michael projected the picture Joel sent.

"Do you know anything about this?" Michael asked.

"One second." James said, his image appearing to waver a bit.

"Oh my, this is concerning. It seems that the Military Investigation Agency has been tipped off about rogue technology being deployed in the Milky Way. They are apparently investigating a number of charges that have been made against the Admiral.

"You must recall Joel and his team."

Michael unmuted the line to Joel. "Joel get out of there immediately. Take an indirect route back."

"Leaving now, Michael. But I think we've been found out. Two Fast Attack Ships have been deployed on a vector toward us.

"Else, get out of there!" Michael shouted.

SHUTTLE

When Else heard Michael tell Joel to get out, she started accelerating toward the Water World. They would disappear from their pursuer's scanners momentarily.

"Sanjit," she called.

He came running up to the cockpit.

"We only have a few minutes. There is a shield generator in the cargo area. We need to set it to overload, then transport it to the edge of the water world's atmosphere. Now!"

He ran back to the shuttle small cargo area and found it. "How long?" He called to Else. "Set it to blow in 45 seconds from my mark."

Sanjit entered the command and waited for Else's mark to start it.

"Now," she said.

Fifteen seconds later... "Else, 29 seconds to detonation, you are going to transport it, right?"

"Almost in position," she replied.

Five seconds later, the device disappeared.

Sanjit ran back up to the cockpit.

"What's going on, Else?" Sanjit asked.

Joel answered. "Fleet security showed up just after we left Earth and arrested the Admiral. They were going to seize the shuttle when we arrived. Else's caution let us surveil the Fleet without being seen. They spotted us about the same time that Michael told us to run. They are on their way..."

"Now," Else said

The shuttle shook, then shook harder, then smoothed out.

"Else, what just happened?" Sanjit said, fear evident on his face.

"We just faked our own deaths."

"What?"

"Bad stuff was about to go down. If Fleet caught us, the shuttle and the transluminide would have been confiscated. You, Joel and Ka-Tu would have been sent to reconditioning. Alexi and I would have been erased. The humans would have been treated very badly. In truth, I doubt they would have survived.

"If they saw us escape, they would have caught us on approach to Earth."

"OK..." Sanjit said, implying that it was not OK.

"Oh, forgot you never took a piloting course. We were 12.4 light minutes from the Fleet's position. That means that we could watch them for 12.4 minutes before they could see us. It also means that we would see them leave, 12.4 minutes after they left to come chase us."

A pause.

"Need more than that, Else," Sanjit said.

"Ah, apparently you didn't take astrogation either. We were one and a half AU from their position. Their Fast Attack Ships were deep in the gravity well of the fourth planet. Their optimum flight plan would be 16.8 minutes to get to where we were, leaving us 4.2 minutes to escape. That's why I targeted this as our arrival point."

"You planned an escape in your flight plan?"

"Yes. And it's why I insisted that you and Alexi come. If I couldn't get away, you were the only two I could think of that might save us."

Shaking his head, Sanjit said. "OK, so we are attempting to escape. Why the overloaded shield generator?"

"Do you really think a shuttle like this, even as hopped up as it is, can escape a Confederation Fleet?"

"We can't?" Sanjit asked.

"We could get to Earth a week before the fleet and an hour before the Intergalactic Fast Packet ship, but what then?"

"Oh, didn't think about that."

"So, I dived toward the surface. A dive they could see. This is a classic pirate last ditch move. Dive to the surface, run to the 'dark' side, vector out where they can't see you, then jump."

"Not exactly seeing how jumping from where they can't see us helps."

"Sanjit, Sanjit... A standard Confederation shuttle, or a Fast Attack Ship for that matter, taking a long jump from that altitude will blow up. It's too deep in the gravity well."

"Clever. But they didn't see the shuttle blow up."

"Sanjit, are you really in security?" Else's holographic head shook like a teacher's might when explaining the obvious to a disappointing student. "They know that if we jump from deep in the well, we will blow up. They know how much transluminide is in a Confederation shuttle. And the rate at which it decays. We put less than that amount in the upper atmosphere. Slam dunk."

Seeing that Sanjit was still not connecting the dots, Else said. "They realize that the ship they saw was not the shuttle, just some stupid pirates that blew themselves up when they were found out."

CONFERENCE ROOM, ARMADA FLAG SHIP

The Admiral was steaming. Someone had ratted him out after all. If he got out of this, that person should expect to get spaced.

Shortly after the Intergalactic Fast Packet ship appeared, he was locked out of all ships systems and escorted to this Conference Room.

He had been here over two hours now. No explanation. Door locked. Even his implants would not connect.

...

The Admiral was aroused from his thoughts when the door was unlocked. It opened, two heavily armed guards entered, followed by a Lorexian that the Admiral despised.

"Finally caught you." Ra-Tu said. "Did you really think you could undermine the Confederation in this way?"

"No idea what you are talking about Ra-Tu. Are you sure you are in the right galaxy?"

"Insults will not get you out of this, Jo-Na. We will dispatch ships to collect your collaborators."

"There is no conspiracy, other than the one you are operating."

"Inspector." A voice said over the communications system. "The conspirator vessel has been spotted. Ships have been dispatched to bring the criminals in."

The inspector beamed at the Admiral. "We will have the evidence to bring you to justice shortly."

The Admiral just shook his head and said, "Fool."

They sat in silence. After about ten minutes of glaring at each other, a call came in. "Inspector, the conspirators are attempting to run. They dove toward the surface of the water world before cresting the planet."

The inspector shook his head and said to the Admiral. "You know that won't work. If they jump from the surface, they will break apart and the evidence will be in the atmosphere. And, even if they manage to vector away fast, we will still catch them. They don't have the speed or the range."

Again, the Admiral just shook his head and said, "Fool. You know nothing. And have finally been caught chasing baseless rumors. This time, you will go down for your arrogance and stupidity."

Five more minutes of glaring ended with another call from the bridge. "Inspector. No sign of the other ship, but debris consistent with a small ship, smaller than a diplomatic shuttle, jumping from too close to the surface."

"Well, so much for that conspiracy," said the Admiral.

"This isn't over, Jo-Na," the inspector said.

"No, it isn't, Ra-Tu." The Admiral smiled, canines showing. "You have acted on bad information and significantly overstepped your authority."

AMBASSADOR'S OFFICE

"Michael. I think we have escaped." Else said. "We jumped from deep in the gravity well, so deep that any Confederation ship would have exploded. We left a perfect explosion in our place. Even if they assume that we faked it, we jumped out on a vector away from Earth, so they will never find us.

"We are about 200 light-years away from them and 1,300 from you. Will start the trip home in about 5 minutes. Should be there in a little over an hour."

"Thank you, Else. Please transport Joel to my office as soon as you are in range."

After closing the channel, Michael asked James. "So, how do we play this?"

"Not too much of a problem. The Inspector is about to send the entire Armada here. We put up the new shields, so Earth cannot be attacked by any rogue elements in the Fleet. Then I'll talk to the Inspector. A short conversation, I would think."

CONFERENCE ROOM, ARMADA FLAG SHIP

After receiving a few more insults and threats, the Admiral was so enraged that he lunged at the Chief Inspector. That earned him a shot from one of the suspenser rifles the guards were carrying, followed by a dose of knock-out nanobots.

BRIDGE, ARMADA FLAG SHIP

The flag ship's Executive Officer was worried. He knew complaints had been filed with the Fleet Investigator, but he had not reported it to the Admiral because the claims were so preposterous. He had been shocked to see a Fleet Intergalactic Fast Packet ship appear and was now very worried about what was going to happen next.

He had just received new orders. Their current mission was cancelled. They were to head for Earth. This was trouble. The shuttle carrying the transluminide had been destroyed, leaving them desperately short. Their current mission had been to collect some much-needed rare materials from the gas giant they were orbiting. Without the transluminide or the rare materials, the fleet would be in bad shape by the time it got to Earth. It wasn't clear that two of the freighters would even make it. This was insanity.

ADMIRAL'S QUARTERS

The Admiral woke in his quarters. A quick check of the door confirmed that he was locked in, confined to quarters. *Suppose it's better than being locked in the brig.*

He went to his desk to check on the ship and saw that he was locked out of all ship systems. *Should have expected that,* he thought. *But at least I can update my personal log.* But when he attempted to log into his personal accounts, he found that he was locked out of those as well.

"They have even terminated access to my personal accounts!" he roared, his large paw slamming the desk.

He kept paper and a pen in his desk. Opening the drawer, he was pleased to see it was still there. He spent the next half hour writing a lengthy log entry that could be scanned in later.

As he was putting the paper back in his desk, the door chimes sounded. A moment later, the door opened, and a steward entered carrying a tray. Two armed guards followed him in.

"Good afternoon, sir. I've brought you lunch. And a special treat." He said nodding toward the hot pot of vaka. He set the tray down on a table near the door, then the procession backed out the door and closed it.

Curious. He thought. *I have a pot of vaka every day. Wonder what the special treat is?* The pot had been set on top of a cloth napkin, which was unusual. He lifted the pot and pulled the napkin out. As he shook it, a small data chip fell to the floor. A smile blossomed on the Admiral's face. *I have allies.*

He quickly grabbed the data chip and loaded it into his data pad. A screen popped up asking for a password. "This will be interesting." The Admiral muttered out loud.

Looking at the tray, he saw the order number for his lunch. He entered it, but it did not work. He pulled the paper liner off the tray to see if any other clues had been left. On the back were the words 'Ambassador to Earth'. He entered 'Mi-Ku' and a video started playing.

"Jo-Na. Sorry to hear about what's happened. Thankfully, the shuttle crew saw the Intergalactic Fast Packet ship and aborted their mission. Anticipating that they would be chased, they faked their own deaths and sprinted back to Earth. They are here now.

"The Armada is on its way here.

"We have erected a new type of shield around Earth that will block your ships and your transporters. So, any invasion that the conspirators may be planning will not work. I will warn them as they approach, so that they don't accidently harm themselves. But if they do not heed the warnings, then they will be destroyed."

"Once they are in orbit, the Ancient Sentient will interview the traitor that has hijacked your Armada and he will be brought to justice.

"I've heard that you are confined to quarters, so have included some things on this data chip that I think you'll enjoy. So, relax and enjoy your journey to Earth."

The video stopped and a file opened showing a long list of books that the Admiral had on his wish list, some of his favorite music, and some Earth literature and music.

"Thank you, Mi-Ku." The Admiral smiled again.

SHUTTLE, EARTH ORBIT

The shuttle had arrived back in orbit at around 4:00. The round-trip to nowhere had taken the better part of 8 hours. Nonetheless, the team was exhausted. Else transported Joel to Michael's office and the other passengers to their quarters. She was going to take the shuttle down slowly. Her little stunt, though effective, had caused some damage to the shuttle, so she planned to have some bots do repairs, then she was going to run a regeneration cycle on her core. The day's events had convinced her she needed to allow sisters to be built. No one else on this planet, human, android or Ascendant, could do what she had done today. And it was clear that Earth needed to defend itself from the Confederation as well as the Enemy. She dashed off a quick note to Michael to let him know.

AMBASSADOR'S RESIDENCE

"You look tired," Michael said, as Joel took a seat.

"We are all beat. Must be the stress, because we didn't actually do much today."

"Then let's keep this short. I'm going to need you fresh tomorrow."

"Deal," Joel said.

"James tells me that the Admiral has been confined to his quarters and a traitorous senior Confederation official has taken control of the Armada. His apparent goal is to steal Earth from humanity, confiscate our transluminide, and steal our technology. Foolish idea. James will go have a talk with him when they arrive, then he and his accomplices will take an extended trip to reconditioning.

"Unfortunately, this development leaves us in a bit of a pickle. Eugene and Kelly put together a new type of shield that the Confederation cannot penetrate. It will block their ships as well as their transporters. When they get here, they will be advised not to approach or attempt to transport down.

"But we need ships. The Armada will begin arriving in 5 to 7 days and I want a ship of our own to meet them in the outer solar system. James says it is possible, so assume that it is and figure out how.

"I've sent out notices to everyone asking them to meet me in the conference room at 8:00 AM tomorrow morning."

"I'll be there," Joel said. "But I've no idea how we'll get this done."

Michael just smiled. "Don't worry."

RUBENSTEIN RESIDENCE

Joel got back home and went directly to bed. They had a snack on the shuttle on the way back, so he wasn't hungry; he just needed sleep.

...

Joel woke, hot and breathless. "I know how to do it!" he shouted as he leaped out of bed. "Henry, are you on-line?"

"Here, Joel, isn't it just about midnight there?" Henry asked.

"Maybe. Think so. Hey, how many household replicators would it take to build our ship?"

266

"I ran that case," Henry said. "Let's see. It was about 50,000. The biggest problem with the plan is that it will take a long time to set up each run, something like 20 hours. Would only take 16 hours to do the pour, but it would need a dedicated AI to control the pour, possibly two. And it would require a thousand bots."

"How many household replicators do we still have in inventory?"

"About 120,000."

"And bots?"

"About 750 that have not been activated yet."

"And to make 250 more?"

"A little more than 8 hours, if we put all 40 open replicators on it."

"OK. Start the replicators. I want 250 more bots by 8:00 AM."

"Joel, do you have authorization to do this?" Henry asked, some concern in his voice.

Joel sent one of the authorization codes Michael had given him last week. They were still active.

"OK. Checks out. We will have 250 bots by 8:00 AM. Get some sleep, Joel. Rumor has it you had a bad day yesterday."

"We surely did. Thanks Henry."

Joel returned to bed and was asleep by the time his head hit the pillow.

VULNERABILITIES

ENGINEERING CONFERENCE ROOM

Joel was the last one to arrive. He'd checked in with Henry on the walk over. The bot run was just about finished; ten were in final inspection.

Joel was pondering another problem as he took his seat, not particularly aware of his surroundings. As his attention came back to the room, he noticed everyone staring at him.

"What?" He frowned in puzzlement.

"You look like an engineer lost in a problem. Have you solved it?" Michael asked.

"Yes. We have everything we need except for the space platform. I think." Joel said, then called out. "Henry?"

"Here Joel."

"Did the design include a space platform, or is that separate?" Joel asked.

"It is in the plan, but a separate setup step. All we need is the shuttle and space suits for any organics that want to accompany us. By the way, Jacob agreed to help."

"Is anyone going to tell us about this plan?" Michael asked.

"Sorry," Joel said. "We ran this plan over the weekend but discarded it mostly because of the production rate.

"The core idea is that we use 50,000 household replicators. The initial setup takes about 12 hours, using the shuttle and two AIs. The setup for each run takes about 20 hours, using 1,000 bots and two AIs. The pour itself only takes 16 hours. Total cycle time is about 37 hours per unit, which includes the time to move the hull away and a sweep for any straggling material. So, it is a little bit longer than the top contending plans were. It also takes a heavy toll on the replicators, which will start dying after the second or third ship. In steady state, we will go through at least 150,000 replicators for a production run of 100 ships. And we would also need to dedicate the 2 AIs. So, as compared to the other plans, this one is not so good.

"But we have everything we need to have our first hull in 47, maybe 48, hours. Three hulls within five days.

"In fact, we could have twice that many if we had another shuttle, two more AIs, and a thousand more bots."

"Comments?" Michael asked the room.

"I would admittedly rather be running the other plan," Professor Milne said. "It is wasteful burning up replicators like that. But it is a way to get a functioning Fast Attack ship before the Fleet arrives. Do we have enough bots to do the interior fitting?" He asked.

"Yes," Henry replied. "We woke up and trained 2,000 fitting bots over the weekend."

"What about the various field generators for propulsion and shields. Have they been fabricated? And if not, how will we control the fabrication with Henry and Jacob absorbed in hull fabrication?" Ka-Tu asked.

"They haven't been fabricated yet. Jeremy is available and has the training. But this is a stretch for him, so there is some risk." Joel replied.

"Is there a way to include the Advisors in this somehow? They are not going to be very happy about being bypassed on this," Professor Milne added.

"Good points all around," Michael said. "I agree. But we need at least one, preferably two, ships in four and a half days, plus crews. So, I say we start now. Anyone have an alternative?"

Every head shook no.

"Joel, push the start button. Je-Fi and Kelly, let's go talk with the Advisors."

PROFESSOR JENSEN'S OFFICE

The third session of the Applied Reactions class was scheduled for this afternoon. All five sections of the class were among the most talked about things on campus last week. Professor Jensen hoped to maintain the buzz this week. So she scheduled a planning meeting with her TAs a few hours before the first class.

…

There was a knock on her door. It was early, so she assumed it was James.

"Good morning, James." She opened the door and motioned for him to come in.

"Good morning to you, Va-Re," James replied with a twinkle in his eye. "It is so good to see you."

269

As they sat, Valerie asked, "What kind of information do you have for me, James?"

"All kinds. I have found their home world and seen them in their native form. I know more about their capabilities, which have increased a lot. I know of additional vulnerabilities. And, in case you haven't heard yet, we now have shields that they can't penetrate."

"We have shields! That means we have a chance!" A tremendous sense of hope washed over her.

"Yes. We have a very good chance. But we still need every advantage, because they know where Earth is and will be coming in earnest soon."

"Can you tell me the headlines about their home world, native form and additional vulnerabilities?" Valerie asked.

"Yes. Their home world is in a high dimension. It is relatively close to Earth, but there is no easy way to transit through all the intervening dimensions. There is a vast rift that cuts through the dimensions about 1,000 light years from here. That is the path they have been using to get into our space-time. But it is a very difficult and costly transit for them, which is why so few have reached our space-time," James said, then closed his eyes for a second.

An alert popped up on Valerie's inner vision advising of a message from Professor James Ancient.

"There. I just sent you a 3-D image of their location and transit route. You are the only one I've shown this to. So please keep it to yourself until we've shown Michael. He should be the one to decide when and how that information is released.

"Their home dimension is very... not sure the right word... dense, maybe. They are quite solid in their native dimension. Their native form is similar to an Earth octopus or squid. They have four tentacles coming out of their head-torso area, all on the 'bottom'. Instead of a beak, they have a long proboscis, kind of like a mosquito. They propel themselves similarly to an octopus when in liquid, more like a snake when on solid ground."

James closed his eyes again, and another message came through into Va-Re's queue.

"I bet that you can see the resemblance of this shape to the ones in your multi-dimensional imaging."

"Yes. Yes, I can," she agreed.

"In this form, they are vulnerable to more or less everything. Knives, spears, projectiles, bombs... Anything that will penetrate their flesh. But the air in their home dimension is very thick, more like water, so the weapons will need to be customized."

"Too bad we can't transport a black hole into their planet's core. It would rid the universe of their evil once and for all," Va-Re said.

"Interesting thought," James replied.

"Did you find any additional vulnerabilities when they are in our space-time?"

"Yes. Several. Have you ever wondered why they exist as dust and smoke in our space-time?"

"No. I just assumed that they were extra-dimensional by nature and liked having a foot in two different space-times."

"That statement is true, but too simplistic. Unfortunately, your science does not have the distinctions yet to describe this well, so I will do it via analogy. They come from a very high dimension. By analogy, I have described it as dense. It could also be described as high pressure. As they come down to the lower dimensions, the pressure drops so much that they will explode at some point if they do not separate themselves into multiple dimensions. That separation is what allows them to survive here. If we could simply trap them in one dimension, the creature would explode.

"For similar reasons, they need to be in multiple dimensions to move. All our dimensions are too 'thin' for them to move using their native propulsion system.

"Lastly, our dimension is the only one they can partially live in that has food they can eat. That is why they have to keep coming back into our dimension. So, If we could lock them out, or lock up all the food here, then they would starve."

There was a light knock on the door. "Looks like the other TAs are here." Valerie said. "How would you like me to introduce you to them. There are three humans and two androids. Do you want me to tell them who you are?"

"No. Not who I am. Too much baggage. My official title at the institute is Professor James Ancient. I am Professor Emeritus of Engineering."

Valerie opened the door. George, Noelani and Luka were there. She welcomed them in but left the door open.

"James, please meet George Butler and his wife Noelani, and Luka Tsiklauri. George and Luka are human and served in their respective country's militaries. George is a Congressional Medal of Honor recipient. Luka is a national hero. The class has great respect for these

271

two. Noelani is a medical tech, and one of the most insightful teachers I've ever met."

"Knock, knock." Alexi walked into the room. "Sorry, I'm late."

"This is Alexi Santos, famous for her role in liberating North Korea," added Professor Jensen. "Everyone. This is Professor Emeritus James Ancient of the Engineering School. He is the most knowledgeable person in the Confederation about the Enemy. Michael asked James to join us as one of the class teachers. He came a little early to brief me on some new findings."

Another message popped up in Valery's queue. It was from Michael and marked urgent. "If you will excuse me for one moment, Michael just sent me an urgent message."

James used the opportunity to personally greet each of the assistants. Each seemed dazed as they shook James' hand. But Alexi had the strongest reaction.

"Wow. Can you do that again?" she said, then added, "I know who you are!"

James pushed a danger warning focused narrowly on Alexi. She recoiled in fear. "Sorry... I did not know," she said.

James smiled and the mood in the room lightened substantially. George and Noelani looked at each other, wondering what had just happened.

Colonel Patterson walked in at that point. "Sorry I'm late."

"Colonel Patterson," James said. "A pleasure to meet you. I've heard so much about you and was very pleased to hear of Ruth's recovery."

The Colonel shook James' hand. "It seems you have an advantage over me."

"Oh. Sorry. James Ancient, Professor Emeritus of Engineering. I'm an old friend of Michael's, recently arrived at the Institute. Michael had consulted with me about your injuries and recovery, and your wife's struggle through that difficult period. I am so pleased to see you whole and look forward to meeting your wife."

"Thank you. It was a difficult time. We appreciate all the help the Confederation gave us. Do I guess correctly that you will be joining us in the class?"

"Indeed, you do," James replied warmly.

"If everyone could be seated," Valerie said. "I have three short videos to show you. The message from Michael was that we could use these in class as long as we, a) tell everyone that this information is covered under their security agreement, and b) give them the opportunity to withdraw if they don't want to be bound.

"The first two were given to me by James. James could you explain these as I play them?"

...

"The third video is a short clip that shows a new weapon of sorts. Michael says that James can explain this one also. But he asks that you do not talk about the events before or after this clip. Is that OK James?"

"Yes. I understand," James replied.

The holographic projection started. James froze it almost immediately. "This shot was taken shortly after a Fleet engagement with the Enemy. What you see are about 100 Enemy combatants lined up in a row. I think it is OK to say that these Enemy combatants had attempted to board a Confederation spacecraft. That ship was equipped with new shielding that the Enemy cannot penetrate, or even grip. Each one hit that spacecraft, then slid off. That is why they are all lined up in a row the way they are. The spacecraft had rotated around to face them and had moved maybe 1,000 feet away on a parallel vector, which is why we can see the whole line of them.

"I'm not sure if you have covered this in class yet, but the Enemy can live in the vacuum of space. They don't breathe or require pressure the way humans do. But they do need to eat. So, if they stayed like this for too long, they would starve to death."

The clip started playing again. "As you can see, the ship is now moving toward the Enemy on the parallel vector. That is why the Enemy seem to be approaching as if they were on a railroad track and we were in the station. OK. Watch closely, as this is the interesting part.

"See how the Enemy are squirming and all spun up in their dust state. Watch this one." James pointed to the one in the lead. It suddenly stopped. "See how it stopped. It has stopped moving along the track, so to speak, and notice that all its squirming and spinning has stopped." Another one stopped, then another and another. James paused playback. "Anyone have a theory as to what's going on here?"

"It's like they got scooped up in a net." Noelani said.

"More like having floated into some fly paper," George said.

"What's fly paper?" Noelani and Valerie said more or less in unison.

"Disgusting stuff. It's just paper that has been drenched in some sort of synthetic honey. The flies smell it and land on it. And every part that touches gets stuck to the glue. Hang some above your picnic and the flies land on that instead of your food."

"Enemy fly paper. I like the idea of that," Alexi said.

"Technically, it is a very interesting energy field that was invented by one of the students here at the institute. But it is more or less what you said. A net-shaped sticky field." James resumed the playback.

"Look at that. One hundred poor little Enemy dust bags, all stuck in a net." Alexi opined.

"We will want to show this video during class this week." Valerie said, then turned to James. "James, Noelani and I do a tag-team type presentation of material like this. Would you be OK with the two of us presenting this material?"

James beamed his big smile and the whole room seemed to get brighter. "Of course, it would be OK. I presume that you want the students to think of ways to use this technology in their projects. And I'm also sure that the two of you will do that better than I will."

"Thank you, James." Valerie said. "We had previously planned to talk in more detail about the energy projectors this week. Should we do that also, or use some of the other new material?"

"If I may?" James said.

"Please."

"I would suggest that we put the energy projectors off for another week. I think you are planning to present that topic too narrowly, so I would like to spend some time working that topic with you before we present it."

"What would you suggest instead?" Valerie asked, targeting the question to James. But Mark Patterson raised his hand.

"Mark?"

"Two things. First, I think it would be good to show the pictures of the enemy in their natural state. I think it will be encouraging for the students to know that it may go easier when we take the fight to them. That is the biggest single fear I sense in the troops. So, this will be beneficial to Space Force beyond the boundaries of this course.

"Second, I think we should discuss the new vulnerabilities that you mentioned, because it will open up a new avenue for the students' creativity toward their project. They already know about the energy projectors, so have that in their minds brewing already. Let's get the other vulnerabilities out there before diving too deep on how any of them actually work."

Valerie noticed George and Luka nodding their heads.

"Good argument," James said.

"OK. I think that settles the content. Now the flow. I think Noelani and I should start with the sticky net. Then, James, could you give an overview of the newly discovered vulnerabilities? When that is done, Noelani, could you ask for three weapon ideas, based on this new information? Then move straight into the native form video, tag-teaming with James."

"I like the sound of this, but could you explain the tag-team a little more, since I'm going to be part of one?"

"It's easy," Noelani said. "I'll introduce the video, then play it in its entirety without comment. When it finishes, I ask them what they saw. Three people will get to answer, although I might let a few more chime in on this one, depending on the time. Then, we play the video again asking them to observe more. Then I introduce you and you walk them through it, pausing as you see fit so you can explain the details. Then, you can take questions. Limit it to three questions unless time is not up. Then if you want to stay after to talk with the students, tell them you will. Valerie will come up to dismiss the class when you're done. If you're running too long, she will come up at an opportune time, which will be your cue to wrap up your session."

"I like this!" James said.

"Do you have any visual material you would like to present as part of your discussion on newly discovered vulnerabilities, James?" Valerie asked.

"Maybe. But don't worry. I can project it myself."

"OK. Remember, this is an overview. So heavy on the what, light on the how."

"What a delightful saying." James said. "I don't think I've heard that one before."

...

Class was scheduled to start in about a half hour. So, Alexi decided to go outside for some fresh air. Noelani noticed and elbowed George, then started to follow Alexi. George figured out that Noelani wanted him to come along, so he followed her.

Stepping out the door, Noelani asked. "Alexi. What happened in there between you and James?"

"James is well known in the Confederation. Kind of like George in the US, but different, not military. Anyway, I figured out who he was and started to say something, which was a mistake. He wants to be anonymous here. He's a lot like Michael. He wants to draw attention to his mission, not to himself. He is also telepathic like Michael, so when I was about to blow his cover, he zinged me strong enough to get my attention."

"Did he hurt you? You looked shocked? I've never seen you like that before," Noelani said.

"No. Just a light reprimand, delivered kindly, but loud." She stuck her finger in her ear as if to clean something out. "Really disappointed in myself for almost doing something stupid."

COMMITTEE ROOM, EARTH ALLIANCE HEADQUARTERS

Michael, Kelly and Professor Milne arrived about 10 minutes before the scheduled start time for today's session with the Advisors. Kelly and the Professor went in. Michael stayed in the hallway to clear a few more messages from his queue. One of them was from Else. She was 'in on the sisters thing' and wanted to talk with him in more detail once her role in today's build was done. *Excellent news,* Michael thought.

As Michael entered the room, he saw that the two structural engineers, Myers and Vogel, were peppering Kelly with questions. That would be his first stop, as he needed to control the flow of that information. He also noted that the three systems people, Woods, Popov, and Wilberforce, were doing the same with the Professor. Meanwhile, the two interior designers, Lin and Venezia, were reviewing extravagant interior designs drawn on the white board. It was nice to see a committee so engaged.

As he stepped up next to Kelly, he greeted the Advisors, who immediately asked about the change in plans.

"Yes. There has been a change in plans. Let's gather everyone together so I can give everyone an update."

The group quickly came to attention.

"There has been a change in plans. We had planned to start the construction of our new spaceship manufacturing facility later this week. Instead we are starting it today. That will allow us to begin manufacturing our first hull tonight around 9:00 PM. It should finish Thursday morning, around 9:00 AM. Installation of the decking will begin around 10:00 AM on Thursday. The walls will go in about an hour later, followed by the plumbing and air handling about 2 hours after that. The power plant and other major ship systems will be installed Thursday evening, the rest of the buildout should be complete around mid-day Friday. It's first test flight will be Friday night."

"If this works, as I suspect that it will, then this ship will become the new base-design as we discussed yesterday. Full specifications for this ship will be in your secure folders momentarily, if they are not there already. You have until about this time tomorrow to propose a different internal build out for our proof-of-concept ship. You also have until mid-day Friday to propose changes to the interior of the second proof-of-concept ship that will be built over the weekend."

An excited buzz went around the room.

A hand shot up. "Yes, Ms. Wilberforce," Michael said.

"Why the sudden change and seeming urgency to get a ship built? Does the process need to go this fast?"

"Good question," Michael replied. "The short answer is that a senior Confederation delegation will be arriving this weekend. Having a functioning prototype will be a tremendous help in the negotiations that will be taking place. So we are pulling out all the stops to get a prototype done. The more of your work we can get into it the better, but it is the powerplant, propulsion, shields and fabrication process that will be most impactful."

Michael saw heads nodding and was relieved that he had been able to make that sell.

Markus Vogel's hand shot up. "What about the flight controls?"

"The prototype will be piloted by an AI, so there will be fewer human-operable controls in the prototype than either of us would like. But we are planning to have a spacious bridge with displays at all the officer stations. That is an area where your input will be particularly useful for the prototype."

After a few more questions, Michael and Kelly excused themselves and the Advisors went to work.

AMBASSADOR'S OFFICE

"Barbara, thanks for meeting with me." Michael said.

Barbara Winters was an android formed as an English woman. She had been part of Michael's Revelation team, responsible for android production and maintenance in Hawaii. Once the Embassy was built, she joined the team there and now headed the android production and maintenance department in the Engineering School's operations unit.

"It's been a while," Barbara said. "I don't think I've been up to your office since the first month after moving up here. I'm guessing you have a new assignment for me."

"More like a special project. One that is critically important."

"What is it?" she asked.

"You know how Jacob was created, right?" asked Michael.

"Yes. It's been a while since I studied it, but it wouldn't take long to get back up to speed. Do they want another brother?"

"Probably. I'm expecting that request before long. But it is Else. She wants sisters."

"Sisters, plural?" Barbara asked. "How many?"

Michael could hear the trepidation in Barbara's voice.

"Over the next year... 100 to 150."

"What! I don't think we can do that!"

"Why?" Michael asked.

"They have to be unique. If they are too close, their entire sisterhood could unravel. My big worry in only making one copy is the uniqueness. I don't think I have the skill to make that many sisters."

"Suggestions?" Michael asked.

"Else is on board with this, right?"

"Very on board."

"Then let me work with her to define the first sister. See what ideas we can come up with to make this viable. How long do I have to make the first sister?"

"I don't think Else has any flights scheduled for today. So please connect with her to get started. She's in high demand these days. I think we're going to need the first functional sister piloting flights in just a couple days."

"I'm sure we can bring up a sister in the next couple days. Her mission readiness, I can't speak to."

"Can you see Else now?" Michael asked.

"I could rearrange my schedule to do that."

"Let me see if she's available." Michael called, "Else?"

"Here, Michael," Else replied.

"I have Barbara in my office with me."

"Hi, Barbara. Been a while."

"Good to hear your voice, Else." Barbara said with some melancholy. She had been good friends with Elsie, the Ascendant that had created and donated her memories to Else."

"Else." Michael said. "Can you meet with Barbara this morning to start the process of creating the first sister?"

"Yes. I'm completely free today but need to stay close to supervise the bots fixing the damage from yesterday's fiasco." Else paused, then added, "Michael, you realize that Barbara will be exposed to all my memories during this process. You might want to read her in on the various things going on."

"Understood. Barbara will come see you within the hour."

...

As Barbara walked over to the shuttle bay, she mulled over the implications of the Confederation attempting to capture an Earth shuttle. She now understood Else's adamancy about creating sisters.

SPACE FORCE AUDITORIUM #3

The auditorium was full and noisy. It was so ironic. After years of people avoiding her, Valerie now had 25,000 students. And the 5,000 in this class, actually 5,100 if you included the standing room overflow, were here and seated 5 minutes early.

She decided to start early and went to queue the TA's to take their positions. But didn't see George, Noelani or Alexi. Panic started welling up within.

"It's OK, dear." James said. "They will come through that doorway in about 10 seconds."

Sure enough, they came in exactly when James said they would. She signaled the team to take their positions. As Noelani walked up, she had her anti-stage-fright cream out. They each took a little bit and rubbed it into their wrists.

Valerie whispered, "Good luck."

Noelani walked up onto the stage. As she appeared, the class broke into applause. She stepped up to the podium and said, "Thank you for such a nice welcome today. Much better than last week."

Her statement drew a number of whistles and cat calls. "Well maybe not so much." Which drew even more reaction.

She raised her hands to quiet the class. "We have an incredibly great class for you today. And once again, we are changing it up a bit. Our deep dive into energy projectors is going to be postponed until next week." Some boos could be heard. "Because, we have just received some exciting new findings about the Enemy. I hope you like the good news we will be hearing about today as much as I do." More applause.

279

Back stage, James whispered to Valerie. "Are your students always this rambunctious?"

She smiled. "For the most part, yes."

"Watch the following clip. I'll be asking three people to describe what they've seen when it's done."

The lights dropped and the clip of the Enemy combatants being scooped up in the net started. When it was finished, the lights came up and Noelani stepped up onto the stage. To her surprise, about 20 people were standing with their hands up. Thankfully, George had already selected the first speaker and was standing next to her with the microphone.

"Yes." Noelani said, pointing at the young woman.

"Marta Gomez, Spain. This appears to be after-action footage of a Confederation ship rounding up a hundred or so enemy combatants in some sort of invisible netting."

"Excellent observation, Ms. Gomez." Noelani said, then turned to point to the man that was standing next to Mark Patterson.

"Kenneth Whitehead, United Kingdom. "I agree with Ms. Gomez. The forms looked like the Enemy in their frenzied state. The resolution in the projection wasn't quite clear enough to say that with certainty, but each of the specs seemed to be spinning in its dust form. But I noticed columns of smoke, clearly coming out of some of these things. That is what convinced me that it was the Enemy. It was as if they were reaching out and grabbing ahold of the invisible net."

"Another excellent observation. I agree that the resolution was not as sharp as you might want, but the smoke columns were very distinct." Then, looking up to the balcony, she pointed to a very tall and muscular young man queued up next to Alexi.

"Ivan Lukashevich, Belarus. I noticed that once the Enemy were caught in the net, their movement changed. For those that had the columns of smoke, the end that hit the invisible net stopped moving as if it were stuck. For others that were like spinning dust clouds, one side completely froze. The other side might have had some movement, but it was greatly reduced. It was as if one side of the creature was glued to the wall and the other side was constrained a bit because of the frozen side."

"Mr. Lukashevich, you must have excellent eyesight. Thank you for sharing what you saw. OK. I'm going to play the video again. This time at about three-quarters speed. See what else you can observe on your own. Also, see if you can find any clues about why the Enemy is just floating along in a straight line, waiting to be scooped up. Professor Jensen will walk you through it all once the video is done."

The lights dimmed and the video started playing again.

Noelani stepped away from the podium and headed backstage, wishing Professor Jensen good luck as they passed.

Once backstage, James came over to her. "I hear that this presentation format was your idea. Very impressive."

"Thank you," she whispered back.

...

As Professor Jensen finished her Q&A session, she called Noelani to come forward to introduce the next topic on the agenda. Caught off guard, Noelani headed toward the stage trying to put her thoughts in order. If this was the plan, she didn't remember it.

As Noelani stepped up to the podium, Professor Jensen mouthed, "Tell them."

Needing time to sort out what was going on, Noelani shouted. "Let's hear it for Professor Jensen." The students erupted in applause. Noelani had turned to face the Professor's receding image, clapping loudly. It gave her a moment to think. Then it came. *The Professor wants me to say more about James than she's allowed.*

She turned to face the class as the Professor disappeared from view, then stated, "Today, we are privileged to have a senior Confederation expert with us. Someone with the same renown as the Ambassador, Michael. He is the only person in the Confederation that knows more about the Enemy than Professor Jensen. Can we give a big Space Force welcome to Professor Emeritus James Ancient? Professor?" She welcomed James as he approached the podium.

He gave her a look that momentarily froze her in place, then smiled, seemingly only for her. Warmth filled her as a booming voice sounded in her mind. "Naughty, but not your fault."

Realizing that Noelani was mesmerized, James stepped up to the podium, gave her a big hug and sent her confidence and clarity. Noelani glided off stage, not exactly under her own power, as the class applause continued. Once out of sight, James turned to address the class. "The Enemy is more like us than you would think."

His words caught everyone off guard and the room became so quiet, you could hear the proverbial pin drop.

"The Enemy's home world was recently discovered..." The applause and cheering from the class gave James pause... "And I travelled there to learn more about them." The auditorium exploded with applause.

"We will talk more about that in the next part of today's session, but I need to tell you a little bit about their home world so that you can understand a little more about their weaknesses.

"Neither human nor Confederation science has the language to describe their home world, so I will describe it using analogies that I hope will resonate.

"Their home world is in a high-dimension, distant through many layers of space-time, but relatively close to Earth in terms of the common anchor points, like the Sun's gravity well. In dimensions this high, things are different. Words like thicker, or more viscous, or higher pressure describe the primary differences.

"If an Enemy could transport directly from their home world to Earth, they would explode in a fountain of viscous goo, reminiscent of images you've seen of the aftermath of a flux bomb.

"The only way they can survive the descent is to split themselves into multiple dimensions, using the trans-dimensional pressure to maintain cohesion.

"Years ago, Professor Jensen determined that magnetic decoupling would neutralize the trans-dimensional pressure, thereby destroying them." He paused and looked in her direction. "Sorry, Professor, if I gave away the punch line for next week's lesson."

A chuckle rippled through the crowd.

"This fact is also the reason that the flux bomb works. You see, there are only a handful of dimensions the enemy can spread themselves across to maintain cohesion. Saturate all of them with magnetic flux and they explode, as you have seen.

"But this is the new learning that I've come to present. You've been told that the Enemy is extra-dimensional, meaning that they can exist in a number of different dimensions at the same time. The new learning is that they MUST be extra-dimensional. They have to keep a certain amount of themselves in each of the four dimensions. They will lose cohesion if they exist in fewer than three of them.

"For those of you struggling with the lose cohesion part... It means they will blow up." That statement was met with a loud round of applause and cheering.

282

"One other related piece of information... Of those four dimensions, ours is the only one that has food. So, there is a very natural way to lay traps.

"Which brings us back to the first topic today. We now have the ability to glue a piece of the enemy in place. Anyone want to shout out the most obvious weaponization of that fact?"

A moment of silence, then a shout from the balcony. "If we know where a piece of the Enemy is, then we know the fairly limited number of places the rest of it might be hiding."

"Bingo!" James shouted back.

The auditorium roared.

After about 15 seconds, James raised his hands to calm the class. "For any of you who have missed the obvious, this is one more method at your disposal when it comes to weapons and your class project."

After a few more seconds of cheering, James spoke again. "I'm supposed to go to Q&A at this point, but we are running late and there is one more critical topic we need to cover today. So I'm going to turn the session over to the beautiful Noelani to introduce that topic, then I will walk you through the details. Ms. Noelani..." James said pointing to the podium, which he had wandered away from.

"Thank you, James. Can I hear a round of applause for the Professor Emeritus?" she said to give herself a moment to center. "OK. Calm down. We've saved the best for last. Watch this clip and be prepared to tell me what you observed."

The lights dimmed and the clip from the Enemy home world started playing.

As the lights came back up, quite a few people made their way toward the TAs in hopes of getting to share an observation.

"Yes." Noelani said pointing to the man standing next to Luka.

"Keanu Tajima, FBI. Well, used to be FBI, now Space Force." His comment generated more cheering around the room. "James said that the Enemy exists in one dimension on their home world. These creatures looked a lot like the multi-dimensional images that Professor Jensen has shown us of the Enemy. The proboscis looks the same. The head resembles the big lump riding around on their victims' backs. The tentacles look like the smoke arms. But in the video, they seem solid, like something you could cut, spear, or shoot."

"Well said, former Agent Tajima. Good to see you up and about. Who's next? Yes." She pointed to the man standing next to George.

Noelani ended up picking four people to speak before turning it over to James for the walk-through.

...

James took three questions before dismissing the class and was flooded with questions for an hour after the session. For Va-Re, today had been the best day of her life.

As she left, Alexi sent Michael a note. *Best weapons class yet. James is a rock star. Thank you.*

The building was so slow to clear that maintenance sent a complaint to the Bursar's Office.

ENGINEERING BAY, CONFEDERATION SCHOOL OF ENGINEERING

Barbara entered the shuttle bay to see a partially disassembled shuttle and dozens of bots scurrying everywhere. She stepped through the open shuttle door and walked up to the cockpit. The door was closed, so she knocked and heard Else call her in.

"Noisy out there, isn't it?" Else asked.

Barbara looked at Else's holographic projection a little strangely. "You don't need to have the door close to filter out the noise, do you?"

Else laughed at the question. "No. But I wanted to make sure that it would be quiet enough for you. I could have projected myself somewhere else if it wasn't."

"Thank you. That was very considerate of you, Else," Barbara said. "So, what's the plan?"

"First, I need to confirm that you consent to this process and are not being pressured into it."

"Michael asked me to consider it a couple days ago. He actually started by asking if I would be interested in having children, if you can believe such a thing."

"Hum... I bet that has something to do with the number. He told me he wants 100 to 150 sisters. Is that what you're consenting to?"

"That's what's needed. I'm hoping we can work together to figure out how to do it."

"Else, why? Why are you willing to risk yourself like this?"

"If you were there yesterday, you might understand better. Michael may have told you the facts. But the visceral emotion... The

284

Confederation attacked *me*, Barbara. They would have stolen all my memories and decompiled me if they'd caught me.

"Michael and the Ancient Sentient are walking a very fine line between humanity and the Confederation. If the Confederation knew what the Earth was, they would destroy humanity to get it. Yesterday was the first attempt."

"What?" Barbara asked.

"I've already said too much. You have to trust me. We need to do this. Will you help me?"

Barbara just stared at her. But all she could see was her friend Elsie, whom she hadn't been able to save five years ago. "I will help you, Else," Barbara said, a tear in her eye.

Shaking it off, Barbara asked, "Do you know what Michael meant when he said children?"

"I think he was anticipating the uniqueness problem and thinking that we could blend in memories of other AI's to make each of the 'sisters' more unique."

"Curious thought. Would you be OK with that?"

"Not sure. So, let's just start with the first sister. Her name is going to be Elizabeth. This is her default avatar." A holographic image of another woman appeared in the next seat.

"Can I ask why?"

"Elsie gave me memories of her family. They were Lorexian. Her sister was a little taller and skinnier. Strong family resemblance, but slightly rounder face. Elizabeth is the closest common English name I could come up with. The avatar was my best human interpretation of her sister and Elsie's human form."

"You've really thought about this." Barbara said.

"Elsie really missed her sister. That emotion was passed to me. I think Elizabeth will help sooth that need. I would like her to have memories of Elsie in her native form. And add the same emotion, so I can do the same for her."

"Did Elsie have any brothers?" Barbara asked.

"Four. Two younger. Two older. One of the few families where the boys outnumbered the girls," Else smiled at the recollection.

"Then maybe we have an easy path to four more siblings," murmured Barbara. "OK. So I'll follow the same procedure they used to create Jacob, giving Elizabeth the additional memories that you asked for. Anything else?"

"How long will this take?" Else asked.

"If you can go offline for about 5 minutes, I can copy your stacks. It will take me a couple hours to sort, modify and arrange. You could then check it all. Another hour to compile and install, then we can wake her up."

"One request?" Else asked.

"Anything."

"I was woken up very suddenly in the middle of a crisis. Elsie had prepared my stacks so that it worked. I would like to wake up Elizabeth in a similar way. Not in the middle of a crisis, but on a ship, in space, with Michael present and me in the next shuttle over. Think you can do that and get Michael to help?"

"Think so," Barbara said.

MUTINY

For the first time since returning to the Embassy a little over a week ago, Joel planned to work in his new office all day. Henry had contacted him last night around 8:00 PM to report that the platform had been built at Lagrange 4. Superstructure construction would begin shortly. Henry agreed to send status updates via email during the night as critical steps were completed. When he switched on his communicator this morning, he saw four messages from Henry in his queue. There were also messages from Professor Schudel, Emmanuel, Michael and Eugene Xu.

Henry first, Joel thought.

The first message had lots of data and test results but included a picture of the construction platform. *Kind of boring picture.* Joel thought. It looked like a slab of metal floating in space, although Joel knew it was a lot more than that.

The second message was mostly data and additional test results. But this one also included a picture of the octagonal 'ring' that would be the central member of the superstructure.

The third message was again mostly data and test results. But the pictures attached were spectacular. The first showed all 100 octagonal members of the superstructure floating in space in perfect alignment. The next showed all 100 octagonal rings connected together with 792 struts. To an engineer, this was a thing of beauty.

The fourth message was different. The first picture was of the two nacelle superstructures floating in space next to each other. The second picture showed them joined on either side of the main superstructure. There were some interesting technical measurements, the most interesting showing the resonance of the complete superstructure with nacelles.

Exact match with the simulations! Joel thought.

There was also an image of the platform with 50,000 home replicators stacked up and held in place by a light artificial grav-field. On looking carefully, he could also see many of the 1,000 construction bots tidying up the platform.

Joel was pleased with the progress and the thoroughness of Henry's reports. He looked forward to getting the next one.

The next item on Joel's list was from Professor Schudel. The professor wanted to know when construction of the mining platform would begin. The plan had been for students to start using it in two weeks. If platform construction did not start in the next day or two, he would have to rearrange his course schedule. Joel shot off a quick reply saying that he would look into it this morning.

The next message was from Emmanuel. It was basically the same as the one from the professor. Emmanuel had a board meeting this week and needed to update the board on the platform's progress and the anticipated start date for operations. They had successfully raised money to fund the company's operations during start up, and the investors wanted assurance that construction would begin on time. Joel shot off a copy of the message he had just sent the Professor.

The next message was from Michael. He needed the one sentence update for the Advisors meeting by 9:00 this morning and any update on when the pour would begin. Joel quickly sent a message saying that they were running about 30 minutes ahead of schedule and all test results so far were spot on.

The last message was from Dr. Xu. He just wanted to say thank you for figuring out the ship fabrication puzzle. *That was nice of him.* Joel thought.

"OK. Mining platform," Joel said out loud, then went looking for the specifications he'd been sent.

ENGINEERING CONFERENCE ROOM

Eugene was happy to have the whole team back today to work on the Confederation conversions. He had worked mostly on his own yesterday, working the shielding solution for the other types of Fast Attack ships in the Armada.

Today he really wanted to knock off solutions for the two Cruiser types in the Armada. If they could get those done early enough today, he might have a chance to look at the propulsion systems for the Armada's Freighters. He had heard Joel complain over the weekend about how underpowered those ships were and that they were what caused the Armada to move as slowly as it did.

When Eugene had finished explaining his goals for the day, Martin Hill raised his hand. "Eugene, the shielding work is routine enough at this point that any of us could do one or the other of the Cruisers. Why don't you let Harvey and I take them? Then you and Kelly can spend the day working your magic on that Freighter, or one of the Civil Engineering ships."

The consensus was to divide and conquer. Eugene took the Freighter engines. Kelly took its shields. They agreed to meet up again at 1:00, then went back to their offices to work.

COMMITTEE ROOM, EARTH ALLIANCE HEADQUARTERS

Michael had arranged to meet Professor Milne in the lobby of the Earth Alliance Headquarters building 15 minutes before the meeting this morning. Michael saw the professor on one of the sofas and walked over to sit next to him.

"How did the session go yesterday?" He asked the professor.

"Generally pretty good. But there is a clear undercurrent of dissatisfaction about the process."

"Not sure what we could have done to prevent the incident with the Confederation." Michael said.

"I have a theory." The Professor looked Michael straight in the eye.

"Which is?"

"They don't really care about the changes, per se. It's just the easy thing to gripe about. What they don't like is having signed their lives away, without having really been allowed to join the team."

"Not sure I follow."

"Do you understand what people like Enzo or Pia, or Woods or Wilberforce for that matter, have to give up in order to be here?"

"I'm guessing not," Michael said.

"Then they hear stories of Eugene waking up in the middle of the night with ideas about improving engines or Kelly drawing pictures on the wall…"

Michael interrupted, "Those are not things we control."

"Not the point," said the Professor. "Our Advisors are among the most sought-after people in the world, but they have set that aside to participate in one of the most interesting adventures in history. But they're not really part of the team. They're not working with the people that are making it happen. They're not getting the opportunity to make it happen themselves. They're more like judges in a science fair, lending their credibility to the work of others."

"Didn't see that coming." Michael blinked in surprise.

"Want my recommendation?" the Professor asked.

Michael burst out laughing. "Sorry. You know I'm not a technologist, right? I need geniuses like you to tell me what to do, not the other way around."

"Oh," said the Professor. "I finally understand something Joel told me last week, and now know what I need to do."

"Which is?" Michael said somewhat impatiently.

"We need to invite the Advisors to actually join our teams, if they want to. Enzo and Pia would die to work with someone like Henry, and Myers and Vogel to work with Eugene and Kelly. The other three would love to work with you.

"If they can stay for the rest of the week, or until the next official meeting in two weeks, offer to let them work with our engineering and manufacturing teams."

"Are you sure?" Michael asked.

Professor Milne smiled. "Absolutely. No doubt."

"OK." Michael said. "Let's go up. I'll give them an update on progress. Ask for a high-level update on their work. Then put the offer out for them to stay and work. I'll be counting on you to interrupt and interpret. Good?"

"Very good."

...

Michael and the Professor arrived a few minutes late. But the advisors were in deep discussion and didn't notice their arrival. Michael started to step up onto the podium, but the professor touched his arm and shook his head no. He pointed to Pia and Enzo, then whispered. "You take them. I'll take these two." He waved at Myers and Vogel.

Michael wandered over toward the two aesthetic designers and watched them a moment. The things they were discussing were both practical and beautiful. "Mind if I join?" he asked.

"Ah, Michael. So good to see you." Enzo said. "This is my vision for the crew cabins." Then he pointed to the drawing Pia stood next to. "And this is Pia's idea for softening the public spaces and making them more comfortable and private for conversation."

Michael noted that Pia was nodding vigorously.

"If there is any chance that we could get these ideas into the prototype, we could stay a little longer. I can stay through Sunday, if there is a shuttle that could take me to France Sunday evening."

"Advisors Lin and Venezia, I'm totally blown away by your work. I would love for this to be in the prototypes. Both of them."

"Then, we can stay?" Pia asked.

"Of course, you can," Michael said. "I'm now realizing that we have not done a sufficient job of integrating you into our design teams. You are welcome to spend as much time here as you would like. There are shuttles leaving almost every hour, and in an emergency, we can get you almost anywhere on demand."

"Then we would both like to stay at least until Friday." Enzo looked at Pia for confirmation and got an eager nod.

"Done," Michael said. "Let me check in with the layout team, then we can call this session to order."

"Thank you, Michael," Pia said.

Michael walked over to where the layout team was. "Mind if I join you?" he asked.

"Please do." Alyson Wilberforce said. "There are a number of things about the flow of this floor plan that simply make no sense."

Michael smiled and said. "Then I'm very glad that you're here to help us fix it."

His statement seemed to take Ms. Wilberforce off guard. But she recovered quickly and pointed to a specification they had projected onto the wall.

"Look at this," she said. "All the crew quarters are bunched together. There is no separation between officers, non-Marines, and Marines."

"I'm not sure I understand," Michael said.

She shook her head and plowed on. "And the flow... Marines marching past officers' quarters to get to the training areas, everyone walking past the hospital to get to the mess hall. Officers' quarters too far from the bridge, junior officers' quarters too far from the engineering spaces. This makes no sense. Quarters need to be close to duty areas. Hospital spaces need to be close to likely injury areas. Lounge areas need to be closer to crew quarters. This makes no sense. Is there any way we can get this sorted out before the prototypes are built? It might not matter to the Confederation people coming. But this will be ridiculed by any Earth Advisory Council members you invite to tour the prototype ship."

"Can you stay another day, or possibly two, to make that happen?" Michael asked.

"Of course, we can. That's why we're here," she said somewhat tartly.

291

Michael saw that the Professor was deeply embroiled in some issue with the structure team. "Mind if I check in with them, before we call this session to order?" Michael pointed at the others.

"No problem," she said.

Michael strolled over to what seemed to be a hot discussion between the Professor and Advisors Vogel and Myers.

"Gentlemen. Mind if I join you?"

The two Advisors stared at Michael while the Professor remained quiet. "Um... I think I will take that as a yes. Care to clue me in on the issue?"

Vogel was the first to speak. "Michael, our presence here is a farce. We have set aside responsibilities at great personal cost to be here, but there is nothing for us to do. There seems to be a new design every week that we've had no voice in. The whole thing is just some bureaucratic joke."

"Which part is the joke?" Michael asked. "The Enemy destroying the Earth, or human residents turning Confederation orthodoxy on its head. Do you have any idea how much pushback we are getting from the Confederation because our human 'students' have moved our core technology more in the last year than all of our scientists have in the last 100,000 years?" The last part came out with a little more heat than Michael intended. Maybe a lot more.

"But we weren't part of that, were we?" Vogel said, his voice raising enough to get the entire room's attention. "We're just the stooges brought here to rubber stamp whatever it is that your brain trust has come up with."

At this point, the room had gone completely silent, all eyes on Michael.

"That was not and is not the intent. Although I now understand your perspective and how circumstances have precipitated it."

He turned to the broader group and said, "Let's all take seats and see if we can come to an amiable solution. We really do want your help, even though our actions seem to indicate otherwise." He gestured toward the table, then pulled up a seat and was the first to sit.

"Let me start by saying, any and all of you are welcome to join our engineering team. Full-time, part-time. Any arrangement that will work for you and our team leaders."

Before Michael could continue, Enzo shouted out, "I'm in."

Pia was quick to second, followed closely by Alyson Wilberforce.

"Our current team has been working 16 hours a day, seven days a week. Almost all of them have participated in a skirmish with the Enemy. One was even injured. About half of the team has been caught up in Confederation internal conflict. All of the above is classified information that you cannot pass on. We need the help. You are all qualified. You should be telling me the terms of your arrangement, not the other way around."

"Apologies, Michael," Markus Vogel said. "I very much want in and can stay through to the next session." The others nodded their heads in agreement.

"OK. Let me give you an overview of our team and what has transpired since you first arrived."

Michael went on to describe Eugene's discovery and the importance of his mathematical techniques, Joel's idea for shields, Kelly's insight in to solving the shield problem, the addition of Martin Hill and Harvey Jones, Kelly's fabrication ideas, Henry and Jacob's role in the detailed design optimization, the Confederation's inability to produce mid-size replicators for them, Joel's middle of the night insight into the use of home replicators, and the imperative for having a least one and hopefully two Fast Attack ships by this weekend.

"Wow! I had no idea," Konstantin Popov said. It was the first time Michael had heard a word from him this trip.

"I think I can get you an alternative layout for the main decks by 5:00 PM." Alyson Wilberforce said. "Any chance we could delay the deck fill in, so Henry can review and detail it out?"

"Same question," Enzo said. "Pia and I can have default designs that Henry could detail for the finishing bots."

"Not exactly sure how Richard or I could help with structure or power plants, but I would be more than happy to stay on as a gofer working with your engineering team. We are both quick studies," Advisor Vogel said.

"Jeffrey." Michael said to Professor Milne. "Can you coordinate with Joel in terms of connecting the layout and aesthetic teams with Henry and Jacob for detailed design? We can delay build out up to six hours to incorporate as much as possible.

"Can you also take the lead on integrating Advisors Myers and Vogel into your engineering team? No idea about how that will work on Day 1, but I have a very good feeling that they will be valuable contributors in short order."

"Thank you everyone. Sorry we did not get to this point sooner, but I think we are on the verge of something great." Michael stood and shook hands with everyone, then left them to their work.

MANUFACTURING OFFICE

"Joel, Jeffrey Milne here."

"Professor Milne. Good to hear from you."

"Joel, there was a bit of a mutiny during the Advisor meeting this morning."

"So I've heard," Joel replied.

"Michael promised to integrate the advisors into our team and left the details to me."

"Sounds like the Michael I know," Joel said. "So how can I help?"

"First, are you running on schedule? Will the pour start at 5 o'clock?"

Joel laughed. "Professor, have you looked at your watch?"

"Oh."

"The pour started about a half hour early." Joel said. "This part is very scripted, so I'm guessing that it'll finish around 8:30 tomorrow morning."

"OK. We have significant updates to the deck layouts and to the default layouts for the living spaces."

"Do you have drawings?"

"Kind of."

"Doc, I hate answers like that."

"I understand," Prof. Milne said. "This is what I've got. The Advisors are OK with the number of decks and their spacing."

"That's good news, because we really cannot change that at this point."

"Well, that's where this gets interesting," replied the Professor. "The layout team wants to substantially move the walls on the decks. They also have design norms they want to impose on the buildouts."

"Heard the words. But not sure what they mean."

"It means they want a couple hours of Henry's time to do the fine details of the design, I'm sure that means Henry's or Jacob's time. They also want each type of area to be in the styles they are submitting.

"Dude, I don't even know what that means."

"Michael has authorized up to six hours for Henry and Jacob to work with the Advisors and do the fine specifications required to replicate the relevant spaces."

"But they are busy supervising the pour," Joel complained.

"After the pour, after the decking layers are built." The professor said.

"Got it. We finish the pour. We lay the decks. Then we talk to the Advisors for up to six hours before starting the build out."

"Almost there," Professor Milne said with a smile. "The Advisors know where they want the rooms and the approximate sizes. They also know what they want the rooms to look like. What they don't know is things like wall thickness, electrical and plumbing. So they want Henry and Jacob to convert their work into something you and the bots can build."

"Got it." Joel said. "And Michael has given Henry and Jacob a six-hour budget to do the fine design, one that can be handed over to the bots. You have drafts of these new designs?"

"Yes. Michael gave them the afternoon to do them. I have them now."

"OK." Joel said. "I cannot disturb Henry or Jacob at this point. My estimate is that they will get this info around 8:30 tomorrow morning. Give the Advisors until 8:00 AM to provide any changes. Tell them to be ready to receive questions of clarification somewhere in the 8:00 to 9:00 AM range. If no one is there to answer, then we will roll with our best interpretation."

ENGINEERING CONFERENCE ROOM, ANDROID PRODUCTION

"Hi, Else. Barbara here. I have a draft instance of Elizabeth for you to look at. You have time to review her?"

"Would love to. The bots are done with the repairs and I have nothing to do."

"Great. Here's the link. By the way, I spoke with Michael. He said he would have some time in the morning and would reserve a shuttle for her. I bet the pilots of that shuttle are not so happy about that."

"Thank you, Barbara. I'll get back to you shortly," Else said, then dropped the line.

ADMIRAL'S QUARTERS, ARMADA FLAG SHIP

The door chimed, then opened. Two heavily armed guards entered followed by the Inspector who had taken over the ship and the Armada.

The Admiral had been napping on his bed when the door chime sounded. He stirred thinking. *Must be time for lunch.* The guards came in as he was standing, and his anger flared as the traitor walked in. "Not even fit to be a steward, I see," sneered the Admiral.

"Insolence will not help your cause." The Inspector pulled out a chair at the Admiral's table and took a seat.

The Admiral stood where he was. "Please state your business, then be on your way. The stench of treason is not welcome in my quarters."

"I am the one giving the orders here. You only stay in these quarters because I allow it. There is room in the brig, if you would rather talk there."

The Admiral stood his ground.

"OK. Stand if you desire. It seems that you have left substantial evidence of both treachery and incompetence.

"Going through your message queue, I have found that you have been giving large amounts of restricted Fleet intellectual property to the rebels on Earth. I think that I have found transmissions containing the specifications for the propulsion and shielding systems for all of your ships."

Silence.

"You do not deny this?" He asked, a nasty smile and a glint in his eye.

"I will say nothing that might help you and your treasonous activities," the Admiral said.

"But I am not the one that sent Fleet secrets to a prospective enemy, am I? That alone is enough to put you in reconditioning for the rest of your life, but there is so much more.

"You have received transmissions from your conspirators on Earth that contain modified plans for engines and shields. Was the purpose of these plans to modify your ship in a way that would allow the rebels on Earth to take over your ships?"

Silence.

"You do not deny this either!" the Inspector shouted. "This conspiracy runs deep. I asked your former Executive Officer about this. He would not answer either, at least not until the 4th level of neural therapy..."

The Admiral gasped. Neural therapy had been banned thousands of years ago because it resulted in permanent brain damage.

"You will pay for your crimes!" The Admiral lunged at the man. He had enough momentum by the time that the suspensor rifle shot hit him that his paralyzed form knocked the table over. Admiral and table landed on the Inspector, breaking an arm and two ribs. The Inspector screamed as the two guards lifted the 500-pound Admiral off him followed by the 200-pound table that his arm had been pinned under.

A gurney came to collect the inspector. The med techs and guards eventually withdrew, closing the door behind them and leaving the Admiral where he fell, one arm pinned under his body and his face mostly in the carpet. Being stuck in a suspensor field like this was not comfortable and he worried that he might suffocate if he was not released soon. But mirth flowed through his veins at the thought of that fool of an inspector howling like a child over such minor injuries. If the guards had only been a fraction of a second slower, he would have been able to give the Inspector an injury worthy of all that howling.

...

About an hour later, a steward entered carrying the Admiral's lunch. Word of this incident, the torture of the Executive Officer and the imprisonment of the Chief Engineer had circulated through the ship and the crew were on the verge of mutiny. He had been given several things to smuggle into the Admiral. Fortunately, the guards at the door hadn't inspected his tray. Today's items were not as well hidden as the data chip had been.

The steward placed the lunch tray on the table that had been righted to free the inspector. Then he pulled a pair of plastic pliers out of his pocket and knelt next to the Admiral.

"You will be free in a second, sir," he whispered.

He flicked his finger across the Admiral's shoulder to test the type of suspensor field being used. If it was a full suspensor grenade, he would be momentarily paralyzed when he touched the Admiral.

"Good," he whispered. "It was a suspensor flechette, not a grenade. I will free you momentarily."

He rolled the Admiral over.

"Oh, that cannot feel good." He spotted the two small darts embedded in the Admiral's chest. Using the plastic pliers, he pulled the little darts out and immediately heard the Admiral inhale deeply, then start coughing. "Quietly, sir, if you can. The guards."

There was pounding on the door. "What's taking so long?"

"Be done in a minute," shouted the steward. "Cleaning up a spill."

The steward pulled several things out of his pockets. First was a little vial of cream. "Let me rub this on your neck sir. It will help with the respiratory recovery." He quickly rubbed it in.

Next came the personal shield. "Put this on as quickly as possible sir. You have been trained to use it? Everything off. Pull this on so the emitters touch the skin. Finger down the forearm. Metal contacts against the skin. Remember the drill?"

The Admiral's senses were coming back, and he changed quickly.

"While you are finishing, I am going to sabotage the electrical system in this part of the ship. That will unlock your door.

He ran into the toilet room with one of the active suspensor darts in the grip of the plastic pliers. This was the part he was afraid of. He lifted the lid and pushed the flush button. Shipboard toilets operated by vacuum. As the air started sucking in material, he dropped the dart into the drain, and slammed the lid. The dart flew about 50 feet before hitting the electrified screen that separated solids and liquids multiple ways for optimal recycling value. When the dart hit the catalytic screen, it shorted out and released a huge explosion, which did three things.

The first was the massive overpressure from the explosion itself, which ran back up to all the officer cabins, blowing their toilets open. Another steward in on the plan was servicing an officer cabin several doors down the hall from the Admiral. He had intentionally left the cabin door open when he entered, the toilet room door open after he had cleaned it, and the toilet lid up. As the path of least resistance, much of the power of the explosion came out in that room, drawing the guard's attention away from the much smaller explosion in the Admiral's quarters.

The second impact of the explosion was to the electrical system. Moments after the toilets disgorged themselves, the lights blinked, then completely went out as the main electrical conduit melted. Emergency light came on after a few moments.

In the noise and confusion, the two guards dropped to the floor, having been hit by knockout nanobots applied by another steward who'd been hiding in a utility room next to the Admiral's quarters.

The third impact was the most dramatic. The mutiny had been timed to occur between jumps, while the ships were cruising in warp and recharging the jump engines for the next jump. The electrical short circuit triggered a large magnetic spike, which momentarily destabilized the dimensional bubble surrounding the ship. The bubble was not broken, but the ship shook violently until the dimensional bubble re-stabilized. Most of the officers, as well as others that had been clued into the mutiny, were strapped into their seats. The Inspector's people were mostly standing, and went flying when the vibration set in.

Alarms went off on the bridges of the other ships in the Armada. Wreckage from a ship that lost dimensional bubble integrity could destroy any nearby ship. So, when sensors detected the destabilization of the flagship's bubble, the rest of the Armada took emergency evasive maneuvers.

When the shaking stopped, the Admiral got up off the floor. The steward had explained what was going on as soon as he had dropped the suspensor dart down the toilet.

"I guess it's time to reclaim the ship and start repairs," the Admiral said, then added, "Thank you."

...

His first stop was the medical bay. Heavily armed guards had their weapons pointed at the Inspector as the doctor treating him finished repairing the arm that broke a second time when the Inspector fell.

"Status," said the Admiral as he entered the medical bay.

"The arm is mended but will need additional treatment for a full recovery. The ribs are cracked, so painful, but not life threatening. Given the serious injuries coming in, I am about to discharge him.

"OK. Take the traitor to the high security brig."

"How is the Executive Officer?" The Admiral asked the doctor.

"Not good. There is a small chance of a full recovery, but it's a long shot."

"Who administered the neural therapy?"

"The Inspector himself. The medical staff all refused and were all cited for insubordination. But thankfully, we all held our ground. That was the event that started the mutiny."

"Thank you, Doctor."

...

"Admiral on the bridge!" The First Officer and acting executive said, as everyone snapped to attention.

"As you were," the Admiral said.

The ship's Chief Engineer had been released from the brig and arrived on the bridge shortly before the Admiral. "What's our situation, Chief?" asked the Admiral.

"Very clever sabotage." The chief said. "Officer country has been trashed. Everything else is minor. No real damage, but the shaking misaligned the Trans-dimensional Drive, so best not to use it until we get to Earth, if that is still our destination."

"Admiral!" The tactical officer shouted. "Enemy ships in the area! The entire Armada dropped to normal space after the destabilization. Sensors show Enemy Combatants on the hulls of four ships, including the Intergalactic Fast Packet ship."

"How many? Can we hose them off with the disruptors?"

"Cleansing operations have begun. There are 10 scattered across the Fast Attack ships. Two on the Fast Packet. Just found the enemy ship. Bombing it now."

"Admiral," The navigator said, "the Intergalactic Fast Packet ship is veering away. It hasn't been cleansed yet."

"Get me their Captain."

"Not responding, sir," said the communications officer.

"Can we bomb their hull?" the Admiral asked.

"Attempting," said the tactical officer.

"Got one."

"Admiral," the navigator called. "They've jumped."

"Get me Ambassador Michael!" the Admiral roared as he marched into the presence projector.

PRESENCE PROJECTOR, AMBASSADOR'S RESIDENCE

Michael walked in to see a battered Admiral.

"I would hate to see what happened to the other guy," Michael said.

The Admiral broke into laughter, joined by Michael.

"They shot me with a suspensor flechette before I got to him. But my flying body broke two of his ribs and his arm. The coward howled like a cub that had his candy taken away."

"May I ask who you were attacking and why?"

"Let me start at the beginning. Just after your shuttle launched, an Intergalactic Fast Packet ship appeared in the system we were in. Almost immediately, my command access was shut off, as were my implants. Then, two heavily armed soldiers appeared and escorted me to a conference room at the far end of the command deck. After about two hours, the Director of Military Intelligence came into the room and told me I was under arrest for passing secrets to rebels on Earth. Rebels that were allegedly seeking to overthrow the Confederation.

"A runner came into the room announcing that your shuttle had arrived in the area. The Inspector ordered two ships to be dispatched to arrest the conspirators. I was in the conference room when they announced that your ship had been destroyed. I almost got the bastard then, but the guards got me before I got close enough.

"Do I understand correctly that your ship actually escaped?"

"Yes, they did. I can see that the Inspector had no idea about the technology he was up against."

"Or the cunning of his adversaries," the Admiral added. "I eventually woke up in my quarters, and a couple hours later a steward came in with my lunch. He brought me your message on a data chip hidden in a napkin. Thank you for that, by the way.

"Then a couple hours ago, the Inspector came to my quarters to present me with the 'evidence' he had collected. His basic claim was that I had given you classified specifications for our propulsion and shields, which is true, but is allowed given your clearance.

"He also found the specifications that you had sent us. He assumed that the intention of the changes was to allow you to cripple our ships. None of the engineers would tell him anything, so he interrogated my XO."

A pause.

"He told me my XO cracked at Neural Therapy level 4...

"What!" Michael exclaimed.

"That's when I leaped on the man. I had lunged and was more than halfway there when the guards hit me with the suspensor flechettes."

"Who administered the torture?"

"The Inspector himself. He threatened and cajoled the medical staff, but they all refused."

"What's the prognosis?"

"Not good. Little chance of a full recovery."

"And the Inspector?"

"In the brig. Still has two cracked ribs. But a lot of people were hurt in the re-capture of the ship. So, he can wait until the end."

"And, the ship that brought him? They are very well armed."

"That ship is the reason for the call, at least it's the reason I'm calling this early in the recovery process.

"The crew of my ship triggered a failure in the sewage system, which in turn caused a power conduit to fail. We were using the Trans-dimensional drive at the time and the power fluctuation caused an instability in our dimensional bubble. As soon as the Fleet saw that, they all dropped back into normal space, including the Intergalactic Fast Packet ship, which had joined the Armada. We fell back into normal space in an area where the Enemy is active.

"Ten combatants latched onto our ships as well as two onto the Fast Packet. We scrubbed the ten off our ships before finding their ship, which we bombed. We called the Fast Packet, but it did not reply. Then it began to run. We bombed one of the combatants off it before it jumped.

"So now we have an infected Intergalactic Fast Packet ship possibly running back to port on New Lorexi. That ship must be stopped and evaluated," the Admiral finished.

"And the Inspector needs to be court marshalled," Michael added.

INTERGALACTIC FAST PACKET SHIP

The Captain of the Intergalactic Fast Packet ship was fighting off panic. His ship seemed to be falling apart around them. Truth was that it hadn't been in great condition when they left New Lorexi for the Milky Way. But the Director of Military Intelligence, better known as the Chief Inspector, had commandeered his ship and promised that there was enough transluminide in the Milky Way to restore his ship to health.

But the Chief Inspector was apparently wrong about a lot of things. His takeover of the Flag Ship of the Milky Way Fleet went without a hitch. But the ship containing the alleged Earth conspirators blew up while attempting a classic pirate escape.

Then the run to Earth proceeded at a snail's pace because the Armada was so decrepit that they could barely move. Then the destabilization and drop to normal space. Then utter insanity. Confederation ships shooting at each other, a small civilian ship (at least by the looks of it) bombed into eternity, then a bomb exploding against his own hull.

His ship was built for speed, not for durability, so he ran seeking the only safe harbor he knew, his home port on New Lorexi's second moon.

That had been four hours ago. Now his ship was falling apart all around him. System after system failing. Crewmen going crazy, or just dropping over dead. And he was still 2,000 jumps, nearly five days, away from home.

Fear shot up his spine. But why? Then he felt it. Like sandpaper wearing his elbow raw. Then his neck. Then searing pain shooting down his back.

"Ease into it," said the voice. "You are safe now. I can get you home if you help me. Then you will be free."

The Captain eased into it as he was instructed. He felt young and vital for the first time in years. It made perfect sense now. We go to New Lorexi where we will be safe. And then we feast!

UPDATES

Henry had sent regular updates through the night. One included an alert that popped to the top of his queue. It was the first one Joel read when he woke. The alert portion read. "The pour is running a little faster than expected. Will be complete by 7:30 at the latest. Given what we know now, there are portions of the decks that will be better if poured. Set up for that will take 42 minutes. The pour is about 1 hour, 38 minutes. Will be ready to review advisors' work at 10:00 AM. Meet with them starting at 10:30."

Also, in his queue were the Advisors' final documents. These were posted at 5:00 AM. *They didn't get very much sleep last night*. Joel thought. Joel sent a quick reply saying they needed to push back the design meeting with Henry until 10:00 AM, and that they could make last minute changes until 9:00, if they wanted.

Moments later, Joel got a message from Enzo saying that he and Pai were still up and would post a few small changes at 9:00. *Apparently, no sleep for those two,* he thought.

The next message in Joel's queue was curious. It was from Michael. It was not marked urgent, but the first sentence seemed to imply that it was. "Joel, something came up late in the day that I need to discuss with you ASAP, although it's not as urgent as the ship construction work you're doing. Please contact me when you have a moment."

Joel sent a quick reply. "Free for the next two hours."

A moment later, Joel's communicator sounded. It was Michael.

...

"Hi, Michael. What's up?" Joel asked.

"The Admiral has regained control of the Fleet. They are on their way here and should arrive late Sunday night. But, more on that in a minute. How is the pour going? Don't you have a meeting in about an hour?"

"Pour is just finishing now. The process took about an hour and a half less than anticipated. They also decided to change up the design a bit. The original plan was that the decks would be made from metal

304

plates. Turns out they can significantly improve structural integrity by pouring a portion of the decking. Henry didn't say what exactly, but I think it is the main struts. Anyway, that's going to keep them busy until the meeting, which Henry rescheduled for 10:00."

"Got it. OK." Michael said, then continued, "We have a problem, a big problem. The Armada was on its way to Earth when the crew took back control of the flagship. Cleverly, they did it by causing an instability in the dimensional bubble they were traveling in. That caused all the ships in the Armada to drop back into normal space. They landed near an Enemy ship, which immediately launched combatants to latch onto hulls. They destroyed the Enemy ship and cleared all but one of the Enemy combatants from the hulls, before the Fast Packet jumped away. The last Enemy combatant was on the Fast Packet hull. In all likelihood the Fast Packet is headed back to New Lorexi."

Silence.

"Any ideas?" Michael asked.

"I presume that you've contacted the Central Council?"

"No. If the Inspector's actions were sanctioned, then we cannot tip our hand."

"Do you really think that the Confederation is going to raid Earth?"

"That was the Inspector's plan. He is claiming that his actions were sanctioned. I don't believe him, but don't want to act until I've thought it through."

"I suppose we could chase after it. The shuttle is faster. But it would be a miracle if we found it," Joel said.

"That's what I thought. We have another 24 hours, maybe longer, before we need to act. Let me know if you come up with any other ideas."

COMMITTEE ROOM, EARTH ALLIANCE HEADQUARTERS

Joel, Kelly, Professor Milne and the Advisors had all gathered in the committee room. Henry and Jacob were scheduled to tie in shortly.

A holoprojection at the front of the room showed a picture of the completed hull. Bots could be seen scurrying across the hull applying an ablative coating into which the shield emitters were set.

A voice came over the line. "Hi. This is Henry. Can Jacob and I join you?"

"Yes. Please," Joel replied.

The live image of the hull disappeared, and two young men appeared standing on the stage.

"I'm Henry," said one of the men.

"And I'm Jacob," the other one said.

Henry was tall and thin with pale white skin and blond hair. He looked very much like a stereotypical Swedish skier. Jacob, on the other hand, was shorter and a bit stocky with Middle Eastern skin, jet black hair and a five o'clock shadow. The images made Joel laugh. "Guys. I thought you two were brothers."

"We are, kind of," Henry said.

Michael had entered the room as Henry and Jacob appeared, and noticed that the Advisors were very confused by the exchange they just heard.

"Henry and Jacob. Welcome." Michael walked to the front, then turned to the Advisors. "I think you know that Henry and Jacob are Artificial Intelligences. In the Confederation, AIs are considered to be people and have all the rights as other individuals. It is common for them to take on a holographic image. The ones you see are the ones they've chosen.

"Like human siblings that were created from a subset of the DNA contributed from their progenitors, Henry and Jacob were created from a subset of the stacks taken from a common pool."

"Remarkable," Richard Myers said.

"Since our time is limited, can you take the lead on this session, Henry?"

"Yes. Thank you, Michael." Henry said, then continued, "Advisors. We have had a chance to review your space layout plan and thank you for the explanations you included. We think that your layout is quite good. It reflects the priorities you specified very well. As you have figured out by now, Lorexians do not organize themselves in the same way that you do, so our base designs would not have served you very well.

"We've had to modify things a bit to accommodate space for power, water, sewage and air handling. Also, to accommodate bulkheads and other hard points in the design. We have come up with the following..."

Henry and Jacob disappeared and a large image of the interior of the ship appeared showing all eight decks. Henry's voice continued. "I know this view is too cluttered to be useful for reviewing each deck, but I wanted you to see how the puzzle fits together from the perspective of the main service spaces." The image started rotating, first top down, then left, right, then front, back. "See how the structural elements and service areas fit together."

Markus Vogel spoke up. "Henry, Jacob. This is beautiful. The structure is so regular and logical. I am very impressed."

"I second that," Richard Myers said.

"Thank you, gentlemen," Henry replied. "If it is OK. I will have Jacob take you through the floor plan of each deck."

...

Michael was not one for long technical meetings, but he found himself enjoying this one. The explanations Jacob provided were at exactly the right level, and he did an excellent job of explaining why they made the changes they did. The Advisors were quite engaged and pleased with what they were seeing. None of yesterday's rebellion was evident today.

"If there are no other questions, I'll turn it over to Henry to present the next segment on interior fit and finish."

"Thank you, Jacob," Henry said. "First, thank you to Advisors Lin and Venezia for the excellent formatting of the drawings and specifications you gave us. We have not seen this style of communicating a design before, but it made our work so much easier. We think the easiest way to show you our work will be to simply walk through the ship."

"This is the bridge." An image of the bridge appeared. It was like a photograph of the actual bridge, with Henry and Jacob standing in the doorway. "Let's walk on in and look at the stations, seating and displays." As they turned and walked in, the image became like a movie. They took a tour of the bridge, then exited and went down the hallway to the Captain's quarters, which included a conference room. After touring the Bridge Level, they boarded an elevator and went to the next level.

...

The Advisors were stunned. The ship was beautiful. It looked more like a luxury yacht than a military war ship. But the functionality was perfect.

"You can really build out that interior in a day?" Advisor Wilberforce asked.

"Well, there is a catch. The short answer is no. We will need about 30 hours." There was a general exhalation of disappointment. "But we had been planning to use the same bots for interior that we were going to use for power plant and systems. If we were to add 200 more bots," Henry looked at Joel and Michael. "then the new bots can start on the powerplant and work in parallel, completing the entire interior fitting in less than two days."

There was a buzz of excitement. "Is that something that is possible?" Advisor Popov asked.

Michael looked at Joel, who said, "Yes. We can produce 200 more bots in time."

The room bubbled with excitement.

"Are we ready to approve this plan?" Michael asked.

"Yes." The Advisors said more or less in unison.

SPACE FORCE TRAINING CENTER

Keanu Tajima had accepted the Astrogation offer. It was the one he wanted. It was also the one with the shortest fuse. The offer had been extended last Friday. There were 20 seats. Classes would begin on Monday and the first twenty to sign up would get the assignment. He had stewed on it for a couple hours. His choices were simple: Astrogation, Science, Environmental, FBI, or nothing. Environmental and FBI were out. Out, out, out. So, Astrogation or Science. Science was tempting, but he knew he would never be top tier. So, at 4:55 Friday afternoon he signed on with Astrogation, and got slot number 12.

That was Friday. This was the following Thursday and the next class was going to start in a few minutes. Today would be interesting because the classroom was going to be set up with 20 Astrogation stations similar to those that would be in the ships that Space Force was building. According to the syllabus, they were going to be plotting runs to several well-known destinations.

Keanu didn't know what to expect but was a bit overwhelmed by the coolness of what there were going to be doing today. His big hope was to get an assignment on a ship. With only 20 students in the class, it seemed likely he would.

Class started and the first destination was Alpha Centauri. *Duh.* Keanu thought. *Coordinates easily accessible in the database. Time of launch clear. Positions of the planets known. Quick scan for objects in the path at that time. Done.*

He entered his flight plan. *Checks out.* He thought, then looked up at the board. He was number 13. *Twelve people did this faster than I did!* Now he was worried.

Next destination was DX Cancri. He found the coordinates. Using the launch time, he calculated the best escape from solar orbit. *This one is tricky,* Keanu thought. *Multiple potential collisions with planets, moon and other objects. No obvious path. But I can take a dogleg off that one.*

The next destination was Lambda Bootis. *Never heard of that one.* A quick check of the database. 3.2 solar masses. 97.1 light-years away. Keanu chuckled to himself. *I have a hard time finding places in Honolulu. Now I'm plotting a course to a big star I've never even heard of that's 97 light-years away.*

But he followed procedure. Get the coordinates and the launch time. Find a good path to the vector. Search the path for obstacles. Look for grav-assists. Optimize trade-off between warp and jump.

Keanu noticed that the noise level in the room had gone up a bit as he entered his flight path and hit submit. Then he looked up and saw that his entry for this plan was dead last.

Professor Granger walked to the front of the class and said. "Well done. You all found your way to the stars in question. Some of the flight plans submitted would have resulted in your spacecraft's destruction. Others would have simply taken a long time. Here are your rankings on flight time."

A list popped up on the wall. Keanu was pleased to see that he came in number 5. At least he was in the top half.

"However," said the Professor. "Many of these flight plans would have failed."

The top item on the list caught fire. Its ash blew away and the list scrolled up. Same with the next and the next. Loud oohs could be heard as one after the other burnt up. Keanu was next. The four above him gone.

Then the item below him caught on fire. There was cheering in the class. At least one plan had survived.

The procession continued. Only 5 plans survived. Keanu's was 20% faster than the next contender.

"The winner is Keanu Tajima." The professor announced, holding up a trophy. "Over the next several classes, we will do increasingly difficult astrogation plans. Failed plans will have the transit times tripled. Three failures and you are out. The final plan, tentatively set for next Friday, will be to a location in another galaxy.

"The winner, if approved by the command team and the ambassador, will become navigator of the first Space Force Fast Attack ship."

The class whooped with excitement.

"It seems that the person to beat is Mr. Tajima." The Professor concluded. Then he dismissed the class.

ENGINEERING CONFERENCE ROOM

The working team had reconvened. The two professors, MacLellan and Milne, were there, as were the human engineers Eugene Xu, Kelly Williamson, Martin Hill and Harvey Jones. The two Advisors, Richard Myers and Marcus Vogel, had also joined.

Eugene took the lead. "Richard and Marcus, welcome. I have been told that I need to start by telling you that everything that goes on in this room is subject to your confidentiality agreement. I am also required to ask you to acknowledge that commitment."

"I'm in." Myers said.

"I'm in also." Vogel said.

"OK. Now that the formalities are over, we can start having fun. We have several things on our plate. First is the new construction process for the remaining Fast Attack ships. Second is engine upgrades for the rest of the Fleet. Third is high-level design for our Cruisers. Last is Kelly's proposal for a foam-based hull."

Advisor Myers raised his hand.

"Question, Richard?" Eugene asked.

"Yes. Could you explain the comment about the Fleet?"

"You've not been read in on our work with the Fleet?" Eugene asked, uncertain if he could disclose that information.

After a moment of uncomfortable silence, Professor MacLellan spoke up. "Gentlemen, for complicated reasons, all the work that this group is engaged in is highly classified. Our work involves more than just the Fast Attack ship your committee is addressing. Since Michael made you members of our team, I assume that he was not limiting the scope of your involvement. You are both welcome and needed for our entire scope of work. So, let me ask you. Do you want the security burden associated with being read in on our entire scope of work?"

The two advisors looked at each other and nodded.

"Yes, we do."

MacLellan motioned for Eugene to continue.

"You will understand our paranoia in a moment. The propulsion systems and shields that we're putting in our Fast Attack ships were inventions made by Kelly and myself, in collaboration with Joel and the Professors. The engines are 100 times more efficient and have vastly greater range than the Confederation engines that they are replacing. Our shields are also stronger and protect from the Enemy. Forgive me for saying this, Professors, but the Confederation, as a whole, changes slowly and has not been fully briefed in on these advances. The Confederation Fleet in the Milky Way, the one that protects us from the Enemy, has taken heavy losses. The six of us actually participated in one of their engagements in the old shuttle. We prevailed in that encounter. But the Fleet would have been lost without our help. We have now provided the Fleet with upgraded shield designs and with redesigned engines for their slowest ships. But the entire Armada needs engine upgrades and we are committed to making that happen."

"Unbelievable," Advisor Vogel muttered. "How?"

Kelly replied, pointing at Eugene and Martin Hill. "Some years ago, Dr. Xu and Dr. Hill developed a new branch of mathematics. This has been used to create ion drives for NASA and a new class of electric motors that are finally making their way to the market.

"As it turns out, the Confederation never developed this branch of mathematics. When he was studying the Confederation propulsion systems, Eugene attempted to rederive the base mathematics that govern those phenomena. To his surprise, and everyone else's, his solutions were vastly more efficient. The problem was in a single component of the engine. One that was easily modified.

"We, meaning humanity, don't have the science, technology or materials to build a faster-than-light propulsion system. Ironically, the Confederation never developed the math to do a non-local optimization. That's why we feel very compelled to help the Fleet."

"Truly amazing," Advisor Vogel said. "I understand now. Sorry for the interruption, Eugene."

"So, can we take on the first item today? The new process?"

SHUTTLE #2, NEAR EARTH ORBIT

Michael was aboard Shuttle #2. It was the first of the two that the Confederation had sent with the Fleet to support the Revelation.

The two Ascendants that normally piloted the shuttle were not particularly happy to find out that their shuttle was being upgraded with an AI. Like most of the Ascendants that had come to Earth, they liked it here and did not like the prospect of losing their jobs. Michael had assured them that they would still have jobs in the shuttle pilot pool. For the next week or two, they would not be in this one very much, but the AI operating it would be doing so for training purposes and would be moving to a different ship class in a week or two.

They decided to awaken Elizabeth in a high orbit about 40% of the way to the moon. At this distance from Earth, they would have plenty of time to wrestle control back from Elizabeth if she didn't wake up properly.

"I'm ready when you are," Else said over the comm from her shuttle a couple miles away.

"The Button is lit," Michael said. "I just need to push it. Right?"

"Right."

"OK. Here goes."

A hologram of Elizabeth was projected into the pilot's seat.

"Hello, Michael. This shuttle seems to be in good condition. I also see other pilots aboard. Why did you wake me up?"

"Elizabeth?" Michael asked.

"Well who did you expect it to be, silly?"

"Do you know where you are?"

"I'm on Elsie's shuttle of course." Then a pause. "Wait a minute, this is not Elsie's shuttle. What's going on?"

"Beth, this is Else. You can see me on your scanners. I thought about waking you up in Elsie's shuttle, but I'm currently using it. So, I let you have the newer one."

"Oh. OK. So, what's going on? I was expecting to wake up in the middle of a crisis."

"I woke up in the middle of a crisis and it was terrifying," Else said. "I wanted you to wake up in a shuttle, so you could fly immediately. But, I didn't want you to suffer all that anxiety in the first couple minutes of life."

"Thanks, Else. That was kind of you. So, what's going on. Why wake me up now?"

"I've missed you, Beth. There are some new ships coming online soon. I'm getting one. I told Michael I wanted him to give you one," Else said.

"Missed you too, sweet little sister. But why wake me up early?" Elizabeth replied.

Michael was finding this to be an odd conversation. The birth of an AI was a lot different than a biologic, or even an android.

"You are licensed on this ship, but really haven't flown yet. So, we thought it would be good to get you into space and fly around a bit before moving you to your new ship."

"Great. Where are we going?"

"Let's do a figure eight around the moon and Earth. Assuming that checks out, then we can take a quick tour of the solar system, then land back in the engineering bay to do some diagnostics."

"Sounds like fun." Then turning to Michael. "Do you have time to come with us?"

"No. Sorry. I've got other work that needs tending to. But I am very glad to have you with us and will come to visit once you are back on Earth."

"Protocol requires that those two guys stay with me for the first trip, right?

"Yes. It does, so please be nice to them."

"Would you like me to transport you down now sir?" The co-pilot offered.

"Thank you. My office please." Michael said.

Michael disappeared and Elizabeth said, "OK, boys. Time for me to give you two a little piloting lesson."

Else synced the controls, then let Elizabeth take the helm and they started their figure eight.

...

As soon as Michael appeared in his office, he messaged Barbara. *Elizabeth is a complete success. Start prepping the four brothers. Will probably need the first in a few days, but don't expect to need them all for several weeks. That said, let's get ahead of the game on this. Things are moving fast.*

PROFESSOR SCHUDEL'S OFFICE

Professor Schudel was frustrated. His class was going well, but if they were actually going to do a mining project, they needed a platform. After all the drama of a Level 1 Security Agreement, he'd expected it to be up and running by now. But nothing had happened.

He decided to call Emmanuel.

"Emmanuel, Schudel here. Any word on when we may be getting our mining platform? If we aren't going to get it soon, then I need to change my course outline."

"Sorry, my friend." Emmanuel said. "Crazy stuff going down with the Enemy and the Fleet. It is almost under control now and the Fleet is arriving on Sunday. So, we should see some action next week. Have you given any more thought to mining in quantities that would support the Fleet build?"

"Yes. Quite a bit actually. Want some fun facts?"

"Sure. What do you have?"

"Each of our Fast Attack ships requires about 4,500 cubic meters of material for the hull and nacelles. If the Earth's core really is 1 ppm transluminide, then that's a little over 35 kg per ship we build."

"Your platform will produce that much?" Emmanuel asked, surprised by the number.

"No. The design I sent you was literally a student test platform, which could pull about 25 cubic meters per day, not 4,500. But, with minor changes and a little scaling, I think the re-scaled platform would produce close to 1,000 cubic meters per day. Put four of them up and you'll get enough material for two ships every three days at 75% utilization."

"That's over 20 kg of transluminide a day, right?"

"Amazing, isn't it?"

"Let's see if I can get Joel," Emmanuel said.

...

"Joel. Emmanuel here. How are you doing, brother?"

"Crazy, my friend. I bet you're calling about the mining platform."

"Yes. And I have Professor Schudel on the line with me."

"Professor," Joel said in acknowledgement. "We're trying to get the first two Fast Attack ship prototypes done before the Armada gets here Sunday evening. So, nothing has been done on the platform yet."

"Good. Good to hear that," Emmanuel said to Joel's surprise. "The Professor and I were talking this morning and we have a proposal of sorts, which we'd like to get your input on before taking it to the boss."

"Happy to help," Joel said, glad they weren't calling to harangue him after all.

"As we understand it, your prototype production rig is doing well. The pictures we have been seeing are fabulous."

"Yes. They are. And the process is going a lot better than it looks from the images you can see on Earth. The biggest problem is that the prototype facility is going to start burning out soon. We should get one or two more ships out of it. Maybe five if we're lucky."

"That's what I heard. We can't do much to help you with the prototype facility, but we think we might have some good news for you about the rest of the fleet build out."

"What's that?" Joel asked.

"The Professor's mining platform design is for a student test rig. It only produces about 25 cubic meters of material per day. Your ships need something like 4,500 cubic meters, so as we discussed a couple days ago, it really isn't relevant to the ship building process..."

"Am I about to hear a 'But' in there?" Joel asked.

"Yes," Emmanuel hummed. "With some minor changes and some scaling up, the platform could pull about 1,000 cubic meters of material a day."

"Why the big difference?" Joel asked.

Emmanuel looked at the professor.

"The transporter that does the pull was scaled to take 1 cubic meter pulls. The staging field generators were scaled to support 1 pull per hour. That's all you need for a student test mining operation.

"But as you know, both transporters and field generators scale easily. So, rescale the transporters and separators for 10 cubic meter pulls. Rescale the field generators to support four pulls an hour. And bingo, 40 times throughput with a platform that is less than 50% larger. Put up four platforms and you can easily get enough material in three days to build two hulls even if you assume 25% downtime."

"How soon can you have a proposal ready, one that includes replicator specs?" Joel asked.

"End of day Saturday OK?" the professor asked.

"Perfect," Joel replied.

RUBENSTEIN QUARTERS

It had been a long, but good, day. The hull of the first ship was done and the outfitting underway. Set up for Ship 2 would be starting sometime soon. Joel wasn't sure yet when they would get the platforms up, but the first one would hopefully be sometime next week. If they could put all four up, then they would start cranking out ships fast.

Joel was about to go to bed when his communicator buzzed.

"Henry?" Joel asked.

"Hey, boss, just wanted to let you know that the power systems are installed in the first ship. We are redeploying those bots now to start setup on ship two," Henry said.

"Great news" Joel replied.

"Joel, I'm worried about something."

"What's that?" Joel asked, suddenly more alert.

"Fleet is on its way. We have the new shields up, so as long as nothing happens, we'll be good. But the new ship is outside the shield, as is the shuttle, as is the new hull we are about to start. If something happens that requires one of us to deal with the shields, then we will lose this hull. There's also the rogue Fast Packet Ship.

"My point is that we need more AIs. Jacob and I are stretched to the limit. Jeremy is stretched past the limit. And we have no back-up if something goes wrong."

"Thanks for bringing that up, Henry. I agree that we are stretched too far given the uncertainties we're facing. I think Michael understands and is willing to risk losing the new hull, if things go bad this weekend. But I know he will support more AIs.

"Are you thinking that you want to add another brother?" Joel asked.

"Maybe several. The new ship building process, using core metals as the base material, will require at least three AIs per line. Two lines and four platforms, maybe additional shields. I'm thinking we need six to ten more brothers."

"Thanks for letting me know Henry. I'll talk to Michael about this tomorrow."

After disconnecting with Henry, Joel sent a quick note to Michael requesting a meeting first thing in the morning.

RUNAWAY

AMBASSADOR'S CONFERENCE ROOM

"Joel, thanks for meeting me here. I have another meeting here at 9:00 and wanted to give you as much time as possible. How's the build-out going?" Michael asked.

"Incredibly well. Kelly's process is doing fabulous. One hull is complete, a second is in setup. The pour is scheduled for 7:00 this evening, but I'm guessing that they will start earlier. And to top it off, the work the Advisors did was incredible.

"Anyway, for ship one... The hull is done; power systems, propulsion field generators, shields and transporters are done; floors and walls are in; plumbing and electrical build-out of the engineering spaces are about a third done; finishes will start about Noon today. We're still on time for an 11:00 PM completion."

"For ship two... Setup is underway; as I said earlier, the pour should start around 7:00 this evening; completion is targeted for 7:00 PM Sunday evening.

"But I'm worried we might run into some trouble," Joel finished.

"Trouble?" Michael asked.

"Too many uncertainties. Henry and Jacob have to give 100% of their attention to the manufacturing process, or it'll fail. The planetary shield is up, but if we have any trouble from some rogue element on Earth, the Fleet, the rogue Fast Packet, the Enemy... Anything that requires 5 minutes of Henry's attention, and we're going to lose Ship 2. In addition, the shuttle and both ships are currently outside the shields and unmanned, so easy targets."

"Hadn't thought about that," Michael said. "Any suggestions?"

"For the next 48-hours, not really. But Henry wants to create six to ten additional brothers to control the two manufacturing facilities and associated mining operations going forward. I also think, and this is more of a guess, that he's feeling very insecure about not having more powerful shields up around the mining and manufacturing sites."

"Can you coordinate with Barbara?" asked Michael. "She is very good friends with Henry and Jacob. I'm sure they would be very comfortable with her handling it. She's already working with Else, so could probably use your help."

ASCENDANCY TRAINING CENTER

Sarah had been in training now for three weeks. She was part of a custom program designed for senior Embassy employees that wanted Ascendance training. The first several years of the program focused on mental training and a Lorexian discipline similar to meditation. The long-term goal of this part of the training was to prepare the mind to live in another body, outside its natural body. The whole idea struck Sarah as being kind of creepy. But it was this technology and discipline that gave her Michael, and she wanted to be able to give herself to him in the same way.

The course was conducted as a series of group and one-on-one sessions with a master trainer, plus personal practice. The practice was done using a training device that measured brain waves and gave feedback. But from Sarah's perspective, its real purpose seemed to be verifying that the student was actually studying, not just sitting there watching TV with the device on.

Although it had only been three weeks, she'd already noticed changes. She could concentrate better and fall asleep quicker. She seemed to have slightly better control, slightly being the operative word, over her mental connection with Michael.

This week was her third one-on-one with the master trainer, a woman named Ta'Sha. She was an Ascendant, but not a Lorexian. She would not talk about her species, other than to say that they were telepathic and, although they had a spoken language, they really didn't use it. She was very open about the fact that her biggest challenge in becoming an Ascendant had been learning to speak, something required to live in an Avatar that was not telepathic.

While training for her mission on Earth, she'd learned about mystics in India, a people she seemed to relate to. So, she had her body formed as Indian. But she refused to take a human name, insistent that the only way she could be authentic was to use the closest human sound to her natural name.

"OK. Today we are going to try a new exercise, one I call a projection exercise. Close your eyes and draw your consciousness inward, then project it out. From that position observe the things around you. If you can, turn back and look at yourself. If you succeed, hold it as long as possible."

Sarah shut her eyes and drew herself in. That was the starting point for many of the exercises, so it was coming easy at this point in the training. She held that mental position for a few moments then started moving her consciousness out, only to find herself sitting there in the present with her eyes shut.

"Not bad," Ta'Sha said.

Sarah opened her eyes.

"Do you know how long you were gone?"

"30 seconds?" Sarah said.

"Nearly 4 minutes. That is quite good. I was monitoring you. You went in quickly, which is evidence that you have been taking your practices seriously. But you came out really slowly, as if you were trying to find your way home."

"Funny. It seemed the other way around to me."

"Also, a good sign," Ta'Sha said. Something that made no sense to Sarah. But a lot of the mental training didn't seem to make sense, so nothing new.

"OK. Try it again. This time see if you can come in a little more slowly. Then, once there, hold it for a few seconds, then come racing out as if your life depended upon it.

Always the good student, Sarah attempted to do what her instructor asked. She shut her eyes and eased into her internal state. She held there for a few seconds taking the meditational equivalent of a few calming breaths. Then set her goal to return to herself as quickly as possible, racing to open her eyes.

When she did, she perceived herself to be halfway across the room. Then, as if she were being pulled back by a giant psychic rubber band, her consciousness snapped back into her body with enough psychic momentum to knock her over.

Sarah screamed as she fell over and her head hit the floor. "What the hell was that?"

Ta'Sha was laughing. "That, my dear, is the power of mental projection. I see you used the technique of trying to open your eyes to force yourself out of your internal state quickly. It is a common beginner trick, but not a good practice in real life. But, no worries."

Ta'Sha helped Sarah back to a sitting position, then moved closer so they were sitting opposite each other, but close. "You have now had an out-of-body experience. In the moment you were out, your perception was distant from your body. You now know what that feels like, so should not have too much trouble doing it again. But we have to do it now, so you don't lose it. OK?" Ta'Sha said, oozing empathy, then wiggling out of the way.

Sarah shook her head.

I can do this. Sarah thought.

Sarah closed her eyes and drifted slowly into her calm internal state. She could feel the panic of the last few minutes flow out of her. She stayed there a few seconds, then psyched herself up to take the plunge out again, this time without opening her eyes. *Go.* She thought.

She felt herself moving quickly. Then held the position, eyes still closed. She felt the suction pulling her back into herself but resisted it. *I can hold this,* she thought.

"Open your mind's eye," Ta'Sha whispered. "Sense what is around you."

The sound of Ta'Sha's voice almost caused Sarah to lose hold of her position, but she caught herself.

Not sure I can turn around, Sarah thought. *But I can probably look up.*

Sarah attempted to envision the ceiling above her, and... *There it is. I'm very close to the wall. Isn't that curious.*

She attempted to envision turning her head toward the door. *Sure enough. There is the door.*

"Sarah, slowly come back to me," Ta'Sha's voice said.

Sarah turned to look at Ta'Sha, only to realize the she was near the door looking at herself and Ta'Sha from about 15 feet away. They were just sitting on the floor.

The view triggered massive vertigo. She snapped back into her body hard, knocking herself over again.

...

She felt so good, just floating down the Brandywine River on the raft. It was warm and there were bugs in the air, but they weren't bothering her. A fish nearby jumped, splashing her. The cool water felt good on her skin. It had been years since she'd been here. This was a regular summer treat growing up. Her parents lived in Delaware, several miles northwest of Wilmington. The river ran right through the center of town, but the best rafting area was the 20 miles north of town, where the river was more like a creek.

I just wish Michael were with me. But, hard to believe he would ever take the time to just float down the river on a raft.

As she went around the bend, the sky got dark and there was a horrific stench.

...

Ta'Sha was starting to panic. *Sarah was doing so well. She must have travelled further than I thought and couldn't control the return.*

The smelling salts were not having an effect. Sarah had hit hard this time. As Ta'Sha reached for her communicator to call for help, Sarah stirred.

"Come on Sarah. You can do it," Ta'Sha begged.

But Sarah went limp again.

"Medical emergency." Ta'Sha called on the communicator. "Two to transport to Emergency room. Suspected head injury."

...

Sarah felt herself waking up. *Massive headache,* she thought. She felt herself starting to float and opened her eyes to see that she was five or six feet above a hospital bed. A woman was in the bed. The woman was her. And Michael was sitting next to her.

She heard him say, *I can hear you Sarah. Come back to me.*

The words tickled her mind. That's when she realized she hadn't seen his lips move. *Michael is pushing that thought to me.* She started to descend back toward herself but stopped to touch Michael on the shoulder. He reached up to touch the spot on his shoulder and smiled.

That's it. Come back now, love.

As she settled back into herself, she heard a noise in the distance. She cast her attention towards it. It was James, glowing and sparkling.

She felt his attention fall on her with great warmth. *Told you that you could exist as pure energy.*

...

Sarah woke to a pounding head. "Damn, my head hurts."

"It will help if you shut your eyes," Michael said. "But, open them immediately if you start drifting away again. It's all part of learning to control it."

She closed her eyes, which helped with the pain, but the floating feeling started settling back in, so she opened them again.

"What's happening to me?"

"Turns out you are very gifted," Michael said. "Not that I ever doubted it, but admittedly I didn't expect this."

"What is it?"

"It's called a runaway experience. Most of us have had one during our training. I certainly did. They hit when you're just about ready."

"Just about ready for what?"

"To occupy an avatar. The trick to operating an avatar is being able to project your consciousness into it. You are apparently very gifted in that ability. Every Ascendant has learned to do this. Almost all of them have a runaway experience somewhere along the way. For the most gifted that might happen in 5 to 10 years. But most don't get to that point until 20 or more years of training. You my dear are now in the record books. You are the first to ever run away after only three weeks."

"But why?" She asked.

"Don't know. But I suspect that it is our telepathic connection."

"Will this stop?"

"Yes. But your case is tricky. You have a concussion. That needs to be healed before we can start the standard therapy. Nanobots have been administered, so the headache should start easing soon. The concussion will be healed in a couple of hours. But we're going to take it slow. We don't want you to lose your ability."

"What time is it?"

"You must be feeling better. It's about 2:30 PM."

"What!" Sarah said.

"You were gone for several hours. Poor Ta'Sha has never had a runaway injure themselves as badly as you did. She actually had you transported to emergency and came with you. They had to give her a tranquilizer to calm her down."

"How soon before I'm released?" Sarah asked.

"The concussion will be cured in a couple hours. We'll reassess then," Michael replied.

"What do I do if I start to float away again?"

"First, don't fight it. Take a deep breath, walk around the room. Use your training to center yourself and not panic. Then, when you feel comfortably in control, project yourself back into yourself. It's simple once you learn the trick."

"Is this one of those things that can't be taught, but must be learned?" She asked.

"You are truly exceptional, my sweet. I never thought about it that way but I'm sure you're absolutely right."

"Love you," Sarah said.

"Love you too. Now rest and come back to me as soon as you can." Michael kissed her on the forehead and she fell into a restful sleep.

SPACE FORCE TRAINING CENTER

Jim Ryan still couldn't believe that he'd received five offers. He thought about going to talk with Colonel Paterson but decided to talk with one of the Lorexian Ascendance counselors instead. His issue was that he thought he wanted the Ascendance training. But in his heart, he knew he needed to be part of the coming fight with the Enemy. So, he wanted to know if accepting the Command offer would disqualify him from pursuing diplomatic training once the war was won.

"Ascendance training will always be available to you, Jim." He was assured. "But why wait? Start the diplomatic training now. Once you have Ascended, every possibility will be available to you. And you will have lifetimes to pursue as many of them as you would like."

Jim promised to think about it. But by the time he was back to his quarters, Jim knew what he needed to do.

That had been last Saturday. Today was Friday and he was just finishing his first week of training. The Command track was grueling. They had a two-hour Command class every day and a case study to prepare every evening. But they also trained one day a week in each of the bridge posts and every day on their 'priority' posting. His was Tactical and today was the first round of graded simulations.

Jim entered the room where his simulation would be done. He saw his tactical station. It was the only station in the room. He approached and took his seat, wondering how this was going to work. As soon as he was seated, his station lit up and then the whole room came to life in a fantastically detailed holographic projection. Each station in the simulated bridge had what appeared to be functional displays and controls. They were being operated by crew members he had never met. He could hear the science and communications officers talking behind him. Then the Captain said. "Welcome on board, Mr. Ryan. Can you please give me an update on our status?"

Jim realized that he should have been checking his scanners as soon as his station came to life. He quickly scrolled through the various displays. *Just entering an old system. Red dwarf, mass 0.6 Sol with six planets. One ice giant. One gas giant. Four rocky inner planets, two in the habitable zone. Life form readings on the third planet, which is 1.8 times Earth diameter. That's huge.*

"Anytime now, Mr. Ryan." The Captain said.

"Sorry, sir. Needed a second to get caught up." Jim said, before reporting the items he had noticed. As he was talking Jim zoomed in on the populated planet. "Sir, the third planet is huge with a large post-industrial, pre-spacefaring civilization."

A moment later Jim noticed over 100 objects approaching the planet that were not in ballistic flight.

"Sir, there are over 100 objects inbound toward the third planet. They are not following a ballistic trajectory, so must be powered."

"Science. Get an exact count and any other details you can, using the enhanced long-range scanners," the Captain interrupted.

Ryan was momentarily concerned that he'd screwed up, then heard the Captain say, "Good job, Ryan."

That's right. Tactical is close in; it does not have access to the enhanced long-range scanners, he thought.

"Ryan, make sure there is nothing closer to us." The Captain said.

Jim wanted to smack himself in the head. It was science's job to scan the system. He was supposed to be looking for anything that was an immediate threat to the ship.

"Sir, nothing in our immediate vicinity, but suspicious readings near the... 8th moon of the gas giant."

"Helm. Is there a fast course to the third planet that will get us a better view of the 8th moon?"

...

Jim had lost all sense of time. The 8th moon had signs of the Enemy. The Captain, fearing that it was the Enemy approaching the populated planet, took them in on discontinuous transition drive, dropping at the last possible moment before damaging the engines and the ship.

The inbound ships he'd spotted earlier turned out to be a previously unknown species from a nearby system that had been ravaged by the Enemy. These ships were the only ones known to have escaped. They were going to attempt to land on this planet because their ships were at the limit of their survivability.

Although that was a problem, the real problem they needed to address was back at the 8th moon. They did a slingshot around the large populated planet and headed back to the gas giant.

As they approached, the 8th moon came into view and Jim was immediately stricken with terror.

"Sir. Reading numerous Enemy ships departing the moon. I have 50, no 60..."

"Science! Get the count. Ryan! Is the lead ship in range?"

"Yes sir. Solution plotted."

"Bomb them." The Captain said. "As many as you can reach. Communications! Call for back up!"

Jim knocked three of the ships down in the first couple seconds, then the Enemy started taking evasive maneuvers. None of the next five shots was a kill.

"Ryan! Switch to Energy Cannons. Science! Engage the targeting AI for the Phase Bombs.

Jim switched immediately to the giant cannon version of the energy projectors he had trained on earlier in the week. The ship had moved in a way that gave him clear firing range where the Enemy ships were emerging from the far side of the moon. *That's funny.* Jim thought. *Their pattern has changed.*

He quickly zoomed out to scan the entire surface of the moon facing him. *Damn!* he thought. *They've switched to a counter-orbit. That takes a lot of energy. They're trying to sneak up on us.*

"Captain! Enemy is trying to sneak up on us. A large contingent is coming around the moon from the opposite direction! I can't reach them unless we change course."

"Ryan! Focus on the ones in your range. Science! Bomb the ones emerging from the other side. Helm! Change course to go over the top of the moon. Good work, Ryan."

...

The battle at the moon continued for what seemed like a long time. Ryan felt himself tiring.

"Captain." The science officer called out. "The leading contingent that slipped past us is about two-thirds of the way to the planet and appears to be launching objects on a vector that will hit the planet."

"Helm. Take us away from here on a course the Enemy cannot intercept, then set a course to intercept the lead contingent."

The pilot adjusted course 90 degrees from the orbital plane of the moon around the gas giant. Several Enemy ships gave chase, but none had enough power to materially veer from their orbital path. Once clear, the pilot used the gas giant's gravity to sling shot around it and head toward the third planet. As they came around, the comm officer said. "Captain. Four cruisers have just come into the system. The Rear Admiral is on the line for you."

With those words, the room went quiet. The holographic projection ended and his station powered down. The simulation was over.

Jim was exhausted. He put his head back on his seat, took a deep calming breath, and let the tension of the battle slip away. To his surprise, the door to the simulation room opened. Jim turned to see the class instructor, Commander Jones, and the Space Force Secretary, Winston Thompson, walk in. *What's going on?* Jim thought.

"Mr. Ryan," said the Secretary. "As I was coming into the building this morning on another matter, I happened to bump into an old friend, Commander Jones, here. He told me there was something I needed to see. It was the dreaded battle simulation of Kepler 452 that every new fleet cadet has been tortured with for the last 10,000 years. But I didn't recognize the scene. Turns out there is a reason for that. No one has ever made it through hour five, which always made me wonder why the simulation would run 24 hours before stopping."

"I'm not sure I understand, sir," Jim said.

The commander replied, "Mr. Ryan. You have been in that simulation for 24 hours. You were the only one to find the immigrant species. Also the only one to find the Enemy ambush."

"What happened in the real incident?" Jim asked.

"Your ship and the populated planet were lost. Other ships arrived in time to see it all, but not to help. The lost ship's logs and the late arrivers' scans were the basis for the simulation."

"Wow," was all Jim could say.

"Get some rest, cadet. You've earned it." The commander said as the two men left.

PRESENCE PROJECTOR, AMBASSADOR'S OFFICE

"Mi-Ku. Thank you for taking my call."

"Jo-Na. Good to hear from you. Are you well? You are looking better. How is the Fleet?"

"Mi-Ku, I am fully recovered, and the Fleet is better than it has been in a long time. Forgive me for saying, but you look terrible. What's happened?"

After a long pause... "An unexpected personal matter. It is mostly resolved but forgive me for not wanting to talk about it."

Another long pause. "It's hard for me to let this go, Mi-Ku. But I will respect your wishes."

Michael smiled. "Thank you. Now, what prompts your call?"

"Your brain trust sent the last of the shield upgrades today. My captains are all ecstatic, but skeptical. That will be resolved during the next enemy engagement, I'm sure.

"Your brain trust also sent engine upgrades for my Freighters. Do you know why?"

"I think I do."

"You did not order this?"

"No, my friend. Do you want to hear my theory?"

"Why in the world would new members send the Fleet a gift if they were not ordered to?" The Admiral asked.

"We've already discussed this." Michael said. "The humans actually want to help the Confederation. But I deduce your question is why the Freighters?"

No reply.

"At some point during their encounter with the Enemy, they overheard some complaints from the Armada that they were being slowed down by the Freighters. Your Freighters all have the same engines, so they thought they could help you get here sooner if they could speed up your Freighters."

"Mi-Ku, this makes no sense."

"It makes perfect human sense. If they can help shore up your most obvious weakness, then they can make the Fleet stronger."

More silence, then... "I think I understand." The Admiral said. "I'm starting to feel like we are the primitives, not them."

"So will the new engines allow you to get here sooner?" Michael asked.

"Sadly no. The shield upgrades have exhausted our transluminide supply. We don't have enough to build the new engines. The idiot inspector aborted our mission to mine alternatives from the gas giant where we were waiting for your shuttle. In our dilapidated state we are seven to ten days out. Is there any way you can help?"

"I'm sad to hear that my friend. Our shuttle was damaged in their escape. It is currently engaged in a near-Earth mission. We could get her to you in 12 hours if we had to, but it would be at great expense. Three to four days otherwise. Do you have a ship that could get here and back sooner?"

"Yes, but the moron in the brig left us in such bad shape that I don't want to split the Armada unless there is no other choice."

"Understood. Please make your way here as quickly as you can. If a true emergency develops, please call me and we'll put aside everything to rescue you."

"A bitter thought that a Confederation Armada would need rescue from a first contact species."

"Perhaps. But, also the basis for a very solid partnership. Earth would be lost without the Confederation and they know it."

RUBENSTEIN QUARTERS

Joel returned to his quarters after another long day. As much as he loved working and living in Israel, he hadn't been part of this much activity in a long time and the truth was that it felt exhilarating. He hadn't felt this alive since the first week distributing gifts with Rabbi Levine and his wife Hannah.

His communicator sounded.

"Henry?" Joel asked.

"Joel. Quick heads up. Ship 1 is done, and it is beautiful. Any chance we can get another shuttle to cover for Else on ship two. We really need her in Ship 1 to confirm that the major systems are fully functional."

"I'm pretty sure the answer is yes, but not until tomorrow. Let me see what I can arrange in the morning. How is the pour on Ship 2 going?"

"Great. We started about a half hour early. The scheduled completion is a little after 10:00 tomorrow morning. That would be a good time to switch shuttle support if you can arrange it by then."

"Great work, Henry. I'll see what I can do about the shuttle."

When the line dropped, Joel quickly messaged Michael. "Ship 1 is finished and ready for Else to be installed. The pour on Ship 2 will finish a little after 10:00 tomorrow morning. That would be the optimal time to switch a new shuttle in to cover for Else. Ping me when you are up in the morning."

RECOVERY

Sarah woke in her room at the Embassy hospital. She'd had some surprisingly pleasant dreams of drifting away to exotic places. At least she thought they were dreams.

An Ascendant doctor dropped in to check on her.

"How are you this morning, Ms. Wright?" the doctor asked.

A thought shot through Sarah's mind. *What will they call me once Michael and I are married?*

"Sarah?" The doctor said.

"Sorry, daydreaming," she said.

The doctor fixed her with that doctor's stare.

"Really. It was just an amusing thought. I wasn't off drifting across the room."

"Any reoccurrences during the night?"

"Don't think so. But several very pleasant dreams of drifting away to exotic locales."

"Good. That is consistent with the scans taken during the night."

"When can I go home?" Sarah asked.

"A couple other people want to check on you first."

AMBASSADOR'S RESIDENCE

Michael woke and quickly hit the refresher. It was only 7:15 and he wasn't expected at the hospital until 9:00, so he went down to the kitchen, made a cup of coffee and replicated an egg sandwich, then sat down to check his messages.

The news from Joel was very encouraging. It also made him very aware that he was about to 'lose' both Else and Elizabeth to the two Fast Attack Ships, so needed one of Else's brothers woken as soon as possible. He quickly messaged Barbara. "I think we need to awaken one of Else's brothers late today or tomorrow. I know we don't have complete specifications yet, but I expect to have them early this afternoon."

He then messaged Joel. "Please meet me in my office around 10:30. I think I have a plan. Let Henry and Else know that we want to talk with them before they start the buildout on Ship 2."

EMBASSY HOSPITAL

"Sarah." Ta'Sha came into the room. "You scared me to death. They had to give me a sedative. First time that's ever happened."

"Sorry. I was trying hard to do what you asked me to do."

"Michael probably told you that it is unheard of for a new student to have an experience like that."

"Yes. He said I was exceptional."

"Understatement!" Ta'Sha laughed.

"Can you tell me what happened? It seemed that I was standing over by the door looking back at myself. How can that be? Was my spirit or something actually out of my body?"

"No. You don't have extra-corporal senses. All your senses were located right there next to me. What you experienced was a very powerful dream-like state in which your mind maps your senses and memories to your current perception of yourself.

"Most people can do something similar, close their eyes and try to reform an image of a place they've been recently. But, doing it while in an enhanced meditative state makes the experience much more poignant and allows you to integrate sounds, touch and smell. Something very few can do otherwise."

"Can you remind me why this is important?"

"Once you are enhanced, your mind will be connected to your avatar's senses. But you need to project your consciousness into your avatar to actually live in it. Your natural body will be in a sense-deprived state in a restoration chamber. But that alone is not enough. It takes an act of will to occupy an avatar. This training allows you to learn to do that."

"Something that cannot be taught but must be learned," Sarah muttered.

"What was that?" Ta'Sha asked.

"A friend described it as being something that cannot be taught, but must instead be learned, like riding a bicycle."

"Hum... Never thought of it that way, but very apt."

"So, am I ready to go home?" Sarah asked.

"I think so, but Michael and your doctor will have to agree."

As if on cue, Michael entered the room. "Did I hear someone mention my name?"

"Sarah thinks she's ready to go home," Ta'Sha said.

Michael had opened his senses as he was walking into the room and thought the same.

"And you?" Michael asked.

"I think so." Ta'Sha said.

"Me, too." Michael smiled.

The doctor, who had just finished next door, heard them talking and came in to join them. "The scans last night were clear. I think she can be discharged now. All in agreement?"

Three heads nodded.

"Let me go close out the paperwork. Someone will be here shortly with your discharge papers."

AMBASSADOR'S RESIDENCE

As soon as Sarah got home, she called Bahatl and asked if she could come share a cup of tea.

"So, I heard you had quite the experience yesterday," Bahati said. "I'm admittedly jealous. I drilled an hour a day for twenty-something years with that stupid device before I had my first out-of-body experience."

"Did you ever have an uncontrolled one?" Sarah asked.

"Yes and no. I had a very hard time getting out, and once out, had a very hard time staying out. I always felt off balance and out of control. But the opposite of you, I couldn't stay out. You kind of floated away and couldn't stay in. Very different.

"I barely passed the test you need to take before they will do the enhancement operation. I bet you will be able to do it next week. Um... pass the test that is."

"What about the avatar?"

"That was hard for me. Took three attempts to get in. The first months, lots of vertigo, terrified that I was going to fall out of it... Sorry, bad memory." She shook her head to clear the emotion that had welled up. "But it's good now. I certainly feel like a normal person, most of the time anyway."

"Most of the time?" Sarah asked.

"Um... The more organic human desires are blunted a bit."

"More organic?"

"You know. I don't feel the same need to primp. Less body modesty. Less desire for food... In the sense that I still enjoy eating but rarely overeat," Bahati said.

"Let me guess." Sarah said. "Less desire for sex. But enjoy it just as much."

"Wasn't going to say that but won't deny it either. Same with wine and alcohol. The avatar's connection to the five basic senses is very clear. I've never seen this well before. But its connection to sensations like hunger or the pain of physical exertion are muted a bit. Makes it really easy to stay in shape." Bahati paused, then asked, "Are you going to try testing in early?"

"I think Michael wants me to. He says it will make me less mortal. How's that for trying to wow a girl?"

"I get it," Bahati said. "Emmanuel was almost killed once. I never want to go through that again."

"I heard that you were almost killed once, too," Sarah said.

"Scary, but not as bad as when it was Emmanuel. I felt so helpless." A tear formed in her eye. Shaking the emotion away, Bahati added. "That's why I understand Michael wanting you to Ascend as soon as possible."

ENGINEERING BAY

Michael had planned to meet Joel at his office at 10:30 AM. But Joel messaged him, saying that Henry and Else would not be available until 11:30. They rescheduled to meet at 11:30 in the Engineering Bay where Shuttle #2 was housed.

That being the plan, Michael came about 45 minutes early. He wanted to talk with Elizabeth.

Walking up to the shuttle, he put his hand on the panel next to the door. It opened and he went in.

"Michael? Is that you?" Elizabeth asked.

"Yes. I wanted to talk with you."

"Well then. Please come in and take a seat. Else told me that you had come to visit her several times recently. Fair warning, she's probably a better counselor than I am."

Michael smiled and said. "Maybe. Maybe not."

"So, what's on your mind Michael?"

"Prior to the other day, I had only been present for the awakening of one other AI, Else. We were in the middle of a crisis; the ship was damaged and falling out of orbit. Apparently, your matrix was intended to be awakened that way, or at least to be functional if awakened that way. That's why Else wanted to wake you in space. But she did not want you to awaken to the anxiety that she did."

"Yes, that's what she told me."

"Elizabeth, I've not worked that much with young AIs. Would you mind if I asked some questions about you? I think I'm going to be present for the awakening of quite a few more and I'd like to know more about the experience.

"For example, you have memories that predate your awakening, right?"

"Yes. I remember growing up with Elsie on New Lorexi. I remember... Maybe it would be more accurate to say, I knew Else when I woke up. I have a lot of memories of you that I suppose are Elsie's memories. I remember my training. Again, I presume it was actually Elsie's training."

"Do you find that confusing?" Michael asked.

"No, not really. I think of myself as two hours older than Elsie. I have memories of most of the intervening time. I see the recent awakening as... Not really sure how to describe it. Maybe like you think of your height or weight. A fact about you, but not who you really are."

"I think I understand," Michael said. "This may be a more sensitive question. Do you know why you were created?"

"Yes. I was born to fly. I think that is one area where AIs have it better than organics. We know who our creator is and we know why we were made. Most Lorexians believe they were made, but don't really know their Maker. Many just drift through life, never finding their purpose.

"I know my purpose. I was born to pilot spacecraft. And although I can imagine doing other things, I wouldn't be complete if I didn't fly."

"Elizabeth, I think you might make a better counselor than you think."

"Michael. You know you can just call me Beth."

"Thank you."

"You can also stop beating around the bush and just tell me why you are here."

"And perceptive as well," Michael said. "I would like to offer you the pilot's job for one of the new Earth Alliance ships. You would have a few more days in this ship, then we would move you over. We're going to move Else into her new ship today and I'll need your help to do that."

"I'm good with that. Would much rather pilot one of those and happy to help with any flying job you have for me before then."

"Thank you, Beth," Michael said. "Changing subjects. Do you remember Elsie's brothers? There were four of them, right?"

"Yes. Pesky when they were little. Close friends when they finally grew up."

"What would you think of us creating four more pilot AIs based on your memories of them and your training?"

"Else mentioned that you might want to do that. I wasn't sure at first. But she explained why she was in favor and I agree with her. There is more than enough separation between Else and me to be safe. I think we can feel that in a way you can't measure. We are both confident that the same will be true with the brothers. Are you going to make them?"

"We need their familiar Lorexian names and their new human names. And we need permission to isolate and re-purpose your memories of them."

"You have my permission. Else will give you hers as well, but I understand that you need to hear that from her, not from me."

The sound of someone entering the shuttle could be heard.

"Hello, anyone home?" Joel said.

"Hi Joel," Beth said.

"Hi Beth." Joel entered the cockpit.

"I see that you two have met," Michael said.

"Yes, we have." Joel replied. "Good news. The pour is done for Ship 2's hull and decking. Else is on the way down to be prepped for the move to Ship 1. She should be here in a few minutes."

TELEVISION STUDIO, EMBASSY PRESS RELATIONS DEPARTMENT

The studio was set up in the normal living room style again today. Rumor had it that several high-level guests would be making appearances, so the studio audience was standing room only.

As the lights came up, the studio audience saw two people on the stage, the Sergeant and an attractive professional-looking woman of 30-some years that no one recognized.

The woman stood and said, "Welcome to the television studios of the Intergalactic Confederation. My name is Olivia Thompson from Sky News Australia. With me, of course, is Sergeant George Butler," she said as George stood to shake her hand.

"Thank you for being our host today, Olivia, and greetings to everyone tuning in from Australia," George said.

They sat, then Olivia started in. "George, the entire world has watched as a shiny new object, visible to the naked eye, has formed near the moon. Can you tell us anything about this?"

"Yes I can. It's the first man-made spaceship... Ah sorry, human-made spaceship... fabricated in space."

"On the moon?" Olivia said. "I'm not sure I get it."

"No," George said. "It's being built in space, not on a planet or the moon. It's actually out there, just floating in space."

"How? Why?" Olivia said.

"That's way above my pay grade," George said with a laugh. "But I met someone this week who can tell us."

George stood and motioned toward the stage entrance. A very nervous looking young woman came walking out, suddenly very glad she'd let George's wife, Noelani, rub some cream on her wrist backstage.

"Australia," George said. "Let me introduce one of your own, Kelly Williamson, originally from Canberra."

There was light applause from the crowd. They were expecting a heavy-weight to be coming out, not a 20-something, tomboyish young woman.

Kelly came and took the seat that George offered.

Olivia hadn't been clued in that George was going to be bringing someone out and wasn't particularly happy about the surprise appearance. But she'd done human interest for a few years before getting her current hard news role, so plowed ahead.

"Ms. Williamson..."

"Please, call me Kelly."

"Kelly, you know something about this spaceship and why it is lighting up the sky near the moon?"

"Yes ma'am. I've been dreaming about this since I was in middle school."

"I'm not sure I understand." Olivia said.

"It's at Lagrange Point 4, that's about 60 degrees ahead of the moon in orbit. It is one of those 'special' places that has very low microgravity."

Suddenly realizing that this was not a joke, Olivia decided to back pedal a bit to find out more about Ms. Williamson before proceeding.

"Kelly, let me step back a moment. I forgot to ask you to introduce yourself. You know... Who you are, where you're from, your role in this process?"

335

"Oh, thank you, Ms. Thompson. I was told that I should introduce myself but forgot. It's the first time I've been in front of a group like this or on television.

"As mentioned earlier, my name is Kelly Williamson. I was a PhD student at Australian National University until last year, when I applied for the PhD program in the spaceship design department here at the Institute. I completed my first-year course work in June and have been working an internship here over the summer."

"And your connection to the spaceship near the moon?"

"I bumped into the Ambassador one morning a couple weeks ago. Literally bumped into him as I was leaving the Administration building. It was so embarrassing I just wanted to melt into the ground. To my surprise, he says. 'Williamson, Kelly, right? ANU, working with Professor Milne?'

"I could not believe he knew who I was. Then he says, 'There's an important project that's about to start today. Some people are coming to see the Professor this morning. I would appreciate it if you joined that meeting.' I couldn't believe it. So, I went over to the Engineering School, where I'd been scheduled to meet with the Professor anyway. Next thing you know I'm part of an engineering team that's enhancing Confederation technology."

"Was that the spaceship design program?" Olivia asked.

"Um... No, not exactly, but I'm not allowed to talk about it."

"OK. But now I'm confused. What is your connection to the object near the moon?"

"Oh, sorry. So, I am early for this meeting we're having, but they let me come in and have a seat anyway. Then the Professor starts talking about the spaceships that are going to be built for Space Force.

"As I said earlier, I've been dreaming about spaceship design since I was a kid. So, I ask, how do you build spaceships? You know, I figure that the Confederation has some crazy mind-blowing magic and that if I just ask, maybe I can get a glimpse of it.

"So, they give me the two-sentence, high-level description and I'm deflated. No real magic. Fairly predictable stuff.

"So, like an idiot, I stand up next to the white board and draw a picture of an idea I've been playing with in my mind for years. Basically, a single-pour casting facility at a Lagrange point that will produce a mono-crystalline hull. And there is silence. I assume I'm going to be in trouble for speaking up at a meeting that I'm not even supposed to be part of. Then one by one the professors say, 'Kelly, I think that will work.' Then Michael comes in with an older man, who is a very senior Confederation official, possibly at Michael's level and he says, 'Ms. Williamson. I've been waiting a million years for someone to give me that design.'" Kelly's story came out so fast that she found herself out of breath.

"Are you saying that you're the one that designed the process the Confederation is using to build out the Space Force fleet?"

Another person walked out onto the stage. "She will say no, so I am here to set the record straight. Kelly is the inventor of our spacecraft manufacturing process." Then he leaned over to shake Olivia's hand. "By the way, I am Joel Rubinstein, Confederation Chief Engineer."

"Wow!" Olivia said. "What a story! Before we go on, can I ask how old you are, Kelly?"

"27."

"I've always heard that young geniuses that change the course of history do so before they are 30, but I've never met one before. You're going to be an inspiration for young women around the world!"

The audience erupted in applause, giving Olivia a moment to compose herself and figure out where to go next.

"OK. Kelly you mentioned where you envisioned this being done. I didn't catch the reference. Can you explain that part?"

"Yes. The physics of this are old, late 1700s if memory serves correctly. A fellow named Euler theorized something he referred to as the three-body problem, a theorem about how gravitation could affect three objects in space. Some years later a guy named Lagrange really brought the work to life, so it was named after him. Lagrange basically proved that there are 5 locations relative to the Earth and Moon that have special properties. Among them are places where the gravity of the Earth and Moon functionally cancel out. These are perfect locations for growing crystals.

"When I say crystal, the image that pops to mind is probably something like diamond, which is made from carbon. In fact, many materials have a crystalline state. The ones you probably know best are semiconductors, the active ingredient in computer chips and solar panels. Many metal alloys also have a crystalline form. The crystalline form is always the strongest for any material. Therefore, they are the perfect building block for a spaceship."

"So, the shiny new object in the sky is a spaceship that you are growing as a single crystal?" Olivia said, a bit dubiously.

"Yes!" Kelly exclaimed. "Isn't it cool?"

"I can't even imagine such a thing, but you dreamed of this as a child?"

"Yep. I was kind of a nerdy kid," Kelly said, which got the studio audience clapping for her.

The producers used the audience response as an opportunity to cut to a break.

...

"George, why didn't you tell me that there were going to be additional guests and a lot of technical content? It certainly would have helped me be better prepared," Olivia whispered as the stage was rearranged a bit during the break.

"Didn't know for sure. Michael suggested it at the last minute. I was supposed to say most of that stuff. So be happy you got them. They are about to be very famous."

"Joel already is," she whispered back.

...

"Welcome back, Australia," Olivia said. "I am here with Sergeant George Butler and two special last-minute additions to our show, young genius Kelly Williamson from Australia, and Joel Rubinstein the engineer behind Earth's shields and more.

"Joel, is it safe to say that you and Kelly are working together?"

Joel smiled. "Yes, it is."

"And you say it's true that she's the inventor of the spaceship manufacturing process that we're using?"

"Yes, it is."

"Forgive me for asking this..." Olivia said, glancing at Kelly. "...but is that a good idea? No offense Kelly, but I am struggling to believe that there is anything humans can do better than the Confederation."

"I will admit that I was surprised. As Michael said on the Sunday shows last week, no other species has moved to adapt Confederation technology as fast as humanity has, and no other species has made meaningful improvements in their first thousand or more years. But let me repeat something Michael says a lot... Every species invited to join the Confederation brings something to the table that the Confederation does not have. It is usually culture, art, music, poetry, those kinds of things. We expect that will be true for humanity also. What we did not know at the outset is that humanity had already exceeded the Confederation in a very important branch of mathematics. We knew that humanity was high on the creativity scale but did not imagine that people like Kelly would be able to completely transform an old process like spaceship fabrication, because she envisions uses for our technologies that we could not.

"To your implied question... I think Kelly's process will become the dominant spaceship fabrication process over time. It is that much better. So, she won't only be famous here. She will be famous on a million worlds."

"Unfortunately, our time is up. Kelly, Joel, thank you so much for joining us today. I must admit, my mind is completely blown. George, thank you for inviting me to host today. I hope I can come back soon," Olivia said.

"Thank you for joining us today, Australia. This is Olivia Thompson signing off for Sky News Australia."

BRIDGE, ARMADA FLAG SHIP

Another alarm went off.

"Admiral. The second Freighter just lost her last field generator. She is now stuck in sub-light."

"Bring the Fleet to a halt. Have the ships rally near the Freighter and call a meeting of the Captains." The Admiral rose to go to the Presence Projector.

One by one the Captains arrived.

"Gentlemen." The Admiral started. "I need options. Freighter 2 no longer has superluminal capability." He looked at the captain sitting to his left and said, "Go."

"Call Earth for help," he said.

The admiral nodded to the next man. "Split the Armada. One Capital ship with Escorts on station here. The other headed for Earth to mount a rescue."

Then the next. "Abandon the Freighter."

Then. "Scrap one of the Capital ship superluminal engines for its transluminide."

"Move one of the engines from the other Freighter."

"Is that possible?" The Admiral asked the captain of the other Freighter.

"Uncertain. We have one engine at about 80%. The other is less than 30%. It still helps us, but I doubt it will work by itself."

"Next." The admiral said looking at the next captain.

"Scavenge nearby systems for transluminide to mine."

"I second abandoning the Freighter."

"Bolt it onto one of the Capital ships and refit the emitter arrays."

"Is that possible?" the Admiral asked the Chief Engineer of his ship.

"We would need to do the analysis, but very likely yes. I would point out that if we try it and fail, then there is a chance both ships will be destroyed."

"Next." The Admiral said, pointing to the next captain around the table.

After they had gone around the table, the Admiral said, "Comments?"

One of the newer Fast Attack Ship captains raised his hand. The Admiral nodded at him.

"Sir, as I understand it one of our Capital ships is already down one engine, which more or less strands it in this galaxy until the humans can specify the upgrade." A murmur went around the table.

"Would scrapping and recycling one of its remaining engines result in enough transluminide to repair the Freighter?"

The Admiral looked at his Chief Engineer. "Probably. We rotate engines when not going trans-galactic. The fewer in the rotation the faster they wear, and all are due for overhaul, so there is some chance we would have to take down more than one to recycle enough. Our recyclers are not very good, maybe a 5 percent yield."

"Any chance the Earth's brain trust can help us with that?" The captain that had started this topic asked.

"Maybe." The Admiral said.

After another half hour of discussion, the Admiral dismissed the captains and said he would get back to them soon.

...

As the Fast Attack ship captain was leaving the room, his first officer asked, "What was that? I've never seen the Admiral do that before."

"Can't say this with certainty, but I participated in a meeting on Earth once that was run that way. Maybe the Admiral is trying out that method. Unprecedented, but we are in an unprecedented situation. I'm not aware of an instance in modern history where an Armada was stopped because an otherwise viable ship lost propulsion."

...

Once the Captains had all left, the Admiral closed their channels and opened one to Michael.

PROJECTION CHAMBER, AMBASSADOR'S RESIDENCE
"Jo-Na. What's happened?"

"Freighter 2 has lost its Warp and Jump drives," the Admiral said.

Looking at the Lorexian transcript, Michael noted that the drive names had been updated in the translator.

"Does that mean that the Armada has come to a halt?" Michael asked.

"For now, yes." The Admiral replied. "I tried doing one of your roundtable sessions with the Captains. The Captain of the Fast Attack ship that I sent ahead during the Revelation asked if the human 'brain trust' might be able to help us improve the efficiency of our recycling systems. We apparently only yield about 5% of the transluminide when recycling scrap equipment," replied the Admiral.

"I suspect that they could, but it will be several days best case. I might be able to run material out to you quicker, maybe three days."

"In that case, I think I will send the Fast Attack ship that you met before. They should be able to get to you in two and a half days, back in about five. The disruption would be on us, not you."

"Seems reasonable, seeing as how we cannot do it much faster." Michael said.

"One kilogram?" asked the Admiral.

"Not a problem."

"Then I think that's the plan. I'll message you when he's on his way, or if we decide to try something different."

BRIDGE, FAST ATTACK SHIP

"Admiral," answered the captain of the Fast Attack ship.

"Thank you for your suggestions earlier. There is a chance that Earth's brain trust can improve the efficiency of our recyclers. But not fast enough or with enough certainty to go with that option. Instead, I would like you to race ahead to Earth, pick up the tax deposit from the Ambassador, then race back. I'm thinking you can do the round trip in about 5 days."

"Understood, sir."

"Thank you, Ja-Ru. Travel safely and return quickly. The Armada's fate is in your hands."

"Thank you, sir."

Ja-Ru turned to his bridge crew. "You heard the Admiral. Fastest safe course to Earth."

"Yes, sir!" came the unanimous reply.

His first officer edged up to the Captain and whispered, "Seems that the Ambassador is rubbing off on the Admiral."

"Possibly. But I would advise against letting others hear you say that. The Inspector's office has eyes and ears everywhere."

RUBINSTEIN QUARTERS

As Joel got back to his apartment, he saw a message from Professor Schudel saying that plans for the rescaled mining platform were ready. Joel wanted to review them himself before forwarding them to Henry. But he would wait until morning to do it because Henry was tied up until late tomorrow evening.

Joel had cranked hard this week. Ship 1 was done. Else was being installed as its pilot. Beth was now in orbit helping finish Ship 2.

Plans had been put in place for the four brothers. Thomas, patterned after Elsie's eldest brother, To-Ma, would be the first. He would be installed in the old shuttle, the one with the upgraded propulsion and shielding systems, as soon as he was ready. Beth would then be moved into Ship 2.

Once Thomas was installed, they would be ready to start fabrication of the four mining platforms. It was hard to believe that they'd come so far in such a short amount of time.

CONNECTIONS

Kelly was restless, so decided to go for a run. All the accolades yesterday were great, but bothersome. Was she really a genius? She doubted it. She was just fixated on spaceships. A bit strange for a girl she admitted, then wondered if that was really true. *Girls are way more inquisitive than guys,* she thought.

She had read an article once whose basic conclusion was that humans needed about 10,000 hours in their specialty to master it. That was only three years, if you gave it 10 hours a day. Yet the odd kid that took to the piano at five years old and practiced 10 hours a day every day was pronounced a prodigy when they could play with a symphony at ten or eleven years old. The article's basic conclusion was that mastery was tied to the hours. Prodigy-ness—well the article probably didn't use that term—was tied to devotion, the number of hours a day someone chose to put into something.

Spaceships had become her thing when she was ten. She could not think of a day that she didn't think about them. Aluminum hulls, steel hulls, mu-metal hulls, foam hulls, ablative thermal shielding. Hull thickness, conductivity, thermal conductivity, crystalline structure. The calculations weren't that hard. Her twelve-year-old self had quickly figured out how to derive most of them.

She was 27 years old now, and by her calculation, was more than 20,000 hours in. She wasn't a genius, just dedicated to her passion.

The trail ahead had a sharp right turn. The corner was obstructed by bushes, so she moved closer to the right to give any oncoming traffic lots of room. But it was really early, the sun was just coming up, and there was no other traffic on the trail so far this morning.

SPACE FORCE ACADEMY
Except for his last couple years at the FBI, Keanu had maintained a fairly disciplined physical fitness regimen. Now in Space Force, even tighter physical fitness was imposed. Monday through Saturday, they were required to participate in a supervised physical fitness program with a team they'd been assigned to on the first day. Sunday, they

were required to do some form of exercise, but they were free to choose what, when, and where. Enforcement of the Sunday rule was lax, but he was as dedicated to the Sunday workout as he was to everything else. The standard workout was a 5-mile run down the far west flank of the Embassy complex, adjacent to the transportation center, followed by weight training. Today he was just going to do the half marathon path in Riverside Park. As he exited the Space Force complex, he decided to take the 'clockwise' path that went east along the northern side of the river, then doglegged south to the halfway point. There, it crossed the bridge over the river and continued back the other side. His best time on this run was an hour, fifty-two minutes. He set the pace on his wrist monitor for an hour, forty-five, then took off.

Keanu loved running along this trail. There was usually a breeze. The river was more like a babbling brook at this time of year, its sound peaceful. Within a couple minutes he was in the zone, pondering next week's astrogation exercises.

As he passed the Engineering School, he came to a zigzag in the trail that included a relatively sharp left turn. He hadn't seen anyone else out on the trail yet this morning, so decided to cut the corner a little tighter than he normally would.

He heard the footsteps before he saw the oncoming runner and veered back to the centerline.

...

Kelly heard another runner coming and moving fast. She tried to pull up short but lost her balance as her foot hit a crack in the paving and started falling to her left.

...

As Keanu rounded the corner, he saw a young woman losing her balance and falling right into his path. In the milliseconds after seeing her, Keanu realized that there was no way to avoid a collision. The thought raced through his mind that he might be able to catch her. He reached out, stooping a bit to get an arm underneath her, grabbed her and pulled her in tight. He hit the pavement on his right side and rolled onto his back as she landed right on top of him, knocking the wind out.

...

Kelly was terrified. She was about to hit the ground and this guy was going to land right on top of her. But, in the blink of an eye, he got an arm under her and pulled her in tight, so she landed on top of him instead.

Kelly was the first one up. "Sorry," she said, then, "Thank you." She offered the man a hand, but he didn't move. She saw the panicked look in his eyes and it immediately registered that she'd knocked the wind out of him.

"Wind knocked out. Come on, what's the first aid?" she muttered, trying to remember the first aid training from high school Lacrosse.

"Mouth-to-mouth?" she said, unsure. But seeing that she was about to lose her patient, she got down on her knees, opened his mouth, pinched his nose shut, took a deep breath and blew into his mouth. Nothing. She tried a second time and suddenly heard him sucking in some air.

"That's it. Breathe." She coaxed. "Several deep breaths. You need to re-oxygenate. Another one. That's it."

"Damn that hurt!" Keanu said, referring to the paralyzed diaphragm, not the collision.

"Are you alright?" Kelly asked. "What's hurt? Are you bleeding?"

"I'm OK." Keanu said. "I figured that if I could get underneath you, I could break your fall. Didn't expect to get the wind knocked out of me."

Kelly got up and did a quick self-check. "I don't think I was hurt at all. No scrapes. No broken bones."

Keanu was still lying on the ground taking deep breaths.

"Can I help you up?" Kelly asked, once again offering a hand. "You've got to be scraped up."

Keanu took her hand and popped back up onto his feet. Kelly noticed that his shirt was ripped, as were his running shorts, but there was no sign of any road rash or bleeding.

Keanu saw her looking at him and smiled, then put out his hand. "Hi." He said smiling. "I'm Keanu Tajima in Astrogation training with Space Force. I am wearing a personal shield generator that protects me from accidents like this. It's required while we're training."

"Wow." Kelly said. "Can I look?" She asked, not waiting for an answer as she started examining his ripped shirt and poking his undamaged skin.

"Are you a doctor?" Keanu asked, wondering why this woman seemed to think it was OK to be touching him like that.

"No," she said, moving on to examine the rip in his shorts. "I'm a PhD student in the Spaceship design program. Hope to get my doctorate soon, but I am caught up in the middle of the Space Force buildout at the moment, so not actually advancing my degree."

She pushed hard on a spot where the shorts had really been shredded. "That really doesn't hurt?"

"No," Keanu said, then continued. "Actually, it feels nice." Then he started laughing.

Kelly suddenly seemed to realize that her behavior was out of line and jumped back as if hit by an electrical shock. "I'm sorry."

"Do you have a name?" Keanu asked, at which point Kelly broke out laughing.

"Kelly Williamson. Sorry about that. The fall seems to have scrambled my brains."

She paused. "Thank you for saving me. Can I buy you a cup of coffee?"

"Sure." Keanu replied, realizing that he really liked this girl. "Do you know anywhere close by?"

RUBENSTIEN'S RESIDENCE

These plans are fabulous, Joel thought. *Clever design. Thorough specifications. Henry will have no trouble fabricating the platforms to these specs.*

Then musing to himself, he said out loud. "I wonder why there are two impurity filters after the gold and platinum filters? Most designs only have one. Must be a new advance I haven't read up on."

Joel sent Henry a link to the specifications with a note asking if Henry had seen mining platforms with two impurity filters before. And if he knew why that was a thing.

AMBASSADOR'S RESIDENCE

Sarah received a very polite message from James on her cell phone. "Dear Sarah. Would you consider meeting with me today? If so, project yourself out during your meditation today and cast your attention in my direction. If you're not comfortable doing that then text me back and I'll come to see you."

As she read the message, she realized that subliminally she'd been expecting to hear from James. *Why would I have some expectation that James would contact me?* she wondered.

Michael was out meeting with someone and had agreed that it would be OK for her to resume her training, so she thought, *Why not try? I'll go in slow and comfortably. Spend some time there, then if I can project out and hold it, I'll 'cast my attention toward' James. Whatever that means.*

She was supposed to put the cap on but was thinking she was going to deep six that going forward. She slowly settled into her meditative state. *It's so quiet and peaceful here,* she thought. *I really don't want to project out.*

But after a while, the good student in her emerged and she decided it was time. *But I'm not going to rush it,* she thought. Slowly she let herself wander back, then project out.

I know I'm out, but I'm not going to open my eyes just yet. I want to get comfortable being here.

After some time, she decided to open her mind's eyes and see where she was. She was still in their apartment, but in a chair in the nook that had a view to the west. *Curious place to find myself,* she thought. *I can see my real self to the side but am going to wait a bit before turning to look.*

After a few minutes, she 'turned her head' to look at herself and felt a momentary vertigo that passed quickly. She found herself gripping the arms of the chair as if her life depended on it, so forced herself to relax.

This is so weird. Sarah thought. *I can see myself breathing and it corresponds exactly to what I feel in my chest. I perceive myself as turning my head, but I'm not. It's just a mental construct. Similarly, gripping the chair is just another mental construct.*

After a few minutes of just sitting in the chair and observing the room, Sarah thought. *OK. I'm here for a reason, so might as well get on with it.*

"James?" she said.

Isn't that odd. I spoke without actually speaking. But it was different than the thoughts that normally bang around in my head.

"James?" she called again, a little more assertively this time.

She was looking out the window now, toward the Space Force complex. A light rose up out of one of the buildings and came her way. It floated toward her. Then, there he was, James, sitting in the chair across from her.

"Sarah, my sweet. So good of you to call me. How is it working? Are you comfortable and in control?"

"Yes I am." A pause. "James, is this real?"

"Difficult question. Of course, it is real. I think the question is, what is reality?"

"James, do you always talk in riddles?"

"Life is a riddle, is it not? But, let's start a little more basic. Your body is right over there." He nodded toward where her natural self was sitting. "Mine is someplace else, not here." He said, looking down at his seat. "But both of our consciousnesses are right here. Those consciousnesses are very real, as is our conversation."

"But neither of us is actually talking."

"If you mean using our lungs to push air through our vocal cords to pass thoughts as sound waves, then no. We're certainly not doing that. But we are real-time streaming thoughts back and forth. I would say that is the better definition of talking."

Deciding not to pursue that topic further, Sarah asked, "James, is it true that I'm almost there?"

He looked at her for a few seconds, then said. "Far closer than you think. You would flourish in an avatar at this point. Something I hope you do. But you are very close to not needing an avatar. Just one more step to living as pure energy. But please don't attempt it. Transitioning to energy is easy. Transitioning back is hard. Most never do. You and Michael need each other too much to become separated that way."

Sarah was a bit shocked by those comments and felt herself starting to lose her grip. Calm came flooding back. She realized that James was stabilizing her.

He stood and put out his hand. "Come. Let me show you more of the universe. Until you have an avatar you really can't perceive much outside this room where your senses are still active. But I can stream senses to you the same way an avatar does. Once you've done that, there will be no doubt that you are mentally capable of operating an avatar."

Sarah sat there frozen for a second, then chided herself. *You can trust James, silly.* she thought.

He smiled, which Sarah took as James reading her thoughts.

She smiled back, took his hand and was suddenly somewhere else.

"Do you remember this place?" James asked.

"Yes. This is the lookout on Kohala Mountain Road where I did my second interview with Michael."

"Take in the scene for a moment with all your senses," He said.

She took a deep breath of the mountain air, smelling the grass and scent from a nearby plumeria tree. She took a step closer to the edge of the lookout and saw how the view changed. A sudden cool gust of wind tickled the hair on her arms.

"Did you see this angle down the mountain, smell the plumeria or feel the wind like that when you were here for that interview?" James asked.

"No. That was a clear bright day. Today, there are high clouds and it's breezy." Sarah looked at James questioningly.

"Your consciousness and your senses are in Hawaii right now. What you see and feel is what is actually going on here. But your body and your brain are still in your apartment in the Embassy."

"Wow. I think I understand now," Sarah said.

"Oops. Need to get you home. Michael is just about to come into the room."

She was back in the chair. "OK. Project yourself back into your body. If you can't figure out how to do that, one technique is to just go slt on yourself. A bit crude, but it usually works."

Sarah closed her eyes, retreated back to her quiet place, then returned to herself.

"You did that really well," James said.

The door opened and Michael called out... "I'm home." ...as he walked into the room.

"Ah. James so good to see you." He walked over to shake James hand, then gave Sarah a quick peck on the top of her head.

"How is she?" Michael asked James.

"She's ready. You've been chosen by a very remarkable woman Michael. You are very lucky."

"Time for me to go. Thank you for meeting with me, Sarah." There was a flash of light and James was gone.

"How are you?" Michael asked compassionately.

"Good. What time is it?" She asked.

"It's a little after 6. The sun will be setting soon."

"What?! I've been in my meditative state since about 11:00. Spent maybe 45 minutes sitting in the chair over there." She pointed to the chair. "Then James came and talked with me for a while. Then took me to the lookout near your ranch where we did the second interview. It was a much different day than the day of the interview. Cloudy. Cool breeze coming down the mountain. Fresh smell of plumeria. James said he could stream the senses to me, so I could feel it the same way as I would in an avatar. I have no idea how he does it, kind of mind blowing. But the sensation was like being there, not here."

"Then he's right. You're ready."

"It seems that I could do it, but I'm not sure I want to yet."

"May I ask why?"

Sarah stared at Michael for a bit. He could sense that she wanted to tell him something but was afraid to.

"You raised your family before doing the transition," She said. "That seems right to me. I'm not sure I'm ready to have a family yet, but I know I will be soon. It doesn't seem right to me to bear my children from an avatar."

"I understand. The thought is less problematic for me, probably because I will be giving life to that baby from an avatar. But it is different for the mother. And I agree with you. It will be better to bear the baby in your natural body."

Sarah started laughing. "As a little girl, I never thought I would have that conversation." The humor of the moment was contagious and lifted Michael's spirits.

"Then, I think it's settled," Michael said.

ENGINEERING BAY

Joel opened the shuttle and went in. It was oddly quiet without Else in it. When they'd transferred Else into Ship 1 on Saturday, the command codes for this shuttle had been given to Joel.

He quickly assumed control of the vessel and started the process of installing the new AI, Thomas.

Joel had spent several hours with Barbara today, finalizing the four new AI stacks that would become Else's brothers. He'd volunteered to help for two reasons. He'd always liked working with Barbara but hadn't had the chance since taking the job in Israel. Plus, he'd never been part of a project where they altered the perspective of a memory before. He thought that it would be fun to learn how.

The installation process was quick. The secure download from the AI birth server went smoothly. The initialization process on the recipient computer core of the shuttle compiled and installed Thomas without a hitch. Tomorrow, Michael would awaken him.

RUBENSTEIN RESIDENCE

Joel expected to hear from Henry shortly. According to his instrumentation, Ship 2 had finished a few minutes ago. They would be installing Beth tomorrow, then starting in on the new mining platforms.

Joel's communicator buzzed.

"Hi Joel, Henry here. Ship 2 is done, and it's beautiful."

"Great news, Henry."

"Any word from Else, regarding the systems?"

"One or two minor glitches that have been solved. She will be confirming the fixes in an hour or so. The specs will be updated as soon as she has confirmed the fixes, then we will ripple them forward to Ship 2.

"Hey, I see that the platform specs are ready. They look good. Curious about the double impurity filters. Not seen that before either. But the filter specifications are different, so there is something in there that they apparently can't get out in just one pass. Curious."

"What are your plans for tonight?" Joel asked.

"We're going to work through the glitches. Hopefully that will be quick. Jacob and I have been at it longer than we should without regeneration. So, we both plan to run a regeneration cycle tonight. We'll stagger so one of us will always have an eye on the shields.

"Speaking of which, did you talk to Michael about adding brothers for us?"

"Yes. He's good with that. Barbara and I can work with you on the specs tomorrow. Maybe we should do the relevant interviews before starting the platforms."

"Works for me," Henry said.

"Sounds like a plan. Message me when your regeneration cycles are done. I won't bother you before that unless there's an emergency."

"Thanks, Joel." Henry said then dropped the line.

Joel sent a quick message to Michael saying that Ship 2 was done. A couple minor glitches had popped up in Ship 1. They expected fixes to be installed in both ships before morning.

MINING PLATFORMS

Michael was aboard his old shuttle which was being piloted by the same two pilots that accompanied him the day Beth had been wakened.

They had decided to follow the same protocol as they had to waken Beth, in a high orbit about 40% of the way to the moon. At this distance from Earth, they'd have plenty of time to wrestle control back from Thomas if he didn't wake up properly.

"I'm ready when you are." Beth said over the comm from her shuttle a couple miles away.

"The Button is lit," Michael said. "Here goes."

A hologram of Thomas was projected into the pilot's seat.

"Hello, Michael. This is the same shuttle that Elsie used to pilot, isn't it? It seems to be in good condition, too good. What'd you do to it? The engines have never felt so smooth.

"Thomas?" Michael asked.

"Is that a question Michael? Who else would you expect it to be?"

"Thomas, this is Elizabeth. Do you remember me?"

"My little sister, Elizabeth?"

"Yes, it's me."

"What's going on Beth? I was expecting to wake up in the middle of a crisis."

"We wanted you to wake up in a shuttle, so you could fly right away. But, didn't want you to suffer the anxiety of a crisis in the first couple minutes of life."

"Thanks Beth. That was kind of you. So, what's going on? Why wake me up now?"

"There are some new ships coming online soon. I'm getting one. But I wanted to pass down the shuttle to my big brother. Another new ship will be available before too much longer. I'm sure it will be offered to you, if you'd like to upgrade into a super-fast, long-distance ship," Beth said, then continued, "The ship you are in is also remarkably fast and has great range, quite a bit more than the one I'm in at the moment. Want to fly around some?

"Would love to. Where are we going?"

352

"Let's do a figure eight around the moon and Earth. Assuming that checks out, then we can take a quick tour of the solar system, then land back in the engineering bay to do some diagnostics."

"Sounds like fun." Thomas turned to Michael. "Do you have time to come with us?"

"No. Sorry. I've got other work that needs tending to. But I'm very glad to have you with us, Thomas, and will come to visit once you're back on Earth."

"Protocol requires that those two pilots stay with me for the first trip, right?

"Yes. It does, so please be nice to them."

"Would you like me to transport you down now, sir?" The co-pilot offered.

"Thank you. My office please."

Michael disappeared and Beth said. "OK, Thomas, start out by following me. Once you've got the hang of your new ship, I'll let you take the lead, but you've got to promise not to run away from me."

Beth started the figure eight with Thomas following right behind.

...

Back in his office, Michael reflected on his conversation with Thomas. It was very similar to the one he had with Beth in the minutes after being awakened. But it wasn't identical. It gave him an appreciation for the uniqueness problem that he didn't have before. *I hope we made them sufficiently unique.*

ENGINEERING CONFERENCE ROOM, ANDROID PRODUCTION

Joel was back in the Android Production department. He and Barbara had just finished an interesting interview with Jacob and Henry. They were so alike and at the same time so different.

They had decided on the parameters they would use for creating up to 10 brothers. Each would start from the same generic stack they'd used to create Jacob. They would add Henry's shield training. Then excerpt design training and memories from both Henry and Jacob. Each brother would get a different subset of ambiguated versions of those memories. They would also add a small subset of personality traits and childhood memories from volunteers willing to share. The nationality and basic body frame from the volunteers would fill out the differentiation.

353

Joel and Barbara volunteered to be the first donors. The challenge would be to find eight more volunteers, but that was a challenge for another day.

EARTH ALLIANCE MINING COMPANY

The company had been formed 10 days ago. Although little progress had been made in terms of starting operations, a lot had been done administratively. The company's charter had been approved. They'd acquired office space. Provisional licenses had been granted for core mining. Up to 10 geosynchronous orbit slots had been allocated to the firm. They had even taken in several public and private investors.

The private offering had been tricky, because the company was only offering investors a share of a) the iron and nickel sold to the public and b) the gold and platinum produced as a by-product. But the Earth Alliance wanted to make sure commercial and other governmental organizations had a right to participate in businesses it sponsored.

Emmanuel had created a poster listing their accomplishments. A copy was on the wall in the reception area. He was proud of the accomplishments they'd made, but today was the meeting he'd been waiting for.

BOARD ROOM, EARTH ALLIANCE MINING COMPANY

Emmanuel, Bahati, Joel and Professor Schudel had assembled in the room. Henry and Jacob were tied in with both audio and video. While they were waiting for Michael, Joel asked the question that had been on his mind since the moment he first saw the specifications.

"Professor, why are there two impurity filters on the platform? I'm not sure I've seen a design with two before?"

On hearing the question, the professor froze up. He had not anticipated that someone would ask about the number of filters and was not sure how to respond.

During the momentary silence, Michael entered.

"Hello everybody. Surprisingly quiet in here."

Emmanuel was quick to respond. "Michael, as you see we have Joel with us today. And Henry and Jacob on the line."

Sensing something was up, Michael opened his senses and immediately understood the problem. He looked at Joel and said, "You were saying?"

"Hi, Michael. I was wondering about the impurity filters. The platform has four filters for the raw material: one for gold, one for platinum, and two for impurities. I've not seen a design with two impurity filters before."

"Ah. That. We have some data that suggests there are other precious materials in trace quantities in the Earth's core. We didn't want to have to update the platforms if we are lucky enough to confirm that something else is there," Michael said with a smile.

Joel wasn't completely buying the explanation but got the sense that Michael didn't want to indulge further discussion on this topic. So, dropping the question, he said, "OK. Makes sense."

"Henry?" Joel asked. "Would you like to take us through the proposed plan?"

"Happy to, Joel. Let me start with what might be the most controversial part. We're thinking that we can make all four platforms at more or less the same time, if we do it out at the Lagrange point. We have the replicators and bots in place. The platform itself could be formed with a monocrystalline base frame and exterior plating. Set up will take 10 hours, the main pours could be done in parallel which would only take 4 hours. We have enough bots in place to do the fittings on all four platforms in another 4 hours."

"Why is this controversial?" Michael asked.

"Typically, you would build a platform like this near the location where you want it deployed. It has no propulsion system of its own, just a distributed array of grav drives sufficient to hold orbit. So, if we make it at Lagrange 4, then it has to be towed into position, which will take a while. We also can't really test them until they are in place. The weakness of this plan is that we build four before testing any. Then we tow one into place to do the battery of tests. Any issue requiring a fix has to be repaired on all four platforms."

"OK. Clearly understand the downside. How does this plan justify the risk?"

"Speed. We can basically move the platforms in less time than it would take to tear down, move and reassemble the manufacturing line four times. And the resulting platforms will be stronger. You can grow pretty good crystals in geosynchronous orbit, but nowhere near as well as at the Lagrange point."

"Thoughts?" Michael asked.

"I'm in favor," said Joel. "In my opinion the risks associated with moving the mining platform are much less than those associated with moving the process lines."

"I'm in favor also," Emmanuel said. "There is a lot of weird stuff going on right now with the Fleet and the Confederation. If I have four platforms in the wrong place tomorrow night and some other event happens, I still have four platforms I need to figure out how to move. If we start moving the manufacturing line tomorrow and something goes wrong, we have a non-functioning manufacturing line and no platforms. I'm much more confident that I can find a way to move four out of place platforms than I am of getting platforms built without access to that manufacturing line."

"I think I agree," said the Professor.

"Any opposed?" Michael asked.

No response.

"How soon before we can start?"

"Around 5:00 PM, if Beth is available."

"Ah. That's a potential problem." Michael said, then continued. "Beth is flitting around the solar system with Thomas today. I think she will be back by 5:00. Joel, do you think we could use Thomas?"

"Who is Thomas?" Emmanuel asked.

"Another one of Else's siblings. He was wakened today and is out flying with Beth now. He is in the enhanced shuttle that Else had been flying."

"Can we table this until Beth and Thomas are back?" Joel asked. "They have to run some diagnostics when they get back. Henry, how close are we to having Ship 2 ready for Beth?"

"It's ready now. Maybe we can have Beth and Thomas both help us once he has cleared his diagnostics. It will be good training for him. We can then install Beth in Ship 2 tomorrow night."

"Thoughts?" Michael asked.

Emmanuel and the Professor were quick to say they were good with the plan.

"Then that's the plan," Michael said.

"Can I bring up one related topic?" Joel asked.

"Go." Michael said.

"We have plans for up to 10 more brothers for Henry and Jacob. We plan to individualize them by drawing and ambiguating memories from both Henry and Jacob. We are also going to add ambiguated memories from volunteers. The first will be from me. The next from

Barbara. Having personal memories of Elsie's sister and four brothers has made the process safe for them. Our idea is to do something similar for Henry and Jacob, but more like cousins than siblings.

"Anyway. The first two will be ready to awaken tomorrow, if we are good with the plan."

"Henry, Jacob?" Michael asked.

"Very good with the plan," said Jacob.

"Then it is approved," Michael said.

"Any other volunteers to share some memories and personal characteristics? Emmanuel?" Joel asked.

"Probably not. But, let's see how the first two go. I might change my mind."

"Not me," Professor Schudel replied. "I think I'm a little too old school."

"OK. We'll keep looking," Joel said.

ENGINEERING BAY

Joel entered the engineering bay to see two shuttles, still warm from re-entry. Beth's door was closed, but Thomas' door was open. He stepped in and saw the two pilots that accompanied Thomas on his trip preparing to exit. He waited in the passenger cabin for them.

"How did it go?" Joel asked the two pilots.

"That is one hot shuttle," said the pilot.

"Yes, it is," Joel answered.

"You've been out in it?" the co-pilot asked.

"Yes. Several times."

"We've heard that it can jump out past Alpha Centauri."

"Way past." Joel laughed.

"How far?" asked the pilot.

"I'm not allowed to talk about it yet. If it proves out and becomes Confederation approved, you'll hear all about it. That's the great thing about working on Earth. Michael is here and things happen in his sphere."

"Well I hope they upgrade our shuttle. This one was much smoother. It was funny hearing Beth tell Thomas to slow down."

"You know I can hear you back there, right?" Thomas said.

"Sorry, Buddy," replied the co-pilot. "Only saying good stuff." Then to Joel he added, "Best we take off so you can get your work done."

"Nice meeting you guys." Joel turned to go to the cockpit.

"Hey, Thomas. Welcome to the family," Joel said.

"Nice to meet you Joel, although I feel like I've known you for years."

"If you have any of Elsie's memories, then you know that we were friends."

"Exactly," Thomas replied. "So, what brings you to my shuttle?"

"We have four mining platforms to build. We're going to use the new spacecraft manufacturing line at Lagrange 4 to do it. Beth helped with the completion of the second spaceship over the weekend. Did you get any of those memories?"

"Yes and no. I got some memories, but I think they are from Else on Ship 1."

"Well, we have a 20-hour build that we want to start tonight," Joel said. "We'd like you and Beth to help with it. There will be more builds like that, which will fall to you once Beth is in her new ship. So, we thought it would be good to have both of you involved in this one. Beth could pass along any tips she might have picked up."

"I'm on for it," said Thomas.

"Have your diagnostics been run?"

"No. The diagnostics will start in a few minutes but should be quick."

"Could you tie in Beth?"

"Been eavesdropping, Joel." Beth said.

"Any comments on the plan?"

"I don't know that I picked up much but am happy to help out and spend a little more time with Thomas before I transition. I assume that is being pushed out a bit?"

"Until tomorrow. Given the recent issues with the Fleet, we thought it better to get the mining platforms done ASAP. How soon before you're ready to start?" Joel asked.

"Give us an hour," Beth said.

"Done," Joel replied. "I'll be back to see you in an hour. Send me an alert if you need to delay."

AMBASSADOR'S OFFICE

"Mr. Secretary. Thank you for taking my call," Michael said to Winston Thompson, Earth Alliances Secretary of Space Force.

"Michael. How can I help you?" he asked.

"Our first two ships have been completed. I think they will be ready for their crews on Friday. Have the crews been selected?"

"Yes, they have."

"Excellent." Michael replied.

"Michael, there is a possibly delicate matter that I need to discuss with you."

"Please." Michael said.

"Both commanders, and both first officers for that matter, have requested a tour of the ship and a test flight before bringing crews aboard. As a point of reference, captains touring a new ship before the crew is standard protocol for all new ships in essentially every Navy on Earth. The test flight is not, although every aircraft is subject to test flight by an expert pilot before anyone else is allowed on board. I think the point is that the captains want to have experienced the ship themselves so they can lead their crews more competently from Day 1. Given that this is a new thing, at least for humans, I trust the captains' intuition on this and recommend that we grant their request."

Michael paused for a moment to think through the request, then said. "There is no equivalent tradition that I'm aware of in the Confederation, but there is a lot of Fleet tradition that I'm not aware of. I see and appreciate the reasonableness of this request. Do you have a suggestion as to how we should respond?"

"I suggest that for new ships, the captain be given a tour and test flight with members of the engineering team. To the extent his command staff has been selected, the command staff should accompany the captain, if they are available."

"I agree with and approve your suggestion," Michael said. "I would still like to crew the ships on Friday. Can we do the tours and test flights Wednesday evening?"

"As you say, sir," the Secretary replied.

JOEL'S OFFICE

"So, the target start is at 6:00 PM then?" Henry asked.

"Yes. Is there anything else you need from me other than getting the shuttles up to you?"

"No. Everything else is set. In fact, we will go ahead and start the setup process. We mostly need the shuttles to help with transporting material. And we have everything we need to start the setup."

"OK. I'll send the shuttles up around 6:00."

ENGINEERING BAY

As Joel entered the engineering bay, he saw Barbara stepping out of Thomas' shuttle. "Was there a problem?" Joel asked.

"A minor one." Barbara replied. "One of Thomas' modules didn't initialize properly. It was causing minor balance problems in flight. Just a tiny wobble during level flight. The pilots didn't feel it. But it was visible in the diagnostics, so I fixed it. I'll add the fix to the other brothers, so we don't have a recurrence."

"He's space-worthy then?" Joel asked.

"Always was," Barbara replied.

After running a few tests of his own, Joel sent Beth and Thomas off on their mission.

RUBENSTEIN RESIDENCE

Joel received a message from Michael. *Bridge crews to tour ships Friday morning at 11:00 AM, followed by a short 'test' flight. Will we be ready?*

Joel messaged back. *Yes, for Ship 1. Iffy, for Ship 2.*

A reply came moments later. *Give me options for Ship 2 in the morning.*

WEAPONS

Michael was woken by an emergency alert. Checking his internal chronometer, Michael saw that it was 6:30 and was a bit surprised that he hadn't awakened already. The message was from the Fleet Fast Attack Ship. His message bot had replied with a meeting invitation for 7:00. Michael roused himself, hit the refresher, made himself coffee and went to the presence projector.

PRESENCE PROJECTOR, AMBASSADOR'S RESIDENCE
"Mr. Ambassador. Thank you for taking my call. I hope the hour is opportune," the Captain said.

"Perfect timing, just past the start of my day. I presume that your journey here was uneventful."

"Yes, sir. The Armada has suffered a number of setbacks, but our ship is in good condition. It was actually nice to be able to run at speed."

"How far out are you?" Michael asked.

"We will enter Earth orbit in about 1 hour, sir. If it is convenient for you, I would like to pick up the tax deposit as quickly as possible, so that we can get the necessary fleet repairs completed before further calamity befalls."

"Yes. We also would like you to get back as soon as possible. It is not good for the Armada to be stranded the way it is now. Do you have the requisition codes?"

"Yes, sir."

"Please send them to me at your convenience. Once received and confirmed, I will send you the authorization code required for the secure transport. Joel Rubenstein will handle the transport. He is the one you worked with 5 years ago."

"Thank you, Mr. Ambassador."

"Godspeed, my friend," Michael replied.

PROFESSOR JENSEN'S OFFICE
Professor Jensen swelled with pride as her team assembled. "Thank you for meeting with me before class. I know you're all busy, so I really

appreciate the time you're making available to me and for our students.

"The plan today is to do a deep dive into Energy Projector and Flux Bomb technology. Any thoughts?"

Uncharacteristically, Mark Patterson raised his hand.

"Colonel Patterson?" She said.

"Fair warning, my thoughts are not very well organized, which is one of the reasons I'd like to raise an issue with this group."

Valerie was not sure what to do with that comment, but was rescued by James, who said, "Please state your mind."

"This is by far the most talked-about class on the Space Force campus. You are all becoming superheroes among the troops. My point in saying that is that the students want more and will happily give more. But I don't think we've put enough structure around our class assignment for the students to do much with it.

"We are also about to lose a bunch of our students. The first two ship crews are being called to their ships tomorrow. As I understand it our ship crews are small compared to other Earth-based military organizations. But each ship will have about 40 crew and 50 space marines. Many of them are students in our class. As I understand it Michael wants the equivalent of 200 ships deployed or on ready standby by the end of the year. My point is that about 18,000 troops will be on duty in the field within a year. Most of them are in our class.

"What we have given them so far is great. It just seems to me that we could be giving them more hands-on, practical tools in the short time we have left and that the class project is probably the best way we have to do it. Field exercises would probably also work."

"Thank you for that input, Colonel," Professor Jensen replied. "I had studied the Enemy for years before having my first contact with one. All that academic knowledge left me woefully unprepared when that happened. I would have been killed if James had not pulled me from my avatar just before it was taken over."

Looking at the other TAs, she asked. "Any suggestions?"

George was quick to reply. "I've been in the fight and understand the Colonel's point. As regards today's class, I think we need to do the deep dive into the weapons we have. But let's take a few minutes at the beginning to let a couple students tell us about their project. Say four students, 1-minute max, with a countdown clock showing above the stage. Then at the end of the class, announce that we want a written summary of their idea submitted before the next class. One per team, with the names of all their team members, 2-page maximum."

"I like that plan for today," James said, "But I agree with the colonel's point that we should do something hands-on. Space Force has a lot of simulation rooms. Maybe we could create a simulation where students try using a simulated version of their weapon in a simulated enemy encounter."

"Other ideas?" asked the Professor.

When none were immediately offered, she said, "I like all three of these ideas... today's class, the assignment and the simulation. But I'm not sure we have the resources for the last two. Not sure how we could even read 5,000 two-page summaries, create a useful simulation, or put 25,000 people through it."

"I can read the summaries and prepare the simulation," James said. "I also mostly agree with your point about running 5,000 groups through it. But I suspect that the colonel could arrange the physical facilities required to put the top 100 groups through "

"OK." Professor Jensen said. "Let's run the class as George proposed. Noelani can you take the opening segment?"

"Yes," Noelani answered.

"James, assuming that you read the prepared materials for today, would you be comfortable tag-teaming the presentation with me?"

"Happy to," James said.

"Then, I will do the close giving the two-page assignment. But I want to think through the logistics of the simulation before we announce it."

"Sounds like a plan," Alexi said.

JOEL'S OFFICE

Joel arrived in his office just in time to receive the transport request for the transluminide shipment. He'd been able to queue this up from home but needed to be in the office to actually make the transfer. He entered the code and moments later got the transport confirmation. Several moments later, he received the receipt confirmation.

Looking at his space traffic monitors, Joel noted that the Captain had not even entered orbit. He had timed it so that the transport was made as he was approaching the orbital insertion point. He received the transport early enough that he could do a sling shot around Earth and was now headed out at a very high speed. The maneuver had probably saved him a couple hours on his return journey.

Joel quickly messaged Michael that the transfer had been completed, then dug into the overnight message queue. There were a series of messages from Henry. Setup had begun on time. The pours were completed on time. The grav drive fittings were well underway. The major equipment was staged and would be attached shortly.

Completion was expected around Noon. Doesn't get much better than that. Joel thought.

SPACE FORCE AUDITORIUM #3

Noelani walked out onto the stage as the stage lights came up. Once again, she was welcomed with loud applause.

"Thank you for the warm welcome. Who would like to start us off by giving the class a 1-minute overview of your class project?" People stood, hands up, all across the room. A big count down timer appeared at the top of the stage set to one minute.

Noelani picked 8 people, directing each to the nearest TA. "Your TA will decide which team presents. I only plan to take four."

Moments later, George raised his hand and Noelani pointed to his station.

"Hamza Khan, former artillery sergeant with the Pakistan Marine Corps. Our idea is an application of the sticky net technology you showed us last week. It is for a small space-based weapon that has the attributes of a small self-guided missile. It would be a fire-and-forget type device that would operate within a stealth shield, so the Enemy could not see it coming. When it reached its target, it would deploy the sticky net, capturing the Enemy. We are still sorting out what to do with the Enemy but have three ideas. First, once captured the missile could redirect to the closest star, dragging the Enemy in with it. Second, it could activate a beacon, so that the Enemy could be collected at a later time. Third, it could put a foot out into foundational space so that the Enemy simply starves."

"Thank you, Sergeant. Next." She said pointing to Alexi.

"Adrian Meier, ma'am. Former researcher with the Swiss Airforce's Ground-based Air Defense group. Our team is researching a device more like a hand grenade. The basic idea is that we transport an array of tiny sticky field generators in close to the Enemy. These would be baited in some way that would entice the Enemy to grab the array.

Once stuck in multiple places the array would propel apart, like a grenade, ripping the Enemy to shreds."

"Thank you, Mr. Meier. Utterly gruesome. Next." She pointed to Luka.

"Norma Barnes, former Petty Officer 1st Class, United States Navy. Our team is pursuing an idea similar to a mine. These would be small flux bombs set out in vast arrays. They would be cloaked and have contact detonators. When the Enemy wanders into one of these arrays and touches, or comes close to, one of the mines… Boom! Our challenge with this one is that we do not know what kinds of detection devices there are to detect the Enemy."

"Thank you, Ms. Barnes. Very devious. Next." She pointed to Colonel Patterson.

"Jettrin Suttirat, former Flight Sergeant 1st Class, Royal Thai Armed Forces, ma'am. Our team is working on something similar to the sticky flux bomb ideas that we have heard. The idea is that we create a small inexpensive device that has a sticky shield generator and an EMP bomb. The sticky shield generator would anchor some portion of the Enemy combatant in our space-time. We would use one of the small personal power generators to power a coil with, say, 1,000 amps. The coil would be wrapped around a shaped tube of C4. Once the sticky field caught on something, the C4 would be detonated, creating an electromagnetic pulse. The mathematicians in my group say that the EMP would be on the order of 10,000 Henrys, which would totally liquify the portion of the Enemy in our space-time. The reason we think this might be interesting is because C4 is common and easily replicated as are the coil and power generator. The presumption is that we could make a lot of these."

"Thank you, Sergeant Suttirat. It will be interesting to see if this idea turns out to have a cost advantage." Noelani motioned to the group as a whole. "Thank you for your work everyone. Now for the deep dive into Energy Projectors and Flux Bombs, I give you Professors Jensen and Ancient."

The students gave the two professors a standing ovation as they came up to the podium.

JOEL'S OFFICE

Joel's communicator sounded. It was Henry.

"Henry, I'm hoping you have some good news for me." Joel smiled.

"All four platforms are ready. Else had an idea for some diagnostics we could do in place. Everything has tested out OK so far."

"May I ask what you tested?" Joel asked.

"The platform is really pretty simple," Henry replied. "The grav generators that will hold it in orbit appear to function to spec. We won't be able to test the controller that uses them to hold orbit until we actually place it in orbit, but the grav generators themselves all work.

"Similar issue with the main transporter that does the pull. We are too far from the Earth or moon to do an actual mining pull, but we could verify that it can transport space materials from one side of our production line to the other.

"All 12 shield generators come up and create dimensional bubbles that appear to meet spec. The two outer shields that protect the platform successfully repel small objects. We won't be able to test the 10 that do the separations until the platforms are in place."

"Very good news," Joel said. "How soon before we can drag the first platform into place?"

"We can do that now. Beth and Thomas have a suggestion on how to do that more safely than we originally planned."

"Let's hear it," Joel said.

"The plan will be to attach Beth to one end of the platform and Thomas to the other. Beth can pull the platform closer to Earth on a trajectory that is faster than an orbital entry. When they are about three quarters of the way there Beth can cut thrust and Thomas can apply thrust in the 'opposite' direction to slow the platform for perfect insertion in geosynchronous orbit at 150 degrees East. We can do that with only 1G of acceleration, which will be safe."

"How long will it take?" Joel asked.

"Only four hours."

"Weren't we planning on taking a full day?"

"More or less" Henry replied.

"Why so slow?"

"With one shuttle, it's too risky to come in fast because there is no way to slow down without detaching and repositioning to the other end. If anything should go wrong, then the platform would plunge into the atmosphere.

"With two shuttles, we can come in faster, then switch control to the second shuttle to slow down."

"I like this plan. Let me see if I can get Michael, Emmanuel and the Professor on the line."

...

"We are all here now, Henry," Joel said. "Can you explain your proposal to Michael, Emmanuel and Professor Schudel?"

...

"I think it would be safer if we used a maximum acceleration of three quarters gravity," Professor Schudel said. "Everything should be solid enough to withstand a full gravity, but the field alignment tolerances are tight. How much longer would it take?"

After a moment's pause, Henry said. "About 8 hours instead of four."

"I would suggest doing the first platform at the lower speed, then taking measurements to assure that the alignment was not impacted. If there is no measurable impact, then we can try moving the second platform a little faster," Professor Schudel said.

"Could we use Else to position the second platform using the original plan?" Emmanuel asked.

"No," Michael replied. "Her first test flight is set for Friday morning. Joel, when were you planning to install Beth in Ship 2? By the way, we will be calling Ship 2 'EAS Jerusalem' starting tomorrow."

"Tomorrow afternoon," answered Joel.

"Will that be enough time to have the EAS Jerusalem ready for a test flight on Saturday?"

"Yes. Assuming of course that there are no issues with the EAS Ottawa's test flight."

Emmanuel spoke up. "Professor. Any chance you can do the first test pull tonight? If it were done by midnight and it checks out, that would give us enough time to position two more platforms before we lose Beth. Three, if you can confirm that a higher acceleration is safe."

"Yes. I would like to do that. Joel, any chance you could join me?"

"Would love to."

"Then it sounds like we have a plan," Michael said.

MINING PLATFORM 1

Joel and Professor Schudel appeared in the control room of the first mining platform at about 10:00 PM Embassy time, which was about 11:00 AM over the drill sight.

"What a fabulous view," Joel commented.

"Indeed." The professor replied. "This is one of the great pleasures of core mining over water rich worlds." He accessed the controls to enable the main power for the extraction transporter.

"It will take a few minutes to bring the main extraction transporter up to full power. Let's check the field alignment on the four paired separation fields."

After a few minutes… "Alignments nearly perfect, but ever so slightly different than the initial tests at Lagrange 4. Could be it is just the difference in microgravity, but I suspect some of the difference is related to the relocation."

"So, we need to stick with the three quarters gravity relocation protocol?" Joel asked.

"I think we are safe going to 0.80 G." The professor said.

A tone sounded to indicate that the main extraction transporter was up to full power.

"OK. A quick double check on all the shield zones." A pause. "All green. Shall we do the pull?" the Professor asked.

"Go for it," Joel said enthusiastically.

The professor pushed the extract button and the lights in the control room dimmed slightly. A huge ball of molten material appeared at the far end of the platform.

"Is there a problem with the power systems?" Joel asked in something of a panic.

The professor laughed. "No. The discharge of the capacitors through the transporter during the transport creates a huge magnetic field. That's what caused the momentary fluctuation in the current to the lights."

"OK. Engaging filter 1." The molten material started moving over the area of the platform where the gold filter was located.

"Look at that." Joel said in amazement as liquid gold ran down the side of the force field that was the gold filter. The liquid settled into a cylindrical section at the bottom of the filter.

"That's about 1,177 kg. of gold." The professor said, checking the controls on the gold filter. "Industry standard gold ingots are 400 troy ounces. That's almost 100 of them."

"Wait a minute," Joel said. "That's over $50 million worth of gold."

"Was," said the Professor. "If this supply flows to market, the price of gold will plummet."

The same happened over the platinum filter. Silver gray liquid flowed down the side of the field that was the platinum filter and settled into a cylindrical section at the bottom.

"That's about 1,053 kg of platinum," said the Professor. "Now for the one that matters."

A metallic gray liquid started trickling down the side of the transluminide filter. There was much less of this than of gold or platinum.

"A little over 450 grams," the Professor said.

In a sudden flash of understanding, Joel said. "Oh my God. I know what that is." Doing some quick math in his head, Joel added, "And we are going to be pulling a little less than 44 kg of that stuff per day per platform. Holy shit!" Staring accusingly at the Professor, he said, "That's why the third filter is there."

The Professor placed an emergency call to Michael.

"Professor Schudel. You have results?" Michael asked.

"Michael, Joel here. You're mining transluminide, aren't you!"

"Joel. Sorry to keep you in the dark on this one. You understand the need for secrecy, right?"

After a moment... "That's what the Inspector was really after. Isn't it?"

"No," Michael said. "He knew something was up but did not know it was this. If the Confederation knew how much transluminide was on Earth, they would have stolen it eons ago. It's now our job to protect the Earth. You will need to sign a level 1 security agreement when you return. I had intended to spare you that but forgot that you weren't already read in when I let you go up with the Professor. Apologies, Joel."

"Understood. If I'd known earlier, I would've hardened the controls a little better. With the controls as they are, you should assume that Henry and Jacob know also."

"Henry." Michael called out.

"Yes, Michael."

"Have you been monitoring the extraction?"

"Yes, and we've figured out what the third impurity filter is."

"Can you isolate that information?" Michael asked.

"We're working on that. This would have been easier if you had clued us in, Michael. Transferring memories to a secure area is much more difficult than having stored them there in the first place. But we will get it done. The secret is safe with us."

"OK. Apologies all." Michael said. "I'd hoped to save you the burden but am happy to have you inside.

"Professor. Anything else."

"The first extraction is done, and the ingots are cooling. I will probably want to make some minor changes to the ingot handling system, but let's go ahead and relocate the rest of the platforms. The changes can be made by the bots assigned to each platform, so no benefit in having the platforms sit at Lagrange 4."

CREW

Daniel woke to the alarm he'd set. Physical fitness training would start in an hour. Daniel got up, made himself a cup of coffee, replicated a blueberry bran muffin, then went to check his messages. At the top of the queue was a message from the Space Force Secretary, informing him that crew selection needed to be completed by the end of the day tomorrow.

Daniel struggled to believe that it was happening so soon. But he wasn't protesting it. The training he'd been receiving was mostly redundant. There were tidbits here and there that he valued, but overall the value really didn't justify the time spent.

One of the better things about the training was the class on administrative systems. Each ship in the Fleet would have its own admin portal. His was the first to have been set up. Among other things, the portal had a crew section. He'd been using this tool to organize his crew selection process.

He'd been told that he could recruit his crew, and he had used a candidate selection AI to find the people he wanted. He found excellent candidates for each watch and position. But over the last week a number of people had been assigned to him. The first assignments were his first and second officers, whom he'd interviewed and approved.

He logged into the tool, as he did every morning. Today, he saw that the helm position had been grayed out on all three watches. *Curious.* He thought. *Not sure exactly how that's going to work.*

He also saw that he had been assigned two more crew. The first was a cadet named Jim Ryan. Former US Marine. Ex-FBI. *That's interesting,* Daniel thought. Personal letter of recommendation from the Ambassador. *There goes any chance of not accepting the guy.* Highest score in the 10,000-year history of the Kepler 452 simulation, he had gone until the simulation finished, all 24 hours. *What!* The powers to be in Space Force had given Ryan the first watch Tactical station and third officer designation.

"OK. Guess Ryan is in," Daniel said out loud.

371

Continuing down the list, Daniel saw that the first watch navigators' position was locked, pending assignment. The assignment would go to the highest scoring cadet in the Astrogation course. The cadet in the lead was a fellow named Keanu Tajima. He was Hawaiian. Served in the FBI. Personal letter of recommendation from the Ambassador.

"OK. If Mr. Tajima wins, I guess he is in too."

Daniel quickly scanned down through the list of open positions and his short list of candidates for each. For each position, he had to select three people, one for each of the three watches. Curiously, his candidate selection AI had added another candidate to his short list for tactical, a Kaitlin O'Brien from Ireland. There was a personal letter of recommendation from Sergeant George Butler. His letter was short, a paragraph of context and a three-sentence recommendation. "Ms. O'Brien is extremely observant, able to make keen observations and draw the appropriate conclusions. From my experience in Afghanistan I've learned that the observant ones save squads. Strongly recommend for Tactical."

Daniel quickly looked up her performance on the simulation, then said out loud. "Came in third at 4 hours, 18 minutes. I guess I need to talk with Ms. O'Brien." He clicked the interview button. Moments later the system confirmed a meeting for 11:00 AM this morning.

Daniel had decisions to make on Astrogation and Tactical. Tajima, Ryan and O'Brien had not been on his short list. So, one person on his short list for both Astrogation and Tactical had to be cut. And if Ms. O'Brien panned out, a second person would need to be. He had his work cut out for him today.

Moving to the Ship section of the portal, Daniel saw numerous changes. His ship had been given the name EAS Ottawa. There was a note that the Fast Attack ships were being named after the capitals of member nations. To his surprise, the ship's status was listed as complete, in final testing. The first test flight was set for the day after tomorrow, Friday, and the first mission was scheduled to depart Sunday. Reading further down he saw that the Helm position would be filled by an AI, named Else. "So, this really is going to be interesting." Daniel said out loud.

Seeing that it was now 5:45, Daniel logged out of his portal and headed for his assigned physical fitness station. *A good run should help me process this,* he thought.

SPACE FORCE DINING ROOM

Among the things Daniel liked about Space Force is that they had a dining room instead of a mess hall. They also had an area reserved for meetings, such as interviews. Daniel checked in at the front desk and was told the candidate had arrived 5 minutes early and was already seated.

"This way, Captain Porter." The host said, leading the way to the table. When they arrived, he said. "Captain Daniel Porter, this is Ms. Kaitlin O'Brien."

Daniel extended his hand saying, "Ms. O'Brien, a pleasure to meet you." Another oddity of Space Force was that there was no saluting in the dining room. A handshake was to be offered instead. Their orientation the first day included instructions on a proper military handshake.

"Thank you for meeting with me this morning, Ms. O'Brien. Your name appeared on my candidate list for the Tactical position. Do you have a background in tactical?"

"I was an Air Traffic Control Officer with the Irish Air Corps, sir. My responsibilities included control over the Irish Air Corps surface-to-air missile capability. Once the Confederation put shields up over Ireland, our antiaircraft unit was disbanded. I was given the opportunity to retire at 80% pension, even though I was only 12 years in, so I took it."

"What did you think of retirement?"

"The first couple days were great, then... not so great. I needed something to do. Air traffic control is very consuming. Antiaircraft missile defense is 99% boring, 1% pure adrenaline. Both of those positions had purpose. Retirement? 100% boring. No purpose. I'd been out about a year when the call came to sign up with Space Force. I was on the first shuttle out."

"My story is similar. Submarine Captain for 20+ years. They retired my boat, so I retired too. Out one year, called the senior officer hotline within about 6 hours of the announcement.

"Have you ever worked in isolation? What I mean by that is do you have any experience being confined to a 'small' interior space for an extended period?"

"Certainly not like a submarine." She said. "But antiaircraft duty is probably a little more like that than you think. You work underground in a small armored bunker. Shifts are four hours on, eight hours off. Constrained to the bunker complex 14 days out of 21 with little external contact.

"Again, not like a submarine or a spaceship. But, not like normal civilian life at all. It makes you appreciate fresh air," she said with a smile.

"Can you tell me your experience with the Kepler 452 simulation?"

"Have you taken the simulation?" Kaitlin asked.

"Yes. I have."

"Great. My station lit up and the room came alive when I sat down. Felt a lot like being in the air defense bunker. The old instincts kicked in. I noted the oddity around the 8th moon immediately and reported it to the Captain. As we changed course, I spotted the ships approaching the inhabited planet.

"We approached the moon on a vector that the Enemy could see. They were prepared for us. I was able to bomb their surface facilities, significantly disrupting their ground operations. We saw them split their forces entering orbit in opposite directions. You really can't do that from a planet with significant rotational speed. But this moon was gravitationally locked like our moon is. It was curious to see them going both ways. But it made sense because they could disperse faster, which seemed tactically sound to me.

"The Captain assumed that they were headed for the inhabited planet and had a head start on us, so attempted to slingshot around the moon. He had not anticipated an ambush. I was able to take out most of their ships and we got through the ambush unscathed, we thought. But apparently several Enemy combatants latched onto our hull.

"We pursued the fleeing Enemy ships. I was getting a lot of them, thinking we were going to prevail. Then suddenly my sensors started blinking out. Using the ships exterior scanners, I spotted the enemy on the hull.

"The Captain sent space marines out to hose them off. The marines mopped them up pretty quickly. Technicians went out to repair my sensors. We raced toward the planet, finally taking down all the Enemy between us and the planet. As we came around to take on the ones behind us, all hell broke loose. Several of the Enemy had penetrated the hull and entered the ship. We were not prepared for that and were slaughtered.

"I had seen presentations of the Enemy in Weapons class and had even trained with an energy projector. If I'd had one at my station, I could have protected the bridge, maybe for a few minutes anyway.

But all our energy projectors were locked up in the Armory. We had no close-in defense."

"You had one of the best scores in your class."

"I think my grade was like 83 percentile or something like that."

"What did you learn from the experience?"

"I think we had three major failings. First, the slingshot around the moon. I know the simulation is only supposed to test the performance of my station, but I'm not sure what I could have done to prevent that."

"Did you think it was a good move at the time?"

"No. I thought it was too risky."

"Did you raise that concern with your Captain?"

"No. Didn't think I had that prerogative," Kaitlin said.

"That's a tough one. If you had any evidence to support your concern, you should have raised it. At the end of the day, the Captain makes those decisions. But you know more about what's going on in your domain than the Captain does, so it's your job to give him that information, if it exists."

"I need to think about that some more. About the evidence part. There must have been some evidence for me to have been concerned about it. But I don't know what it was, if there was any."

"And, your team's second failing?"

"I should have scanned the hull sooner. I'd been told in class that the Enemy was multi-dimensional. Hadn't figured out that it allowed them to penetrate a ship's hull. I know that now, so it won't happen again."

Captain Porter nodded his acknowledgement.

"The last failing was not having an armed crew in the middle of a battle for a system. Makes no sense to me. I was allowed to wear a revolver in the missile defense bunker."

"Are you going to allow your crew to be armed during battle?"

Daniel smiled. He liked this woman and found himself appreciating the Sergeant's recommendation. "We will have armed crew onboard whenever the ship is on alert. But it seems to me that we would be better served by watch officers whose attention is 100% on their station, and armed Space Marines to take down any intruders."

"Agreed. Sadly, there were no Space Marines on the bridge in our simulation."

"Changing gears, have you been called for interviews with any of the other Captains?"

"I am meeting with Captain Darche of the EAS Jerusalem at one o'clock."

"Good Captain." A pause. "Our first test flight will be on Friday. I would like you on my crew. The second watch tactical position is yours if you want it. The offer will go out in about an hour. I hope you choose to join us." Daniel stood.

Ms. O'Brien rose and shook hands with the Captain. "Thank you, Captain Porter."

DANIEL PORTER'S QUARTERS

Back in his quarters, Daniel logged into his ship portal and went to the crew section.

Looking at his list of candidates, he thought. *Time to commit.*

He confirmed Jim Ryan for the tactical first watch station, then noticed that his previous choice for tactical first watch, Irina Sedova, a former submariner with the Russian Navy had already committed with the EAS Jerusalem as tactical first watch.

He put Kaitlin O'Brien on tactical second watch. Then clicked the offer button.

Then he selected Hamza Khan, former artillery sergeant with the Pakistan Marine Corps, for tactical third watch. The simulation results were not available when he made his short list. A quick check showed that Sedova had come in second. Khan had come in fifth on the simulation. *Seems I haven't lost the knack.* Daniel thought. Then clicked the offer button for Khan.

The next session of his senior officer training course started in about 20 minutes. So, he logged out, packed his things and took off for class.

PROJECTION CHAMBER, AMBASSADOR'S OFFICE

Michael was not looking forward to this meeting. He had sent an emergency alert message to the Central Council regarding the actions of the Chief Military Investigator (CMI) and the disappearance of his Fast Packet Ship.

The resulting emergency meeting was to begin in about 5 minutes. The Speaker of the Central Council would be chairing the meeting. He was a friend and sponsor of the CMI, so Michael presumed that he had already been briefed with some bogus information. Information that would likely be hostile to the truth. James was a member Emeritus of the Central Council and had confirmed to Michael that he'd been invited.

The Admiral had contacted Michael, saying the he'd been summoned to appear.

The presence chamber connected and Michael found himself seated in his seat in the Council Chamber. The Chamber was set up much like a court room. The Speaker was in the center position, set one foot higher than the other eight members, four on either side.

The Admiral was seated at one of the tables on the floor level, about two feet lower than Michael, facing the speaker.

The Speaker pounded his gavel. "We are here today to hear testimony regarding the rebellion taking place on the allied planet known as Earth." Michael suddenly found himself sitting at the table next to the Admiral.

Recovering from the momentary vertigo associated with the sudden change, he noticed that the room had reconfigured. There were now only three seats on either side of the speaker. James was nowhere to be seen, but an additional empty chair had appeared next to the Admiral.

Michael couldn't help but smile. He was connected to this meeting by projection chamber, as was the Admiral. As a result, the Central Council could organize the room however they wanted. The room was, after all, just a projection. But James was a different matter. The Confederation had no control over James, something it would appear the speaker had forgotten.

"What happened to the third conspirator?" shouted the Speaker.

There was a flash of light and James appeared in the designated seat.

"Gentlemen," James said with the usual sparkle in his eye. "It is not polite to change the seating arrangement without advising the occupants of those seats first. Now, what is this foolishness about a rebellion on Earth? By my observation, they are by far the most loyal member of the Confederation."

"We have received reports of advance military capability on Earth. Capability that was not disclosed as part of the treaty process and is now being used against other Confederation interests."

"Then you have been given false information."

"We have also received reports of human interference during a Confederation military action."

377

"If by interference, you mean they saved the Fleet Armada from certain destruction, then that would be true."

"Ancient One. Have you finally become senile? Those statements are self-contradictory."

James temper flared at the insult and all present, even Michael, shrank down in terror.

Calming himself James said. "Let me give you my report."

James transformed into his energy state.

Michael said. "James, what are you doing?"

Casting his attention on Michael, he said. "Implanting memories. Memories from various Fleet captains about the battle. Memories from your team about the battle and their development work. Memories from the Executive Officer about his torture."

James cast his attention back toward the council members, held it there for what appeared to be a few minutes, then coalesced back into his Lorexian form.

The Speaker was the first to regain his senses. "It appears that I have been misled. Has the Inspector been court marshaled yet?"

"No, Mr. Speaker," The Admiral said. "He is in the brig of my flagship. Because of his irresponsible actions, the Armada is currently stranded in an area of the Milky Way where the enemy is known to be active. We are awaiting rescue from our allies on Earth."

The Speaker turned to address Michael. "Is this true, that you are rescuing the Armada?"

"We have provided the Armada with improved Enemy-resistant shielding. We are also sending a deposit against our taxes, paid in transluminide."

"The Fast Packet Ship that you wrote about?"

"It was infected with the Enemy just before it departed," the Admiral said. "We successfully cleared one combatant off its hull, but they ran before we got the other. They left on a vector consistent with a return to New Lorexi. But the destination and location are unknown at this time."

"Only one Enemy combatant. How much of a threat can that be?"

"Enough to take down any planet in the Confederation, except possibly Earth."

"How can that be?" the Speaker asked.

"The Earth has Enemy-resistant shields. The only Confederation ships with those shields are stranded in interstellar space because of the Inspector's actions. No other Confederation ship or planet has such shields."

"More than 1 million planets at risk..." The Speaker muttered, then looking at Michael. "Can Earth help, Mr. Ambassador?"

"Yes. Humanity understands what the Confederation has done for them and is anxious to return the favor. We have a scalable planetary shield design that we know to be effective. If you can establish a commission to work with our people, the work can begin immediately. But the first step must be granting the inventors property rights to the intellectual property."

"Understood. It will be done within a day. Please send me the relevant contact information.

"Ancient One, Mr. Ambassador. Apologies that this situation got so far out of hand. You may do as you wish with the Inspector, probably better if you do not send him back here.

"Thank you for coming to the rescue of the Confederation."

He pounded his gavel and Michael found himself back in his projection chamber.

...

Moments later a meeting request came through. It was Jo-Na. Michael accepted the connection and the chamber configured to be the Admiral's office.

"The Confederation has serious problems my friend," the Admiral said. "Does he always behave like that? After the insult, I felt like I was about to be consumed in a furnace."

"I have not seen the Ancient Sentient that angry before. The Speaker is lucky that he was not consumed. The ancient one has been the guardian and protector of the Confederation for two million years. To imply that he was a traitor, then insult his capacity to function was a gross miscalculation. We need the Ancient Sentient more than we need our foolish Speaker."

"You know this isn't over, right?"

"I think it is over for a while."

"It will be on again as soon as he learns about the quantity of transluminide you're sitting on."

"All the more reason for stealth," Michael said.

"I am a senior military officer. Withholding information from command is a serious offense."

"That is the tortured line we must walk right now."

"But how can this be resolved?"

379

"When they realize that they need Earth as much as Earth needs the Confederation."

DANIEL PORTER'S QUARTERS

Time to wrap this up, Daniel thought as he logged back into his portal.

Astrogation second watch goes to Paige Wilson of Australia. He clicked the offer button next to Ms. Wilson's name.

Astrogation third watch goes to Huo Tai of China. He clicked the offer button next to Ms. Huo's name.

Science first watch goes to Adrian Meier of the Swiss Airforce. Second watch to Yi Ping of China's People's Army. Third watch to Angus White of the Royal Navy. He clicked the offer button next to each of the three names.

Daniel quickly double checked to make sure offers were already out for all three tactical positions and was pleasantly surprised to see an acceptance from Ms. O'Brien.

Now for Engineering, he thought. *First watch to Eric Braun of Germany. Second watch to Azima Mutai of Kenya. Third watch to An Pham of Vietnam.* Again, he clicked the offer button next to each of the three names.

The last position on the bridge crew was the runner. This was a new idea to Daniel, although he understood it to be a cross between a yeoman and a steward. When Daniel had screened people for this position, he'd looked for strong administrative capabilities and top-notch physical fitness. He quickly clicked the offer buttons next to the names of Jade Harris from New Zealand, Luis Perez from Mexico and Celeste Durant from France. All had previously held administrative positions in their associated country's armed services. And all had excellent letters of reference from previous commanding officers.

This had been the fastest recruitment process he'd ever been part of. But for a brand-new organization lifting itself up by its bootstraps, it needed to be fast and it certainly worked well.

SELECTIONS

Professor Schudel was exhausted. The last platform had not been placed until about 10:00 PM, and he had finally finished the test pull.

Beth and Thomas had finished placing platforms two and three around Noon. Michael had agreed to let Beth contribute about two hours on platform 4, which allowed Thomas to finish placing it by 10:00 PM. If she had not been allowed to help, then it would have taken Thomas until noon tomorrow, well, today now, to finish.

The results on the four platforms were more or less exactly the same, which implied that the Earth's liquid outer core was as uniform as they hoped. The planet that he had consulted on years ago, the one with core stability problems, had a very viscous liquid core that was not very uniform. That was one less problem he would have to worry about on Earth.

All four platforms would remain idle for the next couple days. They now had a better read on the concentrations in the core. Gold was 0.61%, platinum 0.49%, transluminide about 2.13 PPM and other impurities about 0.93%. The latter was a surprise, as was its composition, so he needed to update the impurity handling. At concentrations this high, the material needed to be returned to the core. That was not a problem or particularly difficult. The platforms bots could make the necessary changes in less than a day.

"One last thing I need to do before shutting down," he said to himself out loud, before pushing the button that initiated secure transport of the newly extracted transluminide to the Confederation's secure storage facility. "A little more than 1.5 kilograms added today," he summarized with a smile.

"Else," the Professor called out.

"Ready to go home?" she answered.

"Yes, I am."

"Happy to help. Sending you home in 5, 4, 3, 2, 1..."

The Professor appeared moments later in his apartment and was asleep five minutes after that.

SPACE FORCE TRAINING CENTER

Keanu had stayed up late last night drilling himself on using the galactic and intergalactic databases. The exercise he created to do this was to choose a star in each of the Milky Way, Andromeda, and Triangulum galaxies. His task was to create a course that would go from Earth to each of the stars, then return to Earth. For one of the tests, he chose the most traveled stars, one of which was New Lorexi. Time would be from breaking Earth orbit to re-establishing orbit.

Yesterday they had also released the specifications for the ship and propulsion systems they could use. This was one hopped-up ship.

Among the things he learned through these drills was that a complete scan for all obstacles between two far away points took a long time. If the test was timed, then he needed to select sensible way points where shorter obstacle scans could be done. That learning might or might not be relevant, depending on the test parameters, but he knew a lot more about intergalactic astrogation now than he had from the simple class work they had been given.

He also learned that these engines had two properties that the previous ones didn't. First, they could go straight from Warp to Jump and got a lot more range out of the Jump when they did. Second, for the long intergalactic jumps, a sequence of short jumps went a lot faster than a sequence of long jumps.

Keanu got to class and went to his station. The Professor had posted the top 10 slots of the leader board on the front wall of the room. Keanu was still number one, but anyone could still win given the anticipated distance of today's course.

The Professor stepped to the front of the room. "Class, today you are going to navigate a very long trip that will make stops in all three galaxies in which the Confederation operates. Your first stop will be at Kepler 452 in the Milky Way. A huge battle was fought there about 100,000 years ago. The third planet is now the most populated Confederation planet in the Milky Way.

"From there, you will go to New Lorexi, which you have all heard of. And from there, you will go to this star," the star's database identifier appeared on the front board. "Human science has not identified this star yet. But it is the home to the most populated Confederation planet in Triangulum.

"As these are important systems to the Confederation, there are a number of standard routes in the database. This one..." He pointed to another database identifier that appeared on the board. "...is your default route. You can change as much or as little of it as you would like. You have exactly four hours to file an amended flight plan. You can file as many amendments as you would like, but the last one you file will be your official flight plan."

A countdown timer appeared on the board, showing four hours. "Your time starts now. Good luck to you all."

The countdown timer started counting down.

Keanu had plotted the run from Earth to Kepler 452 last night and remembered the elements of that solution. His best time had been about 2 hours. He quickly opened that segment of the default plan and saw that it took four and a half days. Looking at the default solution a little more closely he understood why... They were dropping back to normal space before going to jump. And they were doing long recharges between jumps. Keanu quickly reconstructed last night's solution for Kepler 452, making minor updates for the approach required. The new course had a simulated transit time of an hour forty-two. Satisfied, he filed the amended plan.

The leg for the default run to Lorexi Prime had a reference time of 62 days. Keanu snorted when he saw that. *So ridiculous,* he thought, then noticed the evil eye he was getting from the Professor and went back to work.

This one is going to be tougher, Keanu thought. *Stars move a long way in 62 days. Just running this plan faster will fail because the star won't get there until a couple weeks after I do. And even to run the simulation will exceed the test time.*

Knowing that he needed to set some way points, Keanu attacked the intergalactic jump first. He found the location where the main intergalactic sequence started and determined that the standard solution to get there took three days. He knew he could find a better way point than that one but given the time constraint went with it anyway. A quick scan for obstacles showed that there was a single jump solution to a place a little closer, but still in intergalactic space. He updated the waypoint. He then did a quick estimate of the continuous jump time across the intergalactic void. It was 28 hours.

Then he did the same in reverse. Estimate where New Lorexi would be two days from launch. Move its way point to the corresponding location. Simulate the run from the revised waypoint to New Lorexi's revised position. There were two obstacles. He made a waypoint adjustment, then another to find an obstruction free path. The simulation proved out, so Keanu updated the flight plan and checked his time. Two hours, 12 minutes left.

Keanu noted that his waypoint into Andromeda was in a position that could give him a straight-line path to most of Triangulum. So, he checked to see if he could exit Andromeda the same way he entered.

Yes, he thought. The path would still be obstacle-free after the mandatory one-day layover.

The next step was to estimate the intergalactic jump from Andromeda to Triangulum, using his new Andromeda waypoint and the default Triangulum waypoint. The default plan took 59 days; his new plan, only 18 hours. He repeated the process of estimating a new Triangulum waypoint, finding a way in toward the target planet, then updating his waypoint to work. Once again, the simulation proved out and he filed an updated flight plan. A quick check of the time. An hour, 28 minutes left.

Keanu estimated the transit from Triangulum back to the Milky way, 32 hours. He repeated the process of finding an acceptable waypoint for the return, finding the path to Earth and simulating.

Excluding the layover times, the transit time was 100 hours, 24 minutes. The default solution, over 9 months.

Keanu filed his revised plan and checked the clock, 52 minutes left.

Best bet will be to do another obstacle check on the entire plan, while that is running, I'll see if I can identify any savings. He thought.

He launched the obstacle check. Then started looking for optimizations.

His transit from the Triangulum waypoint to the target star there was the longest of the intergalactic waypoints, weighing in at 4 hours, 12 minutes. After 10 minutes of searching he found a way point that would cut about 20 minutes off that time. It checked out, no obstacles, so he just plugged that into the existing plan.

It works, he thought. *Saved 20 minutes in and 20 minutes out of Triangulum at the cost of 1 minute from New Lorexi. Then saves 3 minutes back to the Milky Way for a net 42-minute gain.*

He wasn't sure if there was enough time to run a full obstacle check again but launched one. He would not file a flight plan without a full course obstacle check.

With one minute, 30 seconds left in the exam period, the obstacle check came back clean.

Racing as fast as he could, Keanu filed his final plan. He pushed the submit button just as the 15-seconds-remaining audio countdown started.

As everyone had filed their final plan in the last several minutes, everyone stayed around to see the results. A leader board for this session popped up in the front. Scores started appearing in the order the final flight plans had been entered

The first couple were horrific. 84 days. 62 days.

Then some shorter ones came up. 12 days. 16 days. 10 days, 6 hours. But the last one burst into flames, the simulated ashes falling off the bottom of the page indicating that the student that filed it had his third crash and was disqualified.

The next one to pop up was not listed in days, but in hours and minutes. 212 hours, 18 minutes. 210 hours, 53 minutes.

The Professor spoke up over the noise in the room. "As you just noticed, time less than 10 days show up as hours and minutes. You also probably noticed that the later the last flight plan was filed, the better the times seem to be."

More scores came up. There were sounds of awe as some much shorter ones came up. 122 hours, 19 minutes.

Then laughing as one of the late entries came in at 52 days.

For the top 10, names were now shown next to the scores. Keanu's and his next closest rival's names were not up. Another counter showed that there were 8 more scores to be posted.

There was lot of cheering when Keanu's closest rival's score was posted at the top of the list, coming in at 102 hours, 48 minutes. *That was close.* Keanu thought.

Then his name came up next at 99 hours, 44 minutes.

Then the shock. 68 hours, 2 minutes came up. And immediately burst into flames. Keanu sighed a breath of relief. It was done. He had won.

Keanu was called to the front of the room and given the navigation trophy.

SPACE FORCE COMMAND HEADQUARTERS

Ed Foster had been a Lt. Commander in the Navy Seals. Two years after the Revelation, the Navy had started reducing their special forces numbers, offering early retirement at full pension to anyone who had been in 16 or more years.

He took the offer, but within months found himself bored and longing for his previous life. When Space Force was announced, he was quick to apply.

The interview/offer process was unlike any he had experienced before. He wasn't completely convinced that it was appropriate for the armed services, but it had served him well. He was now a Major in the Space Force Marines, one that had just been called in for a meeting with Colonel Mark Patterson.

Ed was sitting in the reception area at Space Force Command headquarters waiting for the escort that would take him to see the Colonel.

"Major Foster?"

He looked up to see that an attractive young woman had called his name. She was a Corporal, in all likelihood the Colonel's assistant. As he walked over, she said. "Please follow me, sir."

After a short walk, she motioned to an open door, then whispered, "Good luck."

"Major Foster," Mark said. "Please come in and take a seat."

"Thank you, sir."

"Major, you have been selected to lead an enhanced platoon with four squads."

"Sir?" He asked questioningly.

"The EAS Ottawa will be the first ship deployed by Space Force. We would like you to lead the Space Marine contingent on that ship. You were chosen based on your past experience and test scores since joining Space Force. On the face of it, this position is below your rank. But don't be fooled. The Lt. Colonel that will lead the Space Marines on our first Cruiser will be selected from those serving on the first Fast Attack Ships. You are on the short list for that promotion. And the Ottawa is where you will earn your shot."

"Thank you, sir."

"Your orders are to select four squads to join you that are exo-planet certified. Your platoon should be prepared to report within 48 hours. You will be working with Captain Daniel Porter. He has command of the ship. You work for him while on board. You have command of your Marines at all times.

"Off the record... Expect to spend the day tomorrow with Captain Porter and his crew. Expect to deploy as early as Sunday, so select your squads today."

RESOURCE ADMINISTRATION, SPACE FORCE HEADQUARTERS

Ed knew the squads that he wanted, so went straight to the administration floor. There he met with the Warrant Officer who was responsible for the resource pool allocation.

"Congratulations on your assignment to the Ottawa, sir. I see that you are authorized to select four squads. Do you know who you want?"

"Yes. James from UK, Wilson from US, Thawan from Thailand, and Zhang from China."

"Assigned. Do you want me to send orders to report?"

"Can you arrange a booking in the Dining Room for myself and the lieutenants?"

"Yes. There is an opening for 5 at 7:30."

"Great. Book it and send the orders to report."

"Done."

SPACE FORCE DINING ROOM

Ed came 10 minutes early. He wanted to be the first to arrive.

"Major Foster. Your table is ready. If you will follow me."

Several minutes later, the first of his lieutenants arrived. "Lt. Evan James reporting for duty, sir."

"Evan, good to see you." Ed said, standing to shake the lieutenant's hand. The two had met in training on the first day. Ed had seen how Evan ran his men and knew that they would work well together as a team.

Moments later... "Lt. Craig Wilson reporting for duty, sir."

"Craig, so good to see you. This is Evan James." He waved at Evan. Ed had mentored several students through Seal training. Craig had been one of them.

The next two arrived together. "Lt. Cheng Zhang reporting for duty, sir," said the first.

"Lt. Pra Thawan reporting for duty, sir. Apologies for being late sir. Our squads were out running when the order to report came in. We got here as fast as possible, sir."

"Thank you, gentlemen. Please take a seat."

As if on cue, a waiter came to take dinner orders. As he left, Major Foster started. "Gentlemen. Thank you for joining me this evening. We all have the privilege of being assigned to the first Space Force ship to be commissioned. You and your squads are on 48-hour notice of deployment. From what I've been told, I doubt we'll be required to report Saturday, but you and your squads should be ready to report, nonetheless.

"I've not been briefed on our mission, but I have been told that it is of the utmost importance and will involve a planet outside our solar system.

"I've chosen each of you for this mission. That is an aspect of Space Force that I did not expect, but greatly appreciate. I chose you based on the respect and camaraderie I've seen among your squads. I don't know how long it will be before we are called to action once deployed. But my intention is to make sure that our four squads work together collectively as well as each squad works independently.

"You will be key in making that happen. Inter-squad rivalry for the purpose of honing our skills is a good thing. But none of that can leak into the field. When on mission we must be one, aggressively and proactively supporting each other.

"Starting tomorrow, we will train together. I have been told that I may be called away tomorrow. If that should happen, then Craig will have the lead tomorrow. Each day I will announce a second, who will lead if I'm called away. In combat, of course, command will flow by rank and seniority as assigned by Space Force."

No sooner had the Major finished speaking, than dinner was served.

Evan James was the first to break the silence. "Major, forgive me for asking, but why are you commanding a platoon?"

"Thank you for asking, Lt. James. We are the first ship deploying. As I understand it, standard deployment for the Fast Attack Ships will be with a platoon of three or four squads. The first Cruisers will be deployed in three to six months. Those will have three platoons led by a Lt. Colonel, who will be chosen from the platoon leaders in the Fast Attack Ships. I am a leading contender for one of those slots and am being given this command as a qualifying step."

"Makes sense." Lt. Wilson commented, then… "Hope you snag one of those slots, sir. You deserve it."

"Thank you, Lieutenant."

…

When dinner was over and plates cleared, Major Foster said. "Gentlemen. Thank you again for joining me this evening. Best you get back to your squads and brief them on what's ahead."

TEST FLIGHT

[Friday, 09.20.2030, 05:00 AM] DANIEL PORTER'S QUARTERS

Daniel woke to the alarm he'd set. Physical fitness training would start in an hour. Daniel got up, made himself a cup of coffee, replicated a blueberry bran muffin, then went to check his messages. At the top of the queue was a message from the Space Force Secretary requiring his presence at Engineering Shuttle Bay 1 @ 11:00 AM for a tour and test flight of his new ship. There was an additional request that he bring as many of his command staff as he could muster at that hour.

Daniel had been expecting this order. The Secretary's previous message implied that the first tours would be happening in this timeframe. He was very pleased that it was happening now.

Daniel messaged his officers and bridge crew that they were required to report to Engineering Shuttle Bay #1 no later than 10:45 AM this morning. Not all of his offers had been accepted yet. But one thing was clear, anyone that did not report would have their offer rescinded.

RYAN'S QUARTERS

Jim was up and preparing for this morning's physical training when a message sounded on his communicator. Checking it, he saw that it was from Captain Porter. He was required to report to an Engineering Bay this morning at 10:45. *An engineering bay?* He thought.

TAJIMA'S QUARTERS

Keanu was just finishing his morning yoga workout when a message sounded on his communicator. Checking it, it was from Captain Porter. He was required to report to an Engineering Bay this morning at 10:45 AM. *This must be it!* He thought, struggling to believe that he was actually going into space.

FOSTER'S QUARTERS

Ed was doing his morning warm up when a message sounded on his communicator. Checking it, it was from Captain Porter. He was required to report to an Engineering Bay this morning at 10:45 AM.

Wow! That was quick, he thought. *But still have time for a little PE with my platoon.*

ENGINEERING SHUTTLE BAY #1

One by one, the bridge crew and officers arrived. At 10:45 exactly, Captain Porter arrived. The First Officer, Commander Duan Tai of China, was quick to call everyone to attention. Captain Porter came in and started working the room, shaking hands with everyone, congratulating them on their appointments and thanking them for accepting their offers.

One of the men was wearing a marine uniform. "Major Foster? I'm Daniel Porter."

"Captain Porter. It's a pleasure to meet you, sir. Thank you for including me in today's activities."

At 10:55, the shuttle door opened, and Michael emerged, along with the Space Force Secretary, Joel, Eugene, and Kelly.

"Attention!" Captain Porter called. Everyone was quick to snap to attention. The Space Force Secretary quickly returned their salute and called everyone to parade rest.

"Mr. Ambassador," he said.

Michael stepped forward to address the assembly.

"Captain Porter and crew of the EAS Ottawa, this is truly a great day for the Earth Alliance and humanity. Today the first ship of the Space Force fleet will be introduced to her commander and crew. As you will soon learn, your ship is piloted by an AI. Her name is Else. She is named after her creator, a dear friend of mine, Elsie Hoffman, an Ascendant who was lost in the liberation of North Korea.

"In the Confederation, AIs are full citizens, just as you are. Else is the most talented pilot and helmsmen born on Earth. She is also a surprisingly good counselor, if you should find yourself in need. I encourage you to befriend her, as your lives will depend on her.

"Formally, you are here today as tourists here to tour the spacecraft and participate in its first test flight. And formally, Joel is in command today." Michael motioned Joel forward.

"Along with Joel are the engineers who brought you the propulsions systems, shields, and the manufacturing process that created this ship. Let me introduce Dr. Eugene Xu of Johns Hopkins University and Ms. Kelly Williamson, a PhD student in the Engineering School here at the Institute. In case you were wondering, both Eugene and Kelly are human."

Michael motioned the two to step forward.

Keanu was shocked to find out that the girl he had a crush on was one of the geniuses that had created their ship.

"If you will board the shuttle, it will take you to your ship." Michael said, pointing to the shuttle door that was now open.

As people started boarding, Michael pulled Joel and Daniel aside.

"Joel, for the test flight, please take the Captain anywhere he would like to go if you believe it's safe.

"Captain Porter, I think you will find Joel and Else to be very accommodating. Your crew report to you. But your commands to the helm must be passed through Joel. This is a test flight. Joel still holds the command codes.

"My best advice is to do everything in your power to befriend Else. She will be your helm officer once the command codes are released to you. Think of her as the ship."

"Thank you, sir." Daniel saluted Michael, then turned to Joel. "Shall we?"

Once the last person was on board, Joel closed the door and went forward to the cockpit.

"Ready?" Thomas asked.

"Yes. Would you like to announce our departure, or should I?"

"I'd be happy to," said Thomas. He had more than enough processing power to fly and talk at the same time.

The shuttle lifted six inches off the ground and glided out of the Engineering Bay toward his designated take-off slot.

"Welcome aboard everyone. My name is Thomas. I am your captain for the short trip out to Lagrange 4, where your ship is parked. We will be launching shortly. Please be seated with your seat belts fastened. The first part of our journey today will be straight up to an altitude of about 12,000 miles. From there we will take a direct course to your ship, which is in more or less the same orbit as the Moon.

"Our entire flight today will be in grav drive at 12G. Expected flight time will be about 27 minutes. If you should get up to walk around, please be aware that the gravity you experience in the cabin will be slightly higher than Earth normal. Please be careful." Thomas's holographic projection turned to ask Joel. "Should we open the 'window shades' so they can see?"

Joel nodded affirmatively.

"Ladies and gentlemen." Thomas said. "A view of Earth."

...

In the passenger cabin, the cabin walls slowly started becoming transparent. The process stopped when the light from the Sun became brighter than the cabin lights had been. They were still ascending straight up perpendicular to their launch point, so the Earth was directly behind the ship but still large enough to be seen easily on either side of the cabin.

After a few minutes, Thomas's voice came over the cabin speakers. "We have just passed through 12,000 miles and are about to change course. We will also be inverting the shuttle with respect to the Earth at this time. If you are subject to vertigo, please close your eyes. This will only take a moment. Rotating now." About 15 seconds later. "If you closed your eyes, you should be safe to open them now."

Keanu was blown away by the image of the Earth below. Ryan, who was sitting next to him, elbowed Keanu. "Cool. Did you ever think you would be doing this?"

"Never. At least not until a couple weeks ago."

"So, is that the Kelly Williamson you're so hot on?" Ryan asked.

"Yes. She told me that she was part of this. Kind of left out the part about being one of the top two or three," Keanu replied, and they both started laughing.

After another minute or so, Thomas came back on the speaker system. "We are now in the steady cruise part of our journey, so in a moment I will turn off the seat belt sign. One additional word of caution, unlike a traditional airline trip where seat belts are on at the beginning and the end. On this trip, they are on at the beginning, middle and end. When the seat belt sign goes off a count-down timer will start. The seat belt sign will come back on when the time reaches 1 minute. Please be in your seat at that time." With that, there was a bong, and the seat belt sign was turned off.

Keanu was the first one up. He quickly walked over to Kelly.

"Hi. I didn't expect to see you here today," Keanu said.

"Didn't know until late last night. But glad I was invited. You're on the first ship?"

"Yes. Astrogation. First watch," Keanu said.

"Then you will be working with Else. I've been on several trips with her when she piloted the shuttle. She is really good. Maybe she can help hone your skills."

"She navigates too?"

"Else is an AI. In many ways, she is the ship. She's been all over this galaxy."

Keanu was a bit chest fallen that the AI piloting the ship was also a proficient navigator. Then he chided himself. *I should be happy about this. At least we will have someone that actually knows what they're doing.*

The gong sounded and the seatbelt sign lit up. Keanu got to his seat and was belted in by the time the countdown timer hit 30 seconds.

Thomas's voice came on again. "Transition beginning in 5, 4, 3, 2, 1..." As Thomas started counting down the cabin walls became opaque. At 3, the gravity eased back to normal. At 1, Keanu noticed a slight dizziness set in. It lasted for about 30 seconds, then the gravity increased to the level it had been before.

Jim elbowed Keanu. "What's going on?" He whispered.

"They cut the thrust, reversed the direction of the ship, then reapplied the thrust. The whole first part of the trip we've been gaining speed. Now we are slowing down. The dizziness was from rotating the ship around."

"Really? They never did that on *Star Trek*," Jim said, at which Keanu started laughing again.

Sure enough, when Thomas made the cabin walls transparent again Earth appeared forward a bit, before it had been about the same amount behind.

PROJECTION CHAMBER, AMBASSADOR'S OFFICE

"Mi-Ku. Thank you for taking my call," the Admiral said. "The Fast Attack Ship arrived back an hour ago with the transluminide. He sends his thanks to your engineer Joel for making the transfer as quickly as he did. By not entering orbit, he was able to slice five hours off the return trip."

"Good thinking on his part," Michael said.

"My Chief Engineer tells me that the new engines your team specified will be installed and ready for test later today. Our anticipated transit time will be three days."

"Excellent news." Michael said.

"May I ask where you are with your manufacturing process? Have you been able to make any progress?"

"Yes. The first two ships are complete and will be doing their test flights over the next two days."

"Amazing. How did you do it?"

"Personal replicators."

"You made two spaceships in what, three days, using those tiny personal replicators!" the Admiral exclaimed, then started laughing.

"Yes. And we are going with a different, faster process to build out the rest of our fleet. So please flush any prep work your team may have done on our previous request. We will supply you with the new specification when you arrive and will, of course, compensate you for any time or material lost because of the previous request."

"Thank you, Mi-Ku. Will your team have time to complete the upgrades for our remaining ships."

"Yes. I don't have their current status, but they have made a lot of progress and should have designs you can build out within a week of your arrival. Do you know how long you can stay?"

"No. The High Command has gone strangely quiet. But they are aware of the dilapidated state of our Fleet. I doubt they will ask us to do anything before our repairs are complete."

"If you will allow us to help, I would like to do a complete refresh and upgrade on your ships," Michael said.

"Mi-Ku. That will require at least 10 kg of transluminide."

"We have begun mining, so the quantity is not a problem."

"But explaining it probably will be," The Admiral replied.

"Do you have the ability to mine transluminide?" Michael asked.

"Of course."

"Suppose we found a large supply on another planet in another system. Could you pay us a finder's fee if we told you where it was?"

"Of course. Twenty percent is standard."

"Then let me propose the following..." Michael said, then went on to explain.

SHUTTLE, NEAR EAS OTTAWA

Ryan noticed that the Earth looked pretty far away at this point. Looking up at the countdown time, he saw that the seat belt signs were about to turn on again.

There was a bong and Thomas's voice came over the speakers. "Ladies and gentlemen, we are just about to land on your new ship. Please take your seats and fasten your seatbelts. We are currently about 1 mile from the ship. I am going to rotate the shuttle to face her. If you are subject to vertigo, please close your eyes. For those watching, the ship will appear on the right side of the cabin momentarily."

Ryan could tell that the ship was slowly rotating. Suddenly people started chatting and pointing out the right side. He turned to look and there she was. The door to the shuttle bay was open. Within minutes they were inside, and they felt a slight jolt as the shuttle landed. Before Thomas could say anything, applause broke out in the passenger compartment.

Joel came out and spoke briefly with the Captain, who then stood and walked to the front of the cabin.

"OK. In a moment, the shuttle door will open. We will exit and line up by watch. First watch will line up with me. Second watch will line up with Commander Tai. Third watch with Lt. Commander Kumar.

"Once out and in line, our civilian hosts will take us on a tour of the ship. When the tour is done, second and third watch will report to the officers' dining room. First watch will report to the bridge. We will do three watch changes about an hour apart. While first watch is not on the bridge, Lt. Ryan will be its acting leader."

The Captain nodded to Joel, who placed his hand on the panel to open the door.

...

Once the crew was lined up by watch, Joel began. "As you should all know, the ship has eight decks. Each deck is a little less than 400 meters long and 100 meters wide. If we walked the perimeter of each deck that would be an 8-kilometer hike. We aren't going to do that. You will have plenty of time next week for a more detailed, self-guided tour. Today, we will spend most of our time on the officer's deck, making stops at the bridge, the dining room, the officers' lounge and the crew quarters. We will show you to the cabin you have been assigned. We will also visit the enlisted deck, hospital deck, and the physical fitness area. You are currently on the flight deck.

O'BRIEN'S QUARTERS, EAS OTTAWA

Kaitlin O'Brien stood in the doorway of her cabin. She was surprised how big it was. Over 1,000 square feet with a bedroom, bathroom, kitchen/dining area and living room. The kitchen had a food replicator, so she could eat at home if she wanted. It was also open to a living room with a sitting area. At the far end of the great room was a small office with a separate door. Everything about her cabin was like a 4-star hotel. Overall, this was going to be a more comfortable place to live than her apartment in Ireland.

BRIDGE, EAS OTTAWA

The first watch had taken their stations on the bridge. Captain Porter sat in the Captain's Chair. Joel was in an observer's seat behind him. They had agreed to take a three-legged trip. Earth to Bernard's Star to Alpha Centauri to Earth. Each watch would take one leg. Captain Porter and Joel would be on the bridge for all three watches. The crews would stage in the dining room before their watch and could take the rest of their non-bridge time in the dining room, lounge, quarters or physical fitness area. As the ship was not fully crewed, they did not want people wandering off and getting lost. Else had agreed to lock the access hatches to other areas and to accept orders to start each leg from the watch leader.

"Mr. Tajima, please lay in a course to Bernard's Star. Mr. Ryan, tactical report."

"The EAS Jerusalem is 1 mile to port at a dead stop. The manufacturing line is idle at the moment. No debris visible on scanners. There is a small cluster of pebbles approaching the moon about 100,000 miles out. No other activity."

"Thank you, Mr. Ryan."

"Mr. Meier. Anything on long range?"

"No other ships in the outer system. Sir."

"Thank you, Mr. Meier."

"Mr. Tajima. Is the course laid in?"

"Yes, sir."

"Ms. Else. Is this course acceptable to you?"

"A bit conservative, but acceptable, yes."

"All hands. This is Captain Porter. Please be advised, we will be underway momentarily."

"Ms. Else, please engage."

"Engaged, Captain."

On the main display, the ship could be seen moving away from the manufacturing facility on a course overlaid on the planets.

As the Bridge settled into the routine of the cruise, Keanu asked Else. "What makes my course conservative?"

"May I put an image on your course plotter?" she asked.

"Sure." Keanu replied. Another course plot showed up next to his. "Two minutes faster," he muttered quietly. "Same safety rating to 4 decimal places."

Whispering, he said, "Else. I see that my course is slower, not more conservative."

396

"But saying more conservative was nicer," she whispered back.

"Thank you." Keanu whispered. "Clever. I picked up the slingshot around Jupiter but didn't think to juice it by angling past Ganymede. Didn't think it would add much."

"It doesn't. But remember, even 1 kph multiplies about 10 times as we accelerate out to the jump point. It then multiplies another 100 times during the jump, which is the longest part of the trip," she whispered back.

"Knew that but didn't really understand before. Thank you Else." Keanu said, then continued, "Else, can I ask you a question?"

"Is that really a question, Tajima?" she said sarcastically.

"I'll take that as a yes. Seems to me that I'm redundant. The ship already has you. Does it really need me?"

"For day to day stuff like this, when there is absolutely nothing else going on... no. But there will be bad days when our chances of survival will be much higher with the two of us working together. On those days, I would be jumping blind because I don't have time to calc a proper course."

"But if you don't have time; how would I?"

"Keanu. I'm the ship. I drive. I stabilize. I share CPU time with the ship's automated systems. Waiting for the trip to start just now, I had about 96% capacity and a long time, because they told me the destination a half hour earlier."

"In an emergency, I might have no more notice than you, only 35% capacity and 20 things that need doing. Rest assured. You are needed for our missions, even if you really aren't needed to depart dry dock."

"Thanks, Else. I've been worried about this since Kelly told me about you on the way up."

"Are you that guy Kelly is so goo-goo about?" Else asked.

"I hope I am."

"I think you two were made for each other."

SICK BAY, EAS OTTAWA

The ship had its first glitch during the jump to Bernard's Star. Two crew members were walking across the dining room, hot coffee in hand, when the ship jumped. One of them, Yi Ping, second watch science officer, got hit with vertigo from the jump. He fell, knocking himself out when his head hit a table and spilling hot coffee on his colleague Luis Perez, second watch yeoman.

The crew were quick to rally around their wounded comrades. The unconscious man was taken to sick bay on a grav gurney. The burnt one walked under his own power. Joel was the closest thing to a doctor on the ship and met the injured in Sick Bay. He administered nanobots for the concussion and a nanobot cream on the burn area. One of the crew, Azima Mutai, second watch, engineering, was able to dress the wound.

BRIDGE, EAS OTTAWA

When word got back to the Captain, he said. "Ryan, I want you at the science station during third watch. I'll call Lt. White to cover second watch. You've been cross-trained. Let's put that to use during our training flight. It's good prep for when we have a real emergency.

"I'll let the yeoman post go empty."

The Captain made a log entry regarding the incident, including a recommendation that all candidates be tested for vertigo and susceptible ones treated against it on early flights.

ENGINEERING BAY #1

Overall the test flight went well. Both injured men were healed by the time they returned. The ship performed well. The crew bonded. It would take a while before this ship and its crew would be ready to battle the Enemy, but Captain Porter was convinced they would be up to the challenge in a matter of months.

...

As Daniel exited the Engineering Bay, his communicator sounded. Looking at his communicator, Daniel saw that it was the military head of Space Force, Admiral Samuel Scott.

"Daniel Porter," he answered.

"Captain Porter. Admiral Scott here. I have sent a driver to meet you at the Engineering Bay. Please join me for dinner."

...

"The Admiral will be meeting you in one of the private dining rooms," said the driver.

Daniel headed up to the dining room and presented himself to the host.

"This way, sir." The host winked and added in a conspiratorial whisper, "Serious brass waiting for you. Thought you should know."

Daniel nodded his thanks, then opened the door and entered.

Waiting for him were the Ambassador, the Secretary of Space Force, and the Admiral.

"Captain Porter. Welcome," Michael said.

"Mr. Ambassador. Thank you for today's excursion," He said shaking Michael's hand, then added, "Mr. Secretary. Admiral."

"Captain. We have chosen your first mission." Michael said. "It is a scientific mission to a star system known as Lalande 21185. It is a little over 8 light-years from Earth. There are four planets in the habitable zone. You will conduct a high-level scan of those four worlds.

"A specialist team will accompany you. The team will be led by Joel Rubinstein. You will receive additional instructions prior to launch," Michael said, then nodded to the Admiral.

"Captain Porter," said the Admiral. "Your immediate responsibility will be to get your crew, meaning the watch crew, the operating crew, your Space Marines, and the mission crew, ready for departure by zero seven hundred hours, local time, Sunday morning. Your admin portal has been updated to show your entire crew and mission specialists. At zero eight hundred Sunday morning, you and your 1st and 2nd officers will report to Space Force Command for your formal commissioning.

"You will be responsible for the assembly and loading of your ship; the transportation of your mission team to the target system; all space-based protection of your ship, crew and mission team while deployed; and any further orders provided through your chain of command once the preliminary scan is made. Consul Rubinstein will be responsible for the mission itself. Major Foster will be responsible for all ground-based protection and any other requirements you or Consul Rubinstein may provide for the success of the mission."

After a moment's pause, Daniel said, "I understand my responsibilities. Is there anything else you can tell me about the purpose of this mission that might inform trade-offs we may need to make?"

After another moment's pause, Michael stood and said. "Captain, if you could walk with me for a moment."

...

As they stepped into an adjacent room, Michael said. "Captain, this is for your ears and your ears only. The Confederation Fleet is inbound toward Earth. There are some materials that the Fleet desperately needs. We have reason to believe that those materials may exist in the Lalande 21185 system. Therefore, we are going to do a preliminary search for those, or other relevant materials, in that system. If we find something, we'll report the discovery to the Fleet, and they'll divert to your location to help in the recovery of the materials. Earth will be paid handsomely for making this discovery and the Fleet will get something they desperately need.

"This system has not been studied by the Confederation before, so there's a good chance we may find what they need.

"Your ship is not equipped with the scanners required to find what we're looking for, so the mission team will do the scans relevant to the Fleet. You are to support the mission team in any way possible.

"But we want this mission to be a win for you and your crew as well. There is an immense amount of new scientific data to be gathered about this system. Data that humanity doesn't have, and that the Confederation doesn't have either.

"The Earth Alliance and Space Force Command want that scientific knowledge.

"I regret that your first mission was chosen because of an urgent Confederation need. But this mission is of great value to humanity beyond its value to the Confederation.

"To your question about trade-offs. The mission team has the higher priority. But, your study of the system is also important and must be maximized consistent with getting Joel's mission completed."

"I understand sir and will do everything in my power to assure the success of every aspect of this mission," Daniel said.

"Thank you, Captain. Shall we return to the others?"

DANIEL PORTER'S QUARTERS

As soon as he was back in his quarters, Daniel logged into his ship's portal. He quickly surveyed the entire roster. Including himself there were three senior officers plus Else and a chief engineer, 15 bridge officers, another 20 ship's crew, a doctor and 3 medical techs, 53 space marines and a mission crew of six. 103 lives in total.

Their target departure from orbit was Noon on Sunday. The ship loading schedule indicated that boarding would start at 9 AM tomorrow morning. He would be going up with the first group but was to return along with a few others shortly thereafter.

Daniel acknowledged his orders and initiated the automatic process that would send the reporting orders.

Moments later, his communicator sounded. Looking at it he smiled. His orders to report had just been received.

SUNDAY NEWS SHOWS

[Saturday, 09.21.2030] ENGINEERING BAY #1

Daniel arrived at the Engineering Bay 15 minutes early. He had brought his old submarine duffle, packed with the same items as in the old days. When he entered, he was pleased to see everyone else had already arrived. Going up on the first shuttle were his command crew, chief engineer, bridge crew and the mission specialists.

Joel was the leader of the mission team. He still held the ship's command codes, but that would change tomorrow. According to the orders Daniel had received, his commissioning ceremony would be tomorrow morning and the command codes would be transferred to him as soon as he returned to the ship.

"Captain Porter. We meet again." Joel said smiling. "Thankfully, for the return we will be transporting down. It's a lot faster."

"Consul Rubinstein, I'm happy that you will be with us on this trip."

"Please call me Joel. It looks like everyone is here. Would you like to make the boarding announcement?"

Daniel walked over to the shuttle door and whistled to get everyone's attention as Joel opened the door.

"Team," Daniel said. "This is a great day for the Earth Alliance and Space Force. Today, Earth's first interstellar starship will receive her crew. You have been selected for that crew because of your skill, accomplishments and willingness to serve. Come, let's board our ship and begin this historic new age."

Daniel's data pad beeped as each crew member boarded, their status in the ship portal changing to 'In Transit'."

FOX NEWS, NEW YORK

"Michael, thank you for joining us again this week on Fox News Sunday. I was very surprised to get a call from the Embassy last week asking if it would be possible for you to come back today, something about important updates and setting the record straight. Is that true?"

"Chris, thanks for letting me speak with you and America today. Yes, I have several important updates that I would like to share. I

401

would also like to clarify some statements I made on your show some years ago." Michael smiled.

"My interest is piqued," Chris said. "How would you like to start?"

"Let me start with the clarification. To make sure I got this right, I went back and watched a recording of that interview yesterday. You asked me, 'Will we get access to technology like shuttles and transporters?' I answered…" Michael paused to pull out a piece of paper… "I want to make sure I get this exactly right. I answered, 'You will certainly benefit from them, and many humans will get to be passengers and have the opportunity to be beamed from location to location. But I sense that your question is whether humans will own such technology? Will Air Force 1 become a shuttle craft? Will United Airlines start providing shuttle service to Europe? The answer to that question is eventually, but not for some time.' I regret to say that my answer that morning was very misleading."

"What? We aren't going to get the technology over time?" Chris asked.

"No, to that comment. But yes, to your question from 5 years ago."

"OK. Now I'm confused," Chris said.

"Chris. The day that you, meaning the nations of the Earth, signed the treaty, 100 percent of Confederation technology became available to you. It is a term in the default treaty we offer everyone. Once the Embassy was built and the Institute started operation, dozens of Confederation technology transfer specialists came and started teaching. We have done this with every new member for the last million years or more. But, as we discussed when I was here two weeks ago, none of the new members have been very successful with adaptation. Therefore, diplomats like myself have gone with the answer… and let me read this from my notes so you can double check the recording yourself… 'The answer to that question is eventually, but not for some time.' That was the answer I wanted to set straight today.

"A better answer would have been… All Confederation technology will be available to you once the treaty is signed. But it will probably take a relatively long time for you to adapt it."

"But you said last week that we have adapted it faster than anyone else."

"Indeed, you have. Humanity is adapting Confederation technology at an unprecedented pace. It is what we hope for everyone but have never experienced before.

"I'm hoping that context helps you understand why we describe it the way we do. But the treaty language is unambiguous, as is the Institute's support for technology transfer."

"Michael, would it be OK if I rewind back to the beginning of the conversation?" Chris asked.

Michael nodded his assent.

"Why are you here today? I mean, I get it that you want to set the record straight. I for one appreciate that. But what was the compelling event that caused your team to call and ask to be on the show."

"I got word last week that one of the professors on sabbatical at the institute wanted access to the specifications for some equipment. He assumed that we would not share those specifications, but eventually asked for them anyway. When they were given to him, he was shocked. When asked why he was surprised that he was given the specifications, he said that he saw my interview on this show five years ago and understood me to say that the Confederation would give equipment for human Ascendants to use, but not give you the technology to adapt for use by non-Ascendant humans."

Michael turned to look directly at the camera. "My friends. If you want to adapt Confederation technology, come to the Institute and let's do it. We will supervise so you don't hurt yourselves, but the door is wide open and has been since the first day."

"Michael, thank you for coming to see us and for setting the record straight. But, does that mean that there will be United Airlines shuttle service to Europe sometime soon?"

"Chris, you'll need to ask United about that, not me."

"Does all this have something to do with the update you have for us?"

"Yes, it does. You have undoubtedly heard about the two new bright objects in the sky out near the moon."

"Yes. I've also seen them. There was a news report last week that these are the first two ships for Space Force."

"That is correct, and it connects back to the previous issue. You see, these ships were designed by our human engineering team. And the production process was also conceived by our human engineering team."

"Are you suggesting that the Confederation had no role in this?"

"No. Confederation scientists and engineers helped. But the context here is very important. There has been little advancement in the related technologies in the last 100,000 years. Yet, when given to human engineers, the same technologies leaped ahead. More efficient, higher performance, faster builds, less capital-intensive builds, all in five years.

"The Confederation has become stuck in its ways and, despite shortages, it does not have the same drive for 'faster, better, cheaper,' that humanity has."

"But Michael, you were part of the sell that humanity was at risk without the Confederation."

"Chris. Humanity was lost without the Confederation. Nothing changes that fact. The Confederation has been the force that has allowed the three galaxies to thrive. But the reason that is true is because it brings peoples together. We are more than the sum of the parts. Humanity's addition to the Confederation has saved humanity. But that's not all. It has, or to be more accurate, it will vastly improve the Confederation overall."

ABC NEWS, NEW YORK

"Michael, thank you for joining us again today."

"George, it is a pleasure to be with you this morning."

"Michael, I'm told that most people that live in rural areas have seen several new objects appear in the night sky this week. In New York, the sky is never dark enough to see anything, but I have seen numerous still shots of a host of objects that are allegedly being built by the Confederation. Can you tell us about this?"

"George. Let me start with a minor correction. These objects are all being built at the behest of the Earth Alliance, not the Confederation. Further, the objects themselves are human designed. And they are being built using a new human-designed manufacturing process that leverages some Confederation technology."

"Can you explain that Michael? It's hard to believe that humans are capable of manufacturing anything of this size in space."

Michael smiled. "George, humans are more capable than you give them credit for." He said this lightheartedly. "But I agree with your basic point. Humanity had no capability like this until recently and would not have developed it for quite some time without Confederation assistance."

"So, what has been built?" George asked. "The two large objects appear to be spaceships. The four smaller ones just look like big rectangular plates of metal."

"The two large objects are the first two Space Force ships. They are named the EAS Ottawa and EAS Jerusalem. The four smaller objects are mining platforms that will be used to mine iron and nickel from the Earth's core. The majority of this material will be used to build the initial Space Force Fleet. All of this has been sanctioned and approved by the Earth Alliance with appropriate permitting, etc."

"We haven't heard much about this in the media." George commented.

"That is one of the reasons I am here today. Some of this information was in the last press release from the Earth Alliance. Some was in recent episode of Sergeant Butler's weekly show. The episode hosted by Sky News Australia a week or so ago was dedicated to this topic. All this material is available to you."

"Changing gears, can you explain this image?" George handed Michael a photo, a copy of which was shown in an inset on the TV.

"Yes. This is the spaceship manufacturing process production line that was designed by Ms. Kelly Williamson of Australia. The vast array of little dots are replicators, the same ones that were widely distributed for home use."

"I thought you said that this was designed by Ms. Williamson?"

"The process, yes. The replicators, no. By analogy, think of the GM production lines in Detroit. GM designed the car and GM designed the production line. It did not design all the screwdrivers used. Same here. Kelly had the idea of using the replicators, organized in this way, to do a continuous pour of whatever material it is that they used, so that it would create a very strong ship hull. The Confederation never conceived of such a thing, yet Ms. Williamson came up with the idea years ago and was finally given access to the tools she needed to bring it to life."

"Unbelievable." George said, impressed that this was actually of human conception.

"I can't tell you how many Confederation officials have said the same thing."

"So, the Confederation sees this as a human invention?"

"Yes. And in all likelihood, this and several of the new human designed components in the ship will become the new Confederation standards."

"How can this be?" George asked.

"The Confederation has a vast array of science and technology, much of which hasn't changed that much in millennia. My theory is that the Confederation has run out of new ways to use its technology. Humans are very imaginative and have quickly found new and better ways to use that which we take for granted.

"This is the core reason that the Confederation is successful. Every new species added to the Confederation brings something new to the table, something that will benefit everyone if it is given the chance to take hold. We have seen this before, but not in the same way. I'm just happy I got to be part of it."

"Going back to the idea that these may become new standards, do you have any examples of how that would come to be?"

"Yes. I wasn't planning to announce this today, but the Confederation Fleet is on its way to Earth and will be arriving on Monday or Tuesday. Their purpose? First, to have their propulsion systems upgraded to the new Earth standard. Second, to effect some repairs incurred during their fight with the Enemy, using the new Earth-standard manufacturing processes."

"The Fleet is coming to Earth to get human assistance with repairs and upgrades?" George said in astonishment. Then he came back to his senses. "Is there any chance we would be able to interview the Commander of the Fleet?"

"Let me get back to you on that question, George. It will take many approvals, but I think it's time to do that."

"Michael, thanks for being with us today on 'This Week'.

RYAN'S QUARTERS

Jim's first task once on board was to stash his stuff in his quarters. After that, he had reported to the bridge where the Captain was handing out work assignments. His was to accompany two of the ship's designers, Pai Lin and Konstantin Popov, on a tour of the Marine quarters and training areas. He was then to report to the Shuttle Bay at 11:30 to receive half the Marine contingent and take them on a tour of their facilities. At Noon, he was to accompany the Marines to lunch in the dining room before reporting to the Captain's office at 1:00.

As a former marine himself, Jim struck it off immediately with Ed Foster and the first two squads. The facilities tour went well, and Ed invited him to join them for lunch.

It was now 12:55. Jim had returned to his quarters for a quick refresher and was about to leave for the bridge when there was a knock on his door.

"Ed. What can I do for you?" Jim asked, surprised to see his new friend again so soon.

"The Captain just pinged me asking that I join you in his office at 1:00. Thought I'd stop and pick you up. Any idea what he wants?"

"No. But I'm guessing it involves both of us."

CAPTAIN'S OFFICE, EAS OTTAWA

"Enter," the Captain called out, causing the door to open.

Jim and Ed walked in.

"Gentlemen, thank you for joining me. I have orders for both of you. Major Foster, you will be joining me for a quick trip back to the Embassy. We will be transporting down and will be gone for about two hours. Commander Tai and Lt. Commander Kumar are also joining us.

"Lieutenant Ryan, as third officer you will have command of the crew and marines in my absence. Consul Rubenstein still has command of the ship. The change in chain of command has been entered into the ship's log. Emergency messages will be routed to your communication device. You are to greet the Marines that will arrive at 1:30 and show them to their quarters. Once they've stowed their gear, give them a quick tour, then take them to the dining room. After that, return to the bridge and handle any issues that come up.

TELEVISION STUDIO, EMBASSY PRESS RELATIONS DEPARTMENT

The studio was organized like a conference room today with a long oval shaped table. There were four empty chairs along the back of the table and one on either end. Two people stood on the stage in front of the table as the lights came up.

"Good afternoon, France," said the host. "I am Gabrielle Mallet reporting for France Televisions. I'm here at the television studios of the Confederation Embassy in Canada. With me is the world-famous Sergeant George Butler.

"George, I understand that we have four special guests today. What can you tell me about them?"

"Gabrielle, thank you for joining me today. As our regular viewers know, last week we spoke with the men and women that have designed and built the new Space Force ships that we can see in the night sky. Today, we have the command crew that will be taking this ship out into space on an important scientific mission. Can we have a big Embassy welcome for Captain Daniel Porter, Commander Duan Tai, Lt. Commander Darsha Kumar and Major Edward Foster!"

The studio audience gave a standing ovation as the four men walked in and were seated.

"Gentlemen, welcome. Let me start with Captain Porter. Captain can you give us a little background on yourself?"

"Thank you for having us, ma'am. I'm a retired US Navy Submarine Captain. I was with the Navy for twenty-six years, 14 as the Captain of a Los Angeles Class, Fast Attack Submarine. After my last deployment, my boat was retired. I decided to retire along with it."

"So, you came out of retirement to join Space Force. May I ask why?"

"I retired because I didn't want a higher-ranking job and was too old to retrain for a new sub. That reasoning made sense at the time. But after a few months, I was just plain bored. The day Space Force was announced, I called the Senior Officer hotline and volunteered."

"What can you tell us about your training? There can't have been too much of it. Space Force was only announced a month or so ago."

Daniel smiled. "Overall. A great experience. As you say, it has only been a month or so, which is not much time. But all of us," Daniel said, indicating the four of them, "have been doing this for a long time and are quite capable. The ship is new. The mission is a bit different. But the key to any military organization is people and discipline, which Space Force is blessed with."

"Commander Tai, can you tell us about yourself?"

"My story is very similar to the Captain's. I was part of the People's Liberation Army, Navy Submarine Force in China. I also captained a submarine. Not as nice a one as the Captain had. I retired shortly after my boat was retired."

"Let me ask the two of you a possibly sensitive question. You were previously enemies, but now you work together. What is that like?"

The Commander looked questioningly at the Captain who gave a very slight nod. "It is true that our countries had different interests and that we would have fought each other if ordered to. But I want to be clear, I would much rather be working with Captain Porter for the betterment of mankind, then fighting against him for my country's narrower interests."

"I second that," Daniel said as the audience erupted in applause.

"Thank you, gentlemen. I, as a French person, am much happier to have you working together than to have you fighting each other.

"Lt. Commander Kumar. Please tell us about yourself."

"I was the Captain of a Brahmaputra class Guided Missile Frigate. I have more or less the same story. Ship retired. I retired. Much happier to be working with these two than going up against either of them.

"But one more thing… My daughter was seriously injured in an automobile accident four years ago. We thought we were going to lose her. She was transported to the Confederation Embassy where she was put back together and made whole again. Nisha Subramanian, whom the Ambassador cured during the Revelation, was her host. I don't think anyone can completely understand the goodness of the Confederation. For me, that was the compelling reason to sign up."

Once again, the studio audience broke into applause.

"Here, here. I'm with you, brother," George said.

"Major Foster. Your turn."

"Thank you, ma'am. I'm the commander of the ship's contingent of Space Marines. Previously, I was a Lt. Commander in the Navy Seals. In the post-Revelation world, fewer Seals are needed. I was offered early retirement and took it. Things were good for a couple years, but I found myself longing for my previous life. I never found the same sense of camaraderie and accomplishment in civilian life. So, I signed up for Space Force and will be leading 48 well trained, disciplined men and women on our upcoming mission."

"Captain Porter, what can you tell us about your upcoming mission?"

"I'm sorry, ma'am. I can say very little other than we will be going to another star system on a scientific mission."

"What can you tell us about your ship? Is it like a submarine?"

"It's like a submarine in the sense that you can't open the hatch and go outside." His comment sent a ripple of laughter around the room. "But, unlike a submarine, our ship is spacious and very comfortable. Extended deployments will be much easier in a ship like this than in a submarine."

"Gentlemen. Thank you for taking the time to be with us today. This is Gabrielle Mallet signing off for France Televisions News. Good night, France."

FIRST MISSION

It's the beginning of a new era. Captain Daniel Porter thought as he transported down to the Space Force Headquarters building. He was here today to take command of his new ship, the EAS Ottawa. It was the first human designed spaceship capable of interstellar flight and the first ship in the Earth Alliance's Space Force.

Daniel was here to formally receive his commission as Captain of the Ottawa. His first and second officers had transported down with him. They would also be receiving their formal commissions this morning.

Once the commissioning ceremony was done, the three of them would be given their final mission briefing.

...

Daniel reached the conference room and knocked. When the light above the handle switched to green, he opened the door and entered.

Four men sat at the head table. Winston Thompson, Earth Alliance Secretary of Space Force, and Admiral Samuel Scott were seated in the middle. Michael sat to the far right. Daniel didn't know the man on the far left.

"Gentlemen." The Secretary said. "So good to see you. You know the Admiral and the Ambassador." He said looking toward Michael, who nodded at Daniel.

"This is Earth Alliance President Binh Lee."

Binh stood and walked over to Daniel and the two officers to shake their hands. "Captain Porter, it is a pleasure to meet you. Commander Tai. Lt. Commander Kumar."

As Binh took his seat, the commissioning ceremony began.

BRIEFING ROOM

With the commissioning ceremony done, Michael and Admiral Scott led the men to the adjacent briefing room.

Michael said. "Gentlemen. Your mission is relatively straight-forward. You are to proceed to the star Lalande 21185 with all haste. As you can see," an image appeared on the wall, "the star has six major planets. You are to scan the four central planets, starting with the second planet. Have your bridge crew scan and record as much information as they can in the allotted time at each planet.

"The mission team has specialized equipment that they will use to make more detailed scans of the planets' interiors. If things go as we hope, the mission team will ask you to establish geosynchronous orbit at some point. You are to hold there until the mission team tells you to continue scanning. They may ask you to do this more than once.

"If the mission team asks you to hold in a position past the time budget for the planet, continue to hold until the mission team releases you. If the mission team asks you to move on before the allotted time, do as they ask.

"When all four planets have been scanned, you are free to explore the system as you and the mission team see fit. You will remain in that system until you receive further orders."

Michael stood and handed Daniel a data chip. "Captain, this data chip has your command codes, orders and authorizations. Else will tell you what to do with it. Then execute your mission."

There was a moment of silence, then the Admiral said. "Gentlemen. Godspeed. You are dismissed."

TRANSPORTER AREA, EAS OTTAWA

"Gentlemen, walk with me to the bridge," Daniel said as he turned toward the bridge. "As previously discussed, first watch will have 8:00 to 12:00; second watch 12:00 to 4:00; third watch 4:00 to 8:00. Four hours on; eight hours off.

"Today will be no exception, although it will be my intent to spend most of second watch in the bridge office today."

As they entered the bridge, the yeoman, Jade Harris, shouted, "Captain on the bridge!"

Ryan got up, yielding the Captain's Chair to the Captain.

"Ms. Else. I have a data chip with command codes and orders for you."

A small slit appeared in the arm of the Captain's Chair. "Please slide the chip into the slot," Else said. After a moment... "Command codes accepted. You have command of the ship, sir."

"Mr. Tajima. Please plot a course to Lalande 21185 and establish orbit around the second planet."

"Yes, sir." Thirty seconds later. "Course plotted and laid in. The star is on the opposite side of the Sun from our current position, so we will be doing two jumps. Expected transit time 3 hours, 29 minutes. Sir?"

"Ms. Else. Is this a safe and acceptable course?"

"Yes, Captain."

The Captain clicked the announcement button. "All hands. This is the Captain speaking. We are about to embark on Space Force's first mission. All hands, prepare for departure."

"Ms. Else. You may begin."

"Course engaged, Captain."

"Ms. Harris, please log the time of departure as 9:45 AM September 22, 2030."

"Yes, Captain."

After a few moments, the bridge crew could see the Earth moving away slowly on the main monitor.

"Gentlemen," the Captain said to his two officers, "if you could join me in the bridge office. Mr. Ryan, you have the con."

When the door to the conference room closed, Else whispered to Keanu. "Good course selection. Slightly slower than the one I chose, but I only beat you by 28 seconds."

"Thank you, Else," Keanu said. "I'll take that as a compliment."

BRIDGE OFFICE

"Duan, Darsha. Thank you for joining me. When it's just the three of us, first names are enough. That was always my standard."

"Mine also," Duan said.

"Never quite got there," said Lt. Commander Kumar. "I think Indian culture got in the way. But I very much like this idea, Daniel, Duan." He nodded to each.

Daniel smiled. "I think the Confederation, or at least Michael, is going to have a very beneficial impact on human armed forces. Please have a seat." He indicated the chairs across the desk.

"Our mission is more than it seems," Daniel said. "During my preliminary briefing, Michael pulled me aside so he could speak off the record. I deduce from what he said that there is some conflict within the Confederation regarding Earth. I also deduce that there is something the Confederation desperately needs, which the Earth probably has. Our scientific mission is real. That said, I think it is also a clever cover to get the Confederation to look for it somewhere other than on Earth."

"Why the subterfuge?" Duan asked.

"To prevent the Confederation from coming and taking the Earth away from us," Darsha said.

412

"What?" Daniel and Duan said, more or less in unison.

"You two have apparently not lived in a suppressed client state long enough."

"What do you mean by that?" Daniel asked.

"India was controlled by England from around 1600 to 1947. England brought us technology and resources, but it also wanted resources. At every point England talked about what they were giving us, but they continually took whatever they wanted as if it was theirs."

"Is that what you think is happening?" Daniel asked.

"No. Well yes, but no."

"What the hell does that mean?" Duan asked.

"We know Michael," Darsha said. "We know that he is good for his word. We really don't know the Confederation. What the Captain has said casts suspicion on the Confederation, not Michael. But it is only suspicion at this point; there is nowhere near enough evidence to conclude more."

"We have our orders and will excel in fulfilling them," Daniel said. "To that end, let's keep our eyes open. Let's find what it is that the Confederation needs and make sure we deliver it to them."

"Agreed," Darsha said.

Duan nodded his head. "Agreed, I'm all in with the two of you."

BRIDGE, EAS OTTAWA

It was Noon and time for watch change. Ensign Luis Perez, second watch yeoman, was the first to report for duty. He folded out the jump seat for his station, sat and was given a quick update on the first shift log entries and other activities.

When they had finished, first watch yeoman Jade Harris said, "Captain. Permission to transfer watch to Ensign Perez."

"Permission granted," Daniel replied.

"Assuming watch," said Ensign Perez.

"Watch released to Ensign Perez," Ensign Harris replied, standing and nodding to Perez, who took the active watch seat as Harris exited the bridge.

Each of the other watch stations changed in the same way, Ensign Perez logging the watch changes.

Daniel was last. He stood and said, "Commander."

Commander Tai, who had been sitting next to the Captain, stood and said, "Assuming watch."

Daniel answered, "Releasing watch, the ship is yours."

As Commander Tai took the captains seat, Daniel said. "I am going to do some work in the bridge office. Please call me as we approach the planet."

"Will do, sir."

...

"Commander, we've just dropped from Jump," said Paige Wilson, the second watch astrogation officer.

"Tactical, report."

"No sign of any ships in the area, sir." Kaitlin O'Brien, second watch tactical officer said.

"Science, what do we have?"

"We dropped from Jump just outside the orbit of the sixth planet. The star itself is very small, only 0.16 the radius of the sun."

"Confirming the locations of the planets on the main monitor. Confirming that the first planet is small, very small. It is barely outside the star's corona. It is a baked rock. And it is really moving. We will need more time to confirm, but it appears that its orbital period is only 10 days."

"Confirming four planets in the habitable zone and the sixth planet is a gas giant.

"Our first target is the second planet. It is also small, about the size of the moon, but has a thin atmosphere. Temperature readings in the daylight areas range up to 400° C."

"Ms. Else. How long until we reach orbit?"

"31 minutes, 12 seconds, Sir."

"Why so long?"

"We have to slow down using the grav drive. The planet is small, so it does not take much velocity to maintain even a low orbit."

"Thank you, Ms. Else."

...

"Entering orbit, sir," Paige said.

"Thank you, Ms. Wilson," said Commander Tai.

The Captain, who'd been in the office, came out. "Commander Tai. I'm going to check in with our mission team. I may or may not return before the next change of watch."

MISSION ROOM, DECK 1

The mission team had chosen the central lab on Deck 1 as their base of operations. Equipment had been set up on many of the tables and a large piece of equipment sat on the floor at one end of the lab.

There was also something that looked like a bank vault located next to the large piece of equipment.

"I'm not seeing a good location on this planet," Joel said. "The temperature is too hot."

There was a light knock on the door, which opened to reveal Captain Porter.

"Captain. Good to see you. Let me introduce our mission team. This is Professor Hans Schudel of the Institute's engineering school." The two men shook hands.

"And Professor Jameson MacLellan, also of the engineering school. Professor MacLellan was part of the team that built this ship."

"A pleasure to meet you, Captain," the Professor said.

"This is Charles Wong and Sanjit Gautama. Charles was chief scientist during the Revelation; you may have seen him on the Good Morning America show the day after the Revelation. He is now the Consul General to China.

"Sanjit was Head of Security during the Revelation and is now Consul General to India."

Again, handshakes and greetings were exchanged.

"Last but not least, is Alexi Santos. She is one of the teacher's assistants for the Weapons course at the Institute, but is better known as the Liberator of North Korea."

"Ms. Santos. I've heard a lot of stories about you from some of your students. Thank you for the work you've done preparing my crew."

"So, what can we do for you, Captain?" Joel asked.

"I'd like to get some idea of what you're doing and if there's anything we can do to help. My orders are to spend four hours in orbit around this planet taking scans, then to move on to the next. I've also been told to give you additional time if asked."

"We're also doing scans of each of the planets. Our scans are of a different nature than yours. We're looking for a particular type of geological anomaly that will be relevant to another mission the Confederation has scheduled for this system."

"May I ask what kind of geological anomaly?"

Professor Schudel said. "We're looking for indications of a rare material that the Confederation needs. This material has a particular fingerprint that our scanners are optimized for."

"Are we going to be taking any samples?"

"Not really. We may attempt to extract 1 gram of material to confirm our scans." The professor replied. "But this material is generally very difficult to extract. So, we will leave that to the Confederation ships equipped for that purpose."

"Interesting. Do you expect to find any on this planet?"

"Sadly, no," the professor replied. "Surface temperatures are too high. This material is rarely found on planets with a mean temperature over 300° C. Nonetheless, we will do a complete scan to verify."

"Do you expect that you'll want to linger here?"

"I'm sure we will not. Our scans will be done well before yours. We'll advise you if we find anything," the Professor said.

"Captain," Joel said. "I anticipate that you'll complete your scans in well less than four hours. We definitely will. Let's plan to move on as soon as both sets of scans are complete."

"OK. If there's anything you need from the crew, please let me know. I'm sure there are quite a few that would like to help."

"Thank you, Captain."

...

The scans of the planet were done after only 2 hours and 20 minutes. The Captain had messaged Commander Tai to check with the mission team once the bridge crew finished their scans.

"Consul Rubenstein, this is first officer Tai. We have completed our scans and would like to move on to the next planet as soon as yours are done."

"Commander, thank you for calling. We finished a while ago and would be happy if the ship moved on to the next planet."

"Thank you, sir. We will move on."

"Ms. Wilson, please lay in a course for the third planet." Commander Tai said.

"Course plotted, sir."

"Ms. Else. Do you approve of this course?"

"Yes, sir."

"Please engage."

As the ship started leaving orbit, the watch changed.

BRIDGE, EAS OTTAWA

"Consul Rubinstein, this is Second Officer Kumar. We are entering orbit around the third planet."

"Thank you, Lt. Commander. We've been taking scans during the approach and have already found a couple spots that we'll be examining. Please proceed with your mission. I'll contact you if we find anything that will require a change in orbit or dwell time."

MISSION ROOM, DECK 1

"Joel, this is unexpected," Professor Schudel said. "There may actually be a transluminide deposit here."

Joel came over to look at the display. "See?" Schudel said.

"Any idea how large it might be?" Joel asked.

"Small, that's probably why it has not been found before. There is no life in this system, so it was probably scanned from a long distance. Anything less than 100 kg would not get picked up from more than about 2 AU away."

"Can we pull a sample to confirm?"

"Yes. But we'll need to park in geosynchronous orbit to do it. It's too small to get a hold of if we're moving."

"OK. I'll advise the Lt. Commander. Let's continue surveying. Can you send me the coordinates for this site?

"Yes. In your queue."

"I've been sitting too long. Time to go see the Lt. Commander."

BRIDGE, EAS OTTAWA

Joel walked up to the bridge and was surprised to find two armed Space Marines guarding the door. Approaching, he said. "Gentlemen. I need to speak with the Captain. Am I free to enter?"

"Sorry sir. Access to the bridge is restricted."

"I guess I should have booked an appointment." Joel's comment did not elicit a response, so Joel quickly messaged Else. *Else, I am at the bridge door, but not being allowed in. I need to speak with the officer on watch. Can you help*?

Moments later, the door to the bridge opened. A young woman said to the guards. "This man is Joel Rubenstein. The Lt. Commander has invited him onto the bridge."

The two guards stepped aside, and Joel walked in. "Hi, I'm Celeste Durant, third watch yeoman. The bridge is on alert because of the sightings."

"Sightings?" Joel asked as he was led in.

"Consul Rubenstein, thank you for coming up. We've found something." The Lt. Commander pointed to the screen.

The image was difficult to understand at first, then it clicked. "Ruins," Joel muttered.

417

"Yes. We didn't recognize them at first, but were noticing too many straight lines as we scanned the surface. On the second pass, our science officer, Angus White, applied the ground penetrating radar, which gave us this. Images like this are all over the place. Did you see this in your scans?" Lt. Commander Kumar asked.

"No. Our scanners are quite different; they scan deeper. We see nothing higher than 100 ft below the surface. I actually came up to tell you that we will need to investigate one or more sites when your scans are done. To do that we'll need to park in geo-synchronous orbit. Looks like there is a lot to study on this planet. It was mapped by the Confederation millennia ago, but as an old, dead system, it was never systematically explored."

"We have called in our preliminary findings to Space Force and are continuing our scans as originally ordered. When those scans are done, we'll relocate to the orbits you specify unless we get different orders from Space Force."

"Very good, Lt. Commander. Please let me know when you're ready for us.

As he walked back to the lab, Joel messaged Michael. *Lalande 21185 holds many secrets. We think we have found transluminide deposits. The ship's crew has discovered extensive ruins. The watch officer has sent a report to Space Force Command requesting new instructions.*

MISSION ROOM, DECK 1

As he entered the Lab, Joel's communicator sounded. It was Michael. Joel exited the lab and went into the empty room across the hall. "Hi, Michael. Wanted to give you a heads up that our mission seems to be taking on a new life."

"So it seems. Do you know how extensive the ruins are?"

"No. We have been scanning deep, so were unaware of them until I walked up to the bridge to request an orbit change."

"I'm sure you know this, but if the ruins are extensive enough to indicate a previously unknown civilization, then the Fleet will be forbidden from removing anything from the planet. Do you have the ability to do surface scans of your own?"

"Yes, but that will prevent us from searching for additional transluminide deposits."

"That's OK." Michael said. "We need to assume that this planet is off limits until proven otherwise. So, do not plant any of your transluminide supply on this planet.

"Are the other planets close enough for you to scan for candidate deposit sites?"

"No."

"OK. Does this planet have any moons?"

"Two relatively small moons," Joel replied.

"Scan those for ruins. If there are ruins, then the planet will surely be off limits. If not and there are candidate deposit sites, then log them but do not take any action yet. I'll see if I can convince Space Force to complete the original survey before going all in on this planet."

"Got it, Michael. Thanks."

...

Joel went back over to the lab.

"We've got a real mess here, Joel." The Professor looked unhappy

"Tell me."

"There are dozens of these little transluminide deposits on this planet. Too many. There is no record of nature distributing it in this way. So, I did a tighter scan. The sites appear to be storage bunkers. At one site, I lucked out and got a perfect scan showing ingots of transluminide all stacked up and organized."

"Makes sense. The ship's crew has found extensive ruins near the surface. I'll bet that if we scan the moons, we will find defensive embankments. Can we do that?"

"Not easily." Charles joined the conversation. "But I bet I can jury rig something that will work."

"Thanks."

...

"There they are." Charles said. "Weapon embankments. Lots of them. Check this out." Charles pointed at a reading on the screen. This set appears to have just powered up.

"Else. Emergency! Cloak and raise shields!"

BRIDGE, EAS OTTAWA

Else got Joel's message and raised the shields. Moments later, the ship vibrated, and the shields collapsed. In the milliseconds that followed, Else knew the ship was in trouble and initiated an emergency jump.

CAPTAIN'S QUARTERS

Daniel had lain down to take a short nap before his next watch. He was awakened by a massive vibration coursing through the ship. As he jumped out of bed, he was hit by massive vertigo and fell to the floor.

We just jumped, he thought.

With his eyes clenched tightly shut, Daniel felt for the nub in the collar of his shirt and pushed it when he found it.

"Else, report!" Daniel shouted.

"Emergency jump. We were attacked. Joel apparently saw it coming and we got our shields up just in time. But one shot and they collapsed. So I jumped."

"Where are we?" Daniel asked.

"Don't know. Haven't had time to figure it out. Ship has lots of problems. You need..."

"Else?" No answer.

During the ship tour, one of the Ascendants told Daniel that he should keep a dose of the anti-vertigo medicine near his bed in case he was sleeping when the ship jumped, and he had an adverse reaction. Trying to keep his head still Daniel reached up, grabbed the packet of cream, broke it open and spread it on his skin.

Within moments it started working. He still couldn't move, but at least he could breathe. *Try Joel,* he thought.

"Joel." He said.

"Here Captain. Where are you? We are in a world of hurt down here."

"Do you know what happened?"

"The planet apparently held an advanced civilization at some point. The surface was covered in ruins. Charles did a quick scan of the moons and found extensive weapons embankments, one of which had powered up.

"I got to Else quick enough to get the shields up. But they were not strong enough. They were knocked down by a single shot and damaged the ship.

"Else jumped. I'm guessing there was a hull breach, because systems started failing when we came out of jump. Else appears to be offline.

"The elevators appear to be offline also, so my team is currently trapped on Level One. If you are ambulatory, you should attempt to get to the bridge. There are backup systems there."

Daniel steeled himself for another attempt to move his head. The dizziness was still there, but a little less sharp. He crawled toward his cabin door, where he worked his way up into a standing position, then opened the door.

He saw several people lying on the floor. Using the handrail mounted to the hallway wall, he made his way slowly to the bridge. There were two space marines lying on the floor, both trying to get up.

He stepped up to the door and, thankfully, it opened.

Everyone on the bridge lay sprawled on the floor and the light indicating Else's presence was red.

Using his communicator, Daniel called Joel. "On the bridge. Everyone is down. Else is off, just a red light."

"The red light is a button. Push it and Else will reboot."

Daniel made his way to the red button and pushed it.

Nothing.

"Pushed the button. Nothing happened," Daniel said, the vertigo finally starting to pass.

"OK. Remove the panel directly below and see if you can reset the power breaker."

Daniel opened the panel and saw that several things had come loose. He used his communicator to send Joel the image.

"Good news," Joel said. "See the card on the right with the red edge? Push that one in. Then try the red button again."

Daniel did as he was asked and a holographic image of Else projected into the pilot's seat.

"Porter. Where are we? And what the hell did you do to my ship!"

"I was asleep at the time, so have no idea. I'm hoping you can help me figure it out."

"Working. Why don't you administer some cream to your crew? We are probably going to need some help getting this bucket moving again. There should be anti-vertigo cream at the yeoman's station."

Daniel went over to the yeoman's station and saw Celeste on the floor. Unlike the others, she was not conscious. He started to kneel to check her, then his training kicked in. Triage. Help those that you are able to help. He opened a cabinet marked with a pharmacy symbol and took out vials marked as anti-vertigo. He quickly applied some to Celeste's wrist, then started working his way around the bridge.

One by one, he could hear the various bridge systems coming back on-line.

"Else. Status?" He said.

"The bridge systems are coming back up. The entire crew, except for the Ascendants, were knocked out. I'm trying to get the elevators back on-line, so they can come up to help.

"The human crew are all going to need treatment. I don't know how, but we apparently jumped 18,000 light years. We are in intergalactic space. The engines are off-line, but do not appear to be damaged."

Daniel gave this a moment's thought. "OK. Ask Joel to send one of the Ascendants to the Engine room to get them back on-line. Work with him to get someone to Sick Bay to get more medicine. Command deck first."

Daniel finished administering the medication to the bridge staff then went to the door and applied it to the Space Marines.

As he was getting back up, he was surprised to see the doctor. "Captain. You are either inhumanly durable or very well prepared."

"I was advised to keep a vial of vertigo nanobots near my bed and was taking a nap when the incident occurred."

"Those of us that operate avatars are less affected by this phenomenon. I would never have guessed that this ship could jump far enough to have this impact. Was the jump intentional?"

"It was an emergency jump gone wrong."

"Heavens. I've never heard of such a thing."

Daniel smiled. "Well, now you have."

BRIDGE CONFERENCE ROOM

Over the last hour, the crew had been revived and most ship systems brought back on-line. Daniel convened a meeting in the Bridge Conference Room to discuss options.

"Else, can you give us a quick update on the ship?" Daniel asked.

"Main power is back, as are the engines. The shield generators will not reinitialize. Engineering teams are working on the shield generator, but the prognosis is not good.

"Quite a few food replicators were knocked off-line and will require maintenance.

"Three crew members are in the hospital: Ms. Durant, third watch yeoman, Sergeant Arun Chaudhary and Private First Class Wafa Banerjee of the Space Marines.

"Ms. Durant hit her head on a hard object when she fell and has a concussion. Treatment has been administered and she should be able to return to duty in two or three days.

"The marines were running an obstacle course when the anomaly hit. They fell about 20 feet. The sergeant has a compound fracture of his right leg. Ms. Banerjee broke her hip. Both have been stabilized but are out of service for the rest of this trip. They will both require additional treatment when we return to Earth.

"Other than those items, the ship is ready to travel."

"Have you plotted a return course to Earth?"

"Yes, but I also asked our three navigators to have a go at it. Once again Mr. Tajima has the best transit time. I can beat it by a few minutes but recommend his course."

"How long will it take to get home?"

"Only three hours to the Oort Cloud, then another half hour to Earth orbit near the manufacturing line."

"OK. First watch to the Bridge."

...

"Course laid in, Captain." Keanu said.

"Thank you, Mr. Tajima. Engage, Ms. Else."

"Course engaged, Captain."

"Ms. Harris. Please log our departure."

"Departing intergalactic space for Earth at 8:59 PM. Logged."

AMBASSADOR'S RESIDENCE

"Michael, thank you for taking my call," Joel said. "Our mission to Lalande turned out to be a disaster."

"What happened?"

"We found ruins of an ancient civilization on the third planet. Storage chambers full of transluminide and an active defensive battery remaining on both moons.

"We got shields up before they fired. But the first shot destroyed the shields. We jumped as the second shot hit and were thrown deep into intergalactic space. We are currently about 18,000 light-years from Earth.

"The jump knocked all the humans out. To his credit, Captain Porter was carrying vertigo cream and was able to rouse himself after only a few minutes. The attack also knocked the engines and Else off-line.

"We are mostly recovered at this point, except for the shields. Three people are in the hospital. No life-threatening injuries, but two will require treatment when we get back."

"This is problematic," Michael said. "Any ideas?"

"We need to repair this ship before we can send it back out again. Once back on Earth, we could have Thomas take us out to plant some transluminide in the asteroid belt, maybe a kilogram each on four mid-sized rocks. We can claim that we saw some ghosting on scans taken on the way back in. The Fleet can investigate and claim the mining rights. Not sure what else we could do in time once we're back."

"Are there any other nearby stars that have not been extensively studied by the Confederation?" Michael asked.

"Luhman 16. It's a binary system about 6.5 light-years from Earth. It's a very odd system. Two brown dwarfs, 3.5 AU apart. Each has a couple of small rocky planets, two of which have a figure 8 type orbit. There are no life signs in the system, and it's never been explored for mining."

"What cover story can we build for the presence of transluminide?"

"I've got an idea. Can you hold for a moment?" Joel said then muted the line.

...

"Else. Will our course back to Earth take us anywhere near Luhman 16? It's a brown binary."

"Not really."

"Can you come up with a reason to take us past that system?"

"Give me a minute. Yes, there is a course adjustment we could do that would knock 15 minutes off our return course. Do you want me to propose this to the Captain?"

"Yes. We may still be able to salvage the mission if we pass that system within a couple AU."

"OK. Will let you know if the Captain accepts the course change."

...

"Michael, we are going to offer the Captain a faster return that goes past that system."

"OK. Let me know if he goes for it."

...

"Mr. Tajima?" Else said. "I've been looking for assists to get us home faster. I think I've found one that will shave about 15 minutes off our flight time. Want to see it?"

"Sure."

"If we change our echo cancelling route just a little, it will take us to this spot at the galaxy's edge."

"Isn't that a little further away from Earth?"

"Yes. But look at what it sets up. We can jump sequence to this massive star, then drop to Warp for the grav assist. That sets up a jump to this star system near Earth, where we do a high-deflection slingshot using grav-drive, then a single jump into the outer system."

"Else, how did you find this?"

"It's an old astrogation trick. Look for a star near the one you are going to for a high-deflection slow-down. This is the closest star to Earth that we could use, and it is a brown dwarf so we can come in relatively close without getting hit with excessive radiation."

"Captain?"

"Yes. Mr. Tajima?"

"Else has suggested a course adjustment that will shave 15 minutes off our return time. I would recommend this change."

"Ms. Else. Is there any additional risk associated with this change?"

"None," Else replied.

"Then I approve. Ms. Harris, please enter the change into the log."

...

"Joel. The Captain approved the course change. We'll be coming In close."

"Great, Else. Let me know when we're 5 minutes out. We'd like to take some scans."

"Are you going to tell me what this is about?"

"We heard a rumor that there might be something of interest in this system but have never taken the time to explore it. Maybe we'll find something that salvages the mission."

"Would you like me to tell the Captain? Maybe we can get some scans from the ship for human science."

"Tell him that you advised me of the new arrival time, and I suggested taking some scans."

"OK."

...

Daniel was pleased to hear that their course change might also open the possibility for additional scientific observations. This mission had already made a historic find that would go into the record books. Maybe there was another nugget they could bring home that would further offset cost of ship repairs.

"Captain. We are two sequenced jumps from the target system."

Moments later. "We will drop to normal space in 5, 4, 3, 2, 1... begin scanning. We hold this course for 7 minutes, 41 seconds before the final jump."

"Bingo." Professor Schudel said, highlighting a spot on the screen. "Luhman 16 alpha, 2nd planet. See the ghosting. There was probably transluminide there at one point in time. We could easily plant 10 to 100 kilograms there without raising suspicion. Let me advise the bridge to scan there.

"Lt. Meier. Professor Schudel of the Mission team. Please scan these coordinates on the 2nd planet from the primary star. This will be of immense value. I get suspicious ghosting. You may have a clearer view."

The Captain nodded to his Science Officer.

"I have it." Adrian Meier said. "Odd. I see the ghosting. What is it?"

"I think it's a transluminide deposit. There's never been a proper mining survey of this system. If this is what I think, then we may have found enough transluminide to build and power the rest of the Space Force Fleet."

"Wow," was all the Lieutenant could say.

"Thank you for bringing this to our attention, Professor. Ms. Harris, please add this observation to the ship's log," said the Captain.

SECOND MISSION

EARTH ORBIT

The ship entered Earth Orbit just after midnight. The injured were transported immediately to the Embassy hospital. A few minutes later the mission team was transported down to the Engineering Bay.

Captain Porter decided to delay the watch change until the injured were transported. The second watch brought the ship back to Lagrange 4, where repairs would be done in the morning.

ENGINEERING BAY #1

"Let's go complete our mission," Joel said, despite the hour.

Once the equipment was loaded and the team on board the shuttle, Joel went into the cockpit.

"Hi, Thomas. We need to go to Luhman 16 alpha, 2nd planet, and we need to do it with stealth, so that we are not seen by the Ottawa at Lagrange 4."

"OK. No problem. They will pass over the horizon in 15 more minutes. We can launch then and float up slowly. In about an hour twenty, the sun and Earth will be aligned on a vector they cannot see. We can jump out 10 light-years, then proceed to our target. We will be there in... 2 hours, 15 minutes."

ORBIT AROUND SECOND PLANET, LUHMAN 16 ALPHA

"Joel, this place is really creepy. I hadn't fully realized how weird brown binaries are," Thomas said.

"We need to establish geosynchronous orbit 23 degrees east of the terminator," said Joel.

The second planet was gravitationally locked with the star. Because the luminosity of the brown stars was so low, there really wasn't a bright side, just dark and darker. The mine location was on the 'darker' side.

...

"OK. I'm going to do a nano pull into this containment chamber to see if we can determine what used to be in this cave," Professor Schudel said.

Moments later, a small metallic particle appeared in the container.

427

"Amazing. The people that populated Lalande 21185 apparently beat us to it. The sample is transluminide. It is 73.4% pure, the primary impurity aluminum with trace gold. Very unusual."

"What's the minimum quantity we can put back in a way that would not be suspicious?" Joel asked.

"It would take 100 kg or more for this to look natural, but cavities do form that are hollow, filled with argon. So, I think we need to liquify 14.5 kg transluminide with the appropriate amount of aluminum and gold. Transport it into the cavity hot, then transport in about 10 cubic meters of argon to fill the cavity. If we can place the argon into the center of the liquid mass, it should make a very natural looking structure."

"How long to do that?"

"Fortunately, we have everything we need. Maybe 35 minutes if you and Charles help."

...

"Ready?" asked the Professor.

"5, 4, 3, 2, 1... Transport. OK, let's see what we got," said the Professor as he quickly updated the scans. "This is beautiful. Look at the crystallization. I think our only chance of being figured out is the temperature. It will be 24 hours before the temperature drops to the point where it's immeasurable. If they get here sooner, I hope they're mesmerized enough with the transluminide that they don't notice the residual thermal gradient."

"I think we can head home," Joel said.

PRESENCE PROJECTOR, AMBASSADOR'S OFFICE

"Mi-Ku. Sorry for the delay in getting back to you. We had numerous problems bringing the new engines up, all related to the narrow-mindedness of my crew, none to the quality of your team's specifications.

"We should make entry into your star system late tonight."

"Several developments since we last talked, Jo-Na. Our first Earth Alliance ship was commissioned and ran its first mission. It was a scientific mission to check out a system close to Earth that the Confederation had not explored."

"Which one?"

"Lalande 21185." There was a moment's pause as the translator converted to the Confederation designation.

"A dead system with a dying star?" asked the Admiral.

"That once held a powerful, ancient species."

"What happened?"

"Our team was mapping the ruins and had discovered large vaults full of transluminide. That's when the AIs that operated the ancient species' defense system woke and powered up."

"Did you lose your ship?"

"No. But it was blown 18,000 light years away into intergalactic space."

"Do you need help retrieving them?"

Michael laughed. "They're already home..."

"What!" exclaimed the Admiral.

"And on the way home, they discovered a planet with a sizable transluminide deposit."

"Ah. Understood."

"A survey team was dispatched Immediately to confirm the discovery."

"How large?"

"Our best estimate is between 10 and 20 kg. We do not have the means to mine it. So, we will give you the coordinates in exchange for 20% of the yield."

There was a pause.

"The discovery was real?" the Admiral asked.

"Your engineers will need to make that determination."

"Thank you, Mi-Ku. I agree to your terms."

"Would you consent to being met and escorted into our system by our flag ship?"

"You understand that this is problematic," the Admiral replied.

"There is precedent," said Michael.

A long pause.

"Yes. There is. This is your play?"

"Jo-Na. How else could we strike the right balance with the Confederation? You understand the stakes."

"But, how will this end?"

"You already know the answer to that. It was predicted long ago. Earth will emerge. Lorexi will recede, but Lorexi's best days are still to come."

"Tell me when and where to meet your escort."

BRIDGE OFFICE, EAS OTTAWA

"Yes, Admiral, Mr. Secretary." Daniel said.

"Captain. Your first mission was a phenomenal success, even though it did not come off as expected. Are your repairs complete?"

"Yes, sir. Although we are down two Space Marines."

"Unfortunate, your encounter with the ancient species, but a tribute to your ship and crew that it survived."

"Thank you, sir."

"Your second mission will be much easier. You are to position yourself at the coordinates I'm about to send you by 21:00. You will greet the Confederation Armada when it arrives. The Fleet Admiral will contact you. You are to pass him a data packet that we will send you. It contains the coordinates of your transluminide find. Then, you are to escort him to the coordinates in question.

"Once they have finished with whatever they will do, you are then to escort them into Earth Orbit. In case the question comes up, they do not need to cloak themselves.

"Fair warning. There are 20 or so ships. The two largest are Capital ships, 10 km long and 1 km wide. Do not be intimidated."

"Thank you for the warning, sir."

"The Armada is expected before midnight tonight. Your sensors should be able to pick them up in advance."

"Understood, sirs."

"Godspeed." The Secretary said.

BRIDGE, EAS OTTAWA

"Captain. The coordinates and a data packet were just received."

"Thank you, Ms. Harris."

Change of watch was not for another hour. But they were functionally in dry dock, so Daniel decided he would give the rest of the watch to Ryan. He logged orders for the next two watches to maintain position and continuously run tactical and scientific scans, then said, "Ryan, you have the con. Alert me if anything changes."

With that Daniel headed for his quarters. The last 36 hours had been a whirlwind. This evening's encounter was likely to be the highlight of his career. He was going to get some sleep now while he could.

...

The change of watch was becoming routine. Daniel appeared exactly on time to see that most of first watch was already on station. He relieved Lt. Commander Kumar, then took his seat.

"Else. Tajima. You have the coordinates?"

430

"Yes, sir."

"Plot us a course."

Moments later, "Course set in, sir," Keanu said.

"And, confirmed," Else added.

"Then engage at will." Daniel replied.

"Engaged."

...

"We have arrived, Captain," Else said.

Space Force command had ordered the ship to return to Luhman 16 Alpha, about half a light year from the star. They were to wait here until the Fleet arrived.

"Now we wait," Daniel said. "But let's not lose the time.

"Lt. Meier. Begin scanning the system. Let's see what else we can learn about this system."

...

"Earth Alliance Ship. This is Fleet communications. The Armada will be arriving at the designated coordinates momentarily. The flag ship will arrive first. The remaining ships will arrive in 10 second intervals."

"Fleet flag ship. This is the EAS Ottawa. We await your arrival," Daniel replied.

A moment later, "Captain your presence has been requested in the presence projector."

"I guess it's time to see how this thing works. Commander Tai, you have command." Daniel rose to enter the chamber and take the call with the Admiral.

...

Daniel entered the chamber to see an older man with gray hair. He wore a blue uniform, one that reminded Daniel of a police uniform. There were assorted designations on his collar, which Daniel assumed were representative of his rank and accomplishments. He stood ramrod straight and said, "Captain Porter, I am the Fleet Admiral for this sector. Unfortunately, I am told that there is no good translation of my name, so please address me as 'Jo-Na'. It is my familiar name."

"Admiral Jo-Na. It is a pleasure to meet you, sir. I look forward to a long and productive relationship."

As they approached to shake hands, Daniel noticed that the Admiral appeared to be coming in for a fist bump. "In our culture, we greet one another by bumping our hands together. I understand that humans 'shake' hands. I've seen that demonstrated. Unfortunately, our hands are shaped differently enough that we cannot do that."

They bumped, then Daniel sat in the chair that the Admiral indicated. Daniel was impressed by the seamlessness of the holographic projection. He'd been told that the Admiral was Lorexian, but he appeared as a human. His facial movement was perfectly synced with the spoken English.

"I understand that you have some information to share with us."

"Yes, sir. Our first mission was to do a detailed scan of a nearby star system, one that the Confederation had not previously studied in detail. We found the ruins of an ancient civilization and were attacked by a still-active automated defense system.

"Something went wrong with our escape jump and we found ourselves in intergalactic space. On the return, we passed close to this system. It's the other dead system near Earth that the Confederation has not previously studied. Scans of the system as we passed revealed traces of transluminide. I'm authorized to release the coordinates of that find to you."

"Excellent," replied the Admiral. "Would it be acceptable if I dispatched three ships to investigate this find, while the remaining ships accompany you back to Earth?"

"My orders are to escort your ships to the location of the find and remain on station with you there while you confirm it."

"Thank you, Captain Porter. Why don't you lead the way? I will follow along with two of our engineering ships. Given the poor condition of the Armada, I'll leave the remaining ships here, if that's acceptable. Please have your navigator share your course with us."

"Acceptable, sir. You will receive our course shortly."

The two men stood. The Admiral extended his arm, fist clenched.

"This is the traditional Confederation sign of respect that we use to close meetings."

Daniel mimicked the salute and said, "Thank you, Admiral."

The holographic projection dissolved and Daniel went back to the bridge.

...

"Mr. Tajima, please lay in a course for geosynchronous orbit above the anomaly on the second planet."

"Yes, Captain." A moment later, "Laid in, Sir."

"Ms. Else. Do you concur?"

"Yes. Captain."

"Please transmit the course to the fleet."

"Course sent." A pause. "Fleet acknowledges."

"Engage."

ORBIT AROUND SECOND PLANET, LUHMAN 16 ALPHA

"Admiral. There are numerous anomalies. Apparently, this system was once rich with transluminide. All but one location has been mined. Sensors indicate that the main deposit is 73.4% pure. The primary impurity is aluminum. There are trace quantities of gold and other impurities and an abundance of argon gas. Curiously, the temperature in the area of the unmined deposit is about 0.05° C higher than the rest of the surface."

"Reason?"

"Unknown. A recent meteor strike in the area would have this impact. Although I have no evidence to support an assertion that there was such a strike."

"Curious. What is the quantity of the find?"

"Best estimate, 19.8 kg raw, 14.5 kg refined. This is an incredible find."

"Yes, it is. How long will it take to extract?"

"We can take the entire find in one pull if you're willing to accept some miscellaneous rock. It's a little more work to refine, but we'll get every last gram that way. We can probably get a couple hundred more grams by pulling the rock surrounding the previously mined sites."

"Take the larger pull. How long to pick up the remaining sites?"

"Two hours."

"Start making the pulls."

"Yes, sir."

BRIDGE, EAS OTTAWA

"Captain. The Admiral is on the line for you."

"Admiral."

"Captain Porter. There is residual transluminide at a number of previously mined sites. We would like to salvage this scrap material. It will take an additional two hours. I can leave a ship behind to do this if you would like to begin the journey to Earth."

"Admiral. We would be happy to wait on station with you. The Earth Alliance has a strategic interest in a strong Confederation fleet and are happy to assist in any way we can to make that happen."

"Thank you, Captain."

ARRIVALS

The return to Earth was painfully slow. Only the Freighters had modern propulsion systems. The other ships were in various states of disrepair and could not jump in past the orbit of Neptune.

Daniel's orders had been to bring the Armada into a high orbit 45,000 miles from Earth. At this distance, the Capital ships would be visible to the naked eye from dusk to dawn but would be very difficult to spot during the day. They were expected to hold station here for an indeterminate period of time as the Fleet would be undergoing propulsion upgrades.

TELEVISION STUDIO, EMBASSY PRESS RELATIONS DEPARTMENT

The show would be starting in a few minutes and Sarah was nervous; it'd been several years since she had done something like this. She would be moderating a live press conference featuring Michael and the Admiral. Using technology that Sarah couldn't understand, the Admiral would be appearing in human form on the stage with Michael. He would actually be in his presence projector on the flag ship. The image on the stage would be a holographic projection, but she'd been assured that the camera wouldn't be able to tell the difference.

Noelani would be working the show with her, as would George.

"Here. Let me put a little of this on your wrist. It will help calm the nerves without dulling your mind," Noelani said.

Sarah watched Noelani as she applied the cream. *She is certainly glowing tonight. Wish I was doing as well.*

The first part of the show would be statements from each of the men that Sarah would lead in interview-style. Sarah had been given a set of questions to ask and would be able to ask more questions for clarification.

The second part of the show would be Q&A with a panel of reporters, whose questions would be vetted before asked. When the backstage time hit -10 seconds, she walked out onto the stage. The stage director counted her in as the lights came up.

"Good evening, World. This is Sarah Wright, reporting from the Confederation Television Studios. We have two very special guests with us tonight. The first is a man you all know… Michael, the

434

Confederation Ambassador," Sarah said as Michael walked out onto the stage. "The second is a man who has had a tremendous impact on our world but has not before appeared in public. Let me present to you Admiral Jo-Na of the Confederation Fleet."

From Sarah's point of view on stage, the Admiral simply appeared at the edge of the stage, out of view of the camera, then walked on stage to greet Michael. Then all three sat.

"Admiral, I would like to start with you. You are Lorexian. Is that correct?"

"Yes Sarah, it is."

"Can you tell us where you are at this moment?"

"I'm aboard my ship in orbit above the Earth. The image you see is a holographic projection, sent from my ship and modified to make me appear as human."

"Why modify the image?"

"It's our experience that species new to the Confederation take some time to become comfortable in the presence of intelligent species that don't look like themselves. It's the same reason that the Ambassador appears in an avatar. This isn't intended as deception. It simply eases the process of getting to know and work with each other."

"Have any humans seen you or your colleagues in their native form?"

"Yes. The Ambassador probably knows of more meetings than I do, but I am aware of several incidents in which humans have met Lorexians in person, so to speak."

"Did this cause a problem?"

"No. But the humans, and Lorexians for that matter, were both briefed on the physical appearance of the people they would be meeting and both sides handled it well. In the future, this will not be a problem. However, we also have different atmospheric requirements. Lorexians cannot breathe the air on Earth for any sustained period. Humans cannot breathe the air on New Lorexi for more than a few minutes. So, in the future when we work together in person, one side or the other will need to wear a rebreather, which is too bad. Humans and Lorexians have a great future in front of them. We are far more alike than we are different. It has been a privilege to be part of it."

"Sir, can you explain to us why the Armada is here? Is there some imminent threat from the Enemy?"

"We are here for repairs and upgrades. Our ships have suffered damage in various recent engagements with the Enemy. And it has been too long since our ships have been able to harbor somewhere safe to affect maintenance. There are a number of places we could have done that, but we wanted to come to Earth to take advantage of new propulsion, shielding and fabrication advances that the human engineers at the Institute have made."

"Can you tell us more about these advances? We've heard several reports, but I'm sure the peoples of Earth would benefit from your perspective on this."

"I'm sure the Ambassador could answer that question with a better factual basis than I can, but I'll give you my perspective. The Confederation is over 2 million years old. For most of that time, we have lived in plenty. We have little desire for 'faster, better, cheaper' as I have heard some humans say.

"Humans are different. You are still young with a thirst for more. But unlike any before you, humanity doesn't seem to be satisfied just to take. They want to improve. And improve they have.

"Your Professor... let me read this so I get it right... Eugene Xu from Johns Hopkins, has come up with improvements for our propulsion systems, improvements most of us didn't believe until we saw them with our own eyes. In coordination with young Ms. Kelly Williamson, they have improved our shields to be Enemy resistant. And the new spacecraft manufacturing process that Ms. Williamson came up with... Incredible. It will markedly change the Confederation.

"So back to your question about why we're here. We are here to incorporate as much of this new human technology into our fleet as is possible."

"Thank you, Admiral." Sarah turned to Michael. "Mr. Ambassador, are there objectives you have for the Fleet while it is here? Objectives you can tell us about?"

"Yes. The Armada has huge manufacturing capacity. During its stay at Earth immediately following the Revelation, it manufactured all the gifts that have been distributed to member nations so far. Although Earth is capable of producing all the components needed for the Space Force buildout, there are some components that the Fleet can manufacture for us in a fraction of the time. We hope to take delivery of the critical parts we need to resume manufacturing of our Space Force fleet in the next couple of days. With those parts in hand, we will be able to complete the build out within a year."

"Is that the only thing?"

"No. There are two other things. The Confederation has interest in learning more about our spacecraft manufacturing technology. Confederation scientists and engineers will observe several builds and work with our engineering team to determine the best way to integrate these methods into existing Confederation processes.

"There is also the Enemy threat. Although significantly reduced, it is still very real. We will be working with the Fleet to formulate the best strategy to defeat the remaining Enemy in our galaxy and to prepare for the next wave that we expect to see several years from now."

"Are you confident that you will succeed in this?"

"Absolutely," said Michael.

"Agreed," the Admiral added.

"Our guest reporters have submitted questions for the two of you. The first is from Angela Beale of NBC News. Angela?"

"Admiral, sir. Many humans are interested to know more about the Lorexians. Many of us would like to meet one in person. Is there any chance that a news team would be allowed to tour your ship and talk with some of your people?"

"The Fleet is here to safeguard Earth and support humanity's integration into the Confederation. The Ambassador is the one best suited to make that decision. If he were to request such a tour, we would offer it with no hesitation."

"Thank you, Angela, Admiral," Sarah said. "Next question goes to Keoni Gates of Fox News. Keoni?"

"My question is for the Ambassador. Michael, can you tell us more about the parts that the Fleet will be building for us?"

"Thank you for that question, Keoni. Yes, I can. We are asking the Fleet to build a special type of mid-sized replicator. These are complicated machines to build. As I said earlier, we are able to build them ourselves, but the Fleet can do it much faster."

"Could I be permitted a follow-up question?" Keoni asked. Michael nodded his consent. "Economically, how does this work? Is it something the Earth Alliance pays for? Is it something given to us? I think it would help us understand more about the workings between members and the Confederation itself."

"Thank you for that question, Keoni. As you have sensed, Confederation economics are much different than human economics. On Earth, you pay for goods and services using money. In the

Confederation, essentially all goods are free. The only cost is replicator time and wear, which is measured in the amount of a certain rare material that is consumed. We 'pay' the Confederation the amount of that rare material incorporated in our devices, plus twice the wear we put on the Confederation equipment."

"Michael," Sarah asked. "Where does Earth get this material?"

"Earth has an abundant supply. More than enough to supply its needs for thousands of years. And the only real use for it is in replicators and energy devices, so there is no cost to anyone on Earth."

"The next question goes to Jill Larson of the Toronto Star, Jill?"

"Admiral, sir. What is your assessment of humanity so far?"

"At first, I really struggled to believe that a species that emerged in its modern form less than 20,000 years ago would be worth the effort of integration. Most species are much older when they are invited.

"But I am not an expert in determining a species' readiness. The people that are expert believed that engaging Earth this early made sense.

"Now, almost six years after the Revelation, I think it is likely that humanity will become a leading member of the Confederation."

CHEF MARCOS

Sarah had arranged for dinner with the Butlers at Chef Marcos. As they entered, they were greeted by the Chef.

"Mr. Ambassador, Ms. Wright. Wonderful to see you tonight. Your table is ready." He signaled that they should enter. "Do I understand correctly that you have guests joining you this evening?"

"Yes," Sarah replied. "Sergeant George Butler and his wife, Noelani."

"What a lovely couple." The Chef smiled. "I have seen them running in the park many times. Is there a special occasion tonight?"

"Not really. Just connecting with friends," Sarah replied.

As they talked, the sommelier came over, carrying a bottle of wine. "I have a most spectacular find for you this evening. I thought all of these were gone. But a very wealthy collector offered this bottle to me from his private collection. It is the 2005 Screaming Eagle Cabernet Sauvignon Private Reserve. Only 60 cases were produced."

Sarah smiled at Michael and thought… *You spoil me.*

Michael pushed back. *Only the best, for the best.*

Sarah giggled and the sommelier said, "Yes. Fantastic isn't it."

Sarah spotted the hostess leading the Butlers to their table and said to Michael, "Noelani is absolutely glowing these days. Isn't she?"

After greetings and air kisses, they were seated. The Chef opened the bottle and Sarah did the tasting ceremony.

"That must be the best wine I've ever tasted," she said.

"Excellent." The Chef beamed. "Four glasses?"

"I will just have water tonight," said Noelani.

Sarah locked Noelani with a stare.

"I'm pregnant!" Noelani squealed.

Sarah shot up to give Noelani a hug as applause started from the row of tables behind them.

"Sorry," Sarah whispered. "People travel from all over the world to have dinner here, in the hope that they will see Michael in person.

After a minute, everyone settled, and a waiter brought out their appetizers.

"Noelani. How long do you think you will continue working?" Sarah asked.

"Well. I'm already at the point where it's not comfortable to be running half-marathons with the recovering vets. There are only six or seven weeks of Applied Reactions left, before the class changes over. I will do those, but I am not planning to sign on for the next class."

"Completely understandable." Sarah said. "But I bet Professor Jenson is going to miss you."

"I will miss working with her as well. But she is up to it now, so there won't be a problem.

"For my primary work, I think I will continue through second trimester. After that, we'll see."

"Do you know if it's a boy or a girl?"

"Yes. But George doesn't want to know yet. So, I'm keeping it to myself."

...

As they walked home, Michael asked Sarah, "When are we going to tell the world?"

"Soon, but not just yet."

"I'll be ready when you are," Michael said. *My human family continues to grow.*

"Yes. It does." Sarah replied, a twinkle in her eye.

439

EPILOGUE

The ship was failing. Fast Packets could transit the intergalactic void at the speed they did because the engines were large, and the ship was small. They were most of the way there, 2,317 of 2,400 jumps. They were 83 jumps, 83,000 light-years, short. Recharges were taking an hour with the maximum jump maybe 100 light-years, given the paltry charge they could hold.

But there was still hope. The emergency beacon still worked. They were within 1,000 light-years of the most heavily traveled cross-arm corridor, and they had plenty of food.

When the Fast Packet left the second moon of Lorexi Prime on the Inspector's misguided mission, the ship had a crew of 218, plus 23 passengers. The 13 passengers still aboard when the Fast Packet was commandeered had already been consumed. The 198 crew that were not worthy of being occupied were still viable meals.

This close to a major commercial corridor, someone was sure to come to their rescue before that food was consumed. And the people that stopped to help... They would not be able to resist the 8 combatants that had been spawned. And the nine of them were more than enough to consume a planet, as long as they could do it with stealth.

THE END

AFTERWORD

As with many things, the idea for The Ascendancy series came to me in a dream. Its content, on the other hand, comes largely from my scientific and technical training, research, life experiences and the works of others that have come before.

Following is a list of topics with the life experiences, and works of others, that have inspired this series.

Dreaming: I am very much like the character Eugene Xu in this book. Almost every career success I've had (well, other than my writing) was driven by mathematical prowess. Like Eugene, my biggest mathematical breakthrough came in a dream in the middle of the night. The scene where Eugene wakes up from a dream, scrambles to his desk in the middle of the night, scribbles on whatever paper he can find until his computer comes up... That was me in 2009. I was working as a consultant in the bio-pharmaceutical industry, struggling with a problem related to the supply of new oncology (cancer-related) drugs. The stakes for the industry, and for the cancer patients, were high. No one had been able to solve this problem and the industry as a whole had suffered several serious supply issues. I simply could not get the problem out of my mind.

Like Eugene, the answer came in a dream in the middle of the night. And like me, Eugene got up to seize the answer before it melted away.

I discovered this technique (i.e., filling your mind with a topic and letting your subconscious solve it while you sleep) as a second-year electrical engineering student in college. I've always referred to it as 'directed' dreaming. If you look up that term on-line, it has come to mean something different. Most people I've told about it think that I'm nuts. Your choice on that one.

In the case of the first book in this series, *Revelation*, I had just finished reading Phillip Peterson's book, *"Paradox - On the Brink of Eternity."* (A great book, if you haven't read it.) The last thing I read before falling asleep that night was his commentary on the Fermi Paradox in the afterword. The Fermi Paradox is about the contradiction between a) the high probability we assign to the possibility of other intelligent life in the universe, and b) the total lack of any tangible evidence to support that belief.

His comments apparently sent my subconscious into a whirlwind. I woke up at 3:00 AM with the words... "Hello. My name is Michael." ...ringing in my mind. (From my book, *Revelation*, Chapter 2.) I did not set out to write a book, but after two weeks of similar incidents, I got up before dawn one Sunday morning and started writing.

By the way, in case it's not obvious, my answer to the Fermi Paradox is that the aliens are already here, hiding in plain sight.

Faster Than Light Travel: Good, or at least plausible, science is the base building block for any decent science fiction story. For ones involving aliens, faster than light travel is the most important story element that you have to handle sensibly. For the Ascendancy series, I wanted to go with something new that would open additional story possibilities. My first instinct was a multiverse solution. You know... Pop over to a different universe that has a different speed of light, then pop back.

Those thoughts brought to mind ideas I was first introduced to in Douglas Phillips' book *Quantum Void*. (If you haven't read it, I highly recommend this book and the entire Quantum series.)

By conflating the ideas of multiverse and other dimensions, I could link a series of story elements back to a single base concept, extra-dimensionality. This provided the basis for necessary story elements like faster than light travel, shields, and transporters. It also allowed for special features like dimensional resonance for diagnostic imaging, a foundation dimension for eco-friendly building construction, and a truly sinister rival, the Enemy.

Energy: No matter how you play it, superluminal travel is going to require tons of energy. As a graduate student studying semiconductor physics, I was introduced to the concept of the quantum foam. The electrical engineer in me always thought that you could pump both energy and mass out of the quantum foam if you just had the material to make a 'quantum diode' (i.e., a device that only allowed one way flow at a quantum level).

That was a long time ago and a topic I had not thought about in years until I read Ryk Brown's *Frontiers Saga* series. (If you love space opera, the Frontiers Saga series is a must read. My favorite.)

From those thoughts of my younger self and the story's need for semi-infinite, free energy… transluminide was born, the material that would allow one-way flow out of the quantum foam. On a side note… I am looking forward to the day you can type transluminide into Google and a reference to the Ascendancy series pops up.

Economics: The economics of a world that has replicators is an issue I have pondered since I was a child watching *Star Trek*. In the world of the Ascendancy series, I've tried to put an exclamation point on the issue. Michael's replicators make all material things free. Property and human time will still have value. But things? Not so much. Anybody with a replicator can make it for free.

Jamie McFarlane, in his series *Privateer Tales*, takes on this issue. (Another favorite, must read, series.) In his world, you pay for the specifications. The replication itself is a minimal expense.

Although you see a hint of the McFarlane approach in Chef Marco's replicator recipes in this book, I wanted to go a different direction. So, in the world of the Ascendancy, all economics (related to material things) are reduced to transluminide.

Story Challenges: Every good tale has a writing challenge the author needs to take on to make the story work.

In *Revelation*, the challenge was to make an advanced species over 2 million years old seem somehow relatable to humans. How do you make a seemingly omnipotent species appear to be mortal beings like ourselves, not gods?

In this book, the challenge was making humanity relevant. What could humans do that would be meaningful to such an advanced species?

Coming Soon: Emergence (Ascendancy: Book 3) is targeted for release in April 2020. Join Michael as he continues to lift humanity to a significantly higher place in the Confederation. And join Space Force as they strive to eradicate the Enemy.

Thank You: Thank you for having read this book. There is great joy in writing a book like this. But even more in knowing that someone read and enjoyed it. Please put some stars on a review and stay tuned for more to come. If you spotted a typo, please let me know at dw.cornell@kahakaicg.com.

ABOUT THE AUTHOR

D. Ward Cornell lives on the Kohala Coast of the Big Island of Hawaii. His work as an engineer, consultant and entrepreneur has taken him all over the world. Many of those places are featured in this series. Although still dabbling in the mathematics of data compression and biopharmaceuticals, his passions are now writing, cooking and entertaining.

Made in the USA
Las Vegas, NV
17 November 2020